WEDDING TIERS

WEDDING TIERS

Trisha Ashley

WINDSOR
PARAGON

First published 2009
by
Avon
This Large Print edition published 2010
by BBC Audiobooks Ltd
by arrangement with
HarperCollins*Publishers*

Hardcover ISBN: 978 1 408 45972 0
Softcover   ISBN: 978 1 408 45973 7

British Library Cataloguing in Publication Data available

Printed and bound in Great Britain by
CPI Antony Rowe, Chippenham and Eastbourne

With grateful thanks to all the friends and family who have been there to lend a friendly ear when I most needed one. To my son, Robin Ashley, for research help and technical support. Special thanks also to my wonderful agent, Judith Murdoch, and to Maxine Hitchcock, Keshini Naidoo, and all the team at Avon, HarperCollins.

Jean Ashley, 1927–2009, who took joy in my success

Prologue: Ends and Beginnings, 1983

When Josie awoke in hospital, unscathed except for concussion and an impressive array of bruises, she had no recollection of the crash. Granny, red-eyed but stoical, had to break the news to her.

Somehow she managed to blank out most of the weeks immediately following the accident too, so that when she looked back later it seemed to her that one day she was living in St Albans with a full set of parents and several good friends, leavened with the usual teenage-years angst and a heartfelt, if destined to be forever unrequited, passion for Sting, and the next she was being whisked off alone to Granny's cottage in Lancashire, to start a new life.

'It's just thee and me now, flower,' Granny was all too often to remark, though with the best of intentions. But it wasn't likely that Josie would forget *that* fact, even if amnesia and anger were her current first lines of defence. For she was totally and illogically furious, both with her parents for so selfishly getting themselves killed, and with poor, grieving, gentle Granny for being truly ancient, so that Josie was convinced that she would also soon be snatched away, leaving her totally bereft.

It would be better to love no one, to feel nothing at all—much safer.

All that summer, she silently and sullenly followed Granny around the garden while she hoed, dug, planted and harvested, or helped Uncle Harry (who lived next door and was not a real

1

uncle, only having married Granny's cousin) to tend the poultry. And slowly Josie began to gain some comfort from the cycle of cultivation, the clucking hens and the drowsy, contented humming of bees; while across the Green, the ancient church bells repeatedly rang a joyful wedding peal, a signal that hope and happiness still existed and might one day be hers again.

Only in the evenings, lying in her narrow bed among the transplanted possessions of her former life, the mournful screams of the peacocks next door in the gardens of Blessings would pierce right to her heart with unbearable sadness, and she would put a pillow over her head and weep.

*   *   *

She didn't take the bus to her new school on the first day. Instead, Uncle Harry drove her there in the yellow Vauxhall Cavalier that was his pride and joy. And then, embarrassingly, he and Granny both stood at the gates like the oldest parents in the world while Josie went on alone. She turned once, and they waved at her, as she had known they would: it was comforting but deeply uncool.

Catching sight of her, a passing youth—tall and broad-shouldered, with floppy, light brown hair— stopped dead and gave her a big, drop-dead-gorgeous smile. Suddenly breathless, she gazed into his warm hazel eyes, and it was as though she already knew she'd found a kindred spirit, a soul mate—recognised that fate, having taken love away with one sweep of the dice, had then, fickle, tossed her a perfect six.

'Hello!' he said, his voice deep, friendly and

2

confident. 'I'm Benjamin Richards—but you can call me Ben . . . or anything else you like.'

Flustered, she stammered shyly: 'I'm Josie. Josie Gray.'

'Nice to meet you, Josie Gray.' He smiled again before rejoining his waiting friends, who were all nudging each other and laughing.

She was jerked out of her trance by a voice at her elbow saying, 'You've been here five minutes and dishy Ben Richards *spoke* to you? Wow!'

A small, slender, impishly pretty blonde girl was looking her up and down from under her fringe as if she wasn't quite sure what the attraction had been. 'You must be the orphan—only we were told not to mention that.'

'You just did,' snapped out Josie, who had become used to people tiptoeing around her as though she were some kind of delicately balanced explosive device.

The girl shrugged. 'Well, you can't go pussyfooting around things for ever, can you? I'm Libby Martin, and if it makes you feel any better, my mother's an alcoholic slut and I have no idea who my father was.'

Strangely, it *did* make Josie feel better, and she grinned. Then the bell went and everyone started to stream towards the door.

'Come on—Miss Price told me I had to show you where to go *and* I've got to look after you all week,' Libby said. 'God, I'm so glad you don't look naff—apart from that terrible haircut. If we're going to be friends, you'll have to do something about it.'

'Granny cut it and I think it looks cool,' Josie said defensively, then added, '*Are* we going to be

3

friends?'

'Oh, I think so, don't you? Probably end up BF.'

'BF?'

'Best friends.' Her blue eyes went wide. 'Where on earth are you *from*?'

'St Albans.'

'Huh.' Libby looked unimpressed—clearly she'd never heard of the place. 'I'll tell you about my big plan at break, if you like.'

'Big plan?' Josie echoed.

'Well, I don't want to be Libby Martin with the slutty mother from up the council estate for ever, do I? So I'm reinventing myself.'

'Great idea,' Josie conceded, suddenly dying to know what her new friend was going to reinvent herself as, and how she intended to do it. 'What—' she began, but then the bell rang for the second time and Libby grabbed her arm and started towing her along. Practically everyone else had already vanished indoors, including the gorgeous Ben Richards.

'No time now—I'll tell you later, so get a move on or we'll be late. Though come to think of it, I suppose that's OK today,' Libby added, again with an impish smile. 'You're my "get out of jail free" card.'

* * *

At lunchtime Libby outlined her plan, which seemed to be directed at leaving Neatslake as soon as possible and marrying a rich man.

'Isn't that a bit . . .' Josie searched for the right word, '*mercenary*? Out for what you can get? What about love?'

4

'But I wouldn't marry a man unless I *loved* him,' Libby said, looking shocked. 'No way would I do that! But I'm only going to let myself fall in love with someone well off, who will look after me.'

'Right,' Josie said doubtfully, because this kind of ambition had never cropped up when she'd been discussing future careers with her friends in St Albans.

'But first, I have to get ready to live that kind of life—you know, like in *Pride and Prejudice*, when they keep going on about all the accomplishments you need to be the wife of a rich man?'

'Well, yes, but I think they meant speaking Italian and doing embroidery, that kind of thing, didn't they?'

'Yes, but translate that into the twentieth century,' Libby said impatiently. She dug a notebook out of her bag and flipped it open. 'I've got a list of things I need to learn, like speaking without a broad accent. Mrs Springer, the English teacher, is helping me with that.'

'I like your accent,' Josie said.

'You're mad!' Libby said, then moved her finger down the page and continued, 'Horse riding, tennis, skiing . . .' Here she paused, uncertainly. 'Rich people do a lot of skiing, but that could be difficult round here. We don't get a lot of snow and the nearest dry ski slope is miles away.'

'Are you sure you need all of those?'

'Some of them, anyway—as many as possible. You can help me.'

'OK, but I'm not mad about horses—they're so big.'

'Don't chicken out on me before we start,' Libby said. 'What about you, what do you want?'

5

'I don't know, really. My parents thought I ought to . . .' She suddenly trailed off, her voice trembling.

'Look, don't go all wobbly on me!' warned Libby, and to her surprise Josie saw that her new friend had tears in her large blue eyes. 'If you start crying, then I will too, and then everyone will know I'm as soft as butter and I'll be done for. I'm only cool to know because they think I'm hard as nails.'

Josie sniffed back the tears. 'Sorry. My—my parents wanted me to go to university, but I don't know . . . Now I just feel I'd like to stay in Neatslake for ever and help Granny with the gardening and Uncle Harry with the hens. Granny's teaching me how to bake and make jam and stuff too.'

'You can't make a career out of any of *that*.'

'Yes I could. I could be a gardener, and I think I'd like that.' She caught sight of Ben Richards in the distance, in the middle of a group of boys. He was taller than the rest so he was easy to spot.

Libby saw where she was looking. 'Ben's fourteen, in the next year up from us, and he's very popular. His parents wanted to send him to some public school but he decided he'd rather come here with his friends and he's very stubborn. He's brilliant at art—he's done his O level already—but he's totally thick about everything else.'

'I'm sure he isn't!'

'He's good at football,' she conceded. 'I'm not sure how clever you have to be for that, but it makes him popular with the boys too.'

They watched him in the distance and then Josie sighed and said, 'I don't suppose he'll ever notice me again. I suppose it was just because he practically fell over me and I was a new face.'

'Oh, I don't know,' Libby said, looking at her thoughtfully, then added immodestly, 'You're not pretty like *me*, but sort of attractive in a different way. I've never met anyone else with hair that really dark red—or eyes that bluey-greyish-lilac sort of colour.'

'Thanks, but I'm not sure I want to be different.' Her eyes returned to Ben, now playing football with a group of other boys. She was also tall for her age . . .

'Ben asked me out once, but I had to turn him down,' Libby said.

Josie turned and stared at her new friend, feeling a pang of jealousy. 'Not part of the big plan?'

'No way.' She shook her head. 'And I think he only asked me because his friends dared him to. They probably told him I was easy, like Mum. Anyway, I don't want to get tangled up with some village boy; I have to concentrate on the bigger picture. I'm saving myself for Mr Right. Mr Rich *and* Right,' she added, then giggled. 'It might have been worth going out with Ben, though, just to see his parents' faces! They're so snobby and stuck up, especially his mother, they'd have had fits.'

'Oh? What does she do?'

'Absolutely nothing, but Ben's father's a hospital consultant and they live up a lane the other side of Church Green, in a converted farmhouse. Ben's already got his own studio in one of the outbuildings, because his mother doesn't like mess in the house.'

'How do you know all this?'

'One of his friends told me.'

'Granny's house is on the Green,' Josie said.

7

'That pair of cottages by the really old black and white building. My uncle Harry lives next door to us, but he's not really an uncle, he just married Granny's cousin.'

'The old house is Blessings,' Libby nodded. 'It's Elizabethan.'

'Granny says she used to go there to clean, years ago.'

'In that case, don't get ideas about Ben Richards. His parents would probably think a granny who was a cleaner was only one step above a slutty mother.'

'I don't see why,' Josie said defensively. 'Anyway, she was a nurse during the war, but it damaged her back so she took up cleaning afterwards—just light stuff. She still gets a bad back sometimes, but that's probably just because she's really, really old. My mother was a nurse too, and my dad was a policeman. We lived in a police house in St Albans.'

'Well, don't start crying again, or you'll set me off,' Libby said briskly.

Josie gave a watery smile. She'd got the measure by now of Libby's kind heart under her sometimes brusque exterior, and her friend's lovely blue eyes were, indeed, brimming again with sympathetic tears.

'A dad who was a policeman is at least a couple of rungs up from not knowing who your father is— and my sister, Daisy, doesn't know either, except that we have different ones,' Libby pointed out. 'Maybe it's better not to know.'

*   *   *

Libby left the bus before her new friend, at the other end of Neatslake, but Ben Richards and a couple of other boys got off when Josie did, suddenly swinging down the spiral stairs from the upper deck as the bus stopped, and jumping off first.

She didn't think he'd noticed her, but as she turned the corner towards Church Green, he fell into step beside her as if he'd been waiting for her. Which he had.

'I hear your granny makes the best cakes in Neatslake,' he said, with that warm, irresistible sideways smile, and Josie felt the glacier around her heart crack into a million fragments and melt away.

*   *   *

'Well, that's going to put the cat among the pigeons,' Granny said thoughtfully when Ben had finally—and reluctantly—gone off home, full of cheese straws hot from the oven and several slices of butter-rich fruitcake. 'But he seems a nice boy—considering.'

'Considering *what*?' Josie demanded, coming out of a pleasant trance. Her mouth ached a bit from all the smiling she'd done this afternoon, and she wondered if her face muscles had atrophied over the last few months from disuse. She got up and looked at herself in the small, cloudy mirror beside the coat pegs, but it was about as much good as a reflection on water, all ripply.

'If you two are going to be friends, I don't think Ben's parents, especially his mum, will be too pleased about it.'

9

'I've heard she's a snob, Granny. Do you know her?'

'Oh, yes. Many's the time Nell Slattery's sat here in the kitchen with your mother,' she said unexpectedly. 'They did their nursing training together and started working at the same hospital together too, and they were quite good friends in those days.'

Josie frowned. 'So why won't she be pleased if me and Ben are . . .' she blushed, 'friends?'

'Well, flower, for one thing her husband is a consultant pathologist and the very instant the ring was on her finger she chucked the nursing and most of her old friends with it, and got Ideas. And for another—well, her husband fell for your mother first, you see, and Nell got him on the rebound.'

'Ben's father once went out with *Mum*?' Josie said, amazed.

'No, she didn't have any fancy for him, but he pestered her until she met your father and they got married—then he turned and wed Nell instead. Since then she pretends she's never met me if we pass in the village. Cleaners are below her notice. Though I suppose,' she added with humour, 'if she *really* didn't, she'd be trying to employ me!'

'There's nothing wrong with having been a cleaner,' Josie said loyally.

'No, I'm not ashamed of having done good honest work, but I was proud of your mother, getting her nursing qualifications. And she was so pretty too. You look just like her at that age, Josie.'

'But *I'm* not pretty,' she said, surprised.

'Of course you are.'

Josie shook her head definitely. 'No, I'm not.

Libby Martin, my new friend at school, said she thought I was *unusual*. Libby really is pretty—small and blonde and slim.'

'Isn't she Gloria Martin's younger daughter? The talk of the village, that one is!'

'Libby isn't like her mother,' Josie said definitely.

'I don't suppose she is. Neither of the two girls has had a bad word said about them,' agreed Granny fairly. 'The older one is apprenticed to a hairdresser and doing well. What's she called? Some flower name.'

'Daisy, I think,' Josie said. 'So, can I invite Libby to come round here sometimes?'

'Yes, of course you can.'

'Cool!'

'I'm glad to see you making friends already, though I didn't think you'd be starting with the boys quite so quickly!'

Josie blushed. 'Ben's just being nice. I mean, it's not like he's asked me out. He *did* ask Libby out once but she turned him down.'

'Quite right too. At your age, friendship is better,' Granny said firmly. 'I don't mind him coming here to see you, but no goings-on.'

Josie blushed furiously. '*Granny!*'

Later, in her room, she took the framed photograph of her parents out of the drawer where she'd hidden it away and looked from her mother's smiling face to her own serious one in the dressing table mirror. Her mother *was* pretty, even with laughter lines and a bit of extra weight plumping up her cheeks, but Granny was just being kind, for surely her eyes had been bluer and her skin less sallow than Josie's own?

Then she tried to remember what colour her

11

father's eyes had been, but already the memories were fading, along with the first sharp edge of pain and anger.

*　　*　　*

As the years passed, she forged a bond of hopes, dreams and laughter with Libby and moved seamlessly from friendship into love with Ben. But, deep down, she never quite lost that slight feeling of insecurity, the fear that those she loved might just be snatched away from her at any moment.

And she always hated the cry of peacocks.

Chapter One

Cakes and Ale

The Artist has gone off to London again, for the opening night of an exhibition that includes his work. The source of his inspiration may come from the countryside, but these increasingly frequent trips to the metropolis are yet another necessary compromise to our way of life.

We aim to be as self-sufficient as possible—and still the twenty-first century constantly intrudes. Realistically, we're doing well if we can strike an eighty/twenty balance! Even this diary is now written directly onto a laptop and emailed straight off to the editor of Skint Old Northern Woman *magazine, just one example of the constant contradictions involved. And, of course, many of you now subscribe to the online version.*

But it has to be admitted that the Artist has a weakness for all kinds of gadgets and bits of technological wizardry that I don't share even when, with the best of intentions, he presents me with something like a breadmaking machine, which he is sure will make my life easier . . .

'Cakes and Ale: the musings of a backyard good-lifer'

The sun was making a brave attempt to warm a dank and fuzzy mid-October morning when Ben, looking as big, tousled and wholesomely delectable as always, turned on the doorstep to say goodbye.

'Oh, I *wish* you didn't have to go,' I said, putting

13

my arms around his neck to pull him down to kissing level. Honestly, you'd think he was going on some exotic foreign trek into uncharted territory, rather than to stay with old friends in London for a couple of days. I really must get a grip! But these moments do sweep over me occasionally, because when you've been orphaned as a child and then lost the grandmother who brought you up, it's hard not to be afraid that fate might also decide to snatch away the person you love most in the whole wide world.

'You know I wouldn't go if I didn't have to, darling.' Ben enfolded me in a reassuring if asphyxiating hug, like a good-natured grizzly bear.

'Liar, liar, your bum's on fire!' I chanted rudely. 'You're loving your bit of fame, admit it. These days there's a glint in your eye and a spring in your step every time you set off for London.'

He grinned, though guiltily, his fair skin flushing slightly. 'Perhaps—but aren't I always more than happy to be back home again, with you?'

'Maybe,' I conceded, because it was true that he always came back exhausted and more than ready to slip back into the old, familiar rut as if he'd never been away—until the next time. 'But then, maybe you're just missing your home comforts?'

'*You're* one of my home comforts,' he said, squeezing me again and then letting me go. 'I'll ring you as soon as I get to Russell and Mary's flat—promise.'

'That's OK, I don't really think anything awful will happen to you between here and Camden, unless things have changed radically since I last came with you.' I paused reflectively, trying to remember when that was, and then added in

14

surprise, 'Do you know, that must be more than a year ago!'

'Is it?' he said. 'It doesn't seem like that long.'

'No, the time has just flown. I feel I'm losing touch with Mary too, and we used to be such friends, but now if I phone she's always about to go out and never rings me back like she says she will. I really *must* find someone who would look in on Uncle Harry and walk the dog, so I could start coming with you again.'

'You know Harry's too independent to let anyone else keep an eye on him and too frail to leave on his own,' Ben pointed out patiently. 'Anyway, you'll be much happier here, doing something with all those baskets of apples and pears Dorrie keeps giving you.'

'Actually, I always enjoyed my trips to London, catching up with everyone and visiting my favourite places,' I protested, which was true, especially when Libby was in town so we could meet up. 'But you're right, there's a huge amount to do here at the moment. I'm appled out and I still need to get the last of the marrows in, make green tomato chutney and start pickling beetroot—plus I have a really tricky wedding cake to finish icing. It's just that I do miss you when you're away.'

'And I miss you too, darling,' he said, but absently, looking at his watch. 'I'd better go—speak to you later!'

He gave me a kiss and then off he strode across the Green towards the High Street and the bus to the station, swinging his overnight bag, while I mopped a weak and pathetic tear from my eye with the belt of my blue towelling robe and summoned up a bright smile in case he turned round to wave.

He didn't, but that was probably because Miss Violet Grace whipped around the corner on her tricycle just as he reached it and he had to take sudden evasive action.

A collision was averted and Ben vanished from sight. Spotting me, Violet veered rapidly in my direction, the bobbles of her gaily coloured Peruvian-style knitted helmet flying in the breeze.

'Isn't Ben an early bird?' she called, coming to a sudden halt in front of me, so that her hat fell forward over her eyes. She pushed it back and peered upwards, and what with her mauve lipstick, pale complexion and fringe of silvery hair, she would have looked quite other-worldly had it not been for the faint flush on her cheeks engendered by pedalling hard. 'Off to London again, is he?'

'Yes, and I would have driven him to the station in the van, but he insisted on catching the bus. At least, I *hope* he's caught it, because I held him up a bit,' I said guiltily.

Violet had been to fetch the newspaper from Neville's Village Stores. However hard she and her two elder sisters might find it to make ends meet on their pensions, their father, General Grace, had always had *The Times*, so it was unthinkable to them that they could possibly start the day without it.

'Ben is a brilliant artist—*The Times* said so.' She looked doubtful, though willing to believe anything written in that august organ. 'I thought I would just pop across to remind you that there is a wedding at St Cuthbert's today—ten thirty. Will you be there, dear?'

16

The Three Graces and I are all wedding junkies, lurking outside the church as the happy couples emerge, although this was a habit I had so far managed to keep from Ben, who was stubbornly anti-Establishment in the matter of legal wedlock. He hadn't always been so adamant about it; it sort of came over him by degrees while he was a student.

'I'll try, but I have a wedding cake to ice and more green tomato chutney to make. I'll put some in your fruit and veg box later, shall I? And did you say you wanted some frozen blackberries? I've got loads.'

'Lovely,' she agreed, preparing to cycle off, 'yes, please. Dorrie Spottiswode's giving us some apples, so we can make apple and bramble pies. Pansy's knitting her a tam in exchange, from some leftover mohair. We thought that was about equal value in Acorns.'

Pansy isn't some kind of ingenious squirrel— Acorns are simply a unit of currency I devised a few years ago, to help a little group of us to swap produce and services.

'You can have the latest copy of *Skint Old Northern Woman* magazine too. I've read it. And I must finish off the next instalment of "Cakes and Ale" and get it off to them,' I added guiltily. My deadline was always the twentieth of the month, which wasn't that far away.

'Righty-oh, see you later!' Violet cried gaily, and then cycled off round the Green to Poona Place, leaning forward over her handlebars, earflaps flipped backwards like psychedelic spaniel's ears, while I, suddenly shivering, went back inside.

In the kitchen, under a tea towel, Ben had

17

arranged root vegetables and green tomatoes into a heart shape and added a carrot arrow.

It was a pity he'd created this earthy symbol of our love on the immaculately clean marble surface dedicated to making my wedding cakes, but it still made me smile.

*　　*　　*

Later, sitting in our cosy living room overlooking the garden, logs burning in the stove and a glass of Violet's non-alcoholic but fiery ginger cordial by my elbow (three Acorns per bottle), I was trying to wrap up the latest episode of my long-running 'Cakes and Ale' column for the alternative women's magazine.

I'd written the obligatory 'what's-happening-with-the-garden-and-the-hens' bit, describing September's mad scramble to get all the fruit and vegetables harvested and stored, clamped, preserved or turned into alcohol, processes that were still ongoing, if not quite so frenetic. Some things, like the elderberries, were quite over and well on the way to being turned into ruby-red wine.

I do love the season of mellow fruitfulness, and there's nothing quite so blissful as having a larder full of pickles, chutneys and preserves, crocks of salted beans and sauerkraut, and wine fermenting gently by the stove . . . So maybe *I* am the squirrel and that's why my subconscious decided we would call our barter currency Acorns!

Anyway, I finished that part of the article off with Ten Delicious Things to Do with a Plum Glut (crystallised plums—oh, be still, my beating heart!) and then, after an eye-watering gulp of ginger

18

cordial, embarked on the philosophising section, my readers' favourite:

> If we are not quite living off the fat of the land, as self-sufficiency guru John Seymour once put it, we are at least utilising the cream clinging to the edges. And *what* cream, cheese and yoghurt there has been recently, provided by friends who keep goats, and a Dexter cow or two, at their smallholding on the outskirts of the village . . .

Mark and Stella, our friends with the smallholding, are a much older hippie couple, and I've often wondered whether Ben and I were behind the times or ahead of them when, as teenagers, we dreamed of one day being self-sufficient. Whichever, I was more than happy that the way we lived was suddenly very trendy and aspirational so that the magazine, and especially my column in it, had something of a cult following. I love to share— ideas, inspiration, tips, food . . .

Granny and Uncle Harry were a great early influence, managing to produce practically all their own fruit, vegetables and eggs, plus the occasional hen for the pot, just from their combined back gardens in Neatslake, which is quite a large and pretty village in Lancashire, not far from Ormskirk.

Ben and I had more of a country smallholding in mind, even if we were hazy about how we could ever afford it—unless Ben's paintings began to sell really well, of course. That was the dream: we would work our plot together, and he would paint while I baked and bottled and preserved. It

19

sounded such bliss!

But just as Ben was finishing off the final year of his post-graduate course at the Royal College of Art in London, and I was living with him and helping make ends meet by working in a florist's shop, Granny suddenly died and left me this cottage.

Since she'd taken me in at thirteen when I was orphaned, and was my only remaining blood relative, I was absolutely devastated. It brought back lots of long-forgotten memories of my parents and how I felt after I lost them . . . and I know all this orphan business sounds a bit Charles Dickens, but I can't help that—that's the way it was!

But I couldn't contemplate selling the cottage, which was my home as well as a link with Granny, and nor did I want to leave Harry, of whom I was very fond, to cope alone. But then, I didn't want to be parted from Ben either!

I expect I was a bit neurotic, needy and tiresome for a while, but Ben was always there for me, in his strong, silent way. And in the end he came up with the solution, suggesting that he go back and complete the last weeks of his course alone, and then we'd settle down together in Neatslake.

Despite it being Ben's idea, his parents never forgave me for dragging him back from what they were convinced would have been instant fame and fortune in London; but then, they've never thought me good enough for him anyway. At one point they even threatened to cut off the small allowance they were making him, though they changed their mind. I thought he should tell them to stick the allowance where the sun don't shine as a matter of principle, but he wouldn't, so we had one of our rare arguments. I've never used any of the money—it goes straight into Ben's account to pay for art materials and CDs and all those gadgets that mean so little to me and so much to him.

But his parents were wrong, because here we still were, living a version of our dream on a slightly smaller plane than we'd envisaged, perhaps, but none the less very happy, for all that. Perhaps one or two things hadn't worked out how we planned . . . though as Ben said, as long as we had each other, nothing else really mattered.

And luckily, it was all the compromise involved in trying to balance living a greenish life in the middle of a village, against earning enough to pay the inescapable bills, that interested the readership of *Skint Old Northern Woman* magazine enormously. While they didn't pay a lot for my articles, it formed a regular part of my income, and then the icing on the cake came, quite literally, from my hand-modelled wedding cake business, catering for the alternative market—sometimes *very* alternative:

JOSIE GRAY'S WEIRD AND WONDERFUL WEDDING CAKES
Do you want something different? Original?
Personal? Truly unique?
Josie Gray will design the cake of your dreams!

Or at least it *had* formed the icing, until Ben had won a major art prize about eighteen months previously, and his work began to get the recognition it deserved at last *and* fetch much greater prices.

21

Looking back now, I suddenly had an uneasy feeling that the equilibrium of our lives had subtly changed at that point . . . but maybe I was being over-imaginative?

Ben bought me a shiny, expensive breadmaking machine to celebrate his win, which he said would take away all the endless kneading. Though, actually, I always rather enjoyed doing it, going off into a dreamy trance and forgetting time, which made for *very* light bread.

But that, and one or two other little gadgets he'd brought back for me from London, seemed against our whole ethos, though it could be that I was unsettled by them because I simply didn't like change. It made me uneasy. I just wanted us to go quietly on as we always had, happy as pigs in clover.

The wood-burning stove crackled quietly and nearby a door slammed, waking me from my reverie. The top of Harry's felt hat appeared as he shuffled slowly down his garden, hidden by the dividing fence, to feed the hens.

There was an arched gateway between our two plots so we could both come and go freely, for though Harry was nominally in charge of the hens, we shared our gardens and what grew in them. But these last few months, as Harry had grown increasingly infirm after a fall, it seemed I was doing the lion's share of the work.

Ben used to do most of the heavy digging, but lately he'd either been shut up in the wooden studio at the end of the garden, built against the tall stone wall separating us from the grounds of Blessings, or he was in London.

Each time when he got home and enfolded me in

a big, warm hug, swinging me off my feet and telling me he loved me, it *almost* made up for his absence . . . but not quite.

I looked down at the laptop and sighed heavily, having totally lost the thread of what I was going to say to finish off.

The little wicket gate between the two gardens squeaked open and Harry came through, followed by his sheepdog, Mac. Harry carried a hoe in one hand and a stout walking stick with a ram's-horn handle in the other, and I had to give him full marks for effort even if I expected to find him lying full length among the brassicas one of these days. *And* there was the problem of his failing eyesight, so that half the time he was nurturing seedling weeds and tossing the veggies onto the compost heap . . . Still, that wasn't too much of a problem in mid-October, and he was heading for the pea and bean beds, which needed clearing anyway.

Behind him, stepping delicately, followed the pale, speckled shape of Aggie, the escapologist hen. The others were all fat, cosy, brown creatures, whom I couldn't distinguish apart—and didn't want to, since they were quite likely to end up on my plate. But Aggie, with her inquisitive nature and skill in escaping from enclosed places, was different, and Harry was forbidden from even *thinking* of culling her, whether she deigned to lay eggs or not.

Opening the door I called, 'Tea in twenty minutes, Harry?' and he made a thumbs-up sign.

I went back in, took another look at my notes, and then rattled off the rest of my article, before changing all the names as usual. Even though I never tell anyone's secrets, or gossip about local people, I wouldn't feel half as free to write what I wanted if everyone knew it was me, and where I lived!

Then, with a click of a button, I sent it on its way to the magazine.

It was then I suddenly remembered that in the summer, after one of my cakes had featured in the coverage of a terribly smart local wedding, *Country at Heart* magazine had contacted me. They were interested in the way I combined my wedding cake business with the self-sufficiency too—but, of course, they didn't know I was the author of 'Cakes and Ale' in *SONW* magazine, and I didn't tell them!

They interviewed me by email and telephone, and then sent a photographer to take some pics, but I hadn't heard anything since, so perhaps they'd thought better of it, or found someone more interesting to feature.

* * *

'Our Sadie's been after me to up sticks and go and live in New Zealand with them again,' Harry said, selecting a ginger biscuit from the tin after careful inspection, and then dunking it in his mug of tea. A bit crumbled and fell, but was neatly snapped up before it hit the floor by Mac, who lunged silently shark-like from under the table and then retreated again. 'She's sent me a photograph of the extension they're building onto the side of the house, like a little self-contained flat.'

'Granny annexe, they call them. She's obviously very keen for you to go, Harry,' I said brightly, trying to sound encouraging, even though I would miss him dreadfully if he did go.

'She says I should *want* to live near my only daughter and grandchildren, but it was her chose to go and live on the other side of the world in the first place, not me! There's no reason why *I* should have to end my days somewhere foreign.'

'Well, I suppose they've made their life there now and the grandchildren are New Zealanders, and when Sadie sent you the plane tickets and you went out to visit, you had a great time.'

'Liking the place for a holiday isn't the same as wanting to live there, away from all my old friends.'

'I suppose not,' I agreed, though since Harry's old friends were popping their clogs with monotonous regularity, a fact he pointed out with some relish from the obituary columns in the local paper, that wouldn't be an argument he would be able to use for very much longer. The group of cronies he met in the Griffin for a pint of Mossbrown ale most evenings had reduced to three, one of whom had to be helped up the steps to the entrance.

Harry seemed to realise this himself, for he added morosely, 'Not that they aren't dropping like flies anyway. But *I'll* die here, in my own place—and when I've gone, you make sure and give that tin box of papers and medals to Sadie, when she comes over for the funeral.'

'Of course I will—but I hope not for a long time yet, because whatever would I do without you?'

'Time catches us all in the end, lass. You'll find my will in the box too. Sadie'll get most of what I've got to leave, of course. Blood's thicker than water, and you can't get away from that, even if *you've* been more of a daughter to me than *she* has.'

'No, of course not. I'm only distantly related to you through marriage,' I agreed, because Granny and Harry's wife, Rosa, hadn't even been first cousins, so I hadn't been expecting him to do anything else. It was true that I'd been spending more and more time looking after him, but then that was only fair, seeing how much help he gave me and Ben when we moved back here after Granny died. Anyway, I loved him, and he and Granny had been such good friends, widow and widower, understanding each other.

Harry was still wearing his battered felt hat, which I rarely saw him without, though in times when he was pondering some weighty matter he would run his earth-stained finger around the inside of the band, as now.

'I saw a piece in a magazine at the doctor's last week,' he said. 'It said how I could claim a medal for the six months of minesweeping I did right after the war. There was an address to send to—I ripped it out. The receptionist said I could.'

He produced a much-folded piece of thin paper from his pocket and handed it to me. 'What do you think of that?'

I read it carefully. 'Yes, why not? You're entitled to it, aren't you? It did seem so unfair to me, that after being in the navy in the Far East and fighting on for longer than lots of other people, they made you go and do something even more dangerous for six months before they let you demob!'

It was only in the last couple of years that Harry had started to talk about his war service in the

26

navy. A quiet, sensitive man, what he had seen and experienced had harrowed him and driven him into himself, especially after he lost his wife.

'There was never anything fair about the armed forces, Josie. You did what you were told, or else! But having to go minesweeping when I wanted to get home to Rosa—well, that was a bit of a blow. And it was dangerous work. You never knew when a mine was going to go up and take you with it, and in those little wooden boats we wouldn't have had a chance, we all knew that.'

'It sounds dreadful, and you've certainly earned your medal!'

'So you really think I should apply for it, then?'

'Definitely—another one for the grandchildren. Do you want me to write the letter for you?'

'No, that's all right, I'll do that, but you could take it to the post office later.' He began the painful task of hauling himself to his feet, but I knew better than to offer him any help.

'I've left you the hens and the piano,' he said abruptly, once he was upright. 'The piano was my mother's and Sadie won't want to ship it out there.'

'Thank you—how lovely,' I said, touched but not at all sure how I would fit the piano into my small house, or the hens and their coop and run into the vegetable garden. The thought of Harry gone and a stranger one day living next door was very disturbing . . .

'Well, there's no need to cry over it, you daft lump,' he said bracingly. 'You're too soft for your own good, you are. Cry if a hen dies, cry over a dead hedgehog, cry every blessed time that Ben of yours goes off to London!'

A peacock distantly wailed from the grounds of

Blessings, as if in agreement, even though I thought it was a bit of an exaggeration. I'm not that soft.

I dabbed my eyes with the edge of my sweatshirt. 'Of course I'm not crying, it's wood smoke. That last lot I put in the stove must have been damp. And there's no reason for me to get upset, because you've got lots of good years left in you, Harry,' I said, more positively than I felt, because look what happened to Granny, who was several years younger. And now I had only Harry and Ben—and my friend Libby, of course. But not only did she live far away, she was also rather like a cat in that, though fond of me, she had her own agenda and came and went as she pleased.

'I've got thick vegetable soup on the stove—I'll bring you some and fresh bread rolls later, when I take Mac out for a walk,' I said. Harry is fiercely independent, but I fill his little freezer with single portions of soup, casseroles and all kinds of things, with the heating instructions written on the lids. And I make sure he has fresh bread and biscuits— whatever I've been cooking.

'I like that minestrone best,' he said ungratefully, pausing with Mac on the threshold and letting gusts of October air, redolent with autumnal garden bonfires, into the room. 'Got a bit of news, I nearly forgot to tell you. Mr Rowland-Knowles has put Blessings on the market.'

I stared at him. 'But he's only just moved back in!'

'Yes, but he found that stepmother of his had run the place into the ground. She only used the modern wing and let the rest go hang, and you need to keep on top of these Elizabethan houses

28

or they quickly start to go downhill.' He shook his head at the waste of it all. 'He came round yesterday afternoon and asked me to look over some rotting woodwork and tell him what I thought.'

Harry, who'd been an expert carpenter in his time, had done work in most of the old houses in the area, so that made sense.

'It was in a right state—windows blown in and the rain's made a mess of the floor in one bedchamber, not to mention the woodworm taking hold and the roof needing repairing. The poor man's desperate not to part with it, but he can't afford to put it to rights.'

'That's such a shame!'

'Vindictive. His stepmother had the right to live there unless she remarried, but now she finally has, it's a mixed Blessing!' He grinned, happy with his little joke.

'But what will happen to Dorrie's home if Blessings is sold?' I asked, for Miss Doreen Spottiswode was Tim's aunt, his mother's eldest sister, who now lived in a dilapidated cottage in the grounds and, together with an ancient gardener, did her best to stop the place running completely wild.

'I don't think they can get her out. She'll be like a sitting tenant, I suppose,' he said. 'Mrs Rowland-Knowles never managed it, try though she might, for Miss Dorrie had just as much right to see out her days there as *she* had to live in Blessings. But Miss Dorrie's looked after that garden since she came here to live with her sister, just after she married. She loves it, and it will hit her hard if strangers take it over.' He shook his head sadly.

29

'I suppose Tim Rowland-Knowles thought about all that before he came to his decision, and there mustn't have been any option, Harry.' I didn't know Tim well, because he hadn't been near Neatslake since his father died, and not often before that, since he and his stepmother hadn't got on.

But I suddenly remembered the summer when we were fifteen and Libby's game plan (which involved acquiring the skills she thought would be necessary in order to become a rich man's wife) had led her to wangle invites for us to tennis parties at the vicarage. Tim was often there, because the vicar's drippy seventeen-year-old daughter, Miriam, had a crush on him. He's tall and thin, with a shock of untidy white-blond hair and vague blue eyes, and you couldn't imagine him being terribly successful as a solicitor.

At the time Libby was convinced she resembled Debbie Harry, which she didn't, and her efforts to make her cheekbones stand out meant she constantly appeared to be sucking a lemon. As for me, all I wanted was to look just like one of the black-clad female guitarists in the Robert Palmer 'Addicted to Love' video. We were both totally deluded and neither look really went well with tennis clothes, so it says much for Tim's good nature that he directed the occasional kind smile in our direction.

When Harry had hobbled back into the garden I emailed Libby, though I had no idea whether she was in her pretty London mews house or in Pisa, where she had a rather palatial flat complete with a roof terrace covered with lemon and olive trees in huge terracotta pots. Ben and I had been out there a couple of times, for holidays—she's always been terribly generous and her second husband, Joe Cazzini, who died last year, had been a lovely man.

'You remember when we were at school and were taken round Blessings in the fifth year?' I wrote. 'You said you wanted to live there, and one day you'd have a house just like it. Well, here's your chance, because Tim Rowland-Knowles (do you remember we used to play tennis with him at the vicarage?) has had to put it up for sale . . .'

Of course, I didn't *seriously* think she'd want to buy it! Libby's plans had always involved shaking the dust of Neatslake off her dainty feet for ever, and her visits here since her first marriage had been mere flying ones, in and out, to catch up with me. No, I was just using the news as something exciting that might break the monotony of my emails to her, because she's not that interested in making jam and mixed pickles.

Her emails were always much livelier than mine and I always enjoyed reading them, though I wasn't jealous of her lifestyle at all. I much preferred my rooted and settled existence to her butterfly one.

But as I pressed 'send', I realised that my roots were feeling frail and threatened, as if they had been undermined by a stealthy mole and were dangling in the air. I supposed all Harry's talk about dying had unsettled me.

I wished Ben—big, solid and as familiar to me as myself—was home right this second to give me a reassuring hug. He was my rock—and I knew that was a trite and overused phrase, but in my case it was true. But then, our life here kept his flighty

31

artistic soul anchored to reality too, and that couldn't be a bad thing.

Chapter Two

Sweet Music

My wedding cake business, creating personalised fantasies in fondant icing, has really taken off recently. They are based on a rich, dark, organic fruitcake covered with natural marzipan, though there is nothing healthy or wholesome about the icing outer layer! Last week, as I finished off a cake in the shape of a magician's top hat, complete with emerging bride and bridegroom rabbits, it occurred to me that this dichotomy neatly sums up the life we lead—eighty per cent healthy and wholesome, and twenty per cent the enjoyable but unnecessary icing on the cake.

'Cakes and Ale'

The next morning found me putting the finishing touches to a violin-shaped wedding cake, and although I absolutely adore creating something new, this one had *really* tried my skills to the limit!

For a start, I couldn't think how to put the arch in the neck, until I hit on the idea of building it in wedges of cake like a bridge, propped up underneath until the keystone piece was inserted to hold it all together.

Now it was neatly encased in white icing, polished smooth with powdered sugar, and with the name of the happy couple and 'IF MUSIC BE

THE FOOD OF LOVE, PLAY ON' lettered around the edge, subtly highlighted in edible silver.

The strings had also taxed my brain, until I thought of pulling white toffee into long strands, then laying them out to harden on greaseproof paper, before attaching them. I was just completing the last of some spares, in case of mishaps, when the front door suddenly flew open, letting in a brisk breeze, which blew it into a bow.

Three Chanel suitcases in descending sizes thudded onto the mat one after the other, closely followed by the petite but elegant figure of Elizabeth Cazzini, alias Libby Martin, my oldest friend.

I was not really surprised to see her because Libby usually comes and goes as she pleases, without warning, but I yelled, 'Close the door!' as the rest of the hardened toffee strings showed signs of rolling off the counter.

'OK, there's no need to shout!' She shut the door and then regarded me with astonishment while I played a losing game of cat's cradle with the last toffee strand before it hardened.

'Oh, well,' I said resignedly, putting it to one side. 'I already have several spares.'

'What on earth are you doing?'

'Putting strings on this violin cake.' I gave her a quick kiss, at arm's length because of my sticky apron, and said, 'Look, just let me fix them into place with sugar paste, and then the really difficult bit's done and I can relax and have a break. Put the kettle on.'

'OK,' she agreed.

With a bit of concentration I managed to attach the strings, then turned to find she'd made two mugs of strong, steaming tea and was rummaging in the biscuit tin. She came up with a pecan puff. 'How many calories in these?'

'I've no idea. But what are you doing here, Libby, and where did you spring from? I wasn't expecting you, was I? I only emailed you yesterday and I thought you might still be in Pisa.'

'I was. And you *should* have been expecting me, after telling me Blessings was for sale! But I can see if the Griffin has a room free, if you can't put me up? And unless you've done something radical to that Spartan bathroom, it would be much more comfortable anyway,' she added frankly.

'Of course you can stay,' I said, ignoring this slur on my house, which I admit was shabby and comfortable and not terribly modernised. In fact, apart from installing a wood-burning stove in the living room for heating, it wasn't much different from when it was Granny's, right down to some ancient and nameless precursor to an Aga in the kitchen inglenook. 'I just wish you'd let me know. The spare bed isn't made up and it's covered in marrows.'

'How *very* seasonal,' she said, cutting the pecan puff in half and putting the rejected piece back in the tin. Libby is very easy to feed because she will eat anything, but only in tiny, doll's-house portions, which is probably how she retains her figure. 'But it's OK, Josie, I'm going out shortly to look over Blessings—I've got a viewing order—so you'll have plenty of time to sort it out.'

I carefully carried the cake into the larder and came back, removing the headscarf I'd covered my hair up with and the enormous flowered wrap-around pinafore. Freed from the possibility of

34

getting her rather glorious suit stained with foodstuffs, Libby got up and gave me a proper, warm hug that belied her crisp and cool manner, but then I know the real Libby under that sophisticated (and sometimes sarcastic) shell.

'Seriously, Libs, you actually got the first flight back in order to view Blessings?' I asked incredulously, returning the hug. 'Not that it isn't good to see you,' I added hastily.

She sat down opposite me at the big, scrubbed pine table, her forget-me-not-blue eyes open wide. 'Of course! I told you that one day I would like to live there, you said so yourself.'

'Yes, when we were fifteen, and Tim Rowland-Knowles's father let the school take our class round the house, as part of a history lesson, Libby!'

'I remember—the teacher took our class photo in the garden afterwards and I had a Princess Diana haircut while you were a New Romantic. I'm not sure which one of us looked worse.' She shuddered at the memory, but since she looked very pretty in the photo (which I still have) it must have been the thought of *my* outfit that did it.

'Even then, I didn't think you meant you intended living in that *particular* house, Libs, just one like it.'

'Yes, but that was because I never thought that it would come on the market. It was my ideal. And, if I recall, *you* once said you were going to be a gardener, marry Ben, have two children and live in the country—but just because you never did any of that, it doesn't mean that I can't fulfil *my* dream, does it? As soon as I got your email I contacted the estate agent and then got on the next plane.'

35

'I *am* a gardener, Ben and I don't need to get married to prove our love for each other, and Neatslake is *surrounded* by countryside,' I said defensively. I didn't mention the children, which, as she knows, just never came along . . .

Libby, not the most sensitive of flowers, took a minute or two to evaluate what she'd just said, and then apologised. 'Sorry, Josie. I take it Ben is still refusing to have any investigations done to see why there are no *bambini*? That man has a stubborn streak a mile wide!'

I nodded guiltily, because I'm sure Ben would have been horrified to discover that I discussed our private affairs with anyone else. He'd always been a bit jealous of my close friendship with Libs and he tended to say things about her sometimes that made me think that, despite having several weird arty friends from the wrong side of the tracks himself, some of his parents' snobbery must have rubbed off on him. That had certainly never stopped him accepting her invitations to holiday at her flat in Pisa, or to take us out to dinner at the flagship Cazzini restaurant near Piccadilly, the first one that Joe ever opened.

'But it isn't just stubbornness,' I explained, 'it's because he's seen how traumatic the whole IVF cycle thing has been for Mary and Russell, and he doesn't want to put me through that. Anyway, we have each other. That's enough.'

'Yes, I can imagine him saying so,' she commented drily, 'just like when you moved down to London to live with him when he was doing his MA at the Royal College of Art, and he suddenly started saying neither of you need the outdated trappings of marriage to show your commitment.'

36

'Yes, that was a bit odd, when we'd talked of marrying before. We did row about it, because Granny had old-fashioned ideas about things and it would have meant so much to her if we had got married, but he wouldn't change his mind. But then, he does suddenly get ideas in his head and simply won't change them, no matter what—he always has done. I don't see why he won't agree to a few simple tests, though. I mean, it would be good to at least know which of us has the problem, wouldn't it?'

'Sometimes there is no problem,' Libby said. 'It just doesn't happen. But I agree you ought to explore all the avenues before you give up on the idea.' She changed the subject. 'What have you done to the kitchen? It seems to have a split personality. The left-hand wall has gone all high tech, chrome and utility. And isn't that a second fridge and sink?'

'I suppose it does look a bit strange,' I agreed, seeing it suddenly with her eyes. Most of it was just as it always had been, with jars of wine bubbling round the old stove, herbs, lavender and strings of onions and dried apple rings hanging from the wooden rack over the kitchen table, bright gingham curtains and braided rug, and crocks and pots of earthenware everywhere. But one wall had been transformed into an ultra-modern and terribly antiseptic kitchen workstation.

'It's Health and Safety. Even little home cake businesses like mine need to be checked over and meet standards. There are all sorts of rules and regulations! It's not like the days when I knocked out a few cakes and some jam on the kitchen table and sold them at the WI Markets,' I said regretfully. 'Once things took off, it seemed easier to convert part of the kitchen to a sort of production line.'

'So, the bride cake business is booming?'

I nodded. 'It *really* took off last year when I was asked to design a cake for the Pharamond wedding, over at Middlemoss, and there was loads of publicity. It was a bit of a challenge, what with him being a well-known chef and cookery writer and Lizzie a keen cook too. They could easily have made their own, except they couldn't agree which of them was going to do it.'

'Didn't she write those *Perseverance Cottage Chronicles* that you used to love reading, all grow-your-own and recipes?'

'Yes, she still does. It was her books that really inspired me and Ben to try and live as self-sufficiently as possible. The cake was quite easy, three tiers in the form of apple pies.'

'Weird. Why apple pies?'

'I don't know, except that she and her husband had some long-running feud about who made the best one. The cake featured in the wedding pictures in *Lancashire Life*, and so did the one I did earlier this year, when Sophy Winter over at Sticklepond married her gardener. That was trickier—one big square cake with knot gardens in the corners, and a circular maze in the middle, with a bust of Shakespeare at the centre. I told you all about the discovery of a link between the family and the Bard, didn't I? Secret documents in a hidden compartment seeming to infer that the Winters were descended from Shakespeare? It was all a bit Da Vinci code!'

'I could hardly have missed the story! But it

seems very unlikely to me and it's still not proven, is it?'

'No, I expect they'll be arguing about it for years, but Sophy has built a whole business out of it. They get loads of visitors to the house and garden now.'

'You know her?'

'Yes, we got friendly while working out the design for the cake. She's really nice, and so is her daughter, Lucy. Which reminds me, how is my lovely goddaughter these days? And *where* is she?'

Pia, christened Philippa, is Libby's daughter by her brief first marriage. Her second husband, Joe Cazzini, adopted the infant and doted on her, despite already having grown-up children and grandchildren of his own, but her relationship with Libby became increasingly stormy once she hit the terrible teens. Libby tended to be a bit strict with her and I expect having a young-looking, beautiful and glamorous mother around becomes a liability rather than an asset at a certain age. You could hardly have called Gloria Martin a good role model for acquiring parenting skills, either, but Libby did her best.

'God knows where she is,' she said gloomily now. 'I text her all the time, but if I get a reply, it's just something like, "AM OK", which she would say anyway, whether she was or not. I thought you might know—she tells you things she doesn't tell me, sometimes.'

'No, I haven't had an email for a few weeks now . . . and I have a feeling then that she said she was somewhere in the Caribbean, on an island.'

'The Caribbean is all islands.'

'No, I meant a *little* island, belonging to

39

someone.'

'Possibly. Once she came into her trust fund at eighteen and I lost all control over her, she could be anywhere. Joe must have been mad, doing that!'

'Well, remember what we were like at that age? We thought we knew it all! You finished your art foundation year and blagged your way onto a fashion course in London, and I horrified poor Granny by often staying overnight with Ben in his Liverpool digs, when he was doing his fine art degree.'

'Yes, but the rest of the time you were living sensibly at home, working in a nursery garden and studying for your horticulture qualifications on day release,' she pointed out. 'And I was *entirely* focused on my future and getting to where I wanted to be. Pia's quite different—she goes around with a group of complete wasters who seem to have no ambitions at all, other than to have a good time, though she keeps saying she's going to go to college eventually.'

'Well, you did and then you barely lasted a term before you got married.'

'Becoming a student was just a means to an end, to get me to London, and then you have to strike while the iron's hot,' she said, then looked into her mug and reached for the blue and white striped teapot under its knitted hen cosy (one of Pansy Grace's making, in black-speckled white yarn—it looked just like Aggie).

'Phillip was such a sweetie, wasn't he?' I said. 'Once I met him, I knew you were really in love with him. It wasn't just his wealth!'

'Of course not,' Libby said indignantly and I

40

grinned, remembering how I'd asked her when she first knew she was truly in love with Phillip and she'd quoted that bit in her favourite book, *Pride and Prejudice* (which has always been her blueprint for perfection), where Lizzy tells Jane she first knew she loved Darcy when she saw his beautiful grounds at Pemberley!

'I loved Phillip, and I was devastated when he died within a year. And then Joe came along and I fell in love all over again.' She sighed sadly. 'You know,' she confided, 'the trouble with marrying wealthy elderly men is that they've always already signed over their business interests to the offspring of their first marriage, who are usually old enough to be your parents, if not grandparents, and have their own families. So although they've left themselves plenty to live on, there's never an enormous legacy for the *second* wife. Neither Phillip nor Joe left me a huge inheritance, but Joe arranged Pia's trust fund with the rest of the family when he formally adopted her—they always considered her one of the Cazzinis, even though she was no more related to them than I was. She's dark like Phillip, though, so she looks like one.'

'Oh, come off it with the poverty-stricken bit. You're loaded!'

'Comfortable, not mega-rich,' she insisted, though she always seems to me to be fabulously wealthy and able to do anything she wants. 'If I buy Blessings, I might have to sell the flat in Pisa.'

'Or the London house?'

'Tricky. Pia mainly uses that as her home base when she does deign to grace me with her presence. And that's good, because when she's in London, she gets taken over by the Cazzini uncles and aunts and cousins, especially Joe's youngest sister, Maria, and they might manage to knock some sense into her head eventually. She's more likely to listen to them than to me. The relations in Pisa are a bit too distant to have much clout. Anyway, I like having a base in London.'

She got up. 'I'll just go and tidy up a bit and do my face, then I'm off.'

'You aren't letting the grass grow under your feet!'

'I can't afford to. The estate agent said there'd been lots of interest in Blessings already, almost all from the actors in that *Cotton Common* soap series that they shoot in Manchester.'

'I suppose there might have been. They've been moving into the area, especially round the Mosses, in the last few years.'

'Well, they're not moving into Neatslake,' she said firmly. 'Oh, and is Ben home? I forgot to ask,' she added as an afterthought.

She and Ben had a fairly spiky relationship and I thought he was a little jealous of her. But it wasn't like we didn't both have other friends too, though come to think of it, they were mostly couples, like Mark and Stella who keep the goats, or Russell and Mary. Libby—after Ben, of course—was my *best* friend . . .

'He went to London yesterday.' I looked at the clock. 'He usually gives me a ring about this time, if he can.'

'I hope you gave him a clean hankie and told him not to speak to strange women before he left,' she said tartly, before vanishing into the bathroom, which was inconveniently located downstairs, off the living room. As the door closed behind her I

42

heard her exclaim, 'Bizarre!'

I expect she was impressed by my cherished collection of knitted French poodle toilet roll covers. Whenever the Graces seem to be running short of Acorns, I ask for a new one and Pansy obliges, with whatever wool comes to hand. The last one was in glitzy speckled silver yarn.

*   *   *

The post, including a plastic-wrapped copy of *Country at Heart* magazine with the article about me in it, arrived immediately after Libby had left for her viewing. I almost phoned her mobile to tell her about it, but then thought it would wait.

The pictures were rather nice—one of me wearing a big floppy straw hat, digging in the garden, with Aggie waiting for worms, and Ben in his studio painting one of his three-dimensional creations. There was also a lovely one of Harry sitting in a deck chair under the plum tree, Mac curled at his feet, and a couple of smaller shots of me in the kitchen and the wedding cake I had been making (a fairy cake—lots of fairies).

Then I read the article, and really, I don't remember saying most of the things it said I had! How odd. It all looked and sounded terribly idyllic, though.

Chapter Three

Blessings

I'm making a diamond wedding anniversary cake—a stacked two-tier one, with the names of the happy couple around the top tier and 'Diamonds Are Forever' around the bottom one. There will be a pink and blue harlequin diamond pattern all over it too, and some of the original favours from their wedding cake—white doves and horseshoes, mostly. I'd already baked the cake, so today I covered it with marzipan.

After that, I started off some carrot wine and then, being in that kind of groove, made two carrot cakes which I decorated with little carrots made from the scraps of marzipan left over from the cake, coloured orange and green with natural food colour.

'Cakes and Ale'

After puzzling over some of the inane, if not downright daft, things I was supposed to have said about self-sufficiency and nature's wonderful bounty, I put the magazine to one side and retrieved the Violin cake from the larder, looking at it with considerable pride.

The strings were firm and hard, and it was lucky it was an autumn wedding, because with a bit of luck it would be cool at the reception and they wouldn't sag. I threaded a bunch of white and palest pink silk ribbons around the neck carefully, like adorning a medieval troubadour's lute, then covered it and replaced it in the cold larder, ready to deliver tomorrow.

Then I went upstairs to move the vegetables from the spare bed and make it up, though it seemed a lot of bother when Libby probably wouldn't stay more than one night. It was pretty chilly in there, but would soon warm up once the door was left open and the heat from the stove wafted up the stairs.

As I shook out lavender-scented sheets and pillowcases, I thought how horrified Libby would be when she saw the way Blessings had deteriorated. Her recollections, like mine, would be of how it was once, the snowy interior walls of the Elizabethan part of the house studded with plaster emblems and the garden neatly laid out, all lawns, roses and specimen trees.

But Harry had said it was all sadly changed now ... and, come to that, I'd forgotten to remind Libby of Dorrie Spottiswode's existence, though I expect she would find that out soon enough. Dorrie and I had become friends over the last few years, but I didn't think Libby had ever met her.

I wondered what she would make of Tim, for she probably only remembered him as the languid fair youth of so long ago. He's a solicitor in Ormskirk, and I expect he has some private income, though obviously it's not enough to restore Blessings to its former glory.

Tim was in the pub one evening recently when Ben and I were meeting our elderly hippie friends, Mark and Stella (who unfortunately seem to take the smell of goat with them everywhere, though you get used to it after a bit).

I asked him if he remembered playing tennis

with me and Libby when we were teenagers and he said he did—but he was just being polite; I could see he didn't really. But that was hardly surprising, because we were two awkward, immature schoolgirls and he was almost grown up. He seemed very nice, though he has a permanently anxious look in his blue eyes—an eager-to-please expression—and that shock of white-blond hair makes him look a bit startled. He has a nervous habit of constantly trying to smooth it down, though regular haircuts would be a more practical idea.

But anyway, I was right about the eager-to-please bit, because he certainly seemed to have pleased Libby. I'd just started to wonder how many hours it took to show somebody round a house, even a substantial Elizabethan town house, when she phoned to say Tim had invited her out to dinner and she didn't know what time she would be getting back!

If I hadn't been so surprised I would have told her to call in for the front door key on her way, but by the time it occurred to me and I phoned back, she had switched her mobile off.

I went back to marzipanning my Diamonds Are Forever anniversary cake, but I was a bit distracted . . . What *was* Libby up to? Trying to beat the poor man down on the price?

*　　　*　　　*

She staggered in looking glazed at about one in the morning, after hammering on the door to wake me because by then I'd fallen asleep on the sofa in the living room.

46

'Did you have a nice time?' I asked sleepily as she removed her coat and kicked off her stilettos with a sigh of relief.

'Bliss!' she said enthusiastically. 'Sorry to make you stay up, though. I wasn't thinking straight when I phoned you earlier because—well, you won't believe this, Josie, but I'm in love!'

I creaked my eyelids open a bit wider. 'You *do* mean with Blessings, don't you?'

'No! Well, yes,' she qualified, 'it's the sweetest little Elizabethan house imaginable. But I've fallen in love with Tim too. Oh, Josie, this is *it*—love at first sight.'

'Again?' I said, putting the kettle on for cocoa.

'This is different! I fell in love with Phillip and Joe, of course, but not the very second I set eyes on them,' she said indignantly. 'But when Tim opened the door, we just gazed into each other's eyes and . . . well, we couldn't look away. And after that . . .' she heaved a voluptuous sigh, 'we talked and talked. Then we realised how late it was and thought we'd better go out for something to eat . . . Oh, I feel like we've been soul mates for ever!'

'That's a bit how I felt when I first saw Ben,' I said, with a reminiscent sigh. 'Though I suppose I was so young I didn't understand it was love.'

She snapped back to reality, her blue eyes wide, and said, 'No, it was *nothing* like that, though admittedly you and Ben had a bit of a Juliet and Romeo thing going on. Lucky there were family objections only on his side—it takes two families to start a good, tragic feud.'

I let that go. I played Juliet to Ben's Romeo in the school play one year, and I hated the end, though if they had both got up and run off hand in

47

hand, I suppose it wouldn't be a tragedy.

'Did you actually find time to look around Blessings—remember, the house you were so keen to buy that you flew all the way over from Pisa with a viewing order?'

'Of course I did, and it's even more wonderful than I remembered, though it's so run down and shabby! Those plaster walls with funny little animals and shields and stuff moulded into them, and the huge beams and little diamond-paned windows with ripply glass. Tim adores the place and, do you know, he loves Italy too. He's been to Pisa but always wanted to go back for long enough to explore it properly! Isn't that a coincidence?'

'Mmm . . .' I said, starting to feel sleepy again. This was way past my bedtime.

'In fact, we seemed to agree about everything. And the great thing is, there's no need to buy Blessings if Tim and I are getting married so I can spend the money renovating it instead.'

I missed my mouth entirely with the last dregs of my cocoa and it went down the front of my dressing gown. *'Married?* Libby, you only met him two seconds ago!'

'That's all it took for us to fall in love and know we wanted to spend the rest of our lives together,' she said simply. 'Tomorrow we're going to buy an engagement ring and I'm moving into Blessings.'

'Bloody hell!' I gazed at her anxiously. 'Look, Libby, hadn't you better think about it a bit first and not do anything hasty? I mean, I know you fell in love with your first two husbands quickly and married almost immediately, and it worked out fine, but this is *hugely* rash. And he's not rich, either.'

'I know, but it doesn't matter.' Then she bleated, 'Resistance is useless,' in a Dalek voice, and giggled like a teenager.

'You've gone mad, Libs!'

'Yes, but mad in a good way. Tim's handsome, sweet, funny, and kind—everything I could possibly want . . .'

I gave her the sweet and kind, but he definitely wasn't handsome. So it *must* be love.

'We'd like to get married tomorrow.'

'Well, you can't,' I pointed out. 'I really think you ought to consider all this in the cold light of day, not get carried away and—'

'Break out the elderflower champagne and let's celebrate!' she interrupted gaily. 'Come on, Josie, don't I always know exactly what I'm doing?'

'You *did*,' I conceded, 'but that was before you turned into Love-Crazed of Pisa!'

But by then, being Libby, she had taken out a little pink leather-bound notebook from her handbag and started to make a to-do list.

'What's the name of the vicar?' she asked, looking up.

*   *   *

She was still in the same state next morning, except the list was now two pages long.

Over breakfast I showed her the *Country at Heart* article, which she read through twice, and then commented, 'It doesn't sound like you at all!'

'It isn't. I'm quite positive I didn't say most of that. In fact, some of it is quite idiotic.'

'The average reader probably won't think that, and it's great publicity for the cakes—and for Ben

49

too, come to that.' She peered more closely at the photograph of him in his studio. 'I'm not sure about whatever it is he's working on, though. It looks like an explosion in a half-set black pudding.'

'His work has been a bit odd lately,' I admitted. 'I don't like it very much, but it must be good or he wouldn't have won that prize.'

'I tell you what,' Libby said, tapping the page with her long, French-manicured nails, 'I bet lots of *Skint Old Northern Woman* readers get this magazine too, and they will put two and two together. Your cover will be blown.'

'Oh, I hope not. I'd have to be so careful what I said if everyone knew who I was!'

She'd got me worried, but later, when I got Ben on the phone and told him, he said he didn't think the readership of a little niche magazine like *SONW* would be the same as that for an expensive glossy like *Country at Heart*. But he was pleased he was in it, I could tell from his voice.

I didn't mention the Libby and Tim situation. I thought I'd give it twenty-four hours and see if it wore off.

Chapter Four

Love, Actually

A friend is suddenly moving back to the village after dividing her time between Italy and London for several years—in fact, she is here!

She always had a fancy to live in a nearby small Elizabethan house and, when it recently came onto the market, she snapped it up—and the owner with it. Reader, she married him!

I've had to quickly finish off the Diamonds Are Forever anniversary cake I was making (a special order) so I could start on my friend's bridal cake . . .

'Cakes and Ale'

Libby and Tim certainly didn't let the grass grow beneath their feet, and by the time Ben returned from London only a few days later, they were engaged, living together and planning their imminent nuptials.

I'd finally broken the news to Ben on the phone, but I wasn't sure he quite believed me until he got back and I showed him the announcement in the local paper, which had just come out.

'This has to be the most unlikely pairing ever!' I said. 'I mean, "A marriage has been arranged between Mrs Elizabeth Cazzini of London and Pisa, and Mr Timothy Rowland-Knowles of Blessings, Neatslake," may *sound* very well, but everyone around here knows that she started life as plain Libby Martin from the council estate. And

51

if her mother wasn't actually on the game, she sailed perilously close to the edge! Libby doesn't even have a father to give her away; she says she's going to do it herself. Mrs Talkalot at the post office says the village is reeling with shock, but she personally doesn't think Libby is after Tim's money. I told her Libs is much better off than Tim so, if anything, it would be the other way round, but I'm not sure she believed me.'

Even two rich and elderly husbands later, transformed into a wealthy and sophisticated widow, I was sure there would always be people who would try to put her down. Not that they would manage it. Libby might look like the fairy off the top of the Christmas tree, but her backbone is pure steel.

'That sort of class snobbishness doesn't seem to matter so much these days, does it?' Ben said rather absently, staring at the newspaper.

It was on the tip of my tongue to blurt out that it certainly *did* matter to his parents, who had never thought me good enough for their blue-eyed boy, but I heroically managed to stop myself in time. It was mostly his mother's jealousy and spite, anyway.

'I suppose you're right and perhaps no one will take much notice, especially since Libby's mum moved down to Brighton years ago to live with her other daughter,' I conceded, though if Gloria Martin turned up at the wedding—and there is no way you can't invite your own mother, regardless of what you think of her lifestyle choices, is there?—then it might rake things up again. 'Tim doesn't care who her parents are. Dorrie Spottiswode did think Libby was a gold-digger at first, but she quickly warmed to her once she

52

discovered she was a well-off widow, and she's started going on about "vigorous plebeian blood enriching the atrophied Rowland-Knowles family tree", now.'

'Libby's certainly a fast worker; I've only been away a few days.' Ben didn't sound admiring, more thoughtful, but as I've said, he'd always been a bit jcalous of our close friendship. Perhaps it was because Libby and I shared a bond that deep. We both had sadness in our pasts and a yearning for security, even if our ideas of what that entails, and how to obtain it, were entirely different. I often suspected a bit of Ben's parents' snobbish attitude had rubbed off on him too, so no matter how smart and rich she became, in his mind she remained Libby Martin from the dysfunctional family at the wrong end of the village.

'She didn't have to work at it, Ben, because she and Tim fell in love the instant they set eyes on each othcr again. It's *terribly* romantic! He showed her over the house and then they went out to dinner—and by next day they were cruising Lord Street in Southport, looking for an engagement ring, and sending out the announcement to the newspapers. They just caught the deadline for this week's issue.'

'Does she have enough room on her finger for any more rings?' he asked sarcastically.

His attitude was really starting to annoy me. 'Don't be silly. She took off Joe's ring when she put on Tim's, just as she did with her first husband's when she married Joe. The ring's terribly pretty—rose diamonds in a platinum setting.'

I tried not to sound too wistful. The only ring I

53

possessed was Granny's old worn wedding band, upstairs in a box of treasures; but then, when I spent most of my days either up to the elbows in earth or cake mix, it wouldn't be practical to wear jewellery anyway, would it? But it would have been nice to have the option!

'Marry in haste, repent at leisure,' Ben quoted smugly.

'Oh, honestly, Ben!' I snapped. 'What is the matter with you? Libby's married in haste twice before and been very happy, so I think she knows what she's doing. And it will be lovely to have her living nearby—she'll be company when you're away. They've asked us both over for a drink tomorrow evening, so that you and Tim can get to know each other.'

'We do know each other. We've met a couple of times down at the Griffin.'

'Oh, have you? I know we ran into him there once when we were with Stella and Mark, but we didn't talk much.' Ben does sometimes walk down there in the evening with Harry and then stays for a drink, and to most men, exchanging a few words at the bar is enough to constitute a friendship. 'Well, it's kind of them to invite us round for a drink, isn't it?'

He grunted unenthusiastically, but I expect he was just tired. As usual on his return from these trips, he was looking exhausted and glad to be home, but I had a feeling there was also something on his mind . . .

'Libby showed me over Blessings yesterday and the Elizabethan part does want a lot doing to it. Tim's stepmother really let it go. It's not even clean. That Portuguese couple who worked for her

54

don't seem to have been very efficient at all, so I'm helping her have a good spring-clean. Just as well it's not that big a house, more of a town house than a manor.'

'Haven't you got enough to do, Josie? I hardly see you as it is. You're always off looking after Harry, walking the dog, making cakes or doing errands for the Three Graces.'

'But these days you're shut away in the studio working most of the time you're home, Ben, so I don't see much of you either, unless you come to talk to me while I'm gardening,' I pointed out.

'I want to finish that second series of paintings,' he said, 'but if you're out half the time, you aren't going to know whether I've been looking for you or not, are you?'

Actually, I did have a pretty good idea, because once he was down in the studio he was lost to the world until called in for meals or to help with something. He'd even constructed a little lean-to kitchen area at the side, with a cold-water sink and a kettle, and took a Thermos of cold milk down with him for his tea. I kept the biscuit barrel stocked up, and popped down with hot scones and other treats from time to time. Sometimes he used the kitchen area as a darkroom and I lived in fear that one day he'd absent-mindedly make his tea with developing fluid, or something.

If he'd been around more often, he would have realised that I was only usually out in mid-afternoon when I needed a break, unless I crept out to the church gates for ten minutes for a sneaky wedding fix when I heard the bells peal out . . .

'Helping to sort out Blessings is just a temporary

thing and we're having fun!' I said. 'I rang Sophy Winter up and asked her advice on cleaning and renovating old properties, because she's done wonders with Winter's End since she inherited. She was very helpful. And her great-aunt Hebe is a friend of Dorrie's, so when she heard what was happening she sent Libby a big jar of her home-made beeswax polish. Wasn't that kind?'

'I can't see the elegant Mrs Elizabeth Cazzini getting her hands dirty. You'll end up doing it all yourself.'

'There you do her an injustice,' I said indignantly, 'Libby's never minded hard work. She went straight out and bought overalls and ordered the cleaning materials Sophy advised from a specialist firm called Stately Solutions.' I didn't mention the several pairs of thin cotton and latex gloves, with which Libby intended to protect her immaculate nails. 'Dolly Mops, that cleaning agency from Ormskirk, sent a team round to give the modern wing a good going-over, but Sophy advised us to do the rest ourselves. And she knew someone who could come and repaint the plaster walls with whatever authentic gunge they need—you can't just slap vinyl emulsion on them.'

'Oh, well, I suppose it's only a week or two, and I expect you'll both have fun doing it up and planning the wedding and everything,' he said, his usual good nature returning. 'Now I've got this studio space in Camden I'm bound to be away more, so it will be good that you've got company.'

While I was pleased to see Ben slowly warming to the idea of Libby's permanent presence on the Neatslake scene, this last statement dismayed me.

'Away *more*? I thought the stuido was just for

storage, because it would be easier than moving your work up and down between here and London in the van. Are you going to paint there too?'

'Probably just finishing things off. I'll still do most of it here. But the artists at the studios are forming themselves into a group to exhibit together, the Camdenites, and they want me to join them.'

'Ben,' I said, dismayed, 'at this rate we might as well both move down there and use the cottage as a weekend retreat!'

'Don't be silly, you know we both love it here and it's where my inspiration comes from. It's only networking, exhibiting and selling my stuff that takes me to London. Now my name's really getting known, I have to strike while the iron's hot. But this will always be my home, and actually, when I'm in London, I love the idea of you up here waiting for me and everything going on just as usual.'

'I suppose you're right,' I said, slightly mollified, 'and I do see what you mean about striking while the iron's hot. But I don't actually hate London and it's always nice to catch up with Russell and Mary, so I think, although I got out of the habit of coming with you after Harry had that fall, I should get back into it again!'

'But that's easier said than done, isn't it? I do understand that you can't leave Neatslake at present. It's not like Harry can be left alone to look after things any more, and the garden would run to seed now he's too frail to do much. Besides, what about the Three Graces, not to mention Josie's Weird and Wonderful Cakes?'

I sighed. 'I know—it's all so difficult! I love my

57

life here and I don't want to go away. It's just I don't want us to be apart so much, either.'

'It'll get better soon, you'll see,' he said easily. 'When I'm a big name, I can paint anywhere and people will come to *me* to buy my work, not the other way round.'

'I suppose so, and it's some consolation to know we have friends you can stay with. How *are* Russell and Mary?'

In the days when the three of them were at the Royal College of Art and I was looking after us all and working in a nearby florist's, learning how to torture innocent flowers into bouquets and wreaths, we'd all been good friends and shared seedy digs together. Now they're married and have a ground-floor flat in Camden, and they put Ben up in the spare room.

'They're fine,' he said, suddenly looking a bit shifty and evasive. After all these years I recognise the signs.

I narrowed my eyes. '*And?*'

'And what?'

'And the rest—whatever it is that you don't want to tell me.'

For a moment he stared blankly at me.

'Come on, Ben, tell me the awful truth. You haven't fallen out with Russell and Mary, have you? We've known them so long and it's been really useful being able to stay with them.'

'No, I haven't fallen out with them, but they may not be able to put me up much longer because they'll want their spare room themselves.' He got up and put his arms around me. 'Mary's expecting. She says it's all due to some herbal stuff she's been taking, but I suspect it's more because they ran out

58

of money for further IVF treatment, and the pressure was off a bit.'

'Expecting?' I held him off, gazing up into his face, which looked anxious and concerned. 'You mean, it *worked*? What kind of herbal stuff?'

'Something she got from a Chinese practitioner, though I really don't see how a few dried plants brewed up into a tea could make any difference, Josie.'

'Well, something obviously did! How pregnant is she?'

'About three months. I only just found out, but I didn't want to tell you because I knew you would be upset.'

'I'm not upset,' I lied, since I certainly was. And also, I was ashamed to find, jealous—plus deeply hurt that Mary hadn't told me about the Chinese herbalist, when she knew how desperately I wanted a baby, too. 'I'm really pleased for them, but surprised Mary didn't phone and tell me herself.'

'I expect she wanted to wait a bit before she told anyone this time.'

Mary had been pregnant twice after IVF treatment and lost the babies at the twelve-week stage, so that would be quite understandable.

'This Chinese medicine...I wonder where she—' I began.

Ben's arms tightened around me. 'Forget it, Josie. What's meant to be, will be.'

I held him off and snapped, 'That's all very well, but maybe it was meant to be that *I* consult a Chinese herbalist too! Had you thought of that?'

'Now, darling, don't start getting upset about it. I

59

knew this would rake it all up again,' he said, stroking my back in a would-be comforting way that didn't quite cut the mustard this time. My biological clock had been ticking so loudly lately that he must have felt he was being followed around by the crocodile in *Peter Pan*.

'We're happy just as we are really, aren't we?' he added soothingly.

'Yes, but that doesn't mean we can't make the *attempt* to have a family, does it, Ben? I mean, without getting obsessed by it, we could at least explore all the avenues before giving up!'

Not for the first time I suspected that, whatever he said, Ben liked being the centre of my world and didn't want to share it with anyone, even children (or my one close friend, Libby). Like a big cuckoo chick in a nest, really . . .

I wondered if all hugely talented artists were that egocentric.

Ben gave me another squeeze and then, obviously considering the matter closed, sat back down in the rocking chair, his long legs stretched out in front of him. Changed back into old, worn jeans and sweatshirt, his light brown hair tousled, he was the Ben I knew and loved, rather than the distinctly smarter London version who had returned to me earlier that day, but it still didn't stop me feeling exasperated with him.

'It's so good to be home,' he said with a sigh. 'I'm shattered. At least here no one expects anything of me and I can just sink back into my groove.' But then he sat up again as a thought struck him. 'Unless . . . Libby's not staying with us, is she?'

'No, she moved into Blessings the day after the viewing.'

He subsided again. 'That's what I said—fast worker!'

* * *

Of course, I phoned Mary as soon as I had a minute to myself, to congratulate her and, if truth were told, to find out all about the Chinese herbalist.

'This is such great news, Mary! I don't know how you managed to keep it to yourself for so long.'

'Well, I would have told Ben sooner only—'

'I know,' I broke in sympathetically, 'you wanted to hug it to yourself for a while, make sure everything was going well, didn't you?' I suppose that explained why she'd been a bit distant and reluctant to talk to me for ages too.

'Yes, there was an element of that until I was at the three-month stage,' she admitted, 'but also I felt so sick all the time, which was a bit distracting, though that's better now. Just as well, because I'll have to go on teaching as long as I can. The two courses of IVF we paid for meant we had to increase our mortgage, so we still need my income coming in. But afterwards, Russell and I will have to arrange our classes so that one of us can baby-sit while the other is teaching.'

They both lecture part time and since Mary's are mostly evening classes, that should work well.

'I bet Russell's delighted!'

'Oh . . . yes. And relieved, I think.' She gave an embarrassed laugh. 'It's only now it actually looks as if I will have this baby that I realise quite how obsessed I've been with it. It's lucky we've managed to come through it all as a strong couple.'

61

'I thought you'd given up any thought of getting pregnant after the last attempt.'

'Oh, no! I had to give up the IVF—it was way too expensive and the whole regime of drugs and stuff very invasive—but I never gave up hope.'

'Ben said you were taking a kind of herbal medicine?' I prompted.

'Yes,' she said eagerly, 'about a year ago Olivia told me about a Chinese herbalist who specialised in infertility problems, so we went together, for courage.'

'Olivia?'

There was a pause, and then Mary said, 'Oh, she's a fairly new friend you haven't met. But she's in her early forties so she was getting even more desperate than I was. Anyway, we were given this rather foul concoction to take three times a day, plus recommendations to balance our yin and yang and stuff like that.'

'And do you think that's what did the trick?'

'I honestly don't know. It might have been just the relaxing part of it that was crucial, though, goodness knows, we were relaxed enough when we were first married and nothing ever happened then—and we were both younger, so it should have been easier to get pregnant.'

'And what happened to your friend? Did it work for her too?'

'Well, that's the amazing thing. She fell pregnant about a fortnight after I did! But again, who knows whether it was because she stopped trying so hard or due to the healthy regime and the medicine?'

Who knew, indeed . . . but it sounded at least worth a try!

'Mary, do you think you could give me the

contact details for this herbalist? It's all natural, isn't it?'

'I haven't got them by me, but you can look her up on the internet,' she said, and I jotted down the name.

'Thanks, Mary.'

'Are you sure you want to try it?' she asked. 'It's very expensive, though not on the scale of IVF treatment, obviously. And pregnancy does change things. Ben said to me once that he really didn't mind that you hadn't had children because he liked you just to himself, the two of you, and having a family would have changed the dynamics of the relationship.'

'Ben said *that*?' I thought about it. 'He's always gone along with me when I've said I wanted children, but you're right, he's never actually been bothered by them not coming along, except on my account. But then, I suppose *I've* always gone along with things he's felt strongly about in the end, like his going all anti-marriage, even when it upset Granny. She would have loved to have seen me married.'

'Ben does dig his heels in about things sometimes,' Mary agreed, 'and then he never changes his mind. Not that I've seen much of him the last few months. I—' She broke off. 'Sorry, thought I heard Russell come in. What was I saying?'

'That you'd hardly seen Ben lately, but I suppose he's pretty busy when he's down, especially now he's taken on studio space. I take it you are one of the Camdenites too?'

'Yes. Some of my big sculptural ceramic pieces are going into the first exhibition. It's all looking

63

very promising, though in a way we're all currently riding on the coat-tails of Ben's success.'

'I don't think he sees it that way—we've all been friends so long. And it's been kind of you to let us use your spare room. I know I haven't visited for ages, but it's a relief knowing that Ben's staying with friends when he's down in the Big Smoke. But I expect you're going to turn it into a nursery soon, aren't you, so he'll have to find himself another place to stay?'

'I—yes,' she said, and then added hurriedly, 'Look, I've left something on the stove, I'll have to go. But it's been lovely talking to you, Josie.'

'Yes, we really should—' I began, but I was talking to empty air.

What she'd said about Ben not being that keen on the idea of children really crystallised what I'd long suspected myself. He would have accepted it, had it happened, but that was as far as he was prepared to go. And that wasn't far enough.

It would be terribly devious if I did something about it behind Ben's back, but it didn't stop me looking up that website. Mary was right about the expense, but then, we had money in the bank, some of it earned by my cake business, not just from Ben's work. And the regime seemed to involve a healthy diet and destressing more than anything, which could only be good.

It was surely worth a try? And if babies changed the dynamics of a relationship, it was in a *good* way, so if anything came of it, I expected Ben would get used to it. He'd have to.

As I started to bake the first in a series of small, round dark fruitcakes from which to construct the wedding cake of Libby's dreams, I kept wondering if the Chinese medicine had really been what had made the difference to Mary, or if it was just coincidence—or even hope and positive thinking?

It was an exciting prospect, though. All aspects of my life seemed to be exciting lately!

Chapter Five

All Apple Pie

It's been such a good year for the apples and pears that we get from a member or our Acorn barter group, that I'm starting to feel sick of the sight of them! The best have been individually wrapped in tissue and stored in boxes. Festoons of dried fruit rings hang from the kitchen ceiling, there are jars and jars of apple jelly, apple and bramble jam and apple sauce, and one side of my second freezer, in the garden shed, is stacked with pies, crumbles and purée. The apple press has been fully employed and demijohns of wine bubble gently in the kitchen inglenook.

I'm appled out!

'Cakes and Ale'

'Why do you want to do the whole church wedding thing, with a meringue dress and all the rest of it, Libby?' I asked curiously next day. 'I mean, it *is* your third time and you're already living with Tim!'

We were standing in one of the bedrooms in the Elizabethan part of Blessings, the one with the window that had blown in and been left hanging open, so that the rain had made a mess of the floorboards beneath. Harry had been over to mend the catch that morning and we'd just finished pinning a sheet of polythene over the broken panes to keep any more rain from getting onto the floorboards, until they could be replaced.

We were both wearing jeans and jumpers, though of course Libby's was designer, lush oatmeal cashmere, to my jumble sale and hand-knitted (by Pansy Grace). Libby had incongruously topped her ensemble with a long wedding veil and, since it was a dark day, she looked rather ghostly against the pale plaster walls studded with heraldic emblems, most of them grimacing creatures.

She turned to look at me, opening her round, forget-me-not-blue eyes even wider, like a surprised kitten just before it inserts its needle-sharp teeth into your hand. 'Yes, but I'm widowed, Josie, and Tim's ex-wife is a Catholic and managed to get the marriage annulled on some technicality, so we're *allowed* the full monty if we want it.'

'Non-consummation of the marriage?' I asked with interest, that being the only grounds for annulment I'd ever heard of. (And I hadn't known about Tim's brief early marriage before she told me, either—that had been a surprise.)

'Absolutely not!' she said decidedly. Then a soft smile appeared on her face, one that was totally different from any expression I'd ever seen her wear before the advent into her life of Tim Rowland-Knowles. Soft was something she had never been, even as a mother. *Especially* as a mother, since I'm sure she was so terrified that Pia would turn out like her granny that she was often way too strict with her. No wonder the poor child had rebelled!

'Anyway,' she added dreamily, 'this time it's entirely different. Before I met Tim I only allowed myself to fall for rich men—and I *did* truly love Phillip and Joe, you know I did.'

I nodded, because she had been rosy and starry-eyed both times being, despite her crisp-shelled exterior, a romantic at heart.

'But I hadn't realised I could feel so—so deeply head-over-heels, and fluttery in the stomach when I see Tim, and as if everything is new and bright and beautiful. So I want to trip down the aisle looking and feeling like a Madonna—totally pure and *extra* virgin.'

'You will,' I assured her, touched, and I didn't ask which Madonna she had in mind because I thought I could guess. Indeed, she was humming a very familiar tune as she adjusted about three miles of antique gossamer thread veiling, secured by a pearl and diamond tiara, on her natural (if slightly enhanced) golden hair.

It was a Spottiswode heirloom and had been Tim's mother's bridal veil, which Dorrie had bestowed on her earlier that morning, as a familial seal of approval. Libby looked like an angel in it—but actually, she looks like an angel in *anything*. I sometimes wish I did too, but I'm tall, sturdy and grave, with perfectly nondescript blue-grey eyes, a cloud of unruly, fine, dark auburn hair and pale, sallow skin.

'I'll have to take the veil with me when I go down to London to find my wedding dress,' she said, 'or it won't match. It's going to be difficult finding something off the peg that's suitable, especially in petite, but there's no time to have one made. I'll

67

take your measurements with me, Josie, but you're a pretty standard size twelve, so I should be able to find you *something*.'

'I can't imagine why you want me to be a bridesmaid, when you must know hordes of younger and prettier women.'

'Yes, I do, and that's precisely the point: I don't want my thunder stolen and you'll make a perfect foil,' she said frankly, examining her flawless and Botoxed-smooth complexion in a clouded mirror, before pushing the veil back a little so that a few more gilded curls peeped out. 'I'd have had Pia too, but since she put the phone down on me as soon as I told her about Tim and now isn't answering my calls, I don't think she's going to turn up. I don't even know where she is.'

'You're worried about her, aren't you?'

'Of course I'm worried, but what can I do? She's turned eighteen and she's got money—she's out of my control. She hasn't listened to a word I've said since she hit the teens anyway, so it's probably as well I don't know what she's getting up to.'

She shrugged resignedly and returned to the subject in hand. 'You know, Josie, you shouldn't put yourself down all the time, because you *are* pretty in your own unusual way when you scrub up, besides being the only real female friend I've ever had, so I truly want you at my wedding, as my bridesmaid.'

'Well . . . OK,' I said, touched. She had asked me the previous two times, but luckily there had been hordes of little granddaughters of the bridegroom simply *panting* to climb into fuchsia silk taffeta, so I'd managed to get out of it. 'But do you think you could find me a dress in any other colour than

68

pink?'

To be honest, I'm not a terribly girly girl, which is probably just as well. It wouldn't be practical to go all pastel and frilly when I spend most of my time working in the garden in jeans and wellies, and the rest wrapped in a huge pinafore cooking, jamming, wine-making or baking and decorating cakes.

'I suppose blue *would* be better, especially the same dirty French blue as your eyes, and it would flatter your sallow skin more,' she agreed candidly. 'It's a pity the wedding is late in the year, because you look *so* much better in the summer when your skin has a bit of a glow.'

'Thanks.'

'But pink is more weddingy and anyway, it's going to be a question of what I can find in your size. Besides, I'm going to have a hint of pink in my bouquet and in the roses on the cake, so it would tie in.'

'You're quite *sure* about the cake design before I start putting it together?'

Libby had certainly sounded definite about what she wanted—the Leaning Tower of Pisa, with an ascending swirl of blush-pink roses entwined around it. Hence all the little round cakes I'd been baking, ready to stack up high and ice.

'Oh, yes, and I've told Gina to send me some postcards of the tower, to help you get it right,' she said, Gina being her devoted *tuttofare*, or maid-of-all-work, in Pisa.

'If Pia does change her mind once she's over the shock, she could take my place as bridesmaid,' I suggested hopefully, because although I'd always secretly yearned to walk down the aisle, it was as a bride, not an also-ran.

'I hope she will change her mind, but I'm not holding my breath. But look on the bright side, Josie, if Ben sees you looking all bridal, flowery and pretty, perhaps he'll finally decide to tie the knot. And, come on, you *know* you want to!'

'No I don't! We don't need to be married to show we care about each other,' I lied firmly. 'Especially not at this stage. Weddings are for other people, not us.'

Libby, who knew me all too well, blew a raspberry and even as I said the words, I was feeling the familiar pang of sorrow and regret that Granny had never seen me walk down the aisle, as she had so desperately wanted to—and now she never would. It had felt very selfish of us not to give her that happiness—or selfish of Ben, because of course *I* would have loved to . . .

Still, the upside was that at least I hadn't got Ben's ghastly, social-climbing mother as my ma-in-law. I hadn't even seen them since they moved to Wilmslow several years previously, though Ben visited them sometimes. They still thought I ruined his life by making him move back to Neatslake instead of staying in London and becoming famous, which they were convinced he would have been before now. But it was his decision just as much as mine. I sometimes wondered if he had ever told them that. But I expect he had and they just didn't believe it.

'Ben and I've been together since I was thirteen, Libby. That's rock-solid enough, isn't it,' I asked, 'even without a wedding ring?'

She gave me a sideways look from her deceptively innocent eyes. 'But haven't you ever found that a bit smothering? You've never really fallen *in* love, or *out* of love, just jogged comfortably along on a plateau of contentment, doing everything the way Ben wanted it.'

'The way we both wanted it,' I corrected her. 'I'm living the life I always dreamed of and I'm not a slave, even if I do think it's important to create a comfortable environment for him to work in. And, what's more, I did fall in love with Ben, the moment he first spoke to me!'

'Puppy love!'

'Maybe it started that way, but it's still going strong. If you remember, *my* game plan was the direct opposite of yours. I just wanted to stay in Neatslake for ever when I grew up.'

'Which you have, apart from two years in London, while Ben was at college. But while I've just really and truly fallen deeply in love for the first time with husband number three, there you are, still ambling along in your little rut with Ben. I don't suppose you've ever even looked at anyone else?'

'No—well, apart from Sting, before he started to look like that coconut head in the Tom Hanks castaway film. But Ben hasn't looked at anyone else either, Libs. We're fine as we are. Everything in the garden is perfect . . . or *almost* perfect,' I qualified honestly. 'I wish he didn't have to go off to London so much lately, for instance. That is a fly in the ointment.'

'It's the price of fame,' she shrugged. 'You should be glad he's finally made it big and his work is fetching good money. All the more reason to marry him now, before some other woman decides he's a good prospect and snaps him up.'

I smiled. 'Libby, that's not going to happen and you know it!'

'You can't bank on that. He looks pretty tasty in an expensive suit and with a decent haircut.'

'It wasn't expensive. He bought it from Tesco, though it was quite a good fit.'

'The one I last saw him wearing didn't come from Tesco,' she said positively.

'Oh? Actually, he *did* say something about buying another one and he's got some smarter jeans, but he mainly keeps his London clothes at Russell and Mary's flat so I haven't seen most of them.'

'You should see that suit. I wouldn't have known it was the same Ben, when I popped into the opening of his one-man exhibition at the Egremont Gallery in May.' She paused. 'He didn't see me; he was talking to a tall blonde for ages— fortyish, expensive-looking. He seemed quite engrossed in what she was saying.'

I grinned. 'I think I know who that must have been. He told me all about her—he calls her his patroness! I've forgotten her name, but she's an investment banker and nearer fifty than forty, though I expect she's very well preserved. There's family money too, and she must be very well off because she's bought several pieces of his work and he's charging quite steep prices now.'

'Hmm . . . Well, he certainly *looks* expensive these days,' Libby said ambiguously, 'and I still think you ought to go down to London with him more often and keep an eye on him.'

I felt a sudden, unexpected, pang of doubt. It was true that the Ben I knew and loved, the tall, rugged one in hand-knitted jumpers and tattered jeans, with his thick, light-brown hair rumpled and all on end, had to spruce himself up a bit when he was away and often even returned looking like a total stranger, until he'd changed back into his old clothes again.

But I said firmly, 'I trust Ben and he hates having to leave me so often. He phones me up every night when he's away, from Russell and Mary's house. We both enjoyed living in London when he was at the RCA, but it wasn't where we wanted to live for ever, and now we just prefer it for visits. Neatslake is home.'

'Is Mary still making those dreary pots?'

'Mostly large one-off ceramic pieces, and they sell very well. She and Russell have studio space in a converted warehouse in Camden and Ben's just taken one there, to give him a London base to store his stuff. He and some of his ex-RCA friends have formed a group to exhibit together, but of course his inspiration is here, so he'll always want to spend most of his time here.'

'Well, I still think you ought to make more effort, Josie—spice the relationship up a bit. And with men, even old ones, never, *ever* take your eye off the ball.' She thought about that for a minute, blinked her preposterously long, tinted eyelashes and amended, 'Balls.'

She may be the expert on most men, but Ben was different. 'I know you mean it for the best, Libs, but you don't understand. Ben loves me the way I am and we're happily living the life we always wanted. Money, material things and marriage have never been that important to us. Ben's work is, though, and it's wonderful that it's getting the recognition it deserves at last. Besides, even if I

73

wanted to go to London with him, I couldn't keep going off and leaving Harry to cope with everything. He's getting so frail now that I'm always afraid he's going to fall over and really hurt himself.'

'You can't build your life around an elderly neighbour, even if you do have some sort of gardening commune going with him!'

'You know Harry is far more to me than just a neighbour, Libs, and he's been a huge support over the years. But now he's getting too frail even to walk his dog every day . . . and then sometimes he forgets to shut the hens up and I'm afraid that that fox I saw one evening will come back and take them.'

Especially Aggie, my beloved but overly adventurous speckled friend . . .

'Then there are my Acorns to keep an eye on,' I added.

Soon after Ben and I settled in Neatslake I'd been horrified to discover that the three elderly Grace sisters' pensions were barely enough to keep them alive since the General died, let alone warm, amused and well fed, and Dorrie Spottiswode had been in much the same situation. My weekly boxes of fruit, vegetables and eggs, plus anything else I could pretend to have a glut of, helped to keep them all going.

'Dorrie's been really struggling to make ends meet since Tim's father died. She could have grown her own vegetables, but she's devoted herself to trying to keep the Blessings gardens in some kind of order, especially the roses, so she's been bartering things for eggs and stuff instead.' And most of what she had been bartering was the

74

fruit from the Blessings orchard, I thought guiltily, plus the occasional bunch of Tim's grapes from the greenhouse!

'Josie, it's the twenty-first century, and the way you're trying to live is totally perverse—if you can even call all this scraping by on what you can grow "living". And you can't tell me that you're charging enough for your cakes to make a decent profit, either.'

'You'd be surprised! And I only make unusual cakes, which are fun to do. I'm not tied to producing boring, royal-iced, tiered ones—I leave that to the bakery. And I write my magazine piece every month too, which I also enjoy. They're both just a way of making enough to pay the utility bills. And actually, the self-sufficiency, make-do-and-mend, thrifty lifestyle is terribly fashionable again, you know. That's why *Country at Heart* did the piece about us.'

'Yes, but now Ben's raking in the money, you don't *have* to do any of that! Turf the garden, get rid of the hens, and get a life, before it's too late. You could even get a flat in London and use the cottage as a weekend place.'

'I suggested that, now Ben is away so much, but he adores it here too—it's not just me insisting that we live like this! He says when he's in London he loves the idea of me in the cottage, waiting for him. And we *have* a life, and we like things the way they are now,' I said firmly, unshakeable (and probably horribly smug) in my conviction that what I had would endure for ever.

'But something Ben told me when he got back from London has upset me a bit, Libby. Mary's pregnant! It's all through taking some kind of

75

Chinese herbal medicine, apparently, not IVF, and it's stirred up all my feelings again. But Ben was reluctant to even tell me about it and he certainly didn't want to talk about us trying it.'

'No, well, if Ben really wanted children he'd have agreed to have some tests done years ago, wouldn't he?' she pointed out. 'He likes being the cosseted centre of your world, with you running round after him, and I'm sure he'd hate to change that.'

'I've slowly come to that conclusion myself, though he's always agreed with me that we'd like children. I can understand that seeing what Russell and Mary went through, financially and emotionally, set him against taking that route, but now he really doesn't even want to discuss it any more. He goes all hurt when I try.'

'I can't say I ever wanted any more after Pia, and *she* was a mistake,' Libby said frankly. 'Not that she wasn't sweet when she was little, it's just that Joe spoiled her and she turned into a monster once she hit thirteen.'

'I expect she'll grow out of it eventually,' I said consolingly.

She looked thoughtful. 'I have a horrid feeling that Tim would absolutely adore a little Rowland-Knowles. Think what that would do to my figure! At our age, everything isn't just going to snap back into place like elastic afterwards, is it? But maybe I'm past it,' she said hopefully. 'Doesn't fertility decline rapidly after thirty?'

'Yes, but you still have a pretty good chance. I mean, you've already got Pia, so you know you *can* get pregnant.'

'Well, I'm telling you now that if I *do* have to suffer the slings and arrows of outrageous pregnancy, I don't see why you shouldn't too. Shall I talk some sense into Ben and tell him he's being a self-centred pig?'

'Absolutely not! It would have the opposite effect anyway; you know how stubborn he is, and the more you try and change his mind about anything, the more he digs his heels in.'

'Did you get the name and address of that Chinese herbalist from Mary?' she asked innocently.

I grinned, although guiltily. 'Yes . . . she gave me the website address and I got the contact details through that, though I haven't done anything about it. And Mary said it was *very* expensive.'

'Give it to me. I'll find out about it and get you some when I'm down in London, my treat. After all, if it worked for Mary, it's worth a go! And if Tim is insistent, I may have to try it too—but it will be our secret.'

'OK,' I said, because I suddenly realised how unbearable it would be if all my friends suddenly produced a late crop of offspring, just when I thought I'd resigned myself to being barren ground.

Chapter Six

Hippie Chic

On the recycling front, a friend has given me lots of genuine hippie clothes that she wore as a girl and, although I don't really care about fashion, I'm told that this kind of thing is back in vogue again. One of the Acorn members is altering them to fit me and it feels rather decadently pleasant to change out of my workaday jeans into something long and floaty, or sumptuously velvety, in the evening. I don't suppose the Artist will notice . . .

'Cakes and Ale'

Ben was fairly comatose that evening, after a dinner of globe artichokes with melted butter, followed by stir-fried brown rice and vegetables and a blackberry mouse. It made him reluctant to get all dressed up to go for drinks at Blessings, until I pointed out that I'd never seen Tim at home wearing anything other than jeans and jumpers almost as disreputable as Ben's usual attire.

'*You've* got a skirt on,' he pointed out to my amazement, because he doesn't usually notice that sort of thing.

'Well, I do sometimes change in the evening. I don't live in jeans, do I?' I stroked the sumptuous folds of the long, teal-coloured velvet skirt lovingly. 'This is a genuine hippie skirt Stella gave me. She showed me a picture of herself wearing it, circa 1970, with a headband and moccasins, and she looked lovely. But she can't fit into it now and she thought it would suit me.'

In fact, Stella had been sorting out a whole trunkful of clothes, and the skirt was only one of many pretty things she'd given me. 'Fashion's gone boho, so I think I'm actually very trendy at the moment.'

I rather hoped he would think I looked pretty in my long blue skirt and cotton top, but instead he said, with unusual grumpiness, 'If it doesn't matter what I wear, I'll go like this, then,' *this* being his paint-spattered jeans and a sweatshirt up which he had at some time wiped a loaded palette knife.

'Fine—Tim won't notice. Libby says he can't wait to get out of his solicitor's suit when he gets home and out into the garden. He and Dorrie are having endless discussions about how to restore the grounds to their former glory. Now, come on, or we'll be late.'

I put on a long, purple Moroccan cloak with a pointy, tasselled hood (another of Stella's offerings) and picked up a coracle-shaped wicker basket decorated with faded raffia flowers. It contained a bottle of our best elderflower champagne and a Battenburg cake made using natural marzipan and pink food colouring. Libby doesn't know anything about baking, but she can whip up Italian pasta meals at the drop of a hat, especially those that had been her late husband's favourites. I expect she'll now learn to cook what Tim likes, being a great believer in the way to a man's heart being through his stomach. I ascribe to that one a bit myself—Ben loves my food, just as he adored Granny's cakes and biscuits when we were still at school. She used to joke that he had a

79

stomach like a bottomless pit.

Cupboard love.

Ben always says his mother can't cook and on the occasions when he visits them in Wilmslow, they eat ready-prepared Marks and Spencer's meals, though since she's never invited me over for a meal (or anything else), I can't vouch for that. They have never visited this house either, though I gritted my teeth and invited them a few times, until I realised they were never going to accept me—or Nell Richards wasn't. I had a feeling Ben's father, sarcastic and superior though he was, might have weakened a bit, left to himself. But you can see why it was a bone of contention between me and Ben that he still accepted an allowance from them after they'd snubbed me for all these years!

We walked past Blessings and up the little side lane, because no one ever used the front entrance of Blessings: by the time the bell had been pulled and someone had heard it jangle, then unlocked the big, oak door, come down a flight of steps, crossed the little front courtyard and opened the great gate, set in its castellated wall, the visitor would have long since vanished. Instead, a brass plate and an arrow directed you round the back.

Feeling like a slightly Goth Little Red Riding Hood with my cloak and basket, I led the way to the rear gate and up the short gravelled drive past the empty and neglected gatehouse. I was heading for the kitchen wing, but Libby was standing at the French doors that had been rather incongrously let into the back wall of the Great Chamber, looking out for us.

The two men got on fine, as I'd known they would, especially once they'd had a glass or two of bubbly each. Tim might have gone to Ampleforth College and sounded a bit plummy, but you soon forgot that because he was so ordinary and nice.

It still struck me as odd to see him and Libby together, because she'd always gone for more of a father figure before (if not grandfather figure!), and Tim is only a couple of years older than she is. *And* he had a lost-boy sort of air about him that seemed to be awakening an unsuspected and long-dormant maternal streak in her. I was amazed! I'd never seen much sign of it with Pia, even though I knew how much Libby loved her. It was all very strange.

The Great Chamber was the first room Libby and I had started cleaning and it looked much better without cobwebs and a furring of dust along every surface. Like all the Elizabethan part of the house, it had had electricity put in at some time in the dim and distant past and a central heating system of old-fashioned proportions and inefficiency. But apart from that, it was very much as it had always been: a large room with a huge fireplace at one end, dark oak flooring in need of polishing and a central spoked wheel depending from the moulded ceiling, which had probably once been set with candles but now held those dim, twisty little lightbulbs instead. There were several windows with diamond panes of ripply glass, which let in the light but left the view outside blurry. From black, wrought-iron poles hung tattered, sun-rotted curtains and, even after unpicking a bit of hem, we had been unable to decide what their original colours had been.

Many of the rooms at Blessings were plastered and studded all over with moulded heraldic emblems, a bit like extreme Anaglypta, which had been tricky and delicate to dust. We'd used special brushes, as advised by Sophy Winter, and great care, especially where faint traces of bright paint and gilding still clung here and there.

The house seemed to have been updated in the thirties and forties, when the new extension was added. Spartan bathrooms had been created in small chambers, and telephone lines, electricity cables and water pipes run over the surface of the walls, seemingly at random. There had been no attempt to hack into the plaster and hide them, but I expect, from a historic viewpoint, that was a good thing.

We each had a glass or two of elderflower champagne, and then Libby went away to find a knife and plates for the Battenburg cake. She'd just come back when the French doors swung open and Miss Dorrie Spottiswode marched in on a blast of chilly air and stood, hands on hips, surveying us with light blue eyes that were a fiercer variant of Tim's. It occurred to me that Stella and Mark's billy goat, Mojo, had just those same pale, slightly mad eyes, with small dark pupils . . . But luckily Dorrie doesn't smell the same as the goat, just strangely but pleasantly of Crabtree & Evelyn's Gardeners soap, lavender and mothballs.

'Ha—carousing, I see!' she said severely. With her pulled, blue tweed skirt sagging at the seat and worn with purple Argyll-patterned knee socks and stout, Gertrude Jekyll-style lace-up boots, she cut a strange figure—but then, she usually does. In honour of the evening hour, she had changed her habitual woollen jumper for a silk shirt and pearls, but she still wore her French beret, set at a jaunty angle over elf-locks of iron-grey hair.

'Come in, Aunt Dorrie, we're just having a little drink to celebrate our engagement,' Tim said warmly. 'I was wondering where you had got to. Didn't you get the note I put through your door earlier?'

'The cat tried to eat it. I wondered what the soggy bits of paper on the mat were.'

'Well, you're here now, that's the main thing. You know Josie Gray and Ben Richards, don't you?'

'Of course I bloody do—they live a stone's throw away! And anyway, I'm an Acorn.'

'An . . . Acorn?' queried Tim, cautiously.

'It's sort of a barter group Josie set up, darling,' Libby explained. 'They use imaginary acorns for currency.'

'Oh, right!' he said, though he didn't look particularly enlightened.

'Anyway, I'd have to be flaming blind, deaf and dumb not to recognise every living soul in a village this size, after living here all these years, wouldn't I? And there's nothing wrong with any of my faculties.' Dorrie was obviously in belligerent mode.

'Of course not, Aunt Dorrie,' Tim said.

'And if I don't recognise someone, then Mrs Talkalot at the post office soon fills me in, whether I want to hear it or not.'

Mrs Talkalot is the name the postmistress, Florrie James, is commonly known by in Neatslake, and she even good-naturedly refers to herself by it. She only ever stops talking to draw breath and doesn't so much converse with her customers as let loose a permanent stream-of-consciousness gabble. Her husband wears a permanently dazed expression and keeps his hearing aid turned off most of the time.

Dorrie jerked her head at me. 'Old Harry Hutton's her uncle and she's a friend of the Grace sisters. Go there for bridge sometimes. Violet's useless, but Pansy and Lily aren't bad.'

Tim began to open a bottle of champagne that they had ready in an ice bucket. 'Josie and Ben brought us some of their elderflower champagne, Aunt Dorrie, and this isn't going to be half as nice—we should have saved you some.'

'I don't want either of them. I don't like anything sparkling; the bubbles go right up my nose.' She seated herself in an upright armchair covered in tapestry birds and roses. 'I'll have a nice glass of sherry.'

'Ben and Josie tell me they make a lot of wine and beer themselves. They grow most of their own fruit and vegetables too, and keep hens,' Tim said, and Dorrie and I exchanged slightly guilty glances, thinking about all the apples and pears we'd had from the old Blessings orchard.

'I'd *love* to do that,' he continued. 'Maybe I could even keep ducks too, since we have the lily pond. Or what's left of the lily pond. It's very overgrown.'

'I couldn't keep everything up practically single-handed,' Dorrie said gruffly. 'Moorcroft's past doing anything now except mow the grass very slowly, and by the time he's finished he has to start again. Needs pensioning off.'

'No indeed, Aunt Dorrie, you've worked wonders,' Tim said quickly. 'Without you, it would be a wilderness.'

'It's not far off now, though I've kept a firm hand

with the roses.'

'And you don't need more poultry, Tim, you've got peacocks,' Libby pointed out.

'Yes, but they're only ornamental, darling. You can't eat them.'

'I think people used to,' I chipped in, 'but I wouldn't have thought there was a lot of meat on one.' I wouldn't have minded giving it a go—I hated the mournful scream they made. I always had.

'They're stupid creatures,' Dorric said. 'We had two females once, but they wouldn't roost in the trees out of reach of the foxes. Rare instance of the female being stupider than the male, ha-ha.'

Dorrie was a bit of a feminist at heart, but then, after her fiancé was killed in the last war she had parachuted into France to help the Resistance movement as a wireless operator, so she was entirely fearless and self-reliant, and knew she could do anything a mere man could do, only a lot better.

'Ducks should be all right, though,' she said thoughtfully. 'They can nest on the little island in the middle of the lily pond. And if you want to grow your own produce, we could make a vegetable patch at the end of the old orchard, if you like, and put in soft fruit bushes too.'

'And we could trade things,' Ben suggested, forgetting that we already did, unknown to Tim and Libby. 'We have a huge plum tree in Harry's garden but no apples or pears; there isn't room.'

'But we get loads of quinces because they grow all along both sides of the fence between the two gardens,' I put in hastily.

'I like a bit of quince jelly with my salad meats,'

Dorrie said.

'Is it nice?' asked Libby.

'Yes, I'll give you a jar, Libs. I've made loads of it this year, and I'm still making quince wine.'

Dorrie said hopefully, 'Some of the woodwork's rotten on the big greenhouse, Tim, but if you had it repaired, we could grow tender fruit in there. The old vine still produces grapes, but I'm always afraid the roof is going to collapse in on me when I go to pick them. And I have to beat Moorcroft to it, because he loves them. But it's more than time he retired anyway, he says so himself when his lumbago is bad.'

'It would save money,' agreed Tim, 'and I suspect I'll do more at weekends than he manages full time.'

We ate the Battenburg cake right down to the last crumb, and then Dorrie expressed an interest in seeing how Libby and I were doing with the great clean-up. We left Tim and Ben planning out the new vegetable garden.

Dorrie enlivened our tour of the house with her freely expressed opinions of Tim's stepmother and the way she'd spitefully let Blessings decay, but our cleaning efforts and Libby's organisational skills impressed her.

'You're a born housewife, my dear—just what Blessings needs. And a strong character too, which is just what *Tim* needs.'

'Oh, thank you,' Libby said gratefully, turning slightly pink at this accolade. 'I'm going to do my best to make him happy.'

Like me, Libby has never had any great career ambitions: she hoped for love, security and safety, which she found through marriage. I suppose gardening and cooking are my passions, and I'm sorry if that sounds old-fashioned and sad, but there it is. And at least I do seem somehow to have made a successful and lucrative business out of the baking! In any case, it was always clear that Ben would be a brilliant artist, and I truly don't think having more than one genius in the house would work terribly well.'

Libby was pointing out the evidence of fresh woodworm damage. 'We have to move back into the modern wing tomorrow while the treatment is done. Luckily it's only a minor outbreak and it turned out it was still under guarantee. When we can get back in, we need to finish brushing down the walls and ceilings and put the furniture in the middle of the rooms under dustsheets, ready for a man to come and repaint the walls with a special, authentic whitewash—forgotten what they said it was.'

'Limewash?' I suggested.

'Maybe . . . whatever.'

'You don't let the grass grow under your feet, my dear,' Dorrie said. 'Like a breath of fresh air to Blessings, you are!'

'I'm doing my best, though of course most of it will take a long time to put right—and a lot more money than I thought at first, especially to have the roof properly repaired instead of just patched. We've started running the central heating in this part now too, which is going to be very expensive even though it is an ancient system that doesn't get terribly hot.'

'That's probably just as well,' I said, 'because too much heat suddenly turned on wouldn't be good for the place.'

'No, but it needs to warm through and dry out before we move back into the main bedchamber from the modern wing, which Tim is determined to do as soon as possible.'

'The new wing was mainly added for a modern kitchen and utility room, plus an extra bathroom and a couple of spare bedrooms upstairs,' Dorrie said. 'But until Tim's father died, the family always lived in the old part, and that's how it should be. Once you start lighting fires in the Great Chamber, it will carry the heat right through the rest of the house, you'll see.'

'That huge fireplace will take quite a lot of logs to fill,' I said.

'A few of the old trees in the grounds need to come down, or have already fallen down. They could be sawn up and stacked in one of the outbuildings,' suggested Dorrie.

'Yes, that's true,' Libby agreed. 'Waste not, want not—though we'd probably have to get someone to saw them up, because I don't think I'd trust Tim with a chain saw. He's much too absent-minded.'

'It would still be cheaper than buying wood, even so,' Dorrie said. 'Are you going to carry on doing all your own cleaning, or get someone in?'

'Actually, since this is where I'm going to be spending most of my time, I think Gina, who looks after me in Pisa and is something of a Cazzini family retainer, could be persuaded to move here. Tim's stepmother had the chauffeur's flat over the garage renovated for that Portuguese couple she employed and I'm sure Gina would love to have her own little place.'

'That sounds very suitable,' approved Dorrie. 'The gatehouse was formerly a dwelling too, you know, though it has not been lived in for some time. In fact, I think Tim's father's old nanny was the last resident and she passed away several years ago.'

'Yes, I had a quick look round it, but I'm putting off cleaning that out until later,' Libby said. 'The sanitary arrangements are extremely rudimentary and it's tiny, but I thought perhaps if it's done up a bit, it could be let out as a holiday cottage and earn us some money. A romantic getaway for two.'

'I can see you have it all in hand,' Dorrie said. 'Now, perhaps we had better see what those two young men have been discussing. And I am sure you and I,' she added to me, 'have much more idea of what is wanted, regarding vegetable plots, than they do!'

Chapter Seven

Gathering In

By the end of October all was safely gathered in, as the old harvest hymn has it. Or almost all. My elderly neighbour helped me to make a beetroot clamp and then store away the last of the carrot crop in layers of sand, and I'm still pickling and chutney making. I've also dug over the pea and bean beds, set out Brussels sprout plants and divided clumps of chives.

Throughout all this, the Artist could be seen in his studio, working on a new series of three-dimensional paintings. He had to be coaxed out from time to time to help with heavy jobs, like

chopping logs into firewood and hefting sacks of henfood about; but I expect it did him good.
'Cakes and Ale'

Now Ben was home, life should have settled back into the cosy, comforting, uneventful round of cooking, dog-walking and gardening, but I found that I still felt vaguely uneasy.

Of course, the even rhythm of our former existence was bound to change once Libby exploded onto the scene like a demonstration of chaos theory in miniature. But actually, that didn't bother me in the least, for I was used to Libby and very happy that she was going to be living in Neatslake again. No, it was just a feeling that something wasn't *right*, but I couldn't quite put my finger on what it was . . .

Ben, too, seemed even more abstracted than usual and had thrown himself into finishing his latest series of paintings. He tended to work on five or six simultaneously, and I never knew what to call them: paintings, installations, constructions, or just artworks. They all *started* as flat canvases, but then things began to burst out of them, because two dimensions simply weren't enough for Ben and couldn't contain his imagery, which dripped, oozed, sidled sideways or simply exploded into 3-D.

His original inspiration came from our shared love of thrusting, exuberant and earthy nature, full of flowers, rampant foliage and small living creatures. I'd always considered him a brilliant artist and I still did, even though what had been emerging more recently was much darker and (though I hadn't, of course, said so) rather nasty. I

90

hoped it was just a temporary phase.

As I worked in the garden I noticed that he was getting an awful lot of calls on his mobile, which seemed to make him cross, but then, if he didn't want to be disturbed he should have switched it off!

*　　　*　　　*

Once the woodworm treatment at Blessings was done, and the rooms aired, Libby and I returned to our dusting and cleaning, keeping one room ahead of the specialist painters. I was amazed at Libby's stamina. I was only helping out for an hour or two in the afternoons because of all my cake-making and other commitments, but she seemed to be working dawn to dusk.

When we took the old curtains down they pretty well fell to pieces, but she had surfed the internet and found a firm who sold medieval-style crewelwork curtains and fabric by the metre, all curly foliage, birds and rabbits—lovely, though very expensive.

Dorrie brought her friend Miss Hebe Winter (who is my friend Sophy's great-aunt), to look around one day while we were working. The room we were in was a bit gloomy and for a minute we thought we were seeing ghosts, because they walked in wearing Elizabethan dress. Miss Winter, who is tall, grand and aquiline of nose, is a dead ringer for the Virgin Queen, and even Dorrie was transformed by a wide ruff and full skirts, despite having kept her beret on.

It turned out they'd been to a historical re-enactment society meeting in Sticklepond. Lots of the members help out as volunteers at Winter's End in full costume, when it's open to the public. They are very big on the Elizabethan over there, especially since the discovery of that Shakespeare document.

Miss Winter had come out of sheer curiosity to see Libby, I think, the plebeian marrying into the Rowland-Knowleses, and, like Dorrie, she found her not at all what she expected.

I left them having tea (it was lucky I'd taken Libby an apple upside-down cake), passing Hebe's little white Mini car on the drive. How does she get behind the wheel in a farthingale?

*   *   *

Moorcroft, the gardener, was very ready to take a golden handshake and retire, which would be much more economical in the long run than paying him to cut the grass and hide out in the garden shed, making endless cups of tea on a Primus stove.

Tim and Dorrie, full of plans and enthusiasm, began to try to get the grounds into some kind of order and create a fruit and vegetable patch. Tim came over a couple of times to ask my advice—or Ben's, if he caught him out of the studio, which was pretty rare at the moment.

'Tim's passionate about gardening. He's even more dotty about it than you are,' Libby said one day, when we were taking a break from cleaning out what had once been the old kitchen, but was now a kind of storeroom. She straightened up with a groan; she's only about five foot two without her stilettos, so even standing on a stool she'd found, reaching up with the feather duster, was quite a stretch.

'I think he loves flowers and shrubs more than vegetables, Libs, like Dorrie.'

'Yes, but now you've infected him with the self-sufficiency bug he's determined to follow suit.'

'Well, that's OK, isn't it?'

'Yes, as long as he doesn't expect *me* to start digging and jamming and making pies . . . though when Gina's here I expect she'll be quite happy to cook what he grows. It will save us money too, which will be a good thing, because I hadn't realised quite how high the cost of restoring and maintaining a place of this age would be. I know I'm well off, but really, we need to find some way of increasing our income, unless I sell one or both of my other homes. But Tim loves Italy, so apart from our honeymoon being in Pisa, I hope we're going to spend a lot of time there—and it's handy having a *pied-à-terre* in London.'

'Yes, I've been thinking about what you said, and I'm starting to think that's what *we* could do with, though at least Ben hasn't been so eager to rush back to London this time. He's very engrossed in his paintings.'

'Tim hates being a solicitor, so it's a pity we can't find some way of making Blessings pay for itself. But it's a bit too small to open to the public. We live in all of it and we can't just move into the modern wing three-quarters of the time, can we?'

'Perhaps you could open a little garden centre in the grounds?'

'I'm not sure they're really big enough for that, either, but it's worth thinking about.'

'How are the wedding plans coming on?'

Libby pulled a large, folded list out of the pocket of her all-enveloping blue striped cotton apron, which looked like something a Victorian maid might wear. 'Special licence—check. Church, vicar, church bells, organist and photographer—all sorted. Cake—you're doing that. Invitations—already done by those strange friends of yours, though I don't see why the cards and envelopes have to have bits of grass and petals in them.'

'It's because they make the paper themselves, using natural sources and inks,' I explained. 'All recycled and biodegradable.'

'And why does it say on the invitations that confetti will be provided at the church door?' she queried. 'Guests usually bring their own!'

'We don't want paper confetti everywhere. We need to supply a natural alternative, Libby! Perhaps something like millet, which would give the birds a feast afterwards? Yes—a golden shower of millet would be *lovely* . . .'

'I am not emerging from the church to be pelted with handfuls of budgie food,' Libby said coldly.

'No?'

'No!'

'Oh . . . then how about dried rose petals?' I suggested. 'I've heard of those being used.'

'Now, that's more like it!'

'Hebe Winter uses a lot of roses in the products she makes to sell in the Winter's End shop—perhaps she could supply us with rose petals. Shall I ask?'

'Yes, do. If you could sort that out for me, it would be a great help,' Libby agreed. 'Actually, the Winters are on the guest list, since they're friends of both Dorrie and Tim. And I've invited a second

94

photographer, but not an official one—Noah Sephton. He was some kind of cousin of Joe's and a great friend. He'll be staying overnight, but I think I'll have to put him in the gatehouse. I've asked Dolly Mops to come and clean it out and I thought they might as well do the flat over the garage too, though, knowing Gina, she'll scrub it from floor to ceiling as soon as she gets here, anyway.'

'It'll be nice to see Gina again. And I think I've heard of Noah Sephton,' I said doubtfully. 'Didn't he take those lovely photographs of you with Pia as an infant, which are in your apartment in Pisa?'

'Yes, but you should have heard of him anyway, because he's quite famous for his portraits. He has an annual exhibition of his more oddball, black-and-white photos every year too, and they're a sell-out. His last one was called *Fate*.'

'I know all about *fate*,' I said, and, as if on cue, one of the two peacocks wailed. It always gave me the cold shivers. 'Couldn't you *try* eating the peacocks?' I pleaded. 'I hate the noise they make.'

'Don't be silly, they give the place class. Get over it,' she said absently, looking down at the back of the list where she'd jotted the names of the invited guests. 'There are quite a few celebs on here as well as Noah, because Tim knows Rob Rafferty, the star of that *Cotton Common* TV soap and one or two of the other actors, though I don't think *Hello!* magazine will be jostling for my wedding photos any time soon.'

'So you've got it all pretty well arranged?'

'Yes, apart from the reception venue. At this rate, we'll be handing out directions in the church!'

'Still no luck finding somewhere nearby?'

'No, they're all either booked up, can't handle the numbers, or they don't do them at this time of year—or *something*.'

'Oh dear, and it's hardly marquee weather, is it?'

'I expect I'll think of something. I'll have to. I only hope the guests who are coming from a distance can find somewhere to stay on the night of the wedding!'

'Any word from Pia yet?'

'No, still not a dicky-bird since I told her I was marrying again and she put the phone down on me. She's not answering my emails either.'

'She hasn't contacted me for ages,' I said. 'She doesn't usually leave it this long.'

'She's sulking, but I'd like to know if she intends turning up for the wedding. It would have been lovely if she'd been happy about my getting married again and agreed to be a bridesmaid, but it doesn't look likely to happen.'

'Once she gets over the shock she'll probably get back in touch again,' I said optimistically.

'I'd just settle for the sound of her voice telling me she was all right, at the moment,' Libby admitted.

'I'll try emailing her again when I get home, Libs. Perhaps she's still speaking to me.'

'Oh, thanks, Josie—and I *must* take your measurements before you go, because I still have to dash down to London in search of my wedding dress and shoes, and get a bridesmaid's dress for you. I should have gone before, but there's been so much to do.' My practical, hard-headed friend gave a dreamy sigh. 'I hate the thought of being apart from Tim, even for one night. Isn't it

96

strange?'

'No. And now you know how I feel when Ben goes off to London without me.'

'It's not the same. You've never been *in* love with Ben, just loved him with blind, dogged devotion.'

'Not *blind*. You can't live with someone for that many years and not be aware of their failings. But he's such a brilliant artist, a genius, that I've had to be the one to make allowances.'

'I don't see why having any kind of talent should entitle you to get away with behaving badly,' she said, 'or selfishly. Though, actually, it usually does seem to have that effect. Noah—Noah Sephton, the photographer I was telling you about—goes through girlfriends faster than a hot knife through butter. He *says* he's a romantic and believes in true love, but he never puts his money where his mouth is.'

'Has he never been married?'

'Joe said he was, briefly, when he was very young, but she died of leukaemia, so I expect it was all a bit *Love Story* and put him off marrying again.'

'That's terribly sad!' Tears came to my eyes as they usually did when I heard something touching. 'It's probably blighted the poor man's life.'

'No, I don't think so. The loveliest girls seem to fall for him and it all looks really promising, but by the time they start to hint that they're getting serious ideas he's ready to move on.'

I thought about that. 'Perhaps it's because no one is going to measure up to his dead wife? I mean, if they were really young and not married long, the rosy glow wouldn't have worn off and, looking back, she will always seem perfect, won't she?'

97

'Or perhaps whatever he says about love, he just prefers casual sex with no commitment?' Libby suggested.

'That makes him sound horrible—shallow and self-gratifying.'

'Well, actually he's not, he's really warm and nice.'

'I suppose he's good-looking?'

She considered. 'You might not pick him out in a crowd straight away, but once you did, you'd wonder how you missed him. He's about six foot and slim, not exactly handsome, but he's got lovely, light grey eyes and long, long black eyelashes . . . His smile's sort of quirky and goes up at one side too . . . and his hair's almost black and goes curly if it gets damp.'

'You sound half in love with him yourself!' I said, dismayed at this apparent lack of loyalty to Tim.

'Not me! You know I'm a hard-headed, marriage-or-nothing kind of girl!'

'Maybe, but you moved in with Tim the day after you met him,' I pointed out.

'Yes, well, that's different. And he proposed to me before I moved in, don't forget.'

'Come on, you were so love struck you would have done it anyway.'

'Maybe, but so was Tim, so it doesn't matter.' She smiled happily. 'Oh, Josie, it's such bliss! I only hope Pia does come to the wedding and realises how nice he is, then she'll soon get over her huff and we can be one happy family.'

I thought this was more than optimistic. 'You can see her point, Libby. She adored Joe, he was a father to her in every sense. And I think girls often get on better with their fathers than their mothers, until they get older. You were fine until she was thirteen or fourteen, and then she started seeing you as competition.'

'She *was* lovely when she was little,' she agreed. 'Then—bam!—in kicked the hormones and she turned into a sulky monster in a permanent strop.'

'She'll turn back into a human being again any minute now,' I assured her. 'And if she surfaces in London, Maria Cazzini will make her come to the wedding.' Maria, the formidable matriarch of the family, had married the cousin who now ran the family restaurant business. A thought struck me. 'You *have* invited your mother and sister, haven't you?'

'Tim said I had to,' Libby said unenthusiastically. 'I've told Daisy she'll have to keep Ma off the sauce the whole day. I'm trusting her, but I'll have a hire car on standby to whisk them away if she goes off-piste. I've booked them into a Travelodge, where I expect they're used to getting all types, including drunken mothers of the bride.'

'But I thought she'd joined AA and gone teetotal?'

'That's what she says, but Daisy reckons she's just got more cunning about where she hides it.'

'It was very kind of Daisy to move her down there and look after her.'

Libby gave me a scathing look. 'It was Joe's idea. He bought them the house and paid the bills. Now I send money every month and that's another drain on my income, but at least I know Mum is eating properly and living respectably, because Daisy has control over everything.'

It was some years since I'd seen Libby's mother, but even semi-reformed, she was still likely to add

99

a lively touch to the wedding proceedings, not to mention raking up the past in the minds of those villagers who were still finding it hard to accept that any daughter of Gloria Martin could possibly marry a Rowland-Knowles, so I could quite understand why Libby was reluctant to invite her. But Tim was right—it had to be done!

* * *

I emailed Pia and that night she phoned me. It was such a relief to hear her voice, even if she was in a strop.

'How can Mum get married so soon?' she demanded. 'She can't have loved Dad at all. It's indecent!'

'But she did love Joe very much, Pia, really she did. And it's more than a year now. She and Tim just fell in love at first sight, that's all.'

'She's too old to fall in love,' she stated disgustedly.

'Oh, I don't think you're ever too old, darling. And Tim is lovely—quiet and kind. You'll like him, honestly.'

'She doesn't care if I'm there or not. She probably doesn't want me coming along and making three.'

'There you're quite wrong. She does worry about you, and Tim is really looking forward to meeting you. He hopes you'll make your home at Blessings with them.'

'*Blessings?*'

'That's the name of his house. It's Elizabethan, and Libby's currently designing your bedroom in one of the original chambers, so if you don't want to find yourself in a flowery bower, with the gilded rococo bed with cherubs she is talking about shipping over from Italy, you ought to get down here and tell her so.'

'Cherubs?' she said, horrified. Then she collected herself and said tersely, 'It doesn't matter: I'm not coming.'

'Where are you now?'

'Pisa, with Gina. But she says they're coming here for their honeymoon, so I'll have to clear out to London then.'

'Look, do come just for the wedding, Pia,' I cajoled. 'Some of the Cazzinis are—your aunt Maria, for one.'

'Aunt Maria's coming?'

'Yes, she's already sent an enormous Gaggia coffee machine as a present, so I think you can take it that she approves! I'm sure she'll be disappointed in you if you don't come—and your mum will be deeply, deeply hurt.'

There was a small silence. 'I *might* come up from London with Aunt Maria, just for the wedding,' she conceded sulkily.

'I think that would be a very kind and generous thing to do,' I said encouragingly. 'And perhaps you could ring your mother and tell her? She'd love to hear from you and—'

'No!' she said explosively and slammed down the phone, her volatile and passionate Italian side clearly getting the better of her good manners. But I was sure Maria Cazzini would manage to persuade her at least to turn up on the day and be polite. I hoped so, because otherwise Libby would be devastated and it would ruin her big day.

I rang her straight away and gave her an edited

version of what Pia had said, because I knew it would be a huge relief to Libby just to know she was safe and well. Whether Pia turned up for the wedding would all depend on Maria Cazzini's persuasive skills.

* * *

At dinner last night (Spanish omelette followed by a blackberry version of Eton mess), I said to Ben that he seemed to have an awful lot of calls on his mobile lately, and was everything all right?

I could tell something had been on his mind since he'd come back from London, even after he told me about Mary being pregnant, but I thought perhaps it had to do with his parents. He tends not to mention them to me; they're a thorny subject.

He took a deep drink of elderberry wine and said, 'Actually, darling, there is something worrying me and I haven't known how to tell you. In fact, I thought it would just sort of . . . well, fizzle out on its own.'

That was typical of Ben. He'd let problems slide in the hope they'd either simply go away or *I* would sort them out for him, by which time they had generally escalated.

I leaned my elbows on the table and said encouragingly, 'So, what is it?'

'You'll probably think this sounds silly, but I'm being . . . well, stalked.'

'*Stalked?*'

'Pestered—followed—rung up and harassed. By this woman who has been buying my work—you know, the patroness?'

I nodded.

'Now she seems to want to acquire me too. She must have a mental problem, because in her head she's convinced that we're already having some kind of relationship. It's getting a bit embarrassing.' He looked at me appealingly. 'I've tried distancing myself, but it's very awkward.'

'Yes, it must be! The poor thing,' I added charitably, because I could see how easy it would be to fall for Ben and, if you were inclined to mix reality and fantasy, dream up a whole relationship in your head.

'The Egremont Gallery must have given her my number, because she keeps phoning me up. I'm just afraid she might call the house too, and she's so unhinged she sees you as the usurper, darling, so goodness knows what she might say.'

'Do you know, there *have* been a lot of calls lately where the phone's been put down the moment the caller heard my voice,' I said. 'Do you think that might have been her?'

'Possibly.' He leaned back, looking relieved. 'I'm really glad I've told you about it now, Josie!'

'Yes, but shouldn't we tell the police or something? I've read of cases where stalkers can get quite nasty—even dangerous.'

'No, I don't think so. I'm sure she isn't the violent type. And, after all, she's not going to turn up here—it's too far away—and in London I avoid her as much as possible. Let's wait and see,' he suggested.

He was probably right. For all we knew she made a habit of imagining herself in love with personable men and would soon lose interest in Ben and be off after someone new. And since after getting that off his chest he reverted back to being the good-natured, easy-going Ben I was used to, I felt much, much happier.

* * *

On Halloween I had a whole tray of small toffee apples to offer any young ghoul who turned up on my doorstep—and quite a lot did, attracted to my pumpkin lantern like moths to a flame.

I'd dipped the tops of the apples in dark chocolate and they were really yummy. Ben, who has a sweet tooth, ate three before the first trick-or-treater rang the bell, and there were only just enough to go round.

* * *

Since the *Country at Heart* article I had had an increasing number of enquiries about wedding cakes, though luckily once I made it clear that I only delivered locally, most of them lost interest. But not all. I was having to harden my heart and only take the ones I really wanted to do, because I didn't want to spend all my time making weird and wonderful wedding cakes!

At the moment, Libby's Pisa Tower cake was taxing my skills to the limit . . .

Chapter Eight

Snap Happy

Round here, on Guy Fawkes Night, we still tend to carve turnip heads to put our candles in, rather than pumpkins. The smell of hot turnip, the exciting tang of gunpowder in the air and the taste of hard, home-made, splintery treacle toffee—those are the things I associate with 5ᵗʰ November.

Sometimes we go over to the bonfire at Middlemoss, a few miles away, where they have the strange tradition of burning an effigy of Oliver Cromwell instead of Guy Fawkes . . .

'Cakes and Ale'

Libby finally left for her shopping trip to London early next day, which, considering her wedding day was now less than three weeks away, was pushing it a bit. I was not even going to think about what monstrous bridesmaid's creation she might bring back for me . . .

Later that morning I was standing at the sink washing up the equipment I'd just used to make parsnip wine, when I glanced out at the tranquil Green and spotted Aggie, the escapologist hen, wandering up the road. Without stopping to take off my red rubber gloves, I shot out of the front door.

A large, maroon car was sweeping up towards me *and* the unaware hen, who was ambling along in its path in an aimless, hesitating sort of way.

'Aggie!' I yelled, and, without thinking, leaped forward into the road to make a grab for her. Behind me, the car slammed on its brakes with a squeal, but Aggie, squawking loudly, shot off across the grass, with me in hot pursuit.

Luckily, all the titbits I'd given her made her too fat to keep up any kind of pace, so I soon scooped her up and tucked her under my arm. She gave in instantly, and made amiable clucking noises.

The driver of the old Jaguar that had so narrowly missed us was now standing next to it: a tall, slender man with short, ruffled black hair and an olive complexion that contrasted startlingly with his light grey eyes. As we approached, he had the cheek to whip a camera up and click away with it!

I was already cross and this didn't improve my temper, so I marched up to him and let rip: 'Are you mad, driving so fast in a village? You could have killed Aggie—in fact, you could have killed both of us!'

'Ooo-er!' agreed Aggie, softly.

'I wasn't actually driving fast,' he said, with a hint of amusement in those grey eyes that made me feel even crosser. 'In fact, I was crawling—and I'd seen the hen. I just wasn't expecting a madwoman in red rubber gloves to hurtle out right after her.'

Aggie made another throaty crooning noise and he lifted his camera—an old-fashioned one, I noticed, not a new digital job—and clicked the shutter.

'What on earth do you think you're doing?'

'Sorry—habit. Do you mind?' He had a very charming, apologetic smile that titled upwards at one corner, but I wasn't at all beguiled.

'Yes, I do mind!'

'Once a photographer . . .' he drawled, looking at me assessingly with half-closed eyes. 'And you do make rather a unique picture, standing holding that hen.'

I became conscious that my hair was blowing out in the wind like a banner, my feet were bare and frozen, and my red rubber gloves did little to add to an ensemble that consisted of a rather pulled green fleece over torn dungarees. 'Maybe, but you should ask permission first!'

'Sorry, it really was just impulse. Actually, I'm looking for a house called Blessings, if I have the name right. It sounds a bit unlikely.'

'Blessings?'

'Yes. You've heard of it?'

'You're practically next to it. It's that Elizabethan pile over there. Are you . . . I mean, do you know Tim Rowland-Knowles?'

He looked that type—sort of minor public school, comfortably off and assured.

'Not yet. But an old friend, Libby Cazzini, says she's going to marry him, so, since I was passing nearby, I thought I'd pop in on my way back to London.'

'You're an old friend of *Libby's*?' I gazed at him like the halfwit he patently thought me, while my brain digested a couple of things. 'Oh . . . then would you be that photographer she told me about—Jonah somebody?'

'Noah. Noah Sephton.'

'I knew it was biblical. And you're out of luck, because Libby's actually on her way to London, to buy her wedding dress. Maybe you'll catch up with her down there, though she'll be a bit pushed for time since she's coming back tomorrow.'

107

He smiled again, rather attractively. 'And I suppose *you* wouldn't be the mad friend who chose to stay in Neatslake when she could have lived in London, by any chance? I can't remember your name at all, biblical or otherwise.'

'Josie—Josie Gray,' I said, wondering what on earth Libby had said about me. 'Does she talk about me?'

'All the time.' He offered a long, slim hand and, hampered by the hen, I shook it awkwardly. Then he turned to survey the Green and the church behind it, with its strange, rather squat tower and said, 'Well, it's a pretty enough spot, but I always thought she'd had a dodgy start in life here and never wanted to come back again.'

'So did I, but she always loved Blessings and now she loves Tim Rowland-Knowles too, so that's the reason she's coming back.'

I wondered if, perhaps, he had become more than just a friend since Libby's husband had died (I knew her too well to think she would play around while she was still married); but he didn't look upset or even slightly jealous, just interested.

'So it's really love, purest love?'

'Definitely. Tim's such a sweet man,' I assured him. 'They fell for each other the minute they met . . . or met again, because we'd played tennis with him when we were teenagers. I didn't think he would remember us, because he's a few years older and we were just tedious, giggly fifteen-year-olds at the time, but he says he does.'

'Oh, well,' he shrugged, 'it seemed a bit sudden, but she's old enough to know what she's doing. Maybe I'll see her in London, as you say. I'll give her a ring. Should have done before I called in,

108

only I was so near. And I did meet you, after all. I expect I'll see you at their wedding?'

'I suppose—' I stopped, for the Jaguar's passenger door had swung open and a girl with tousled blonde hair and the longest legs I'd ever seen got out. Even dishevelled, without makeup and in Ugg boots and a crumpled denim miniskirt, she looked beautiful. She just had to be a model, she had that 'look at *me*!' air about her.

'Are you going to be much longer, darling?' she asked Noah, ignoring me. 'I'm freezing.'

'Get back in the car then,' he said shortly.

Behind her, Ben suddenly appeared in the cottage doorway, tall, tousled and chunky, a smear of ochre paint up one cheekbone. As always, I felt my face break spontaneously into a smile and my heart melt.

Noah, looking bemused at this sudden transformation from the half-propitiated virago of a moment before, moved aside as I wished him an absent goodbye and went in, hen and all—though not before he had whipped that camera up again.

I heard the whirr of the shutter and sincerely hoped he had forgotten to load it with film, or I might just appear in one of his exhibitions as 'Portrait of the Village Idiot'.

* * *

When I told Ben who I'd been talking to, he was cross that I hadn't introduced him.

'He's very well known and he's photographed a lot of famous writers and artists. If he'd known who I was, he might have taken my picture and it could have done my career a bit of good!'

'He seemed to be more interested in taking mine,' I pointed out, 'and Aggie's.' Under my arm, Aggie crooned agreement.

'I can't imagine why, unless he's doing something on village characters. You do look slightly mad in patchwork dungarees, with a hen under your arm and red rubber gloves,' he added with a grin, and I gave him a dirty look.

Then he compounded his insult by asking, 'Who was the gorgeous blonde in the car?'

'I have absolutely no idea,' I snapped, and stalked past him, heading for the back door with Aggie.

*   *   *

Libby squeezed in a visit to Mary's Chinese herbalist. In fact, she phoned me from there to relay a list of rather personal questions. It was just as well that Ben was shut up in the studio and Harry distantly hammering something in his garden shed. She said really the woman would have preferred a personal consultation, ideally with Ben as well, but she was making me something up to try until my next visit to London.

I told her she'd missed a fleeting visit by her photographer friend, though we didn't have time to chat, she had too much to do.

*   *   *

I went over to Blessings next day and she gave me a package of pale jade-coloured pills and also a sort of herbal tea, with instructions. 'But it can take a few months to work, and if it hasn't by then, it probably isn't going to,' she warned me. 'Ben might be the problem, so you may have to try and persuade him to consult her too.'

'Thanks, Libby. I hope it wasn't too horrendously expensive?'

'No, not really, and I was interested anyway, though I'm not about to do anything hasty unless Tim presses me about having offspring. I'd like it to be just us two for a while, at least—and Pia, of course, if she deigns to grace us with her presence.' She paused, biting her lip. 'You *do* think she will turn up, don't you, Josie?'

'Yes, of course I do,' I assured her with a confidence founded on Maria Cazzini's ability to make Pia behave properly, once she came within her orbit.

It seemed to cheer Libs up, because she stopped looking quite so worried and said, 'Come on and I'll show you the dresses!'

She led the way. She and Tim had already moved into the largest bedroom in the old part of the house, though she insisted on having a new mattress made to fit the ancient four-poster before she slept in it. Of the two small chambers off it, which had probably been servants' rooms, one was now a solidly Victorian bathroom, all brass, and blue and white porcelain, and the other Libby seemed to be using as a walk-in wardrobe. She had installed a couple of long rails on wheels, but her wedding dress hung on a wooden peg against the wall, almost indistinguishable from the plaster.

She unhooked it and, holding it against herself, gave a twirl, so that the full skirts flew out around her. 'What do you think? The colour is the exact match to the veil Dorrie gave me, but it took a bit

111

of finding. You wouldn't think there were so many shades of white!'

'Lovely,' I said, admiring the way the ivory silk and lace was ruched and draped and adorned with tiny crystals and small roses tinged with the palest hint of pink. 'And a very modest neckline and sleeves.'

'Of course! I've no intention of walking down a church aisle in one of these strapless ones, with my baps hanging out. It's not my style at all, and anyway, it would be freezing in this weather. I've got a little fur-trimmed velvet cape to go to church in, if it's really cold.'

It hung on the end of the nearest rail, the fluffy edges stirring slightly in the draught caused by Libby's twirling about. She looked like the governess in *The King and I.*

'It's not real fur, is it, Libby?'

'No, of course not, it's fake. Don't get your thong in a twist.'

'Briefs—cotton midi ones. Thongs are too hideously uncomfortable.'

'Yes, I've noticed the VPL.'

'I think VPL is sexy,' I said firmly.

She gave me a look. 'When I get to the church porch, I'll take the cape off and hand it to you.'

'What do I do with it?'

'Hang it in the porch. I might need it on the way out, though I'd rather have the photographs without. And the rehearsal is the day after tomorrow, at four—is that OK?'

'Rehearsal?'

'Yes, I want everything to go perfectly on the day, so we're going to have a walk-through. There will be me, you, Tim and Nick Pharamond, the best man—he and Tim were at school together. You've met him, haven't you?'

'Yes, when I was making their wedding cake, and of course I've read his cookery articles in the newspapers. I found him a bit scary, to be honest.'

'Tim says he's more bark than bite. We've had Sophy Winter and her husband over to dinner once, but I'm not inviting the Pharamonds until Gina gets here, because I don't think my cooking's up to their standards!'

'I think your cooking is brilliant—or your pasta is, anyway,' I added honestly.

'Pasta is all I do, and I don't even bother with that if Gina's there to do it for me.'

'So Gina is definitely coming to live at Blessings?'

'Yes, she's flying over before the wedding and will stay here while we're on honeymoon. She's packed up a lot of her things and sent them on, so she can make the flat a little home from home.'

'It's lucky Joe's first wife was American, so Gina speaks English well, isn't it?' I said. 'I hope she likes it here in Neatslake, because it doesn't really have the attractions of a city like Pisa.'

'Gina says Britain is a heathen country, but it's her duty to look after me here, though what really swung it was the thought of having her own home, so she can invite her relatives to stay.'

'I'm looking forward to seeing her again,' I said, for when we'd visited Pisa, I'd spent many happy hours in the kitchen with Gina, learning how to do things the Italian way. 'Did you say you'd managed to get my bridesmaid's dress too?'

'Yes, though I think it'll need taking in at the waist. I was in a bit of a hurry after spending all

113

day finding the perfect wedding dress and then visiting the herbalist.'

She took a shrouded shape off the rail and I saw the warm glow of pink through the white plastic with a sinking heart. 'I knew it: it's a Barbie dress!'

'No it isn't. It's pink, I admit, but it isn't the pale pink I wanted, more a pinky-purple old-rose colour—and actually, I think it will suit you.'

The dress was, in fact, much prettier than the stiff, flouncy, satin horror of my nightmares. It was made of fluid velvet, for a start, in a vaguely medieval style—close-fitting to the hips, then flaring out in heavy folds to the feet, with long, tight, pointed sleeves and a gothic sort of neckline.

'That's really pretty!'

'It's the last thing they offered me, in desperation—a cancelled order. Look, just slip it on, so we can see how much it needs altering.'

It wasn't that warm in the room, even with the old cast-iron radiator valiantly clanking away in the corner, but I removed my outer layers and slipped into the stretchy velvet. As the skirts settled around me I found myself automatically standing taller and felt ... well, totally different. I turned to admire myself in the long glass and found that Libby was right—the colour did suit me, warming my skin from its habitual pale winter sallow and flattering my figure.

'It needs taking in at the waist for a closer fit, but other than that, it could have been made for you. No wonder they didn't sell it!'

'Thanks,' I said.

'Well, you've got an athletic sort of build—broad shoulders and long back, legs that go on for ever and not huge in the bum and boobs department.

This makes the most of what you've got.' She frowned. 'You remind me of something . . . a painting, I think . . . can't remember what.' She shook her head. 'It'll come back to me. Now, how are we going to find someone to alter it in time?'

'That's easy. Lily Grace will do it. She's given up dressmaking really, but she still does alterations.'

'Lily . . .' she mused.

'You remember—the eldest one? White curly hair, Alice band with a satin bow on it, taller than the other two.'

'Oh, yes. You know, they called and left me a visiting card while I was away. I'm not sure what to do with it.'

'I think that's a sign of social acceptance and I expect Dorrie suggested they do it. They haven't got any money, but they're still very proud. Really, you ought to return the call and leave a card with them.'

'I haven't got any cards. I could invite them to the wedding, though. It's going to be a bit thin on my side, even if we are trying to keep it small.'

'They would love that—they'd be so excited.'

'Great. We'll write out an invitation when we go downstairs, and maybe you could take it round with the dress, later?'

'OK. What am I going to do about shoes?'

'You'll have to go to a wedding shop and buy ivory satin ones—I'll pay. You can't match that pink in the time, or I would have had them dyed. In fact, on second thoughts, I'll come with you because it would be nice if you had some sort of wreath around your head, or a feather fascinator, or something.'

115

I groaned.

The inevitable list came out of her pocket. 'We'll go tomorrow afternoon. And then that's pretty well everything except for the damned reception venue! I know it will be small, but not small enough to fit into the Great Chamber, and unless we travel more than twenty miles away, there's absolutely nothing to be had locally.'

'It might have to be a marquee then. Perhaps you can get some sort of heaters?' I suggested.

'I don't think it will actually come to that, because on the way back from London I had a brilliant idea. We can hold it in the barn!'

I stared at her. 'What do you mean, the *barn*?'

'The Old Barn, one side of the courtyard buildings.'

'Libby, you can't hold a wedding reception in a barn!'

'Yes I can. Come on, let's go and look at it.'

There's no stopping Libby when she has that determined expression on her face. Snatching up my coat from the back of a chair where I'd tossed it, I followed her out of the French doors in the Great Chamber, past the small, overgrown knot garden, to the U-shaped cluster of buildings near the driveway.

Round the cobbled courtyard was a hotchpotch of buildings that seemed to have grown organically together over time, including the garage, housing an old but very swish Bentley and with the chauffeur's flat over it, soon to be Gina's domain. Then came a row of long-unused stables, tackrooms and various anonymous outbuildings. One entire side of the U was taken up with the Old Barn, dating to the time when the Rowland-

116

Knowles family were local landowners with some use for such a huge structure.

It wasn't by any means as old as the house, but still ancient, with the same stone-slabbed roof and huge wooden beams. Perhaps at one time it had also been used to store carriages, for a huge curved doorway had been let into it, besides a smaller door at one end and several windows of thick, murky glass.

We entered through the small door, and it was almost as cold in there as it was outside. 'You'll be lucky if it doesn't snow on your wedding day, with half the guests stuck in the drifts,' I said. 'And then if they do get here, they'll die of hypothermia at the reception!'

'Don't be such a pessimist. I'm sure it won't snow. I mean, how many times did it actually snow properly in Neatslake when we were growing up? Anyway, as long as Tim and I are here, that's all that really matters. Now come on, look around you—what do you think?'

Great festoons of furred cobwebs hung down from the beams like dirty tinsel and motes of dust danced in the cross draught. The floor was stone and there were more long, narrow windows high up, near the roof.

'Tim says some of the cars used to be garaged in here and he can remember barn dances in it, once or twice. And look—' she crossed to a door at the end and flung it open—'this must have been a tackroom.'

It had a small, pot-bellied stove, a saddle horse, benches, a table and lots of hooks for harnesses.

'I think it needs huge amounts of work just to get it clean, Libs, and it's only a couple of weeks to the big day. It's impossible!'

'No it isn't, and, what's more, I've already asked Dolly Mops if they're up to a challenge. The owner, Anthea, says yes, if she can get her staff to volunteer, because it's a bit out of the ordinary. I expect they will, for double the usual pay. And I've got an electrician coming to put in more lighting tomorrow. *Nothing's* impossible if you have enough money.'

'At this rate, you soon won't have!'

'I know, it does seem to be vanishing scarily fast.' She twirled around. 'But just imagine this place transformed! White painted walls, drapes at the windows . . . and thank heavens they had them put in, because it would have been dark as pitch otherwise. I thought buffet food would be easiest and I can hire tablecloths, trestle tables, cutlery, and wineglasses. And your cake can be on a little side table of its own.'

'But it's the middle of November, Libby. It'll be almost as freezing as a marquee!'

'I'll hire big heaters too. Don't keep putting obstacles in my way.'

'I'm just trying to be practical. At least there's lots of parking in the courtyard, on the drive and round Church Green,' I conceded. 'What about the buffet food?'

'I'm still working on that one, though I'd like an Italian theme. I'm going to ring Maria in a bit and ask her advice.'

'Have you discussed all this with Tim?'

'Yes, as soon as I got back. He thinks it's a great idea, and he says as soon as the barn's cleaned out, he'll whitewash the inside.'

I looked at the cavernous interior. 'I think he

might need help.'

*   *   *

When I got home I read the instructions on the herbalist's packet and pillbox and decided to start right away. I swilled the first pill down with a beaker of the infused herbal mixture, then hid the packets behind one of the plates on the dresser.

It didn't matter so much if Ben caught me drinking the herbal tea, though, because I was always trying some new blend. He preferred to stick to Yorkshire Tea so strong you could stand a spoon up in it and, after tasting this horrible stuff, he might have had a point.

*   *   *

The wedding rehearsal went well. St Cuthbert's is a little jewel of a church and the vicar is very round and jolly, with a big white beard, like Father Christmas.

There was no father of the bride to give Libby away, of course. She would be walking down the aisle in solitary splendour, unless you counted my presence lurking in her wake.

The best man, Nick Pharamond, is scarily attractive in a dark, Neanderthal sort of way, and he'd brought his stepson, Jasper, with him, who also has the typical Pharamond height and colouring: in fact, he's rather handsome.

The wintry sun shone in as Tim and Libby stood at the altar, their fair heads close together, one silvery and one golden, like a pair of love-struck angels . . .

I had to mop my eyes, so goodness knew what I would be like on the actual wedding day! I cry buckets when the wedding bells peal out even for total strangers, and so do the Graces.

Hebe Winter had sent over lots of bags of dried rose petals—the natural confetti. The ushers would hand them out to guests at the door, and Jasper had been roped in for this task. Tim had also asked Ben, so he would have to bring back one of his suits from London for the occasion, but he said he'd have to pop down for a couple of days just before the wedding anyway and could collect it then.

In fact, things were at last starting to come together. Maria Cazzini had even managed to talk some sense into Pia, thank goodness, so she'd definitely be coming to stay for the wedding. She got her to phone her mother too, which was more than I achieved. Libby said it was mainly to veto any floweriness or cherubs in what was to be her bedroom at Blessings, but that was a hopeful sign that one day she might occasionally deign to take up residence there. But she was too late *re* the cherubs, because the lavishly over-the-top bed and dressing table were already on their way from Italy.

* * *

When I got back from the wedding practice, someone from a magazine called *Glorious Weddings* called me, wanting to do a feature on my wedding cake business in their March issue!

They were sending me an interview questionnaire by email, and when I had sent that back they would phone me again about any further points. They were going to send a photographer round to take pics of me with any cakes I happened to be making and I told them about Libby's. Now I had to ask her if she would mind if they dropped by at her reception and took a photograph of her and Tim with the Pisa cake!

When I told Ben about the interview, and that this time they were only interested in my cake-making business, not my whole lifestyle, including him and his wonderful artworks, he was distinctly miffed. But then, he had lots of press coverage when he won that major art prize, and I don't remember much mention of me in all of that!

* * *

Libby was fine about *Glorious Weddings* and I filled in their questionnaire and emailed it back. At least this way they couldn't attribute things to me that I didn't say, like *Country at Heart* did . . . or, at least, I hoped they couldn't!

'Gird up your loins,' Libby advised me before ringing off, 'because from tomorrow, it's operation Libby's Reception, and I want you here helping me every minute you can spare!'

* * *

From that point until the wedding day, Libby was a whirlwind of activity. I helped her as much as I could, although she was terribly efficient.

Dolly Mops went in first and performed heroic acts of cleaning above and beyond the call of duty, transforming the barn into a clean and pleasant

121

place. Apparently they discovered spiders so big they could have saddled them and ridden round the courtyard, had there been any harnesses left in the tackroom.

After that, we all helped paint the rough-hewn walls, including Ben, who emerged from finishing his latest series of artworks in time to tackle the tricky upper bits. When he heard about the Italian theme of the reception, he really got into the swing of it and retired back to the studio to paint a bold backcloth on cotton duck, depicting the Leaning Tower of Pisa. It was hung at one end, behind where the bride and groom would be sitting, and looked rather splendid, especially the opulently rococo clouds.

The electrician had already installed more lighting, including antique-style wall sconces and several power points. The tackroom, too, was being turned into a sort of utility area for food preparation and storage.

Providing the buffet proved to be the easiest thing of all to arrange in the end, once Libby had consulted Maria. It was all to be prepared at the flagship Cazzini restaurant and sent up in a refrigerated van overnight. Giovanni, Maria's husband, now heads the family business and, being too busy to come himself, lavishly gave Tim and Libby the food and champagne as a wedding present.

Background music would be provided by a folk rock group, the Mummers of Invention, whom Nick Pharamond had recommended, but Libby and Tim were to slip away to change and leave by mid-afternoon to fly to Pisa for their honeymoon.

Gina would probably be firmly in control by

then, and able to see that everything was cleared away and returned to where it should be, by the following day, and to look after Maria and Pia.

Tim and Libs were quite soppy together, which made me feel a bit wistful, because I didn't think Ben and I were ever like that, even when we were teenagers . . . and I never got to walk up the aisle in a cloud of love and white lace either.

But I should be thankful for what I had, because love can't be rose-coloured and fluffy for ever, like those clouds in the backdrop; it has to settle into something more everyday eventually—though no less deep and meaningful, of course.

I said as much to the photographer that *Glorious Weddings* sent round, but he was a morose man and only grunted. I only hoped he didn't cast a pall on Libby's reception when he came to take that picture of the happy couple hovering over the Leaning Tower of Pisa with a cake knife.

Chapter Nine

Pisa Cake

I seem to spend every spare moment making parsnip wine lately, though since it is one of the finest wines, the end result is worth it! Not all root vegetables make good wine and, having once tasted Jerusalem artichoke wine at a friend's house, I would strongly advise you against it.

'Unforgettable' would be the politest thing I could say about it.

'Cakes and Ale'

Charlie Rhymer, the editor of *Skint Old Northern Woman* magazine, emailed me to say that she thought my cover was well and truly blown, and thanks to the *Country at Heart* article, everyone had figured out who I was. Then she sent on a load of fan emails that were cluttering up her inbox.

Now they are cluttering up mine.

I think I will have to work out a standard cheery reply to send to them all. Several ask for recipes or advice, and I can't possibly spend all my time answering individually.

It had been so much easier to write my column under the cover of anonymity, like a blog . . . Now I would have to be much more careful what I said!

*   *   *

The wedding was now literally only days away and Libby and I were standing in the Old Barn admiring the transformation.

Carefully angled lighting subtly lit up the beautiful, rough-hewn beams, and rush matting covered the stone floor. Large space heaters stood in the four corners of the huge room, hired for the occasion, like the trestle tables and chairs stacked up along one wall, ready to be set out.

In the tackroom, now turned into a neat and tidy preparation area, were boxes of plates, cutlery, glasses and all the hundred-and-one other things necessary. A huge red fridge, destined afterwards to replace the inadequate one in the Blessings kitchen, stood in the corner.

'It all looks wonderful, Libby! I never thought you'd pull it off, in the time.'

124

'Oh ye of little faith,' she said witheringly. 'And what's more, it's given me another great idea.'

I groaned. 'You haven't got time for anything else, Libs—you're getting married at the end of this week!'

'Yes, but it's not an idea for *my* wedding, it's something more long term. Once I'd realised what a wonderful wedding reception venuc this placc could be, it occurred to me that we could hire out the barn for other people's receptions. There's obviously a dearth of places in this area, since I couldn't find one.'

'Well . . . yes, I suppose you could,' I said, turning it over in my mind. 'You know, I think you've hit on a great idea!'

'Well, you needn't sound so surprised.'

'Sorry, I just hadn't really thought of you as a businesswoman before, that's all.'

'I'm not a complete featherhead, you know,' she said patiently.

'You aren't a featherhead at all,' I assured her. 'I never thought you were. No, it's a really *great* idea, but wouldn't you need planning permission and that kind of thing?'

'Oh, I'm sure we would, but Tim could sort that out. And we'd have to make the tackroom more of a proper kitchen, though we wouldn't cook; it would be buffet-style only. And if they have a small wedding party, couples could even marry in the Great Chamber, if they didn't want a church wedding!'

'I can see you've been really thinking this one out, Libs.'

'Yes, and I think it could be very lucrative. Maybe Tim could give up being a solicitor

125

eventually, which he hates, and just help out and garden. The wedding parties could have lovely photos done in the grounds, once they're tidied up a bit.'

'But you're a bit out of the habit of working, Libby—or of being tied to one spot.'

'I think I would enjoy it. It would be a challenge. And if we only open for the main wedding season, May to September, we'll have lots of time to go and do whatever else we want. Maybe we should open earlier the first year, though, to try and recoup some of the expenses of doing the place up—and, of course, we'll be *very* upmarket and pricey.'

'Would you run it all yourself?'

'Yes, of course. And I'll feature some of your cake designs in the glossy brochure I send out, if you like, so you'll probably get even more orders.'

'Yours has been an absolute *nightmare* to make, Libby. You can't imagine how tricky it was to get the Tower of Pisa to lean sufficiently without falling over.'

'I think they're having that problem with the real thing,' she said absently, jotting something down on the back of yet another list.

When Libby and Tim came over to the cottage that evening to have a private viewing, they both seemed delighted with the cake, so I only hoped subsidence wouldn't affect the foundations before the big day.

* * *

In the morning, when I went next door to collect Mac for his walk, I found Harry sitting in his armchair by the fire, a letter in his lap and his eyes unfocused. Strangely, he always seems more vulnerable when he hasn't got his hat on. Perhaps it's the sight of all those baby-fine silver curls.

'Harry! What is it—bad news?' I was afraid something awful had happened in New Zealand, but was reassured when he looked at me and gave a wry smile.

'No, not really. It's just the Ministry of Defence about that medal. Seems I'm not qualified for it, after all.'

'You're *not*? But you were on the minesweepers for six months, so where's the problem?'

'Apparently I'm seven days short of qualifying. Here, see what they say for yourself.'

He handed me the letter, typed on thick cream paper that had been heavily embossed at taxpayers' expense, and I sat down in the chair opposite. Mac, looking resigned, lay on the mat, though he kept one hopeful eye on me while I read,

Service Personnel and Veterans Agency
An executive agency of the
Ministry of Defence
Ministry of Defence Medal Office

Dear Mr Hutton,

Further to your enquiry concerning the Minesweeping medal, I have assessed the application and can give you the following information.

The Naval General Service Medal with Minesweeping Clasp 45/51 is awarded for *serving 180 days* on a minesweeper from the end of the hostilities in 1945 to 30 September 1951.

Your time spent on a BYMS between 12 June 1946 and 1 December 1946 totals *173 days*.

Therefore I regret to inform you that you do not qualify for the Naval General Service Medal with Minesweeping Clasp.

I am sorry to give what must be a disappointing response and can I thank you for your enquiry.

There was an illegible squiggle for a signature, but underneath was printed, 'Clive Wapshott for Chief Executive.'

I read it twice, in total disbelief, before I looked up. 'You mean, just because you served a week less than the six months, they're not going to give you your medal? After you went right through the war and the Far East and everything, before you did all those months minesweeping? But that's ridiculous!'

'No, that's the Forces for you. Everything has to be down to the precise terms or you get nothing,' he said, seeming, now the first disappointment had worn off, to be amused rather than anything. 'If I'd realised, I wouldn't have bothered applying.'

'And it's a horrible letter, written by some jobsworth enjoying laying down the rules!' I thought it seemed so cruel too, dashing elderly servicemen's hopes like that, however resigned and unsurprised Harry seemed by it.

'Well, that's it,' he said. 'Now, are you taking that poor dog for his walk, or what?'

* * *

That nasty, smug letter occupied my mind all the way through the village, over the fields and back again—and the more I thought about it, the more upset and angry I got.

In the High Street, Violet had to hail me twice from her tricycle before I heard her, and I probably walked straight past several people I knew.

Harry was in his shed when I got back and wouldn't let me in when I knocked, though Mac sidled in through the few open inches of door. I dare say Harry had begun making my Christmas present; he makes the loveliest little wooden boxes and tiny hanging cupboards and things like that.

'Harry, would you mind if I borrowed that Ministry of Defence letter and wrote back to them? I'd like to give them a piece of my mind!'

'Help yourself, our Josie. But it won't get you anywhere, you know. They don't bend the rules, don't the MOD.'

'Maybe not, but *I'll* feel better,' I said, and went home to drink nettle tea and pen a stinging reply to the email address helpfully printed on the letterhead.

Dear Clive Wapshott,

I have seen the letter you recently sent to my uncle, Harold Hutton (your reference above).

Apparently he cannot receive a minesweeping medal because he served only 173 days on a minesweeper, a mere seven days fewer than the required 180 days.

I cannot tell you how disgusted I feel by this

129

piddling, petty-minded, pettifogging and paltry decision. When most people were celebrating the end of the war, he and many others were still fighting on in the Far East under dreadful conditions. Then when he finally got back, he was sent to risk his life again minesweeping around the coast for six months. I don't know what happened to the seven days—perhaps he was suffering one of the recurrent fevers he had for years after the war, probably due to not having enough water on board in the Far East with which to wash down his malaria tablets.

I am sure you are sitting there saying pathetic things like 'we can't bend the rules' and 'oh no, it must be the full 180 days' in a totally jobsworthy way. Perhaps you ought for a moment to contemplate what sort of life you and everyone else working at the MOD would have had (and bear in mind that I and the rest of the taxpayers are paying your wages) had my uncle and many other young men not given up the best years of their lives, and in many cases life itself, to fight that war.

I am quite sure that this letter will get nothing except a brush-off reply, but the almost unbelievably trifling nature of your missive shows such a lack of respect for my uncle's generation that I felt I must express my feelings.

Luckily my uncle, who is now 82 and in frail health, has a sense of humour and has seen the funny side. He will survive the disappointment —he's survived a lot worse, after all. He earned his medal, he doesn't need a bit of metal and a ribbon to prove anything to me or the rest of his family. We know he's a hero.

Yours sincerely,
Josie Gray

I felt a bit better after emailing that off, but not much. Ben agreed with me that Harry's treatment by the MOD was disgraceful, but then what sane person wouldn't?

Ben went down to London yet again, though he assured me he was just delivering the new series of his artworks, which he'd now completed, and would be back almost immediately, together with a suit and shirt suitable for ushering duties.

I thought, he'd better be.

Actually, this time he seemed more resigned to the trip rather than eager to go, which was something, I suppose. But since he'd have to take the van, it would leave me without transport until he got back, unless I borrowed Harry's cherished old Vauxhall Cavalier, which I only do if desperate.

'The Egremont Gallery has got a client who might be interested in buying the whole new series,' Ben explained. 'He likes my work, but he lives in Switzerland and he's only here for a few days. I'll be back before the wedding.'

'I know, I just wish you didn't have to go again so soon. And what about that woman?'

His face went blank. 'What woman?'

'The one stalking you,' I said patiently. Really, he was amazingly single-minded where his work was concerned, to the point of forgetting everything else! He had no idea that I'd told Libby about the patroness. Her advice, predictably, had been to go to London with him and ensure we were seen as a couple everywhere, until the stalker got the idea and gave up.

'Oh, *her*. I think she's over the worst now. She's not ringing me half as much,' he said optimistically, with a charmingly boyish grin, then gave me one of his rib-cracking, but very reassuring, hugs.

This time there was no heart laid out in vegetables anywhere to be seen, but at bedtime I found a tin of chocolate sardines under the pillow that I remembered the Graces giving him last Christmas as a thank you for all the chopped firewood he'd taken them. He must have had them stashed in the studio ever since, because they smelled a bit musty and tasted slightly odd when I tried one, and I wasn't quite sure what kind of message they were meant to convey . . .

* * *

I had lots to occupy myself with in his absence, because as well as the Pisa wedding cake, Libby had decided she wanted a hundred and fifty mini cappuccino cupcakes. She'd seen a photograph in a magazine of little cakes arranged up a sort of spiral stand and ordered two of the stands, though they hadn't arrived yet. The cakes would be made with free-range eggs from Harry's hens, of course, and each was to be topped with an icing rose, tinted blush pink with natural food colouring.

The buffet of antipasti would also include a whole fresh salmon and salads. For dessert, there would be tiramisu or, of course, my little cupcakes. I was to deliver them to the barn very early on the day of the wedding, and then later go across to

Blessings to help Libby get ready, and also to put on my own dress and a bit of makeup.

I did wonder if maybe Libby was right (as she sometimes was) and, if I made a bit of effort, it might stun Ben into seeing me in a whole new light—preferably one coming through a stained-glass window as we exchanged our vows at the altar.

But meanwhile there was work to be done, and I'd just started making the little icing roses for the cupcakes when Violet Grace popped in.

'I don't want to disturb you when you are so busy,' she said, admiring the first row of roses, 'but we would be very grateful for your opinion on our wedding present to Libby and Tim.' She unwrapped the tissue paper parcel she was carrying to display a large, white linen tablecloth. 'What do you think? Will it do?'

The Graces must have stayed up every night since they got their invitations, for the tablecloth not only had one of Pansy's deep, gossamer-fine crocheted edgings, but Lily had embroidered a whole bouquet of flowers in the middle, including lots of fat cabbage roses, and the happy couple's names.

'Oh, it's beautiful!' I exclaimed.

'Do you think so? Not too old-fashioned?'

'Not at all. Retro is back in again.'

'Really?' Violet looked slightly puzzled. 'Lily chose flowers symbolic of love and faithfulness—so romantic!'

'They'll love it. It will be a Blessings heirloom!' I assured her. 'In fact, I've a feeling that once she sees it, Libby will want to have it on the table under the wedding cake at the reception.'

Violet went quite pink with pleasure. 'In that case, we will wrap it up today and take it straight to Blessings. I have some silver tissue paper at home that will do nicely.'

'Did you come on your trike?' I asked. 'Only, if you did, I wondered if you would like to take back a few extra vegetables? I seem to have a glut of some things.'

'Do I have enough Acorns, dear?'

'Yes, loads, because of Lily altering the bridesmaid's dress at such short notice, plus all the Acorns Pansy's earned by knitting me that lovely rainbow cardigan out of leftover wool,' I assured her. 'And my friend Stella's given me lots more of her old hippie clothes and some of them need taking in, if Lily doesn't mind.'

'Oh, no, I'm sure she'll be delighted. This barter idea has been such a godsend, dear. I don't know how we would have managed without it. And being in the co-operative scheme too, so we can club together and bulk-buy things that you can't grow, makes the money go so much further.'

'Yes, it certainly does, and I must go out to Mark and Stella's and pick up the latest order as soon as Ben comes back with the van. Harry's so touchy about his beloved car, I don't really want to load sacks of henfood and brown rice into it.'

I had the Diamonds Are Forever cake sitting in the larder ready to deliver too.

'These icing roses are very pretty,' Violet said. 'They remind me of when I was a girl, and used to do barbola work. One could turn all kinds of old jars and pots into pretty gifts, if you had the knack.'

'I'm baking a hundred and fifty cupcakes for the

reception, and each has to have a flower on top, but they're very fiddly and will take for ever,' I said gloomily—but then what she'd just said sank in and I had a brilliant idea. 'Violet, do you think you could model some for me, if I gave you a finished rose to copy, and some sugar paste? It can't be a lot different from barbola work, can it?'

I'd seen one or two examples of her handiwork about Poona Place, and barbola seemed to be an early type of self-hardening plastic clay.

'Oh, yes, I could easily!' Her face lit up. 'In fact, I would enjoy it.'

So I packed up an example, along with an optimistic amount of icing. 'If you lay them out on greaseproof paper on a tray to harden, like these, I can collect them in the van when I have it again.'

'Give me a ring later and I will tell you how I'm doing with them,' she suggested. The Graces never make outgoing calls, except in emergencies, due to economy.

I saw her pedal off on her trike, the big boot stuffed with spare vegetables, some cheese and vegetable pasties from a freezer batch I had made the day before and, carefully wedged in, the little box containing the rose.

*   *   *

'A hundred and four, dear, before I ran out of paste. Is that enough?' Violet said when I rang that evening.

'Gosh, yes, more than I thought you could make, especially in such a short time! I've done fifty, so that's plenty, with a few spares. And you now have lots of Acorns!'

'Even better,' she said, and rang off, to save me money.

*   *   *

Ben didn't come back on the day I expected him to and, what's more, he wasn't answering his phone either, so I was quite in a panic about what might have happened to him.

When he finally picked up next morning, he sounded sleepy.

'At last!' I said, with a huge feeling of relief. 'I was getting so worried! Where are you, Ben? Are you on the way home?'

'No, actually I'm still here.' I heard him yawn hugely and started to feel cross.

'But the wedding's on Friday—when *are* you coming back? I tried to ring you last night, but your phone was off.'

'Sorry, darling, I was out having dinner with that art collector I told you about. I did try and ring you before I left, but there was no answer.'

'Oh? It didn't say I'd missed any calls.' But then, I thought, it didn't always—or it only tells me about them hours later. 'So was last night's dinner a sort of celebration because he'd bought your work?'

'He's certainly very interested. The Gallery think he might buy the whole new series, but he hasn't quite made his mind up.'

'That would be wonderful! So now, I suppose, you're just about to set off for home?'

'It'll have to be this afternoon because I'm going down to the gallery first, to discuss it with them, then I'll collect my stuff and set off.'

136

'Can there be anything left to discuss? I thought they handled all the sales side.'

'They do, but it's the personal touch that seems to clinch the deal,' Ben explained, 'and it's important to me.'

'Yes, I do understand that, only what with it being the wedding on Friday . . . And then, you've got the van. I could have done with it today to deliver that Diamonds Are Forever wedding anniversary cake, because they live in Mossedge. I had to borrow Harry's car and I'm always petrified I'll scratch it.'

'I'm sorry, that was thoughtless of me.'

'We need to go and collect the co-op stuff from Mark and Stella's too; the order's come.'

'Sorry about that, as well. I know I must seem horribly self-centred,' he added with a rare moment of introspection, 'but I was just so excited about this major collector I forgot about everything else and . . . well, I don't get taken out to dinner at the Ritz every day of the week.'

'I suppose not,' I agreed. 'Swanky!'

'Look, I'll be back early this evening, I promise.'

'You'd better be, Ben Richards,' I said threateningly. 'I'm cooking your favourite dinner, and if you're late, I'll feed it to Mac!'

He laughed, and someone in the background said something—a female voice.

'Is that Mary? Put her on, will you? We haven't had a chat for ages.'

'No, it isn't Mary. Actually I'm at the studios, in the coffee shop-cum-gallery they've set up.'

The voice spoke again in the background, rather insistently. 'Look I'd better go. See you later, OK? Did you want me to bring anything back?'

137

'Just yourself and your suit for the wedding, plus smart shoes, tie, whatever. You're ushering, remember?'

'Umm . . .' he said, his mind obviously drifting elsewhere, which seems to happen a lot with artists, I've noticed.

'Love you,' I said.

But instead of his usual, 'Love you, too,' he simply muttered, 'Damn, the battery's about to run out. I forgot to charge it,' and was gone.

Still, at least I knew he was all right and would soon be on his way home, even if he did sound overexcited and exhausted, like a child after a party. I really didn't think London was good for him.

*   *   *

A pallid young bride-to-be, with blue-black hair, blood-red lipstick, multiple facial piercings and a resigned mother, came to discuss ordering a wedding cake—a Goth one.

She requested purple and black, but left the design to me. I thought a sort of silver stud effect would be nice, using those little silver ball cake decorations or, even better, silver-coated almonds, pointy end out. I would have to order them from a specialist supplier, though. Luckily, it's to be a December wedding, so although it's short notice, I'm unlikely to get many other orders during that month, and it will at least keep my hand in.

I wondered about a sort of half-ruined Gothic tower with a stained-glass window, made like you do traffic light biscuits, using melted toffees—only purples and greens. And maybe a marzipan dragon curled up inside the ruin? The Goth bride had had a dragon tattoo up her arm, so she was presumably keen on them.

I hadn't made a Goth cake before and I found the challenge quite interesting after the tedium of making a hundred and fifty identical cupcakes. I did a few sketches and worked out how many round cakes I needed for the tower, which would not be quite of the same proportions as Libby's Pisa cake.

I might have to make the half-ruined top part, with the toffee stained-glass window, out of biscuit . . . but I could experiment a bit. It would be fun.

Chapter Ten

Slightly Adulterated

I put a couple of new fruit bushes in today, accompanied by the hens—there isn't much in the vegetable garden they can damage at this time of year. As usual, my favourite hen, Aggie, edged so close behind me as I dug that I kept having to shoo her away in case I caught her with the spade on the backward swing.

'Cakes and Ale'

'Ben's on his way back right now,' I said to Harry when he came in that afternoon for a mug of tea and a chat, just as it was getting dark. 'He'll be here for dinner and I've got Lancashire hotpot on in the slow cooker, his favourite. Would you like me to bring you some over when it's ready?'

'No, that's all right. I've a fancy for kippers and brown bread and butter tonight and then I'm going to the pub.'

'Ben might come down for a quick one later too,' I said. He often strolled down to the Griffin about ten, allegedly so he could make sure Harry got safely back home, though I suspected he enjoyed an occasional pint of Mossbrown ale as a change from our own homebrew.

'Aye, I'll maybe catch up with him then—and I'll tell him to stop all this gallivanting off to London, leaving you on your own so much too!'

'He can't help it at the moment, Harry. He has to consolidate his reputation while he can. But soon he—' I broke off as my mobile rang. 'I'd better answer that, in case it's a cake order,' I apologised, 'though most of my calls lately are through that article in *Country at Heart*, asking about cakes for next year's wedding season, so they aren't exactly urgent.'

He got up. 'That's all right. I'd better be off and shut up the hens. It's almost dark. I'll see you tomorrow, lass.'

'Make sure Aggie's in, won't you? I thought I saw her behind the compost bins earlier.'

Harry jammed his old hat on and picked up his stick, and I watched him negotiate the small step down into the garden, followed by Mac, while I absent-mindedly answered 'Hello? Josie's Weird and Wonderful Cakes. Can I help you?'

'Is that Josie Gray?' asked a crisp, incisive voice, the kind that I knew from long experience belonged to the worst sort of mother-of-the-bride: a control-freak who would want to run the whole day with military precision and no margin for

140

errors, or human weakness. She'd be certain to find fault with any cake I made for her . . . in fact, she didn't sound the sort of woman to want a weird and wonderful cake at all.

'Yes, that's right. Were you enquiring about a wedding cake?'

There was an infinitesimal pause. 'No, should I be? I think that's a *teeny* bit premature.'

'Sorry,' I said, 'it's just that I make them, so I automatically assume that it's an order when a strange number comes up. So, how can I help you?'

'My name's Olivia Taunton.'

Olivia? Now, where had I heard that name recently . . . ?

'I don't know if Ben has ever mentioned me to you?'

'I don't think so,' I said, puzzled. 'In what context?'

'Well, we originally met at his first one-man exhibition in London at the end of last year, and since then I've bought several pieces of his work and come to know him *rather* well.'

Now a different picture was forming in my head to go with that brittle, cut-glass voice, and my heart performed a quick, alarmed thump-thump-thump. This must be Ben's middle-aged, blonde stalker, the patroness, out to acquire slightly more than just Ben's art!

'Ah, yes, he has mentioned you,' I said cautiously, 'only not by name. I suppose you want to speak to him, but—'

'No, actually it is *you* I want to talk to,' she interrupted.

'*Me?* What about?' I hoped she wasn't going to

141

launch into some kind of jealous personal attack, though she didn't sound delusional—scarily sane, in fact. I suppose that's how stalkers come across, because their fantasies must seem totally real to them.

She gave an impatient sigh. 'This is *sooo* difficult! Ben should really have told you himself ages ago, but then the poor darling is so soft-hearted, I've realised he's never going to bring himself to do it.'

'Tell me what?' I asked, though it was by now obvious that Ben was right about her, for not only was she losing her grip on her marbles, clearly one or two of the milkier ones had already rolled away into the corners. Perhaps I should just put the phone down?

But before I could do that, she said, 'Look, if you weren't obviously totally dim, you'd have sussed that Ben's been having an affair with me for over a year now. He stays with me when he's in London. He was here earlier when you phoned him.'

'Oh, *really*?'

'Yes, really! I wanted him to ring you right back and tell you the truth, but he couldn't bring himself to do it. He says you're so insecure and needy that you couldn't cope on your own. But after he'd gone, a friend showed me that article in *Country at Heart*, and I could see you're in some kind of la-la land, thinking Ben's going to stagnate in a rural backwater with you for ever! So, obviously, it's unfair to let it drag on any longer and much kinder in the long run to put you out of your misery now.'

'That's very kind,' I said, with as much patience as I could muster, 'but Ben's already warned me about you. Look, Olivia, I've read about older women who stalk attractive men, get fixated on them, think they're having a relationship and then see their wives or partners as the intruders, so I do understand. But take it from me that you're deluded and you need to snap right out of it, because my Ben would never do something like that! And by the way, he stays with old friends when he's in London, not with you, and I frequently phone him there.'

'Mary and Russell? Yes, I've met them, but he doesn't stay there any more. He's moved his things in with me. And yes, you're forever phoning his mobile at the most inconvenient moments, as I know only too well.'

There was clearly no arguing with her and she sounded so calm and rational, but I suppose her delusion was perfectly real to her. 'I'm sorry,' I said levelly, 'but this is all in your head. I mean, look at it logically—you're in your fifties and Ben is—'

'Is *that* what he told you?' She sounded amused. 'Well, I can assure you I'm not in my fifties—far from it. I'm only forty-two. And the minute we first met, the attraction was mutual.'

'In your head,' I snapped, losing patience. 'And I don't care how old you are, he still wouldn't have an affair with you, because he loves *me*—always has, always will. You're fantasising.'

The gloves came off and her voice went steely. 'Look, it isn't me who's delusional, darling, it's you. Get a grip on reality! You must have noticed how different he's been for months? That he can't wait to get back to London? I mean, I know you've had a platonic relationship for years, more like

143

brother and sister, so the lack of that side of it probably hasn't dawned on you yet, but—'

'We have *not* had a platonic relationship,' I said furiously. 'Not that it's any of your business! Ben and I have been together since our early teens— we've always been together, and we always will be, till death do us part. I understand why you're trying to come between us, but it's not going to work.'

'Shut up and listen!' she snarled. 'In front of me I have a scan photograph showing *our* baby—Ben's and mine. You just think about *that* one!' And then the phone went dead.

By then, I was totally unnerved and upset, especially after that last, cruel touch. Logically I knew it was all untrue, but still, she'd sounded so convincing!

Then I thought of phoning Mary. Once she'd assured me that Ben had been staying with them as usual whenever he was in London, I would have proof that everything the woman had said was a tissue of lies, though as I dialled the number with unsteady fingers I felt guilty even doubting Ben enough to need that reassurance.

To my relief, Mary picked up immediately. 'Hello?'

'Oh, I'm so glad it's you and not Russell!' I gasped. 'Mary, I've just had the most ghastly phone call from this mad woman called Olivia Taunton. Did Ben tell you about her stalking him?'

But before she could answer I poured out all the things Olivia had told me, hardly stopping for breath, let alone to let Mary get a word in. 'But he always stays with you, so I *knew* it was all a lie,' I finished, breathlessly. 'It is, isn't it?'

144

There was a long silence on the other end of the phone.

'Mary? Mary—are you still there? Hello?'

'Y-yes, Josie,' Mary said, sounding strained. 'It's just . . . well, I'm so sorry it has to come from me, but actually he hasn't stayed with us since he met Olivia last year, though we've seen him at the studios, of course and—'

'He *hasn't*?' I echoed numbly. Then the penny finally dropped and a horrible, unbelievable pattern began to emerge clearly, making my head reel with shock. 'Wait a minute—you mentioned a friend called Olivia, didn't you? The one who told you about the Chinese herbal practitioner.'

'Yes, and I was grateful to her for that, but I would still have told you about her and Ben, only I didn't like to interfere and I hoped it would just fizzle out—'

But I wasn't interested in Mary's feelings. 'Oh my God! You mean it's all true? *Everything* she said? Even the baby—*Ben's* baby?'

'Yes,' she said in a small voice. 'Olivia was desperate to get pregnant before it was too late. I think that's why she made such a play for him in the first place.'

At that moment my entire life, from that very first meeting with Ben in the school playground to the last time he kissed me goodbye on the doorstep, flashed before my eyes as if I was dying—which, inside, I was. Only what I saw seemed as unsubstantial as stage scenery that trembled with each beat of my heart, and behind it lay only the echoing darkness of the void if it fell. And it was slowly falling now . . .

'Josie, are you still there?' cried Mary.

145

'Yes—and I understand it all now. No wonder you've been avoiding my calls for months. You should have told me. I thought you were my friend!'

'I am your friend,' she said miserably, 'but what good would it have done? Russell and I thought at first the affair would peter out eventually, especially once she got what she wanted, a baby. But instead she's got more and more possessive. She came down to the studios and told Ben she was pregnant, right in front of us, and then said he was moving in with her full time. And he didn't contradict her, he just looked a bit sheepish and harassed.'

There was a voice in the background and she said, sounding relieved, 'Oh, here's Russell now.' Then I heard her whisper, 'Russell, it's Josie and she knows all about Ben and Olivia—*everything*!'

'Josie, my love!' Russell said, in his warm, soft Durham voice. 'I'm so sorry!'

'I just can't believe this isn't some dreadful nightmare and I'm going to wake up any minute, Russell!'

'I told Ben he was mad, going after Olivia when he had you, but he wouldn't listen.'

'But she's having a baby too, Ben's baby. And why *her*, not me?' I choked, which was not at all what I intended to say, but it just sort of fell out of my mouth and flapped about in the air, dying. 'I—oh God, I can't believe this is happening to me! What am I going to do?'

Mary came back on. 'Look, Josie, stay calm, take deep breaths. I really do think Ben is starting to regret it now and that it was an infatuation for him more than anything—and of course he wasn't thinking about the future. I don't suppose he was thinking at all. And now, the more possessive she's getting, the more he backs off. If you play your cards right, he'll come back, you'll see.'

'Come back? I don't think the Ben I loved ever existed in the first place, except in my imagination!' I yelled hysterically and then threw the phone away from me as if it had stung my ear. It hit the wall and fell to the carpet, still quacking, so it wasn't broken—unlike me.

I hurled the bottle of medicinal herbs at the wall too, for good measure, and then followed that by flushing all the pretty jade-green pills, together with my hopes and dreams, down the loo.

*　　　*　　　*

I sat on a kitchen chair, huddled trembling against the stove, listening to the slow tick of the clock as the afternoon wore on into early evening.

Everything was the same—and yet totally changed. Could this truly be happening, or was it just a nightmare? I thought of the day Ben carved 'Ben&Josie4ever' underneath the old bridge, when we were teenagers . . . Of how Granny, not long before she died, had said she wished she could have seen us married, but at least she knew we would always be together.

The cuckoo clock clattered into action and I realised that any minute now he would be home—and what could I say? What was I going to do?

The Ben who would return was a different man from the one I knew, or thought I knew. I wanted the old one back but instead, like some horror story, what would appear at my door would be a

147

ghastly travesty that only looked and sounded like him . . .

I wished I hadn't thought of that one. Shivering, I got up and grabbed a bottle of sloe gin and had a swift gulp straight from the bottle. It burned its way clear down to my diaphragm but didn't warm me. I wasn't sure anything ever could.

Chapter Eleven

Over and Out

Sloe gin should be treated with caution, though there is nothing better for shock than a glass of this seemingly innocuous, pleasant-tasting spirit.
'Cakes and Ale'

'Josie?' Ben called, opening the front door and then switching on the kitchen light. Then he spotted me huddled down in the wheelback chair by the almost-dead stove.

'Why are you sitting in the dark? Are you ill?' he asked, his brow wrinkling in quick concern as he strode across to me, then stopped dead as I leaped up and stood behind the chair, making it a barrier between us.

'Don't—don't come near me! Don't *touch* me,' I said tightly.

'What on earth's the matter, darling?'

'I had a phone call from Olivia Taunton—you know, the rich, elderly art collector you told me about? The one who's been stalking you? Only it turns out that you've been stalking each other.'

148

'Oh God!' he said, the warm colour draining from his face.

'It seems the relationship isn't just a figment of her imagination after all, though I didn't believe it until Mary and Russell told me it was true. She seems to have acquired you as easily as your art, doesn't she? And perhaps I should call her Sugar Mummy now, since I expect she's given you lots of things you've never had.'

'I—no, it wasn't like that, honestly!' he blustered. 'Moncy never entered into it. It was just that . . . well, I fell for her and it was like a fever in the blood: I couldn't help myself.'

'So that makes it all right, does it? No one forced you into it, Ben—you're supposed to be an adult, after all. And according to her, you told her *our* relationship was platonic, almost brother and sister.'

He shifted uncomfortably under my accusing gaze. 'No, I swear I never said any such thing and I made it clear from the start that I'd never leave you. Olivia always said she didn't want commitment anyway, only lately she's changed her mind about that and the more I've tried to shake her off, the clingier she's become.'

'That's probably because she's *pregnant*!' I hadn't realised my voice had been rising until the last word ended on a shriek that echoed round the kitchen.

Ben sank down into the rocking chair and said quietly, 'Oh, darling, I'm so sorry! When I found out about the baby and realised that was what she'd wanted me for all along, I came to my senses and tried to finish with her. I hoped you'd never have to find out.'

149

'Yes, and you even went to the extent of telling me she was stalking you, in case she spoke to me!'

'I was just trying to protect you, Josie, and Olivia *is* deluding herself if she thinks I'm going to leave you for her. It was only ever a physical thing. I don't love her. I've come to my senses now and I know I belong here with you. I promise I'll never, ever, do anything to hurt you again.'

I stared at him in astonishment. 'You mean . . . you imagine we can just pick up our lives as though all of this . . . this *betrayal* never happened? You're so obviously not the man I thought you were, Ben Richards! Just be grateful that Sugar Mummy seems to want you all to herself, because as far as I'm concerned, she can have you.'

He reached out as if to touch me and I snatched my hand away. 'Don't dare come near me!'

'Josie, I can't bear to see you upset, you know I can't. Please, please forgive me?' he wheedled softly, like a small boy who'd shattered a window with his football, instead of the man who'd broken my heart. 'You need me and I need you. This affair was just an aberration, something I should have got out of my system in my teens. It doesn't change my love for you—nothing could change that. I always looked forward to coming back home to you, and I always will.'

'Then you should have thought of that before— only you didn't think, did you? You just did what you wanted, like you usually do. And you know what the final, most humiliating thing about it all is? She's having the child I never managed to conceive, which means *I'm* the barren one, not you. Somehow, I don't think I'll ever get over that.'

His brows knitted, as if he was struggling to

understand. 'But, Josie, if having a baby means *that* much to you, we could try—'

'No, we couldn't try anything now. It's all way, way too late,' I said with weary finality. 'I want you to leave.'

'Leave?' He looked blank for a moment and then his face cleared. 'You mean you want me to go and stay with Mark and Stella tonight? Perhaps that's a good idea, then tomorrow we can talk it all through when you're over the shock and feeling more reasonable and—'

'No, I want you to leave the house, this minute, and not come back! I'll never be in such a reasonable state of mind that you can talk away the affair, or fathering a child with another woman.'

'Josie!'

'This is my house and you aren't welcome in it any more,' I said with finality.

'Look, Josie, how about if I spend the night in the studio, then see how you feel in the morning? I can't let you do this to me—to us!' he said pleadingly, hazel eyes full of hurt—and maybe a dawning of astonishment at finding that suddenly he could no longer twist me round his little finger.

'There is no "us" any more. You can sleep in the studio tonight if you must, but I want you gone by morning. I'll pack your stuff up and put it outside the back door for you to collect—and you'd better send someone to clear out your studio too, before I'm tempted to make a funeral pyre of it.'

'I know you wouldn't do that,' he said, but he didn't sound too certain of it, which enraged me even more. He'd never really known me if he actually thought I could do that . . . and, come to

151

that, it was clear he had never quite twigged how desperately I wanted a baby either, despite all the times I'd tried to discuss it with him.

'*Get out!*' I yelled, because something volcanic was starting to build inside me and suddenly I was on the verge of hysteria and looking over into the abyss.

He got up silently and left by the back door to the garden, carrying the overnight bag he'd arrived with, and as I slammed and locked the door after him I saw the lights in the studio go on and his tall, familiar shape moving about inside.

Sitting on the bottom step of the stairs I gave way to such deep, wrenching sobs that I frightened myself. It was a long, long time before I could stop and by then I was quite hoarse.

*   *   *

I heard the side gate squeak later. Ben was probably off down to the pub for something to eat, and maybe a drink or two to sweeten the idea of sleeping on the old ottoman in the studio, which was lumpy, to say the least. And it would be pretty chilly down there too.

Not that Ben's comfort mattered to me any more . . . though when I thought of life without him, my future seemed to stretch in front of me like a long, lonely road. Could our past have been a total sham? Was it truly me he loved and had I, perhaps, been at least to some extent to blame by staying in Neatslake instead of going with him on his trips to London? Perhaps this Olivia had, siren-like, lured him onto the rocks . . .

For the first time in my life I did the classic

152

suspicious wife thing and went through all his pockets, and then, after hesitating, the small tin box in which he kept odd papers and old treasures, which normally I wouldn't even think of touching. I sat down on the patchwork bedspread and opened it up.

There, right on top, was a picture of me in the garden, wearing the old straw hat that was Granny's and smiling into the sun. I remembered when he'd taken that one, suddenly appearing between the bean canes with his camera. Under it were all the letters and cards I'd ever given him, photographs of us together, Valentine's cards I'd made him . . .

If our love didn't mean anything to him, would he have kept all these mementoes of our life together?

I lifted up one corner of a particularly large Valentine's card I'd constructed out of paper doilies and foil sweet wrappers as a teenager (his to me, that year, had been burned into a slab of driftwood), softening with the memories . . . And then under it I hit paydirt.

'Dirt' was the operative word. Olivia, it appeared, had been in the habit of shoving an explicit little missive into his pocket after his visits, for him to read on the way home, reminding him of what he was missing while back in Neatslake. It was obvious, too, that Ben had talked to her about me—and not in a terribly flattering way either, since she referred to me as 'your comfort blanket', something he clung to simply from habit. In fact, the notes made Neatslake sound like a rest and relaxation facility, with me in the nanny role, where he could retire until he was ready for yet

153

more energetic and innovative sex games.

Any slight sentimental wavering vanished. Shoving everything roughly back into the tin box I went back downstairs and opened the first bottle of wine to come to hand, which was apple, and had downed a couple of large glasses by the time someone knocked at the door a little later.

I ignored it, until Libby opened the letterbox and shouted through it. 'I can see you, Josie. You'd better let me in right now, because I'm not going away!'

I jerked open the door. 'I really don't want—'

'Don't be silly,' she said, enveloping me in a warm hug, which said a lot, because she's not a terribly huggy person, usually. 'Harry just called to tell me he'd heard you arguing with Ben and then crying for ages, and he was really worried. He said he didn't want to come between a man and his wife by interfering—not that you *are*, of course, but the next best thing—so I said I'd come and see what was the matter. Tell Auntie Libby all.'

She held me off, looking at me with worry in her blue eyes. 'You look terrible! What is it?'

I burst into tears again and she guided me over to the table, where I slumped down in a chair. 'Ben's been having . . . having an affair!' I choked.

'I thought it might be something like that.' She poured some more wine into my glass and one for herself. 'Now, just take it slowly and tell me everything.'

I did, every last word I remembered, including the phone call from Sugar Mummy. I'm not sure it was entirely coherent, but she got the gist.

'So I threw him out and he's staying in the studio tonight, though I've told him I want him gone by

154

morning. I'll start packing up his stuff in the house shortly and put it outside. It can all go in the studio until he fetches it, or has it collected, and the sooner the better!'

'Look, Josie, I know you're upset,' she said, handing me a wad of tissues from her bag—she'd obviously come prepared. 'But it does sound to me as though he was just madly infatuated with an older, sophisticated woman. Probably great sex, you know?'

'Obviously not,' I said coldly.

'I expect he was flattered when she showed interest in him too. But once that wore off, and he realised he risked losing you and all his home comforts, he tried to back off. If you throw him out now, he'll probably take the easy option and move in with this other woman, so if you want him back, don't do it.'

'But, Libby, she's having his *baby*, that's the worst thing of all! And when I told him he started to say if it meant that much to me we could try and see if there was anything we could do to start a family, so he can't ever have been listening to a word I said on the subject.'

'He liked being the centre of your world. He didn't really want to change that, Josie, however he justified it as concern for you. But to keep you now, he'll clearly do whatever it takes.'

I knew she was right. 'I thought I knew him as well as I know myself, and now it seems I was totally deluded. He didn't even seem to think having an affair was wrong. He was just sorry I found out and got upset about it!'

'I don't suppose he did think any of it through, because thinking isn't his big thing, is it? I mean,

155

he may be an artistic genius, but he isn't terribly bright otherwise.'

'He didn't need to be,' I said. 'He was loving and strong, supportive and understanding . . . or I *thought* he was all those things.'

'It's easy enough to hug someone and tell them everything is going to be all right,' she pointed out, 'or leave little heart-shaped messages about the place.'

'He left me a tin of chocolate sardines last time he went to London—that should have told me something was fishy.'

'Perhaps his subconscious was trying to confess?' Libby suggested. 'But actually, apart from being so self-centred that he took the way you created the perfect environment for him to work in as his God-given right, he always gave me the impression he truly loved you. In fact, I'm sure he *does* love you, in his way, that's why he doesn't think the affair is important. He doesn't love her, it was just sex.'

'There must have been something missing in our relationship or he wouldn't have done it,' I said miserably. 'Perhaps it's partly my fault, Libby?'

'I don't know how you work that one out, you daft bat!' she said forthrightly.

'But I've been burying my head in the sand. I could see he had another life going on in London that he was enjoying, while mine revolved more and more around Neatslake. And he started buying me all sorts of expensive electrical things, like the breadmaker, which were totally alien to the sort of life we were trying to lead.'

'Well, you can't blame him for wanting to give you a few labour-saving devices, can you?'

'You said you saw him in a wonderful suit in

London and he used to come back in designer jeans sometimes, so perhaps he got hooked on having expensive things? I mean, I know he's always used that allowance from his parents to buy himself electrical gadgets and other non-essential stuff, but apart from that he's always seemed to be as dedicated to living a green life as much as I was. He's *so* not the man I thought he was!'

'None of them are. Like I said, you have to keep your eye on the ball the whole time.'

I looked up, drawn out of my own woes. 'Not Tim—he's mad about you!'

'Well, no, but he's a bit dim, like Ben, so some other woman might decide to try and grab him if I don't watch it,' she said affectionately. 'They probably would have done already, if he'd had any money.'

'Well, it's too late now for me and Ben. I don't want him back.'

'Think about it first, Josie,' she said earnestly. 'Don't cut off your nose to spite your face by sending him right back into her arms.'

'I'm not, and I did start to wonder about whether I might forgive him in time—until I found some notes from her in his keepsake box. He'd obviously described me and our relationship in hugely unflattering terms, because she was spelling out all the things she would like to give him that he didn't get at home, and they made me feel quite sick. I know now that I don't want him near me, ever again.' I shuddered. 'I'm just sorry I wasted the best years of my life on him.'

'*Right . . .*' she said thoughtfully. 'I see what you mean. He's not only betrayed you, he's betrayed everything good that you had together by talking to her about your relationship. But I still don't know how you'll manage without him. He's been the centre of your universe for ever.'

'I'll survive. The house is mine and I don't want any of his money. He can keep it. And I've still got you, haven't I, my BFF?'

'Yes, best friends for ever,' she agreed. 'You know I'll always be here for you.'

'And I've got Harry too. I hope he wasn't too upset?'

'He was a bit, but I'll go there on my way home and soothe him down,' she promised. 'You and Ben splitting up will worry him, of course, but so long as I can assure him you aren't lying on the floor, overdosed on peapod wine, he should be OK.'

'It's apple wine. I *would* be on the floor by now if it was peapod.'

'Will you be OK if I leave you on your own?'

'Yes, I'll be fine.' Things had begun to look a bit swimmy after the sloe gin and wine on a totally empty stomach, but I was far from drunk. 'It's about time I managed to stand on my own two feet and stopped relying on Ben for support, anyway. It just isn't quite the way I would have chosen to do it.' I added resolutely: 'I've got a big roll of recycled bin bags, and I'm going to try and strip all his possessions out of the cottage before I go to bed.'

She looked at me worriedly. 'Perhaps I ought to get my things and stay with you overnight, after all.'

'No, really. I'd rather be alone and I'm going to be really busy.'

'Promise? You won't drink so much you do

158

anything silly?'

'No, of course not. I've too many responsibilities for that and I've got loads to do tomorrow too—all your cupcakes to ice and put the sugar roses on. Did I tell you Violet Grace had made over a hundred of them? I think they look better than mine do,' I added, with an attempt at normal conversation.

'That was kind of her. And the tablecloth they made for our wedding present is lovely. Gina was terribly impressed. I think she intends serving afternoon tea on it every day when we get back from honeymoon. She's convinced all the English do that kind of thing.'

'Tell her I'm looking forward to catching up with her again when she's a bit more settled,' I said, though it seemed unlikely that I would ever look forward to anything ever again.

Before she finally left, Libby made me a mug of very sweet tea, for the shock, but as soon as she'd gone I poured it down the sink and started on a second bottle of wine—more apple, last year's vintage.

Then, in a drunken frenzy, I began to pack all Ben's belongings (including the tin box) in bin bags, which I dragged outside the back door. I stuck a note on one, telling him to put what he couldn't take with him in the studio and to send for the rest as soon as possible, or I would dispose of them.

It was lucky for him it was a dry, if chilly, night. He was back from the pub, or wherever he had been, by then, because I could see him walking up and down in the studio with his phone to his ear, but when he looked in my direction, I went back in and locked and bolted the door again.

What was left of the long night I spent sleeplessly wandering the house, which looked weird, as familiar things in nightmares often do. I felt cold, hollow and shivery, detached with exhaustion and shock, my eardrums vibrating with tiredness.

The alcohol just seemed to increase my sense of alienation and I really, really wanted to get away from myself, especially towards dawn, when one of the peacocks gave its mournful, lost-soul wail. I couldn't stand it any longer and I'd have put my head in the oven if we hadn't had a solid fuel range: I didn't want to be slow-cooked. Anyway, I'd promised Libby.

Instead I poured out about half a bottle of the sloe gin and then downed it quickly, before passing out on the living room sofa . . .

Did I dream that I heard Ben calling my name over and over, or the rattle of the van's exhaust pipe as he drove off, for ever?

*   *   *

When I did finally wake up, it was with a splitting head, furry mouth, seriously creased face and an appalling sense of devastation and loss.

For a moment I was the child Josie, as Granny explained that I would never see my parents again . . . Then memory came rushing back and I remembered what had happened yesterday: Ben, the love of my life, my soul mate, my best friend, the one who shared all my dreams and comforted me through the nightmares, was gone.

It was as though part of me had been wrenched

away, roots and all, and I had the appalling thought, which I was instantly ashamed of, that it would have been easier to deal with the pain of his loss if he had been dead, like practically everyone else I had ever loved.

But overnight it seemed that I'd somehow metamorphosed into a monstrous, alternative Josie, because a desire to get some measure of revenge burned fiercely among the ashes of my heart—and I knew just how to hit Ben where it would *really* hurt.

Chapter Twelve

Stitched Up

I have always found the cycle of nature, the seasons following one another in regular succession, very soothing. But suddenly even nature seems to have turned capricious, so that things flower and fruit earlier than they used to, or later than they used to, and everything's turned on its head. I find that very unsettling.

But it seems all things must change, even those that seem as fixed in time and space as stars . . .
'Cakes and Ale'

Most of the bags of Ben's belongings had gone— and so had the van too, which I hadn't expected. I thought hearing it drive off was just part of a nightmare.

I dragged the two remaining bags down to the studio and booted them through the door. Inside, everything looked much as usual, with new works in various stages of progress, a mess of half-used tubes of paint littering every surface, and three stained mugs left in the little sink in the kitchen/darkroom.

Normally I found the studio smell of oil paint, wood and glue, deliciously comforting when Ben was away. But not now.

The building is made of timber and his artworks and the materials stored there are highly combustible . . . But of course I wasn't going to turn the place into a funeral pyre of our love, tempting though the idea of it was. Ben's moral code might be so low it dragged on the ground when he walked, but still, I respected his art too much to destroy it.

I had a subtler revenge in mind, but first there was something I needed to go out and buy. My eyes were so red and swollen that before going up the High Street to Neville's Village Stores I had to put on sunglasses, even though it was a dark, overcast day.

There I amazed Annie Neville by purchasing a packet of jumbo shell-on prawns from the freezer cabinet, because buying luxury foods was not something I'd ever done a lot of. She gave the dark glasses a strange look too, but when asked, supplied me with a couple of empty cardboard boxes.

Hurrying back home, the prawns clutched to my chest under my coat to start them thawing, I heard a 'Coo-ee!' from the direction of Poona Place in Pansy's high-pitched tones. Breaking into a run I shot indoors, where I locked my front door, panting.

Tipping the prawns onto a dish I set them on top of the warm stove and, while their little ice jackets were defrosting, went through the house on a last sweep, collecting anything of Ben's that I'd missed last night. There was quite a bit, like his collection of old vinyl records culled from car boot sales, and a lot of portfolios of his work in the attic I'd forgotten about, until it occurred to me to check up there too.

I carried everything down to the studio, where I finished by tossing all the tubes of paint and other bits and pieces into the boxes I'd got from Annie Neville.

Then I fetched the bowl of prawns, patted them dry with a tea towel, and ate them while sitting in the old swivel chair in the dead centre of Ben's studio. Having been defrosted on the stove, they were quite likely to give me terminal food poisoning, but I didn't care about that. And I wasn't hungry either; it was just that eating them seemed the logical way to dispose of them. They were extra salty because tears were dripping down on them, though until then I hadn't realised I was crying.

I suppose eating them also added a ritualistic layer of meaning to what I was about to do, one that Ben would come to appreciate, in time.

Eventually the pile of shells lay on one side of the dish, the prawn heads on the other, and I put it down on the floor. A rag of slithery, glistening, dark blood-red fabric still hung like a dead tongue from the old treadle sewing machine in the corner of the room and I tried wiping my hands on it, but it wasn't terribly absorbent.

Going back to the chair I spun slowly round,

examining those artworks he hadn't taken to London for his last solo exhibition, mostly older works, or unfinished. I used to love Ben's paintings when what burst through the canvases were flowers and small creatures and twisting stems. But his recent series reminds me of nothing so much as that scene from *Alien*, where the weird life form rips its way from the host before skittering evilly off. If you were in the room with one of those artworks, you wouldn't want to take your eyes off it: it might literally follow you round the room and jump on you.

Perhaps the way they'd changed had been an indication of how Ben, too, had been evolving into something alien under the façade of his everyday self, if only I'd realised. But I hadn't, and here I was, stitched and stuffed like all his other creations. But not, fortunately, inanimate.

The mobile phone in my jeans pocket rang and I snapped it on impatiently, thinking it was Libby checking up that I was still in the land of the living. Then I heard Ben's voice.

'Josie, are you in the studio?' he said presciently. But then, we always were mentally in tune, right from the moment our eyes locked across the school playground . . . or I thought we were.

Or perhaps he'd developed clairvoyance as well as a chronic case of adultery? (And so what if we were never married in the first place—what we had was *more* than marriage.)

'Yes,' I said, in my new, husky voice. 'What do you want?'

'Josie, don't be like that,' he pleaded. 'I want you to understand what happened—that it was like being offered champagne and caviar after a diet of crusty wholemeal bread and water. They were both good, but one was new and exciting and for a while I—'

'You're making bad worse,' I interrupted, through stiff lips. 'And bad was already the pits of hell, when you let Sugar Mummy break the news you were having an affair and leaving me.'

'I didn't know Olivia was going to do that and, anyway, I never had any intention of leaving you. That's why she told you about the affair, to force my hand.'

'She's got what she wanted then, hasn't she? *Everything* she wanted, if her notes to you are anything to go by.'

'You've been through my things?' he exclaimed incredulously.

'Yes, though porn isn't my usual bedtime reading. Another of my failings, perhaps? Boring old Josie!'

There was a short pause while he mentally regrouped, then he said, persuasively, 'Look, Josie, can we meet up and talk in a day or two, when you feel a bit calmer and ready to listen to my side of things?'

'Oh, yeah, like that's ever going to happen,' I said, and he sighed long-sufferingly, as if *he* was the injured party.

'I've managed to find someone to collect my stuff at short notice and deliver it to the studio in Camden, though it took a bit of doing. They'll be there in the morning and they'll pack the artworks up. You haven't . . . I mean, you aren't in the studio because you're thinking of destroying them, are you?'

'Of course not! Don't be any dafter than you can

help.'

He sounded relieved when he said quickly, 'No, of course you wouldn't, Josie. What was I thinking of? And you could keep the small one in the living room, the one I did at college. That was always your favourite.'

'Not any more. It's here with the others, waiting to go. I'll be at Blessings all day tomorrow—it's the wedding, remember? So tell the removal men the side gate will be unlocked and the studio key will be under the broken flowerpot by the door, though there might be a toad in there too, so they'll have to be careful.'

I clicked off the phone and put it back into my pocket and then, picking up a seam ripper, began the delicate process of opening up a tiny bit of concealed seam in each artwork and inserting a prawn head, before neatly and tidily sewing them up again.

I may or may not have been entirely in my right mind, but look at it this way: I'd added a new sensory dimension to Ben's work that would only emerge in its full glory over the course of time.

Suddenly life stank, and I think that's what I really, really wanted to share with my ex-life partner and one untrue love.

*   *   *

When I came out of the studio, carrying the plate, I came face to face with Harry, who looked at me dolefully, then gave me a hug. Luckily, I didn't think his eyesight was up to discerning seafood remains on pink-patterned china or he might have wondered what I'd been up to.

166

'How are you, lass? I never thought to see the day when Ben would do the dirty on you like this! I thought he was a grand lad, despite his arty ways, and so did your gran.'

Mac licked my hand, which I expect tasted of prawns. It was all too much sympathy and I felt myself on the verge of breaking into sobs again.

'I—do you mind if we don't talk about it at the moment, Harry? I have to pull myself together, because I've so much to do today. It's the wedding tomorrow, so there just isn't time to curl up into a ball in the corner and go to pieces.'

'That's a brave lass,' he said, following me into the house and putting the kettle on. 'Let's have a brew.'

I tipped the prawn shells into the bin, washed my hands, and then got out the mugs and biscuit tin. When I turned he was taking his car keys out of his pocket.

'Oh, I was going to ask you if I could borrow your car, Harry! Ben's taken the van, and I have to collect the co-op order. And then tomorrow I'll need it for delivering the cakes to Blessings, though I could pack them into cake boxes and carry them over in batches, at a pinch, though it might be difficult with the Leaning Tower of—'

He unclipped the car keys from the ring and pressed them into my hand. 'Here. You don't need to borrow it. I'm giving you the car. It's yours.'

'But—Harry!'

'No, not another word. I don't need it. How many times have I used it in the last couple of years?'

'I don't know. I seem to use it more than you do, but even so . . .'

167

'Apart from getting it out to polish, not at all. My eyes aren't up to it any more. And you've got the garage key, so you can still keep it there. After all, if I need to be driven anywhere, you'll take me, won't you?'

'Of course.' I kissed him. 'You're so kind, Uncle Harry. At least I still have you!'

'Yes, well, *I* won't be going anywhere yet awhile, I hope.' He looked a bit sheepish and added: 'I went down to the Griffin last night after Libby told me what Ben had done, Josie-love, and gave him a piece of my mind.'

'You did? And I suppose there was the usual crowd there?'

'I'm afraid so.'

'Oh, well,' I said resignedly, 'at least it will be all over the village already, so I don't have to tell anyone. Mrs Neville did give me a strange look, but I thought that was the sunglasses and the prawns.'

'Prawns?'

'I had to go to the stores and fetch some boxes to pack Ben's things in, and I just suddenly fancied some. A little treat. I'm not feeling quite myself this morning.'

'You need to take care of yourself, our Josie.'

'I need to take care of Mac too. He hasn't had his walk. It'll have to be a short one. I've such a lot to do today and it's getting late.' Mac, hearing the magic word, pricked up his ears and looked up at me hopefully.

*   *   *

After walking Mac I went straight out in the

Cavalier and picked up the co-op delivery from Mark and Stella. I'd rung them up to say I was coming and they had told me where to find my stuff if they were out, which thankfully they were, since I was not exactly in the mood for conversation.

On my way home I dropped off the Graces' part of the order at Poona Place, thinking I was unlikely to get off so lightly there. But I was wrong, for although I was quite sure they had heard all about Ben, they were exercising monumental tact and kindness.

Violet helped me put the trays of sugar roses she had made on the rear seat of the car, and then pressed a bottle of her ginger cordial into my hands. 'No Acorns, dear—it's a gift. Ginger is so *warming* in times of crisis.'

Back home, I wrestled the sack of henfood out of the boot of the car and into Harry's larder, where I tipped it into the big metal bin. There was no sign of Harry, who had probably gone to his dominoes club at the parish hall, but Mac was curled in his basket, guarding a manky-looking marrowbone.

By the time I'd iced a hundred and fifty cupcakes and stuck a rose on each one, there was only time to snatch a quick cup of tea before dashing up to Blessings, where I'd promised to help Libby set up and lay out the trestle tables. She'd already phoned me five times, to see if I was OK, so if I didn't turn up she would be hammering on my door in short order.

By now I was feeling a bit zombie-like, as if I was just an empty shell of Josie going through the motions. My eyes weren't so red and puffy any more, though, so I laid off the sunglasses.

169

I seemed to pass muster with Libby, because after scanning my face anxiously she set me to work, putting cloths on the tables she and Gina had already set up—scarlet ones underneath, and snowy white linen diagonally on top.

I put the Graces' lovely embroidered cloth on the little table meant for the Pisa cake first and then, just when I was unpacking the two spiral stands to hold the cupcakes, Gina came back from the house and, enfolding me in an embrace like a feather bed, kissed me on both cheeks, while commiserating with me loudly in Italian.

That nearly set the tears flowing again, until Libby started briskly ordering us about in her usual way, after which I was too occupied to think about anything else.

Between the three of us, all was soon done and looked lovely and sort of expectant, like a theatre before the curtain went up. The heaters had been on all afternoon to take the chill off the place, and the Pisa backdrop Ben had painted swayed gently in the warm draught . . .

We went back up to the house, because Libby wanted to show me yet more wedding presents she had received, mostly from her extended stepfamilies. She was listing them as they arrived, and wanted me to help her write the thank you notes when she got back from her honeymoon.

I left before Maria Cazzini and Pia were due to arrive. I just felt I'd had enough of trying to put a brave face on things by then and wanted to go home and be by myself. Being by myself was likely to be something I would be doing a lot of, anyway: I might as well practise.

'Noah's probably going to be quite late,' Libby

said. 'I hope he'll be comfortable in the gatehouse. It's a bit basic, but Maria and Pia are having the only two currently habitable bedrooms. Do you think Pia will like her lovely bed and dressing table?' she added anxiously. 'Perhaps they're a bit too *girly*.'

'She'll love them,' I assured her, hoping that if she didn't Pia would at least make an attempt to look as if she did. Libby had gone to so much trouble to turn Pia's room in a very short space of time into a bower fit for a princess, but remembering the last time I saw her, I rather thought her current tastes ran more to black and purple. The bed was really, really over the top, though, so she might just love it.

'I do hope you and Noah are going to get on too,' Libby added.

'I don't think it really matters whether we do or not, does it, Libs? I might think he's a city-bred idiot who drives a gas-guzzling car too fast, but that doesn't mean I won't be perfectly polite to him at the wedding.'

'No . . .' she said doubtfully. 'And you'll soon warm to him, because you've got him all wrong, Josie, you'll see. He's totally charming.'

'I'm sure he is,' I said, and then refused her very pressing invitation to stay for dinner and took myself off home where, since I'd forgotten to stoke up the range, it had gone out.

And there was a message on the answering service too, from Ben, who said tenderly, 'Josie, I'm missing you already. Please call me when you're ready to talk, darling.'

'When hell freezes over!' I muttered, erasing him.

171

I forced myself to eat something, even though I didn't feel remotely hungry, and then I'm afraid I hit the bottle—or maybe that should be bottles—again. Apart from drinking, I didn't know what to do with myself. My usual pursuits had all lost their charm.

Quite late, Russell phoned me to ask how I was, which I suppose was kind, even if it was a funny hour to do it in.

He said Mary was feeling very guilty and upset and I assured him that I didn't blame either of them for not telling me what was happening, even though I do really—Mary especially. But, unlike Ben, I expect I will forgive her . . . eventually.

Chapter Thirteen

Altered Image

Uncle, who, as you know, shares all the gardening with me, has made me a gift of his car, a sunny yellow Vauxhall Cavalier dating back to the early eighties, with amazingly few miles on the clock, considering. The only problem is, I am a bit slapdash in my driving, not to mention loading the boot with henfood and vegetables, so it is unlikely to remain in its current pristine condition for very long . . .

'Cakes and Ale'

For the second night running I didn't fall asleep, I simply passed out. I felt such a strong craving for oblivion, I thought there was a good chance I'd turn into a lush.

I woke up early this time, though, and was immediately crushed both by a headache and a huge sense of aching loss. Hello, heartbreak, my old friend. The pale facc and blue-circled eyes reflected by the bathroom mirror weren't a good look either.

Breakfast was tea and aspirin. I couldn't face anything to eat, which isn't like me. Then with a sigh I got up and brushed my hair, tying it back with one of the brightly coloured knitted hair ties Pansy makes for me, and then went to get the car out of the garage—*my* car. But I firmly blinked back the tears that rushed into my eyes at the thought of Harry's kindness, because once I started I knew I'd never stop. Those huge, gut-wrenching sobs might just tear me apart one of these days. Resolutely, I tried to blank my mind of everything except the job in hand.

This was Libby's big day; I couldn't cast a blight on it by going around looking like a wet weekend.

I know it's only a step or two to Blessings, but it was far easier and safer to transport the wedding cake and the mini cupcakes in the car than on foot. The cupcakes were packed in boxes in the boot and the Leaning Tower, protected by giant bubble wrap, in the passenger footwell next to me. I crawled in second gear round the corner and through the gatehouse arch, and got as close to the Old Barn as I could, though right in front of it was a big refrigerated van. The place was a hive of activity. Clearly the food had arrived and

173

everything was being readied for the reception later.

As I came to a stop and climbed out, Noah Sephton lounged out of the gatehouse, more casually dressed than the last time I saw him, but just as elegant. The inevitable camera was slung around his neck.

'Hello! Libby told me to look out for you and help you with the wedding cakes.'

He seemed to be examining me critically as I opened the boot of the car and I knew I didn't exactly look my best. Nor did I care. But something about my appearance seemed to amuse him, so maybe patchwork dungarees tucked into pink and white spotted Wellington boots, and a quilted jacket featuring big appliqué elephants, aren't everyday wear in London?

His hands automatically went to his camera, but then he noticed my expression and thought better of it.

'Are you still driving that horribly eco-unfriendly car too fast?' I asked pointedly.

'She's parked behind the gatehouse and you know very well I wasn't driving fast,' he said mildly. 'Well within the speed limit. And she may be a greedy gas guzzler, but we've been together a long time, so I don't really think that's good enough grounds for divorce, do you?'

I was diverted. 'You call your car "she"? She has a *name*?'

'No name. But the car's curvy, expensive and purrs a lot—it's definitely got to be female.'

I gave him a look and he grinned. 'Come on, I'll help you carry everything in.'

He took the boxes of cupcakes—I didn't trust

him with the Pisa cake. Inside I could hear Libby, but not see her, but she sounded as if she was in the tackroom, directing operations.

We put the boxes on a table and then I unpacked the Leaning Tower of Pisa and carefully set it down on the Graces' lovely tablecloth, which was spread ready to receive it, while Noah started deftly to arrange cupcakes up the tiered stands that flanked it. He had long, slender hands. You might call them artist's hands, though Ben's are big and square . . .

'How does that look?' he asked, finishing the first stand, and I realised I'd gone into a trance again.

'Fine. I'll help you with the next one.'

Dorrie had a line of small, identical white vases lined up along the edge of the makeshift stage and was swiftly and efficiently making small floral table decorations. When we'd finished with the cakes I went over to admire her skill, with Noah following me.

The back of my neck prickled: I didn't trust him with that camera, now his hands were free.

'These are lovely, Dorrie!'

'Learned it at finishing school, didn't I?' she explained. 'Another bloody useless accomplishment.'

'Well, it's come in handy now. I think you're really clever. Despite having worked in a florist's shop when we lived in London, flowers always look worse when I try and arrange them, than if I simply plonk them in the vase. Not that it's ever mattered, because I've never had any bouquets of flowers. Ben isn't—' I broke off abruptly, my eyes welling.

'Stiff upper lip,' she admonished me.

I gave her a strained smile. 'I'll certainly do my

best not to cast a blight on the day. Now, I'd better tell Libby her cakes have arrived. She sounds a bit frazzled. Oh, too late—here she comes!'

'Josie! I was just about to send someone to see if you were OK, or if the wedding cake had toppled over or—' She stopped dead, staring at my hair.

'What?' I demanded. 'I know it's a mess, but I'm going to go back and wash it in a minute, honestly. And it isn't an illegal act to appear in public with bad hair, is it?'

'It's not that. It's just that you've tied it back with a red sock, Josie. Isn't that a bit weird, even for you?'

'I have?' I put my hands up and felt it and she was right—it *was* a sock. 'I thought it was a knitted hair tie.' I shrugged, because on the scale of recent disasters, this didn't even merit a blip. 'Oh, well, it'll do to keep my hair out of the way until I go home.'

'You might even start a new fashion,' suggested Noah gravely. I hoped I'd only imagined the click of a camera shutter a moment before . . .

'Be at Blessings by ten, Josie. Come right up to my room and we'll sort out your hair and makeup. I've got people coming. You don't need to bring *anything*, just yourself. Don't be late.'

'I'll be there. Did Maria and Pia arrive OK yesterday?'

'Yes, and it was *lovely* to see Pia again, even if she did have purple eye shadow and long black fingernails.' Libby grinned. 'I expect we committed a few fashion faux pas ourselves at that age. Gina's back at the house, catching up with Maria, but Pia isn't even up yet—you know what they're like at that age, practically nocturnal. And she totally ignored poor Tim for ages yesterday evening, but the poor darling looked so hurt and baffled every time she rebuffed him, that eventually she started to come round a bit. I mean, how can you not like Tim?'

'Impossible,' I agreed. 'I'm really looking forward to seeing Pia later, I haven't—' I broke off because I suddenly felt really dizzy—a horrible feeling. I must have swayed a bit because Noah took my arm in a surprisingly strong grip.

'Are you ill?'

'I—didn't sleep too well, that's all and then I wasn't very hungry this morning. I expect that's it.'

'She's being stoical,' Libby explained, looking at me critically and noting the dark-ringed eyes and general morning-after-the-night-before signs. 'She's just broken up with her partner. In fact, I'm going to put *you* in charge of keeping her sane and sober until after the wedding, Noah. That should stop you taking too many candid shots.'

'OK,' he agreed amiably.

'I don't need taking care of. I'm fine,' I lied, removing myself from his grasp. 'Absolutely fine. Where's Tim?'

'Oh, after dinner he went and spent the night in the gatehouse with Noah.'

'Though not in any biblical sense,' Noah put in.

'He's not allowed to see me now until church,' Libby explained. 'It's bad luck.'

'Isn't that going to be a bit awkward?'

'Not really. I'm going into the house shortly and then *he* can come out and help here for a bit. He, Noah and Nick Pharamond were in the Griffin last night, so I expect he's hungover.'

I only hoped they hadn't been in the pub while

Harry was telling Ben exactly what he thought of him! But if they had, Harry would probably have mentioned it.

'Everything's just about ready,' Libby said, looking round the huge room with satisfaction. 'A couple of hired waiters are on their way and the food and drink is staying in the van until later, to keep chilled, though some things are going in the fridge in the tackroom.'

'It all looks lovely, and I have to admit that this was one of your more brilliant ideas,' I conceded.

'I think I've covered all the angles, so long as Jasper can manage as sole usher now Ben's— Oh damn!' she added. 'Sorry, Josie.'

'That's OK. He's not dead, just . . . . gone.'

'I'll usher too, if you like,' Noah said obligingly. 'It's only a few minutes at the start, really, and I've done it before, at a cousin's wedding.'

'Thanks, Noah. You just send everyone to the left or right of the church, according to whether they're from the bride or groom's side, after giving them an order-of-service card and a bag of dried rose petals.'

'Rose petals?'

'Instead of confetti—Josie's idea.'

'That's rather nice.'

'It's certainly better than her first brilliant proposal, that the guests shower us with birdseed,' Libby said drily, then checked her watch. 'Right, Josie, you go back and get rid of the sock, wash your hair—no need to dry it; wrap a towel round it, or something—then come straight over to Blessings. The hairdresser will arrange it to go with the wreath of rosebuds.'

'All right,' I said. I *loathed* that wreath of

178

rosebuds, but what did it matter? What did *anything* matter, except that Libby's big day should go off without a hitch?

Noah helped me put the empty boxes back in the car and then I drove home and went to see Harry, who was ironing a shirt for the wedding—independence is his middle name. Mac was looking hopeful, but there simply wasn't time to take him for his usual walk, so instead we ran right around the Green like mad things and then I threw his ball for him to fetch for a few minutes.

I felt a bit dizzy again after that, but time was rushing on, so I quickly showered and washed my hair and decamped damply to Blessings. I had to run the gauntlet of Gina and Maria, who both embraced me warmly and commiserated over Ben in a way that very nearly set me off crying again, except that I think my tearducts hadn't had time to refill yet. Maybe I was all cried out.

When I finally made it to Libby's room she was already immaculately coifed, veiled and made up, like a fairy princess; but from the neck down, she was still in fluffy pink towelling and bedroom slippers. 'There you are, Josie! We were just going to send out search parties,' she said with relief.

'I had to take Mac for a quick airing, he's got so much energy,' I explained, 'and then Maria and Gina waylaid me in the kitchen.'

'Well, you're here now, and this is Catherine and Paula. They're going to do your hair and makeup.'

I wouldn't let Catherine use anything chemical on my tangled tresses, which put paid to practically every product she had in her box. But after sighing a bit, in a long-suffering and frustrated kind of way, she still managed to tame my cloud of dark

179

auburn hair and then firmly clipped the circlet of dark pink rosebuds onto it.

Then Paula started on my face, which was entirely bare. 'Good skin,' she commented, turning it this way and that and studying it.

'Is everything you're going to use on me cruelty free?' I asked, as she pushed up her sleeves and laid out about a million pots, tubes, jars and plastic boxes.

'Yes!' she snapped, slapping my hand away as I reached out to read the label on the nearest product. 'Now sit still.'

It's very strange having someone paint you as though you were a canvas, and I was quite relieved when at last she laid down something that looked a bit like a shaving brush and said, with satisfaction, 'There—natural but enhanced.'

I'm not sure what I expected to see in the mirror, but after all that work, I still only looked like a smoother, younger version of myself. 'The lipstick colour is really pretty.'

'I'll give you one to put in your bag.'

I had this twee little dolly bag sort of affair, in the same velvet as my dress. I assume they came as a package.

Catherine and Paula stayed to help get us into our dresses without disturbing their handiwork, though first Libby insisted I go and change my undies for a new set she'd got for me. I thought she was a bit thorough when she took my measurements for the dress.

'There's nothing wrong with what I've got on!' I protested.

'Good, solid cotton is all very well for everyday, but to carry off this dress, you need something to

180

enhance your curves, not flatten everything.'

I supposed she was right and I did want to do her proud as a bridesmaid, so I just did what she wanted, right down to the lacy-topped, hold-up stockings.

The dresses were carefully lowered over our heads, and then there we were, bride and bridesmaid, standing slightly stiffly like mannequins in front of the mirror.

Libby looked even more like the fairy on the Christmas tree than she usually did, and stunningly pretty. I wasn't quite sure what I resembled. It was like looking at a stranger.

'I look . . .' I paused.

'Statuesque?' Libby said helpfully. 'The perfect foil—dark and tall, to my small and fair.'

'*You* look beautiful, Libby.'

'You know, so do you, in a different kind of way!' she said, eyeing me thoughtfully, her head on one side. 'I've never noticed before, probably because you don't make the best of yourself.'

'Oh, don't be silly. I know you're only saying it to cheer me up, but there's no need. And by the way, I hope Noah Sephton isn't going to take you seriously and attempt to keep an eye on me, because I'm absolutely fine.' I managed to summon up a little smile from somewhere.

'Hmm,' she said, unconvinced. 'I'm more worried that you'll go to pieces *after* the wedding, while I'm away.'

'No, honestly. I have to keep going for Harry's sake and the Three Graces, and—'

'Are you regretting throwing Ben out?'

'Yes—no—I don't know . . .' I said confusedly. 'I was a bit until I found those horrible notes from

Olivia. Oh, don't ask me, Libby, because it just makes my head spin and I feel sick and . . . and really, it's better to try not to think at all, just live from moment to moment. Ben's sending a van up for his stuff sometime today, because I think he's afraid I might destroy it in a fit of pique, so every last vestige of him should be gone when I get home, which might help.'

'Well, at least Noah can make sure you don't drink so much that you dance on the tables or anything—or not until we've left for Pisa,' Libby said frankly. 'Then it might do you good to let your hair down and get sloshed in company, rather than alone. And it would keep him out of mischief too. Just remember he's a demon philanderer and don't get carried away, will you?'

'Unlikely. He's not my type.'

'He's certainly nothing like Ben, that's for sure. And anyway,' she added, 'he seems to go out with blonde, stick-thin models, so you clearly aren't his type either.'

'That girl he had with him the first time he came to Neatslake looked like that. Do you think she's his current girlfriend?'

'Well, she probably *was* but he may have moved on by now. And come to think of it, he did say last night that if anyone called Anji rang up and asked for him, I was to say he was out, so it looks like another one has bitten the dust.'

She handed me a small box. 'This is for you, a gift from me and Tim, with our love.'

Inside was a pretty little seed pearl locket of antique design, which she insisted I put on straight away. It went very well with the medieval style of my old-rose-coloured velvet.

182

'Thank you, Libs. It's lovely!'

Gina came in with a tray of coffee and Genoa cake, with little napkins to hold under our chins to prevent our dresses getting dripped on. Libby was too nervous to eat and I didn't want to, though she made me.

'I'm not having you swoon in the church,' she said.

'Here, have this big piece,' Gina insisted. 'You are too thin, you need feeding up.'

'Are Maria and Pia ready yet?' asked Libby, putting her coffee cup down and then making sure her lipstick wasn't smeared. 'I thought Pia might have come to see me, before they leave for the church.'

'Maria made her go back to take off the black nail varnish and the dark purple eye shadow, so there may not be time,' Gina said. She picked up the tray. 'Now I take my apron off and put on my best hat, and go myself.'

'God, I need to pee now!' Libby said, looking at me in horror as the door closed behind Gina. 'How on earth do I do that in this dress?'

'I think that's where the bridesmaid comes in,' I said, resignedly.

Chapter Fourteen

White Wedding

My friend's wedding went off without a hitch and she looked beautiful. The confetti was dried rose petals. I had suggested millet seed, so the birds could have a bridal feast too, but that proved to be an ecological step too far . . .

'Cakes and Ale'

Clutching the velvet Dolly bag containing the wedding ring Libby would give to Tim, I followed her down the aisle in a sort of trance, feeling quite divorced from reality.

I spotted Harry's silvery head of curls near the back, and then Libby's mother, Gloria Martin, wearing only half her usual makeup and looking unfamiliarly muted. She was neatly sandwiched between her elder daughter, Daisy, and Maria Cazzini, with Pia on the end of the pew dressed in a funereal shade of dark purple—but at least she was *there*, that was the thing that would matter most to Libby.

Dorrie was seated in the row behind them in her best, heather-blue tweed suit, pearls, and the cashmere jumper she'd got Pansy to darn for her after the moths got at it last year. I didn't spot the Three Graces, but I could hear them twittering excitedly.

We came to a halt, then Libby and Tim turned to face each other, the expressions on their faces so moving that for a moment it broke through my defences. I got a lump in my throat and tears in my eyes.

The best man, Nick Pharamond, gave me a grave smile. He was attractive without being handsome—unlike Noah, who was both. He had greeted us at the door wearing a quite beautiful suit with a rich, subtle sheen and looking, even I had to admit, slim, elegant and entirely delectable, in his own unique way. He might not be my cup of tea, but that didn't mean I couldn't appreciate his charms.

The rest of the service passed like a dream, though I was conscious of a lot of cheerfully uninhibited Cazzini sobbing behind me, together with the occasional broken exclamation in Italian from Gina, when sentiment transported her a little too far.

Then it was all signed, sealed and delivered, and out we poured from the church into a cloud of rose petals, while the bells joyously pealed out.

Noah, his pale grey eyes narrowed in amusement, cast a handful of the confetti over my head and then snapped away with his camera at my bemused face, as I blinked in the wintry sunshine.

There was much kissing and congratulation, and then the official photographer began to marshal us together into the obligatory wedding groups. Even Pia condescended to appear in one of those, after some urging by Maria Cazzini. Maybe the chance to stand near Jasper Pharamond might have helped swing it: she couldn't take her eyes off him. The *Cotton Common* soap star, Rob Rafferty, was a bit of a babe-magnet too, in a lushly golden, ripe-and-ready way.

In fact, there seemed to be an abundance of

185

attractive men about . . . with one notable exception, of course. And perhaps the fact that I'd noticed them was a healthy sign, like going window shopping when you're penniless, to pick out something you might one day be able to buy.

Since it was pretty chilly, most of the guests were soon in full flight across the Green towards the beckoning warmth and shelter of the Old Barn. We were pared down to a final line-up of me, the happy couple, the best man and Jasper and Noah, who were standing at either end of the row like two darkly handsome bookends.

'You look absolutely stunning,' Noah, who was on my right, said in my ear. His aftershave was some deliciously subtle and probably grossly expensive blend that reminded me of limes and cricket fields on sunny days, if you can imagine that. 'You've got a sort of calm, grave, Pre-Raphaelite quality about you,' he added, which just went to show that although I felt cold and distanced from what was happening, I must still have been functioning normally enough to fool most people into thinking I was all right!

'Of course!' Libby exclaimed, leaning forward from my other side so she could see him. 'I knew she reminded me of some painting or other in that dress. It's that one of a woman by a window, stretching.'

Tim, who'd been looking at his wife as though he'd just won a Gold Medal at the Chelsea Flower Show, gave me a kind smile over her head and nodded. 'Oh, yes, I think she's wearing a green dress, isn't she?'

'I know the one you mean, too,' said Noah, 'but actually I was thinking more of those militant

186

Burne-Jones angels in stained-glass windows, holding swords and looking as if they know how to use them.'

I was sort of flattered to be called stunning and then likened to a Pre-Raphaelite *anything*, even if the models they used usually looked sulky—I expect it's the full underlip. I wasn't too sure about the sword bit, though.

'I'm just grateful you didn't say it was that painting of Ophelia, floating down a river covered in flowers and wearing a wet expression,' I said to Libby.

Noah grinned. 'Well, she would if she was in a river, wouldn't she? But I don't see you as an Ophelia. Come on, the photographer's finished here and if we linger any longer we're all going to freeze to death.'

He was right. The sky was going leaden and the cold breeze held a hint of snow, though I hoped it would hold off until the happy couple and most of the guests had left the reception.

Jasper and Nick were already halfway across the Green as I helped Libby put on her velvet cape. She walked off, holding hands with Tim, and I shrugged myself into the wine-coloured cut-velvet jacket she'd loaned to me, and followed them.

Noah, clicking away with his camera again, darted around us like a half-trained sheepdog, until Libby begged him to stop. Then he fell in beside me and put his arm through mine.

'Tell me, do you ever smile?' he asked. 'I mean, I love the serious angel expression, but I'm sure even they cracked the odd grin when no one was looking. You're not still holding the hen incident against me, are you?'

187

'Not really. And I'm so sorry if I'm not exactly a laugh a minute, but do feel free to go and find some more cheerful company when we get to the reception. In fact, I wish you would!'

'Ah, I was forgetting the break-up with the boyfriend,' he said. 'No wonder you're a bit ratty. Though I can't say you look particularly broken-hearted: more devastating, in fact, than devastated!'

'That's because I'm not really broken-hearted,' I lied. 'It was just a bit of a shock, that's all, because we'd been together quite a long time. And I'm *not* ratty!'

I didn't think I was devastating either, but I expect he says that sort of thing to women all the time.

* * *

The barn, with the big portable heaters blasting away in the corners, was bright and warm, and everyone was standing chatting in the middle of the room in front of the stage, where the hired waiters were circling with the drinks.

I took a glass of champagne and circulated too, chatting to anyone I knew, and several people I didn't, as if I hadn't a care in the world—or I *hoped* that was the effect I was giving, anyway. The alcohol on top of an almost empty stomach probably helped, and it got even easier after a second glass, though I don't think bought champagne is half as nice as sparkling elderflower.

Then our attention was called to where the bride and groom were poised to slice into the Leaning Tower of Pisa, while the official photographer

188

took one last picture and then departed, his job done. Then they had to pretend to cut the cake all over again for the morose *Glorious Weddings* photographer, who made the reception in the nick of time. I'd quite forgotten he was coming and so, I was sure, had Libby and Tim.

I expect Noah took some shots too, so this has to be the most photographed cake in the world.

When they were finally allowed to put down the mother-of-pearl-handled cake knife, Nick, as best man, gave the usual short speech, including a couple of anecdotes about when he and Tim had been at school together.

Then Tim, his arm around Libby and beaming broadly, began, 'My wife and I—'

We all drowned him out with cheers.

He held up his hands for silence. 'My wife and I would like to thank you for coming here today. Please now help yourselves to the wonderful buffet and afterwards the Mummers of Invention will entertain us.'

As bridesmaid I was sitting at a table with Libby and Tim. Nick and his wife, Lizzie, were opposite, and Noah was right next to me. He seemed to have forsaken photography for the sake of eating, for the moment at least, for his Leica was laid next to his plate. I still hadn't got much of an appetite, but I'd collected a slice of cold meat and a couple of olives, more for appearance's sake than anything.

I was just pushing the olives about in a disinterested sort of way when suddenly Gina appeared, her feather-trimmed felt hat falling forward over her flushed face. Snatching my plate away, she slapped down another, piled high with food, in its place.

'Eat! Eat! Keep up your strength!' she urged me, before surging off again in the direction of the buffet, presumably to follow her own advice.

'You know, that's probably a good idea, before you knock back any more bubbly,' Noah suggested mildly, and I scowled at him. However, I was afraid that if I didn't eat at least some of her offering, Gina would come back and force-feed me, like a mother bird with one chick, so I had to make the attempt.

The Mummers of Invention helped themselves from the buffet too—*and* from a keg of beer at one side of the stage. Then they began to play a pleasant sort of electric folk-rock and a limp-looking girl started singing.

After a while Rob Rafferty got up on the stage with them and belted out the song 'White Wedding' with a very menacing edge. It seemed an odd choice until he'd finished and explained that Libby had requested it.

Libby is full of odd choices.

I'd forgotten that Rob Rafferty started out in music before turning to acting, and apparently he often sings with the group when he has time, to keep his hand in.

'He's terribly good-looking in a Viking sort of way—even more so off the telly than on,' I murmured. Our table was closest to the stage and I was half-mesmerised by the lithe movements of his admirable body and the way his cerulean-blue eyes seemed to be fixed on me . . . though that was just a trick of the light, of course.

'I wouldn't get ideas, even if he *does* keep looking at you like you're the last sweet in the tin,' Noah whispered in my ear. 'He's a serial

190

philanderer.'

'Aren't you all?' I said bitterly, and he gave me a startled look.

'Has Libby been giving you awful warnings about me, or was that a general reflection?'

'General,' I said, getting up. 'Excuse me.'

Tim and Libby took to the floor for the first dance, and then so did lots of other guests and a good time was had by all—or almost all. *I* was simply going through the motions, assisted by liberal amounts of champagne. I'd lost count of how much I'd drunk, but I don't think bought champagne can be very alcoholic. It doesn't taste like it, anyway.

I talked to Sophy Winter's daughter, Lucy, who was learning to run the Winter's End estate and must be a huge asset to her mother now visitor numbers have rocketed, due to the Shakespeare manuscript discovery. I loved Pia dearly, but I wished she was as sensible as Lucy, though I supposed that might happen when she was a bit older.

I'd registered that Pia had been hanging around Jasper Pharamond like a wet mist, but she didn't seem to be making much headway with him. Then suddenly she abandoned him and flung her arms around Noah's neck instead, in an overly affectionate way, which would have worried me had I not seen her look over her shoulder to see if Jasper was taking any notice.

He wasn't. Noah, looking alarmed, disengaged himself with more haste than tact and made a beeline for me.

'Help!' he said urgently. 'You have to protect me from Pia. I think she's gone mad.'

'Well, I'm her godmother and *I* certainly don't want her getting off with a serial womaniser old enough to be her father.'

'That's a bit strong!' he exclaimed, looking startled. 'What on earth *has* Libby been telling you?'

I ignored that. 'You needn't flatter yourself, anyway. Pia was simply trying to get Jasper Pharamond's attention by flirting with the nearest man, which just happened to be you.'

'Consider my pretensions suitably dampened, then,' Noah said. 'But I'm relieved too. I always thought she regarded me in the light of an uncle.'

I was looking across at Jasper; I didn't think he'd even noticed Pia's ploy. 'Jasper's a serious sort of young man, so I could have told her those tactics weren't going to work. In fact, I wouldn't have thought she was his type at all.'

I lifted another glass from a passing tray and Noah said mildly, 'Haven't you had rather a lot to drink? You didn't eat much lunch and even champagne isn't good on an empty stomach. Maybe Libby was right, and you do need keeping an eye on?'

'I don't. I'm fine, absolutely fine. Wouldn't you like to go off and philander with someone? I could introduce you to the three Miss Graces, if you like?'

'The tiny trio of bewitching creatures with a startlingly original taste in headgear? Better not, I'd be spoiled for choice and might have to elope with all three together.'

'I think Violet's the raciest—she might suit you best,' I suggested. 'She has a wonderful red tricycle called Tinkerbell and when she was young, she told me she used to *smoke*.'

'I smoulder a bit myself—she sounds like my sort of girl,' he said. 'Better keep me away.'

There was a burst of raucous laughter from the other end of the room and Libby caught my eye and made frantic gestures at me.

Obediently I pushed my way down there, where Daisy now had a firm grip on her mother's arm. Gloria Martin was swaying slightly on her stilettos, a wild look in her eyes and a vague smile plastered to her lips. Her makeup was smudged and she had an air of reckless abandon. But then, she usually did.

'Hi, Josie,' Daisy said, 'I'm afraid she gave me the slip when she said she was going to the loo.'

'I did go,' Gloria said. 'Then a nice man outside gave me some brandy from his flask to keep the cold out. Brandy and champagne—there's nothing like it!'

Then she spotted Noah, who must have followed me, and smiled flirtatiously. 'I can still do a high kick with the best of them,' she told him, apropos of nothing. Grabbing Daisy's arm, she began to lift one leg, before almost falling over and dragging her daughter with her.

'I'm sure you can,' Noah said, steadying Daisy, 'but maybe it's not quite the right time now for a demonstration?'

'Mrs Martin, wouldn't you like to go to the house with me and have a cup of coffee?' I coaxed.

'To hell with coffee!' she exclaimed loudly. 'Where's Libby? Where's my little girl? There's something I want to say to her . . .'

She tried to pull away, but Daisy restrained her. 'Now, Mum, you promised me you'd stick to non-

193

alcoholic drinks! You don't want to ruin Libby's big day, do you?'

'Oh, she's always having big days. Never thinks of her poor old mother, stuck down in Brighton with a dried-up stick of a sour-faced daughter. No fun and frolics, no menfriends allowed or—'

'I think it's probably time we went back to the hotel,' Daisy announced brightly. 'Mum gets tired so easily these days. I wonder if you could help me get her to the car?'

'I'm not going anywhere!' Gloria declared. 'Not unless this gorgeous man comes with me!' She made a sudden lunge in Noah's direction. 'I know a nice gentlemen when I see one, one who'll treat a girl right—like Libby's father, he was a gentleman!' She giggled and tapped the side of her nose, then leaned forward and whispered in my ear, 'She and Tim have got more in common than they think, but mum's the word!'

I stared at her. 'What do you mean? Was Libby's father—'

Daisy took her arm and said quickly, 'Come along, Mum. You're talking nonsense and it's time to go home.'

When we'd seen them off, with Gloria protesting to the last, I led the way back indoors, out of the cold, but when I turned round Noah had vanished.

The Mummers of Invention were just about to start up again, having refreshed themselves with beer from the barrel they had brought with them. The drippy-looking girl who sang had been sitting with a strangely foxy-looking young man, but now got up and joined the others.

A large, warm hand suddenly grasped my shoulder and I turned to find myself inches from

Rob Rafferty's bright, intent blue gaze, not to mention all his other impressively sizzling attributes. 'At last! I've been trying to find the most beautiful girl in the room for ages. Where have you been hiding, gorgeous?'

I looked around to see if someone else was standing behind me, but no, he was talking to *me*, Josie Gray. 'N-nowhere,' I stammered. 'I mean . . .'

'I've found you now, so why don't we move somewhere a bit quieter so we can get to know each other better?' he suggested with a bright, white smile.

Something funny seemed to be happening to my knees . . .

'Rob!' said Libby, suddenly appearing. 'The Mummers are playing and everyone is dying to hear you sing with them again. There'll be loads of time to talk to Josie afterwards.'

'Right,' he said, looking flattered. 'Catch up with you later?' he added softly, as he passed me. 'I'll sing the next one just for you.'

I nodded dumbly, fascinated and horrified in equal measure.

'Honestly, Josie, I take my eyes off you for five minutes and there you are in the toils of the biggest womaniser in west Lancashire!' scolded Libby. 'And where's Noah? He's supposed to be keeping an eye on you. I was *afraid* you might do something silly on the rebound, but I didn't expect it to be with Rob Rafferty, of all people!'

'I've no idea where Noah is. *He's* the one who needs a keeper, not me. And I'm not about to do anything, silly or otherwise, with Rob Rafferty,' I said with dignity. 'I was just momentarily . . . well, to be honest, *stunned* that he took any notice of

195

me. And he's a bit overpoweringly gorgeous close to, isn't he? Sexual allure seems to come off him in waves.'

'I did tell you you looked lovely once you'd scrubbed up and put on a decent dress,' she pointed out. 'But Rob didn't suggest you go and find a quiet place so you could have a polite chat, you know.'

'I suppose not. I'm a bit out of the habit of this kind of thing,' I admitted, though in fact I'd never got *into* the habit, having always been with Ben. 'Libby, before Rob waylaid me I was looking for you to tell you that Daisy's taken your mum back to the hotel. She sent her love and said she hoped you had a lovely honeymoon and she would ring you when you got back.'

Libby looked relieved. 'Oh, good. I don't know what I'd do without Daisy looking after Mum. She needs a keeper. But if she's drinking again, I'll book her into an upmarket drying-out clinic and send Daisy on holiday.'

'Stop worrying about everyone and just enjoy your big day,' I urged her, and gave her a hug. 'It's all gone perfectly and Tim is a peach. You'll be blissfully happy.'

'But what about Pia?' she said anxiously. 'I think she's starting to like Tim, but she's barely spoken a word to me all day and—'

'I'll talk to Pia, but I don't think she's sulking, just preoccupied! She's got her eye on Jasper Pharamond.'

It took me a while to find Pia, but she seemed pleased to see me and immediately asked my advice. 'I fancy the socks off Jasper Pharamond, but I don't seem to be getting anywhere. He'd much rather talk history with the vicar than to me!'

She sounded astonished, but she is very pretty, so I suppose being ignored by men was a novelty.

'Well, he's studying history and archaeology, so that figures. And by the way, I saw you flinging yourself all over Noah Sephton earlier.'

She giggled. 'Poor Uncle Noah! He looked quite shocked.'

'Surprised, certainly, but I told him you were doing it to try and catch Jasper's attention—though he's certainly not the type of boy to be impressed by that sort of tactic.'

'You're right, he didn't even notice. I don't think he likes me at all,' she said gloomily.

'I simply don't think you've registered on his consciousness yet. According to his mother, his main interest is in what our ancestors ate and drank, and everyone loves to talk about their pet subjects, so if you have any thoughts along those lines, you could try that angle.'

'What our ancestors ate and drank?' Pia stared blankly at me for a minute, then squared her shoulders and marched away. A few minutes later I saw her gazing earnestly up into Jasper's face with an expression of the utmost fascination.

From what his mother had told me earlier, there was a good chance he was telling her, in great and enthusiastic detail, what had passed through the digestive system of the Vikings and exactly how modern-day archaeologists knew so much about it.

Sooner her than me.

Chapter Fifteen

Undone

There are light wines, strong wines and very potent wines—and then, there is peapod.

'Cakes and Ale'

Noah reappeared in time to see Rob Rafferty wink at me from the stage and murmured as he passed me in the direction of the bar: 'Pot calling the kettle black!' So I expect he now thinks I am a heartless philanderer too—off with the old boyfriend and in search of a new one.

However, it was clear that wild horses wouldn't drag Rob off the stage while he had an appreciative audience, which was a relief, really. I'd never had to cope with the Rob Raffertys of this world and I didn't think I was ready to start just yet. Things were getting a bit blurry anyway. Perhaps someone had topped my glass up again when I wasn't looking.

Libby and Tim must have gone back to the house to change at some point, for they reappeared in ordinary clothes and Nick clapped his hands to get everyone's attention. 'Ladies and gentlemen, the car is at the door to whisk the happy couple away, if you would all like to say goodbye.'

A private plane awaited them at John Lennon airport to fly them off to Pisa and their honeymoon. What it is to have rich friends!

We all trooped out—or staggered out, in my case, for something odd seemed to have happened

198

to my legs as the cold air hit me, though I'd felt absolutely fine until then. The late afternoon was rapidly turning dark, but the carriage lights around the courtyard were lit and a few feathery snowflakes drifted aimlessly down through the warm circles of light.

'Mummy!' Pia called, running out of the barn, and throwing herself at Libby in the abandoned way she used to when she was a little girl, and they hugged and kissed. Then Pia let her go and pushed her in Tim's direction before going back to stand at Jasper's side.

Libby paused as she reached the car to toss her bouquet over her shoulder. Hazily, I watched it describe an arc and then, rather suddenly, drop straight into my arms—or rather *arm*, for I was still holding a champagne glass in one hand. Pollen went up my nose, and I sneezed.

'Bless you,' Noah said gravely, materialising from the darkness beyond the nearest lantern.

Everyone else returned to the warm barn, laughing and talking, while I stood there in the darkness holding a bridal bouquet and thinking I was the last person who should have got it: it wasn't an omen of my future fortunes, more fate's last, ironic taunt.

But I had caught it and now I wasn't quite sure what to do with it. Wired flowers didn't last long, that was for sure. Should I run across to the cottage and put it in water?

Really, I should unwire the poor things, but I wasn't sure if my hand–eye co-ordination was up to it . . . Still, I couldn't just go back into the barn and leave it in a corner to wilt, so I set off for home at a brisk stagger.

The pavement undulated more than I remembered. The council really should do something about that. It was only as I reached my door and fumbled for my keys in the little Dolly bag looped over my wrist that I realised I was still holding my half-full glass. The sensible thing to do seemed to be to drain it, which I did—and then a hand came over my shoulder and removed it from my grasp.

'I saw you leave, a bit like the vanishing bride fleeing the scene,' Noah's voice said. 'Only, since it seemed there was no young Lochinvar—or even Rob Rafferty—to whisk you away, I thought I'd better make sure you got home OK.'

'I'm fine—and I'm no fleeing bride, that's for sure,' I said darkly, trying with immense concentration to insert my key into the door. I could see the key and I could see the keyhole, it just seemed terribly difficult to bring the two together. 'I came home to put this bouquet in water, before the flowers died.'

'Having trouble? Dear me, somebody seems to have rehung your door upside down while you were at the wedding,' he said with awful irony, removing the key from my hand. 'Let's try it this way up, shall we? Ah, yes, that seems to have done the trick.'

'Don't be silly,' I said with dignity, then spoiled the effect by tripping on the doorstep and falling headlong into the kitchen. I might have measured my length if he hadn't grabbed me at the last minute: it was like an old clip of a torch dance I'd seen once on TV in which a man in a striped jumper kept throwing his partner away and then catching her. Someone gave a mad giggle as he

200

reeled me in.

'Were you laughing?' I asked, frowning up at him, my chin pressed against his chest.

'No, it was you.'

'It can't have been. I don't *do* giggling.'

'You probably don't usually drink a bottle of champagne on an almost empty stomach, either,' he said, still firmly holding me upright. He might be slender, but he was surprisingly strong.

'Oh, I'm fine, absh . . .' I paused, and with dignity got a grip on my unruly tongue. '*Abs*olutely fine,' I assured him. 'And you're squishing Libby's bouquet.'

He slowly released his hands from my arms and stepped back, but although the room wavered a bit, I was perfectly steady on my legs as I reached out and switched on the light.

When I turned, he'd closed the door, though unfortunately with himself on this side of it, and was looking round in some surprise. 'You know, my gran's kitchen looked just like this!'

'It *did*? But I thought you were this terribly posh urban type,' I said absently, laying the bouquet on the table and getting out a vase and scissors, though I didn't let go of the vase until I was certain it had made contact with the surface.

He laughed. 'My grandfather was a poor Cazzini cousin. He had a small ice-cream business in St Helens and married a local girl. We've all got to come from somewhere, and whatever I may look and sound like now, my roots are in this area, just like yours. In fact, it wasn't until I came back up for that photoshoot a few weeks ago that I realised how much I missed it. It felt like . . . well, like where I *belonged*.'

201

I wondered if Ben would miss it, this place where he'd always said his roots and his inspiration were.

My legs suddenly gave way and I sat down with more haste than grace on the nearest chair, reaching for the champagne glass that Noah had put there. It was empty. 'You've drunk my champagne!' I said indignantly.

'No, you managed to do that yourself.'

'Oh . . . then would you mind fetching me a bottle of wine from the rack under the stairs before you go back to the party?' I asked, enunciating carefully. 'Top left—the apple and damsh . . . damson.'

'Wouldn't you rather I made you a nice, strong cup of coffee?'

'*No.*'

He looked at me for a moment, one quizzical eyebrow raised, then did what I asked.

'If you want to pour yourself one too, the bottle opener's in that left-hand drawer next to the stove and there are glasses in the cupboard above it,' I said when he returned.

I began to unpick the bouquet. This is a fiddly job even if you haven't got tanked up first, though champagne doesn't have quite the mind-numbing qualities of my apple and damson wine. As soon as I'd finished with the bouquet and got rid of Noah, I intended drinking the rest of the bottle myself until I reached the nirvana of complete oblivion.

Meanwhile, he seemed quite at home in the cottage, even if he did look like a refugee from *Four Weddings and a Funeral*. He undid his collar, took his jacket off and hung it over a chair, then stoked up the range, opened the wine, and sat down at the table with me. After watching me for a moment, he took a flower and began to unwire it.

'What is this stuff?' he said after a cautious sip from his glass. 'It has a kick like a mule.'

'Just apples and damsons—but that's nothing; you should taste the peapod. You'd never find your way to the door after a couple of glasses of that, let alone back to the party.'

'Actually, I've a really hard head for alcohol, plus *I* wasn't knocking it back at the reception like lemonade either,' he said. 'I'm not mad about champagne.'

'I prefer sparkling elderflower,' I agreed, dreamily. I was starting to feel quite warmed all the way through, and much better now I was sitting down and things weren't swaying about so dizzyingly. 'Violet Grace makes a mean rhubarb wine, the one kind I don't make, because we haven't got rhubarb. It's about the only edible thing they've got in their garden. It's a lovely pink colour.'

'Which one was Violet, again?'

'Pale, mauve lipstick, blue velveteen coat and a home-made peacock-feather fascinator. Pansy was the one with red lipstick, black eyebrows, grey hair and a scarlet wool jacket with matching pill-box hat and Lily was in navy and white with a sort of tri-coloured velvet turban. They're my friends . . . my good, good friends.'

'I'm sure they are.'

'Where's your camera?' I asked, peering at him.

'I went and dropped it off at the gatehouse earlier.'

'I thought I hadn't seen you for a while after Daisy and Gloria left.'

'I'm flattered you missed me. I thought your eyes

were glued to the stage,' he said, and I gave him a scathing look and carried on with the fiddly task in hand.

The wine sank in the bottle and the bouquet, unpicked, was finally in the vase. At my suggestion we decamped to the sitting room so Noah could sample one or two more of my home-made wines, especially the peapod, though I *had* warned him about it. I think it was pure bravado on his part.

'And you're missing the party,' I pointed out. 'They'll probably go on for hours. The Mummers are known for having to be dragged off stage once they get going, so long as there's beer.'

'They seemed to have a whole keg of the stuff, so that should keep them going for a bit,' he agreed, then held his glass of peapod wine up to the light. 'This isn't bad at all!'

His light grey eyes looked strangely shiny and silvery, but that was probably because I'd only put on the wall lights.

'I feel fine—you exaggerated its lethal properties.'

'Just you wait,' I said, sipping my glass more cautiously.

'Tell me, do you always drink like a fish, or is it because you've broken up with your partner?' he asked curiously.

'It's none of your business, but I just felt a need to kick over the traces tonight, that's all.'

And probably tomorrow night, and the one after, and the one after that . . .

'So you're not drowning your sorrows, just letting your hair down? That figures. You've looked so calm and composed all day, that I didn't think it could have hit you hard, whatever Libby said.'

'No, it didn't.' I managed a casual shrug . . . I think. My brain and my body seemed to be drifting out of connection. 'The relationship had just fizzled out, really, but I hadn't realised it until he'd left. What about you?'

'Me?'

'Yes, Libs said she's never seen you with the same girl twice.'

'That's a slight exaggeration.' His silvery-grey eyes met mine. 'But it's true I'm not looking for any kind of deep relationship, just . . . fun. No-strings-attached fun.'

'*Fun?*' I tried to remember what fun was like. And then I wondered what having sex with anyone other than Ben would be like—with, for instance, the stranger opposite . . . The absolutely no-strings-attached stranger opposite, who now looked much less unapproachable and distinctly attractive, with his silk shirt undone at the neck, his short dark hair ruffled and a hint of five-o'clock shadow.

He was absently pouring himself another glass of the peapod wine and three was way, *way* too many.

'Too much peapod. Try the elderberry 2006 instead,' I suggested. 'Thash . . . that's nice.'

'No, I think I'll stick to the peapod,' he decided, not slurring his words at all.

'On your own head be it, then.' Somewhat to my surprise, I found that I was sitting close to him, his arm around me and my head on his shoulder, quite cosily.

'No-strings fun sounds like a good idea to me, Noah—and I really don't want to be alone tonight,' I murmured suggestively.

'I don't think you're in a fit state to know what

205

you want,' he said, looking down at me with a grin. '*Or* who . . . though actually, you don't really strike me as a no-strings-attached kind of girl. So that's probably not a good idea . . . or not tonight, Josephine.'

'That was a dreadful joke,' I said severely.

'I know. Come on, I'll help you upstairs and then I'll go.'

He stood up first and staggered. 'Bloody hell!'

I giggled again. I seemed to have turned into someone totally different from the usual Josie, but she appeared to be having quite a good time, whoever she was. 'I did warn you—you've been peapodded!'

'Stop laughing, you terrible woman! Nothing prepared me for *this*!' He hauled me upright and, entwined, we staggered up the stairs, making rather a lot of noise.

'Shhh!' I turned to him halfway up, putting a finger to my lips. 'Harry might be back, and he'll hear us.'

'Who's Harry? Not the boyfriend?'

'No, my uncle who lives next door—the man with white curly hair at the wedding?'

'Ah, yes—I took a picture or two of him. He looks quite a character.'

'He is, and he's also all the family I've got left. I'm *all* alone in the world, all alone . . .' I said sadly, like Little Orphan Annie, as Noah lowered me onto the brass bedstead.

He sank down next to me with a thump. 'I haven't been this paralytic since I was too young to know any better,' he groaned. 'What have you done to me, you witch?'

The mad Josie, the one who'd taken me over and

206

seemed to be having fun, laughed and said brightly, 'I told you, you've been peapodded!' then reached out for him. 'You'd better sleep it off . . . here with me.'

He stood up, but with an effort. 'Look, Josie, that's really not such a good idea.'

'No?' I got up too, not without some difficulty, and stood close to him. 'Then, if you really have to go, could you unzip my dress, first?' I asked innocently. 'I can't reach.'

He sighed and turned me round. The dress, undone, slid down in heavy folds to pool around my feet. I'd forgotten I was wearing Libby's choice of lacy undies rather than my own solidly unexciting ones, so there wasn't a lot between us, other than Noah's unexpected scruples.

My knees begin to buckle . . .

'Oh hell!' he exclaimed, catching me and lowering me onto the bed—but when I pulled him down with me he came, unresisting.

For a minute, propping himself up with an elbow either side of my head, he looked at me with his wry, slightly lopsided smile. 'Libby was wrong: *I'm* the one who needs looking after tonight, not you!'

Then he kissed me and if he meant it as a farewell before resisting my clearly inferior charms, it didn't stay that way.

Soon it wasn't just the wine making my head swim and, if I thought of Ben at all, it was only that this would somehow teach him a lesson . . .

Chapter Sixteen

Peapodded

As November wears on, there is less and less to do in the garden apart from tidying up and picking winter vegetables, as needed. Uncle, as usual, cleaned and oiled those garden tools we wouldn't need until spring and then stored them away, wrapped in sacking.

As I checked over the stored apples today, discarding any that showed signs of decay, my mobile rang, disturbing the peaceful moment. Mobiles are the scourges of the twenty-first century, gremlins constantly interrupting our lives with their inane jingles . . .

'Cakes and Ale'

I woke late the next morning with a thumping head, a furry tongue and naked apart from a pair of lacy-topped hold-up stockings and a dented and battered rosebud wreath. And, while my head felt the worse for wear, my body seemed to be in a state of languorous bliss . . .

My mobile was playing an insistent minuet somewhere downstairs and outside I could hear the clanking of the henfood bucket as Harry made his way up the garden.

For a moment yesterday was a complete and merciful blank—and then a series of appalling recollections began to flash disjointedly across my mind. The wedding reception—Noah—me . . . *Had* I? Had *we*—and *twice*?

'Oh, my God!' I groaned, and turned over quicker than my head could take. But there was nothing unexpected next to me, other than a glass of water, two aspirins and a note on top of the bedside table.

Across the room my crumpled velvet dress hung limply over the back of a chair, like a half-drowned survivor. My bra and pants lay in a heap on the floor near the bed, as if flung hastily aside . . . which they probably had been, and by my own, wanton hands.

Snatching the aspirins, I downed them with one gulp of water, then lay back with my eyes shut and the note clutched in my hand. Then, when I could focus well enough, I read it. I'm not sure what I was expecting, but whatever it was, this casual little missive wasn't really it.

Midnight

Dear Josie, blame it on that peapod wine! I've never drunk anything like it and I never will again (touch wood). And it tasted so innocuous too. But I had a great night. Hope it was for you as well, and I didn't singe your angel wings too much?

Noah XXX

He'd scrawled his phone number down at the bottom of the page too, evidently as an afterthought. It didn't sound like he expected to hear from me again; this was just a polite 'thanks very much and goodbye' note.

If he'd left at midnight, he must have amazing recuperative powers! But, of course, although it had been dark when we came back to the cottage yesterday, it had still only been late afternoon, really. He'd probably woken up after a couple of hours, refreshed by a little nap, and decided to go back to the party!

I lay there, with the aspirin subduing my headache to a dull throbbing and my faculties slowly coming back to life, as if someone was wandering through my brain plugging in the synapses one by one. Once I was capable of any kind of rational thought, I had to admit to myself that the peapod wine, on top of everything else I had drunk, had stripped my inhibitions to the point where I had made all the running and pretty well dragged Noah into bed with me. I couldn't blame him for anything that happened after that.

In fact, the aspirin, water and note were a kind thought, and also, I did seem to recall that he'd attempted to resist me—and even stopped at a crucial point to ask if it was OK—so there you are, it was all my own fault.

Only now, in the cold light of day, it felt totally reprehensible and slutty of me, when I had always loved, and just had my heart broken by, Ben. But a tiny little part of me—presumably the newly discovered slutty bit—would really, *really* like Noah to come back and do it all over again!

I repressed that thought firmly and, instead, wondered if anyone would guess what had happened. But perhaps we hadn't been missed, because a lot of people would have departed just after the bride and groom and it would mainly have been the younger ones who stayed on as long as the music played and there was food and drink to be had.

Oh, I so *hoped* no one knew anything about it!

When I came downstairs, I discovered that Noah had also, just like my own personal house elf, tidied away the used glasses into the sink and placed the empty wine bottles in a neat row on the worktop by the range, before letting himself out. Both the range and the stove in the living room were banked up and gently glowing and the cottage was warm.

The missed call on my mobile had been Ben, just about the last person in the world I wanted to talk to right then. His was the number to come up on the house phone too, when I checked, but there was no message on either.

I opened the front door onto a lovely bright world that hurt my eyes, for a very thin layer of pure white snow lay everywhere, like professionally applied frosting on a cake. It must have fallen after Noah departed last night, for there were no footprints leading from my door. I'd like to think I imagined the whole thing, but evidence is against me. And how, having released my inner slut, am I ever going to get her back into the box? Last night was totally different from anything I'd ever experienced with Ben, especially lately, when he must have been exhausted by his activities elsewhere, and I don't remember making love with him being so full of laughter and . . . well, *tenderness*, I suppose.

And actually, I suppose it *is* flattering that a man like Noah couldn't resist me. Once he got going, he certainly seemed to give the proceedings his all . . .

Now my headache has abated, I am having trouble keeping the smile off my face.

I think I'm going to sign the pledge and go

teetotal . . . when I've finished up our current alcohol stock, which could take a while, though I'm giving my liver a break for the moment, to recover.

*   *   *

I went next door later to sort and date the eggs, and chat to Harry about the wedding and the party, just as if I hadn't got a great big guilty secret, plus the rosy glow of someone who has spent a large part of the previous night making passionate love with a random man. Though I suppose that Rob Rafferty would have been even more random.

But Harry, at least, had noticed nothing odd about my disappearance last night. He'd just assumed I'd had enough and gone home, and since the house was in darkness when he returned after gallantly walking the Grace sisters back to Poona Place (though the other way round would have made more sense), I had gone to bed.

Which I certainly had. I'm sure I blushed when he said that.

Gina, who seemed to have taken rather a fancy to him at the reception, had already been across this morning to chat and had told him that the party didn't finish until she and Maria finally went to the Old Barn and pulled the plugs on the Mummers, about one in the morning.

'She said that actor, Rob Rafferty—the one who sang with the Mummers—was flirting with you, our Josie.'

I blushed again. 'Oh, yes, but it didn't mean anything. I expect he flirts with every woman he meets.'

212

'That's what Gina said. Just so long as you didn't take him seriously, because he's not your type, lass.'

'I don't think I've got a type any more, Harry, but if I had, he wouldn't be it,' I assured him. I'd been flattered by his interest and he was rather gorgeous, but in a scary, out-of-my-league way.

Mind you, I'd have thought the same about Noah before last night.

When I'd done the eggs I took Mac out for a long walk, to make up for the day before and to clear my head. And, if truth be told, to find out if there was any gossip.

But the cold must have kept people indoors, for I didn't see anyone to talk to, not even one of the Graces.

* * *

Ben finally got me while I was in the shed, checking over the stored fruit, but I suppose I couldn't avoid his calls for ever.

'At last! I've been trying to get you all day!'

'Yes, I know,' I said shortly, 'but I've been busy.'

'*And* I called you last night, Josie—and some man answered,' he said accusingly.

My heart stopped beating for a moment. Then I said cautiously, 'A *man*? What time was this?'

'Late—about midnight, or maybe slightly after. I couldn't sleep and I thought I'd just give you a ring and see how the wedding went, and how you were and—'

'You phoned me in the middle of the night?'

'I was missing you. But when this man answered, I was so surprised I didn't say anything and he put

213

the phone down. And then I tried the landline, and no one picked up at all. Who was it, Josie? Are you seeing someone else?' he demanded.

'Not really, it was just some strange man I picked up off the street for a good time. What do you think?'

There was silence and then he sighed. 'Sorry, of course you wouldn't have a man there with you! I must have got the wrong number the first time,' he said, as though it was totally out of the question that anyone would be interested in me, apart from him.

Little did he know . . . My stomach got the hot, churning feeling that letting my mind wander to thoughts of Noah seemed to engender and I hauled it back firmly.

'The first time you rang, it must have been a wrong number and the second time probably the right one. But the reception party didn't end until the early hours. The Mummers of Invention kept on playing until Gina and Maria came out and unplugged them,' I said, which was the truth— except that I hadn't actually been there by then.

'Of course. I'm sorry, I suppose I got hold of the wrong end of the stick and was jealous.'

'Ben, you wouldn't have any right to feel jealous even if I held orgies every night of the week. What I do is none of your business any more.'

'Oh, come on,' he said, laughing. 'I know my Josie!'

'Not any more you don't—and I'm not your Josie. So, did you just phone me up to check if I'd picked up some hunk at the reception, or was there another reason?'

'Well, actually, I'm in Camden, unpacking all the

214

stuff that came down from the studio and there's a bit of a smell, as though a mouse had got into something and died there. Did you notice anything?'

'No, but you've always had a problem with mice trying to move into the studio in autumn,' I pointed out. 'It smelled fine when I packed your paints into some boxes I got from Neville's.'

'Yes, thanks for doing that,' he said hastily. 'I expect it got in afterwards and the smell will go off eventually. I've opened all the windows.'

He lowered his voice tenderly. 'Josie, I really do miss you and I know finding out about Olivia was a shock. Throwing me out was an overreaction, though, because we can work things out, really we can! I still love you, you know that? I think I must have been mad to have an affair with her when I've got you, but now I've come to my senses and—'

'You've made your bed, and now you'll have to lie on it, Ben, because with a baby on the way you have responsibilities, haven't you? And at least *you* have the comfort of knowing *I* was the barren one.'

'Oh, Josie, don't!' he pleaded. 'I'll make it up to you, I promise.'

'You won't get the chance, Ben. Have you told your parents yet? They'll be delighted we've broken up, and adore Olivia. She's rich, well connected and ideally placed to further your career. She might be a bit long in the tooth, but obviously she can still give them the grandchildren I never managed. When's the wedding?'

'Only in Olivia's head—and my parents', now they know the baby's on the way,' he said, sounding harassed. 'But you know what I think about marriage, Josie. Anyway, if I was going to

215

marry anyone it would be—'

'Just don't say it, Ben Richards! You wouldn't even marry me to make Granny happy, because you said it was against your principles, so now it's way too late to change your mind. Just get on with your new life and forget you ever had another.'

'But Olivia was using me! She desperately wanted a baby before it was too late, but if I'd known that—'

'Look, I *don't care*. Nothing's the same any more and I just want to cut you right out of my life, as if you never existed!'

'That's a bit harsh—and I know, deep down, you don't really mean it. We're soul mates, we belong together. Just because I went off the rails a bit, it doesn't mean—'

'You didn't just go off the rails, you crashed the train!'

'Well . . . OK then, but I keep saying how sorry I am.'

I cut him off when he changed the subject and started asking me how the wedding went, as if he'd missed it because he'd been unavoidably delayed somewhere. But the cottage was empty of him, as was the studio—swept clean by the removal men, down to the kettle and coffee cups in the little kitchen lean-to.

You couldn't take away the memories that sneaked in when you least expected them, though, even if they were now tarnished and overlaid with betrayal.

Perhaps *I* was a bit tarnished and overlaid now too? But it didn't really feel that way, for my night with Noah had given me a growing sense of something that was harder to define. Confidence

216

that other men might find me attractive? Release? The capability to move on? I certainly didn't feel cold, hollow and shivery any more, so it seemed to have been a cathartic experience. Perhaps I should thank him. And if he'd released my inner slut as well as awoken me from my frozen limbo, at least I needn't feel guilty, because I was a single woman. I would just look on the experience like a dose of highly strange but very effective medicine and put it behind me.

I'd automatically resumed unwrapping and checking the stored apples while thinking all this over, but now my hands stilled. Medicine had made me think of the herbal remedy, and from there, to remembering Libby's mother's comments at the reception, when she was drunk (and so was I). She seemed to have been implying some sort of connection between herself and Tim's father, but surely not …

I frowned, trying to recall her exact words, then decided I was reading more into it than there was. Gloria's conversation was always full of innuendo. She was simply made that way.

*   *   *

It was only in the late afternoon, when Pia popped over to visit before returning to London with Maria, that I got any gossip at all.

'You left early last night, God-ma,' she said, 'but then, most of the oldies left soon after Mum and Tim did.'

'Thanks for ranking me with the geriatrics,' I said, and she grinned.

'Noah was around quite late. He said he saw you

217

home after Mum and Tim left, because you'd had a bit much to drink. Then you'd insisted on picking Mum's bouquet to pieces and putting the flowers in water, which sounded just like you! He said he helped, and it took for ever.'

'Oh . . . yes, he did. It's very fiddly, but they're half dead now anyway,' I said sadly, looking at the drooping blooms.

'Noah didn't stay right to the end of the party, because he said he had to go to bed and sober up, but not necessarily in that order, so he could drive back to London today.'

'So he's gone?'

'Yes, though not until quite late because he said alcohol stayed in your system for hours longer than you might think. Mum wouldn't have minded how long he'd stayed in the gatehouse, but he has a portrait sitting tomorrow and he's supposed to be going to some charity event tonight with his girlfriend. She's Anji somebody, a model. She phoned him up to make sure he was going to make it.'

I immediately felt guilty. I'd forgotten he might have someone else in his life even if, as he said, he didn't take these things seriously.

'I think her star is on the wane, because he was a bit short with her, which isn't like him.' She giggled. 'But then, he looked a bit rough at breakfast and I've never seen him anything other than smooth and elegant before. I felt a bit jaded myself.' She yawned. 'Gina cooked us all what she called a full English breakfast, though she fries the eggs in olive oil.'

'It's healthier. I like them like that too. I buy gallon tins of extra-virgin olive oil through the co-

218

op group.' I hadn't felt really hungry for days, but suddenly the thought of a bacon sandwich made me absolutely ravenous! There was some organic bacon in the freezer; we share a free-range pig once a year with the Graces and Dorrie Spottiswode.

Pia's voice followed me across the room as I lifted some out and put it on a dish to defrost.

'Jasper is . . . well, he's different,' she was saying dreamily. 'We got off on the wrong foot at first. I must be so vain if I think a boy only has to clap eyes on me and he's mine! But once you told me what his interests were, we got on fine. He has to return to university for a couple of weeks, but then it's the Christmas break and he'll be back at Middlemoss again, which isn't very far away from Blessings by car.'

'I thought you seemed taken with him. But he's a serious boy, not at all the type you've been going around with.'

'I know, he thinks I'm a complete Paris Hilton airhead, but I'm going to change that.'

'How?'

'I'm going to research all the stuff he was talking about on the internet—and I do have some serious friends, you know! And maybe I'll really think about doing something with my life rather than just the party circuit. That was only ever to get back at Mum for . . . well for Dad dying, I suppose, though that was hardly her fault,' she added honestly.

'She did love Joe, and they were very happy together—and she loves you too, Pia. She's always talking about you and worrying about what you're doing.'

'She is?' Pia looked at me doubtfully. 'If you say so. But all she ever seems to do is criticise me, my friends and my lifestyle.'

'Parenting maybe isn't her strong point,' I conceded. 'But then, her own mother wasn't a very good role model and it worries her that you'll turn out like your granny if you go off the rails, so that's why she's so hard on you sometimes.'

Pia giggled. 'I know, Granny Gloria is a complete dipso and even last night she was making a play for anything in trousers, until Aunt Daisy dragged her away. I mean, what *is* she like!'

Pia sounded admiring rather than disapproving, but I suppose being a dipso slut is the norm among some of her circle of friends. When I remember Libby's teenage plans to better herself, ready to marry the Right Sort of Man (kind, solid, wealthy, older) and be a good wife, it makes you think. Nowadays, you just need to be a skinny, uneducated, hard-drinking, fashionista to attract the kind of footballer or TV celebrity that girls of Pia's age seem to want.

'I know you think it's too soon for Libby to get married again, but sometimes you fall in love, just like *that*, and you can't help it,' I told her.

'Like you and Ben—which always seemed a bit Romeo and Juliet, though it was just his parents who thought you were from the wrong side of the tracks for their blue-eyed boy, wasn't it? Your granny didn't mind at all.'

'No. She thought Ben's parents were a pair of pretentious prats, but she would have put up with them if they'd given her the chance, for my sake. And actually, I went round once to see Ben's mother to try if we could get along better, but it

220

was useless. Granny says her husband was in love with my mother first and married Nell on the rebound, but I don't see why she should blame *me* for that.' I sighed. 'Anyway, I tried. They're probably highly delighted that Ben has left me and shacked up with an older, sophisticated and rich woman instead.'

'Is that what he's done? Mum didn't give me the details, just said he'd been having an affair and you'd thrown him out.'

'Yes . . . well, you might as well know, darling, in case you see him in London. It turned out he'd been having an affair with this woman for a year without my knowing anything about it, and now she's pregnant. In fact, it seems that's why she made a play for him in the first place. She's in her early forties, so I suppose it was now or never, if she wanted a baby.'

'I never thought you and Ben would end like this,' Pia said sadly. 'He always seemed to adore you and you shared *everything*.'

'In retrospect, I don't know about "share",' I said thoughtfully. 'My world revolved around him and creating the sort of home life he needed to produce his artwork, but all the things I did, like the gardening and baking and so on, I actually love doing.'

'Maybe he just had a sort of moment of madness and he regrets it now?' she suggested hopefully.

'It was a bit more than that but I don't think I would ever have found out if Olivia hadn't phoned and told me about it. Ben tried to finish with her after he found out she was pregnant, but now she wants to marry him.'

'Perhaps if you hadn't thrown him out, he would

have chosen to stay with you, God-ma?'

'Maybe—but although he says he still loves me, I'll never feel the same way about him again. It was a . . . I don't know how to explain this to you, Pia, but it was a gross betrayal. I might forgive him, in time, but he's not the man I loved.'

'I see what you mean,' she said, 'and let's face it, there *are* still other fish in the sea. You looked lovely yesterday too. Normally you wear such terrible clothes, I've never really noticed,' she said, suddenly sounding just like her mother.

'Thanks,' I said drily, though all this sudden praise made me think I must look a total dog most of the time.

'I wasn't the only one who thought so,' Pia said pointedly. 'I saw Rob Rafferty make a pass at you, and later he was looking for you and asked me for your phone number.'

'I hope you didn't give it to him!' I asked, alarmed and flattered in equal measure.

'No, I told him I'd forgotten it, but he gave me his number to pass on to you if you want it?'

'I don't think so. I've never wanted to live dangerously.'

'He wasn't the only interested man either, was he? Noah seemed to be hanging around—and he walked you home!'

I felt myself go slightly pink. 'Your mother told him to keep an eye on me because I was upset about Ben. He was just being kind—in an interfering sort of way. He saw me home, helped me unpick the flowers from your mother's bouquet, which took for ever, then left. There's absolutely no reason why I should ever see him again.' I sincerely hoped not, anyway! 'Don't try to

222

pair me off with any other men, darling, because I'm done with love. Been there, got the heartache, learned my lesson.'

'I never thought I'd hear you being cynical about love,' Pia said. 'And you adore weddings, you know you do! And what about your lovely wedding cakes?'

'OK, so perhaps true love exists for other people, but not for me. And yes, the sound of wedding bells will always make me go all gooey and excited inside, and I'll go on making brides the cakes of their dreams, even if there is a more than even chance those dreams will be shattered within a couple of years of marriage, at most.'

Pia was shaking her head. 'You're what they call a contradiction in terms, God-ma!'

*　　　*　　　*

I had another call from Russell at ten, just as I was on my way to bed. At least I was sober this time, because I felt so bone-achingly tired I thought I might just drop off naturally.

I suppose it's kind of Russell to keep in touch like this, but I would have appreciated it more from Mary and during the daylight hours.

He asked me how I was and whether I was lonely, and I said brightly that I hadn't had time to be, and anyway I had lots of friends in the village. I'm not sure how convincing I was.

But now I've had my very energetic catharsis, I do seem to have come back to life a bit. I mean to try to carry on as normal from now on, even if Ben's betrayal ripped out a large chunk of me by the roots and tossed it onto the compost heap.

If I keep going through the motions of gardening, preserving and cooking, following the cycle of the seasons, then eventually some kind of tranquillity, even happiness, should return, as it did years before when I lost my parents.

Chapter Seventeen

Off-Piste

Due to one thing and another, I'm a little late in making my Christmas cakes this year. However, by soaking the dried fruit in brandy for a couple of days, I will be able to get that richness of flavour without having to resort to pouring alcohol into the base of the baked cakes later.

The recipe I use is very similar to that of the wedding cake, a mixture traditionally called black cake. You couldn't break one of my cakes over the bride's head without concussing her, as they once apparently did, so I expect the early ones were more bread-like . . .

'Cakes and Ale'

I should have written and sent in the next instalment of my 'Cakes and Ale' column by now and have already had one plaintive email from Charlie Rhymer, the editor of *Skint Old Northern Woman*, asking where it was. I told her I'd had a death in the family, which I have: the death of my love, my hopes and my dreams. But she was so sympathetic that in the end I told her about Ben.

'And now I really don't know what to do, because

224

normally my articles are sprinkled with mentions of what the Artist is up to. I mean, do I now remark casually that the Artist has gone to be creative—and even procreative—elsewhere, or simply never mention him again?'

'I see what you mean,' she agreed thoughtfully. 'I think the casual approach, saying he has moved on, would be best, but I still think you will gets lots of mail from upset readers because they liked the whole idea of you two being self-sufficient together. And Ben was the one who often weakened and bought consumer goods, wasn't he? That made for an interesting angle. But you are the star.'

I smiled wryly. 'I think Aggie is the star, really. Half the emails you send on seem to be about her! But at least she doesn't mind what I write about her, because now my cover is blown I'm having to be much more careful what I say about people.'

Still, I promised to sort it out and get the column emailed out to her by the end of the day. I wish Libby was back, so I could talk everything over with her. My other Neatslake friends are treating me like I'm recovering from some debilitating illness. It's the people who know me best who can see past my calm exterior and know I'm not myself . . . unlike Noah, who took me at face value.

Pansy Grace came across the Green with a home-made, nutmeg-sprinkled custard tart and Harry kept popping in on various pretexts to check that I was not lying in an alcoholic stupor on the hearthrug, though actually I'd gone off drinking to excess.

Even Dorrie Spottiswode pushed a box of strange little pills through the letterbox the other day, with a note saying she'd asked Hebe Winter to make up something. I was looking a little peaky, and these were guaranteed to set me right. I was a bit dubious about those pills, because not only did they look and smell pretty strange, but Hebe Winter has a reputation for dabbling in the darker arts. I expect that's undeserved, though, since she's very active in the Church.

They reminded me of the Chinese herbal pills and medicine, which I'd barely touched before Ben's bombshell. I felt a bit guilty, because if I hadn't destroyed them I suppose I could have given them to Libby eventually, if she really did want to try to get pregnant.

But then, I don't want to encourage her until I've just had a *little* word with her mother about what she implied at the reception . . .

*   *   *

Just after I'd managed to wind up the 'Cakes and Ale' column with a brief phrase about the Artist having flown south, some prospective customers arrived to look at my folder of cake photographs.

It's unusual for both the bride and bridegroom to come together, without even the bride's mother in attendance, but once the happy couple told me what they had in mind, I wasn't surprised she'd left them to get on with it.

They were both keen fans of manga graphic novels, and wanted a single large cake with the top iced to look like a cartoon. They'd brought one or two to show me, in case I didn't know what they meant, thank goodness, because I didn't, really.

'So, you want me to make a square or oblong

cake and then *paint* a comic book image of you both getting married on the top? In natural, edible colours, of course,' I added. 'I don't use any other kind.'

'That's right,' said the girl, who'd managed to apply her makeup in a way that already made her look as if she could have been peeled off a page.

Her fiancé handed me a couple of computer printouts. 'These are our avatar selves—I thought they'd be useful.'

'I know it's short notice, but we'd given up on the idea of a cake until someone told us about you,' the girl said, looking at me hopefully.

It sounded pretty straightforward and would at least keep me occupied. 'I don't see why not,' I agreed. 'I can do the outlining and lettering in black with a liquorice pen, once I've painted on the colours. The cake could be propped up to display the picture for the photographs, before you cut it.'

I'd have got Ben to draw it out for me first, had he not already painted himself right out of the picture.

*   *   *

One of Harry's last remaining cronies suddenly passed away. It upset him quite a bit, though there was still an element of glee that he'd outlived yet another of his friends!

He spent the whole of the next day with the widow, helping her with the arrangements, so I was on hen duty and had Mac with me too. They'd gone off laying and they aren't too keen on going into the run when it's so cold. They fluff out to

227

about twice their normal size, like giant feather dusters.

But the next morning, when Harry resumed his normal round, I baked the manga cake base in my largest rectangular tin and I'd just taken it out of the oven when the phone rang.

I tossed aside my oven gloves and reached for the receiver, only to wish I hadn't when an immediately familiar deep voice said, suavely, 'Hello, Josie? It's me—Noah.'

I felt as if someone had run a cold finger up and down my spine.

'Umm . . .' I managed, after swallowing hard.

'Don't let the wild excitement at hearing from me carry you away, darling, will you?'

'I'll try not to,' I said, finding my voice again now the first shock was over. 'How did you get my number?'

'I ran into Pia earlier today, and she gave it to me. I left you mine, if you recall, but you didn't ring me.' From the tone of his voice, that was totally unheard of. He even sounded a bit miffed.

'There didn't seem any point,' I said briefly, quite surprised because I thought he had a glamorous long-term girlfriend and wouldn't have wanted me to contact him.

'No? Well, after I spoke with Pia I just wanted to make sure you were OK about what happened.'

'Why shouldn't I be?'

'Because, according to Pia, you hadn't just broken up with a boyfriend, but with your long-term partner and the love of your life. She said you were devastated by it, so clearly I misread the situation. I don't want you to think I purposely took advantage of you when you were vulnerable.'

'No, I don't think that at all,' I broke in hastily. 'There's no need to worry, because I'm fine about what we did. It meant nothing to either of us then, and it means nothing now. It only happened because we were both peapodded.'

'What?'

'The peapod wine—my fault, I knew it was lethal.'

'I don't think we can entirely blame what happened on peapod wine, Josie! I—'

'Look, Noah,' I interrupted firmly, 'it was quite nice, but—'

'Nice?'

'Yes, very. In fact, I probably ought to be thanking you, because our encounter was quite cathartic—like a sort of emotional enema, getting rid of the blockage so I could go on with my life. So, thanks and goodbye,' I added brightly and put down the phone.

My hand had gone numb so I must have been clenching it hard, but I thought I carried that off rather well, considering he took me by surprise. I didn't suppose he'd bother getting in touch again.

*　　　*　　　*

Later Ben phoned me up too, so obviously the poet Wendy Cope is quite right about men being like buses, and when one does eventually stop, two or three more will start pulling over and flashing their lights. It needed only Rob Rafferty to run me to earth, to make a full set.

Perish the thought. I'd done with love and, useful though it was, I don't think I'm really suited to random sexual encounters either.

229

'What do you want, Ben?' I said shortly, and was surprised to find his call made me feel irritated rather than anguished. 'I've just spread warm apricot jam over a wedding cake and I want to get the marzipan on. It's a rush order.'

'I've been talking to Harry. I wanted to try and explain things to him a bit, after he tore a strip off me in the pub—not that I didn't deserve it, I know. He told me one of his friends had died. Poor old Bob! It's only a couple of days since I saw him.'

'Yes, it was terribly sudden, though he hadn't been well for ages. He got home from the pub, sat down in his chair and that was it. The funeral is Wednesday and I'll probably go with Harry, if only to make sure he's warmly enough wrapped up and—'

I broke off, realising I'd automatically started chatting to Ben as if nothing had ever come between us.

'I wish I could come, Josie. I—I'm not sure I can function without you and Neatslake and everything. I feel like I've been cut off from some vital lifeline.'

'Maybe you should have thought about that before. But I expect you'll get used to it. You were always pretty keen to get back to London after you'd been home for a while. Now, if you'll excuse me, I've got yet another customer coming to discuss a wedding cake and I need to finish the marzipan on this one before she does.'

He was still saying persuasively, 'But, Josie, darling—' when I put the phone down.

I'm not his darling any more, nor anyone else's.

*　　　*　　　*

230

'So, since we met on the slopes and we're both really keen skiers, what we wanted was a ski cake,' said the bride-to-be, who herself had a long, curving nose rather like a ski slope. 'One with a steep, really twisty run, with little figures, and maybe something written around it, like "Wishing Bev and Steve the run of their lives"?'

'You mean all downhill?' I said absently, fiddling with my pen. My mind had a tendency to keep running over my phonecalls, which had both undermined my hard-won tranquillity a little, but in different ways.

There was a silence and I looked up to find her staring at me rather perplexedly, from boiled-gooseberry eyes. 'Not exactly,' she said. 'Maybe that wasn't such a good idea. But no on-the-piste jokes, either.'

'I'll think it over and see what I come up with,' I promised. 'A ski-run cake won't be too difficult because I can use a lot of Christmas cake decorations, like small pine trees and that sort of thing.'

The phone rang yet again at that moment, but muted, because it was under the thick, knitted hen teacosy.

'Aren't you going to answer that?' she asked.

'No, the chances are it'll only be yet another man I don't want to speak to.'

'Really?' She looked at me doubtfully. I was back in my patchwork dungarees and rainbow-striped cardigan, so I don't suppose I looked much like a man-magnet.

But if she thought I was mad as a hatter, she was still too impressed by the quality of my previous

231

customers and my appearance in the terribly upmarket *Country at Heart* magazine, to take her order elsewhere. Eccentricity was clearly OK in that milieu.

Chapter Eighteen

Mixed Pickles

If you make your own spiced vinegar for pickling, you will find it tastes much better than the bought stuff. I pickle everything, from plain onions, to beetroot, to cauliflower and gherkins, but I can't say I am very partial to pickled eggs. The Artist used to be, but of course now that he has moved on I don't need to bother making them for him, and Uncle prefers pickled red cabbage.

'Cakes and Ale'

There was not so much to do in the garden in late November, but I kept myself busy with my cake making, baking several large square ones and stacking them to make a steep, curved ski-run. There was lots of pickling and preserving to be done, too, plus the next instalment of 'Cakes and Ale' to rough out, so it would need just a polish and a bit of an update before I sent it in.

Libby must have been having a blissful honeymoon, because she didn't phone me until just before they flew back and then only, I think, because she had phoned Gina first. She has a naturally suspicious mind.

'According to Gina, the reception carried on for

hours after we left and the Mummers kept playing until almost one, when she and Maria went over to the barn and told everyone to go home. They were down to the younger guests by then and, since the caterers had long since cleared up and gone, they'd sent out for alcohol.'

'Yes, Pia popped in the day after, before she and Maria went back to London, and said they had a great time.'

'Gina also said she noticed that *you* went home soon after Tim and I left . . . with Noah.' Libby paused meaningfully, but I didn't fall into the trap and rush into speech. '*And* she didn't see him again before she left herself, a couple of hours later.'

'Oh, I expect she just didn't spot him,' I said, though my tummy was doing that hot churny thing it did whenever I thought of that night. 'I had to leave early, because I caught your bouquet when you threw it and I went home to unwire it and put the flowers in water. Noah walked me there and then stayed to help. When he went back to the reception I didn't feel like it any more. I think I'd already had too much champagne. I just wanted to go to bed.'

It was almost true, wasn't it? I was just a little economical with the facts.

'Hmm,' she said thoughtfully. 'You didn't fall for Noah, did you? Only I warned you what he's like.'

'Oh, no,' I said airily. 'I do like him better now I've got to know him, but it wouldn't bother me if I never saw him again.'

'Really?' She didn't sound terribly convinced. 'Well, you *are* pretty sure to see him again, since he's an old friend and likely to visit.'

233

Not if I could help it, I wouldn't! I was sort of grateful to Noah in a way because I'd seemed to turn a corner emotionally after our encounter, but I certainly didn't ever want to meet my catharsis face to face again. I offered Libby a red herring before she could grill me some more. I hadn't decided whether I was going to confess all when she returned or not, but I certainly wasn't doing it over the phone. 'Rob Rafferty asked Pia for my phone number!'

'Oh my God! She didn't give it to him, did she? You haven't been out with him?'

'No, she didn't, and no, I haven't . . . but it is sort of flattering, isn't it, to have a gorgeous man like that show some interest?'

'Men have probably been showing interest for years and you've been too wrapped up in Ben to notice—but I don't think Rob Rafferty is what you need right now.'

'I don't need any men, full stop,' I told her. 'I'm fine on my own. By the way, Pia is really taken with Jasper Pharamond. He's a sweetie, but terribly serious. I wouldn't have thought he was her type at all! She says she's coming back to Blessings for Christmas, because Jasper will be back home for the university hols by then and she hopes to see him.'

'Oh, is she?' Libby sounded pleased. 'That will be lovely! We can have our first Christmas at Blessings as a family. And I'd much rather she fell for Jasper than any of the wasters she goes around with. He seems nice. I think she liked Tim once she got to know him a bit, don't you?'

'I don't see how anyone could dislike him,' I assured her. 'I'm sure she's already getting used to the idea, and Maria was a great help.' Clamping the phone between shoulder and chin, I opened the dresser drawer and fished out a folded newspaper. 'I kept you the cutting from the *Sticklepond and District Courier* about the wedding. Listen to this for excited and overblown local reporting!

'The wedding of the year, between Mrs Elizabeth Cazzini and Mr Timothy Rowland-Knowles, took place on Friday at St Cuthbert's church, Neatslake, and the reception was held in the Old Barn at Blessings, the bridegroom's residence. Celebrity guests included well-known London portrait photographer Noah Sephton and soap star Rob Rafferty, who plays the part of Seth Steele in *Cotton Common*.
 'The happy couple are pictured cutting their very unusual cake (made by local cake designer and bridesmaid Josie Gray, second right in main picture), which was in the form of the Leaning Tower of Pisa. The Italian theme was carried on at the reception . . .

'And it goes on and on, with three pictures. I look sozzled in the one I'm in. Just as well the *Glorious Weddings* photographer took only photos of you and the cake.'
 'You *were* sozzled, but not till later,' Libby pointed out. 'I'll look forward to seeing that article. Tim and I have bought a lovely big album bound in white and gold leather for our official wedding photos, so I hope they've come out well. But I'll have Noah's pictures if not, I suppose—his always *do* come out, even when you wish they

wouldn't! He does tend to catch the oddest scenes and before you know where you are, your intimate moments are blown up in black and white for everyone else to see too.'

'I think that's terribly intrusive.'

'Oh, not really. Most people are flattered that the great Noah Sephton thinks they're worth photographing, even if later they aren't keen on how they're portrayed. It's an honour.'

'It's an honour *I* don't want.'

'I'm afraid you'll feature in them anyway, but he will have taken a couple of frameable wedding pictures too, he promised me,' she said blithely. 'And the wedding photographer will have got *him* in the line-up outside the church—the snapper snapped!'

'I expect the pics are awaiting your return, Libs. You'll be home in a couple of days. Have you had a great time?'

'Yes. Tim had been to Pisa before, but only briefly, and that's never like living in a place, is it? It's so lucky we both love Italy! I already feel that it's my second home and I'm sure Tim soon will too.'

I was pretty positive that Tim would feel like that about anywhere Libby took him to, since in his willingness to please he resembled nothing so much as a big, affectionate golden Labrador puppy, but I agreed that it was indeed lovely that they already had that connection.

'We've been talking over that idea I had of creating a permanent wedding venue in the Old Barn and we're really going to go for it, when we get back,' she said.

'You've definitely made your minds up?'

236

'Yes, and I'll be counting on you to help, Josie, because there will be lots to do if we want to be open for next year's wedding season. I expect we'll need planning permission because of making lots of alterations. There are *so* many things to sort out and I imagine it will all cost a lot of money.'

'Yes, it will be a huge effort to get it ready by then. When were you thinking of opening?'

'Ideally, I'd like to open for business from the end of March to the start of October, just for the first season, to pack in as many receptions as possible to help pay for the alterations. If we make enough during the peak time for weddings to keep us going for the rest of the year, then we can go to Pisa, or ski, or do whatever else we like.'

'You do seem to have it all worked out, and of course I'll help, as much as I can,' I assured her, though inwardly I was wondering where, in my already hectic schedule, I would find the time . . .

'I thought you might be off the whole idea of romance and weddings at the moment?'

'Well, they're not for me, obviously, and nowadays most marriages seem to have a shelf life of about twelve months, but I'm more than happy to help you.'

'You little cynic, you. Do you mean you and the Graces aren't still racing over to the church every time the wedding bells peal out?'

'No . . . but I'm fighting the addiction.'

'Why bother? It's quite harmless. When you're helping me with Old Barn Receptions, you can indulge as much as you want. I'd like the number of your contact at *Glorious Weddings*, for a start, and I'll certainly need you on reception days, as my second in command.'

'I think you mean "gofer",' I said resignedly.

'Josie, we've had such fun working it all out! I'm sure it'll be a real money-spinner and then Tim can give up work and concentrate on helping Dorrie with the gardening. And he can double up as a chauffeur, for those couples who want to marry at the church but not walk back across the Green, like I did—after all, it might not always be a dry day. But I expect a lot will marry elsewhere and just have the reception at Blessings. I'm definitely going to look into offering small wedding parties the option of a civil ceremony in the Great Chamber.'

'Yes, but you'll have to start by sorting out a lot of really basic stuff first, Libby, like toilets.'

'*Toilets?*'

'You may not have noticed, but the one toilet in the stable block was totally inadequate, and since it was so cold, not everyone wanted to trail across to the house to use the cloakroom there. And anyway, if it was strangers, you wouldn't *want* them walking in and out of your house using the downstairs cloakroom, would you?'

'No, I see what you mean, but luckily there's plenty of space in the stable block to create a proper cloakroom, a swish one. And the tackroom will have to be totally revamped into a food storage and handling area. I mean, it will still be all cold buffet food brought in—I'll have to find a local firm who can do that—but it will need finishing touches and refrigeration until it's ready to serve.'

'It would be cheaper to buy your own glasses, dishes, cutlery and tablecloths,' I said, really starting to think about it, 'rather than hire them.'

238

'Yes, and the trestle tables and chairs—they'll pay for themselves in the long run. And we need a glossy brochure of what's on offer, which can feature some of your cakes, so you should get even more orders.'

'I'm not sure I can handle that many more! I used to make one or two a month, just as a little sideline but, especially since that *Country at Heart* article, I'm getting constant enquiries. I don't want to just make cakes all the time.'

'Then double your prices and become more exclusive.'

'I already tell them I won't deliver the cakes out of the area, so that puts off most of the ones who live a long distance away. And I'm hardening my heart and turning down any I don't fancy doing. I don't know about doubling the prices, because I really don't need any more money, Libby. I can't imagine what I would do with it.'

'Buy some decent clothes?' she suggested. 'I'll be paying you for helping me at the receptions too, so you'll have no excuse.'

'I'm not taking any money for that. I *want* to help you!'

'Well . . . maybe at first, until we get a couple under our belts, but then you'll have to accept wages.'

'We'll see,' I said. 'But maybe if I did double my prices, that would cut down the number of orders? Only I would still charge a lot less for local ones, if I really wanted to do them.'

'There you are, you're starting to think it through a bit more. You need to arrange things so you are doing what *you* want, not what everyone else wants.'

I thought that was pretty rich, considering she had just dragooned me into agreeing to help her run a wedding reception business!

'So, what are you doing with yourself? Have you heard from Ben?' she asked.

'Yes, unfortunately. He keeps leaving messages on the phone and when he does get through to me he goes on and on about how he never meant this to happen, and that he misses me. He still seems to think I'm going to weaken and let him move right back in, as if nothing ever happened. I hadn't realised he was quite that stupid, so it was a bit of a revelation.'

'Big, friendly, affectionate, thick but devious— that's Ben,' she agreed. 'But I have to admit he's a brilliant artist even if I don't like his stuff much. I suppose he's living with this Olivia?'

'Yes, according to Russell. And that's another strange thing. Now *he's* taken to phoning me up for late night chats. Don't you think that's a bit odd? It's never Mary, but I think she's still feeling guilty because she didn't tell me about Olivia.'

'He could just be being friendly and supportive?' suggested Libby.

'Maybe . . . The trouble is, I think he's always fancied me a bit. Whenever we used to stay at their flat and he got tanked up, he'd be a bit too huggy and kissy with me. Ben used to think it was funny, but Mary always went tight-lipped, so it was a bit uncomfortable.'

'Perhaps he thinks you're fair game now, then?'

'He'd better not! Not only is he married to Mary, but also I don't fancy him in the least, though I always *liked* him—or I did when he wasn't being drunk and silly. Anyway, I don't want any more men in my life—I keep saying. I'm done with all that!'

'You've left it a bit late to become a nun,' Libby said tartly.

'I'll become the next best thing, then.'

'So, are you already embracing the chaste life and not drinking too much, or sinking into depression?'

'Yes, and I'm so busy I barely have time to think,' I said brightly. 'Harry gave me his car, which was lovely of him—did I tell you? Ben went off with the van and life would just be impossible without transport, because of delivering cakes and collecting the bulk co-op group deliveries.'

'Yes, you can't really heft sacks of rice and henfood on foot, or deliver fragile cakes on the bus.'

'I haven't got the time, either, because when I'm not making cakes I still have to look after the garden and Harry, walk the dog and keep an eye on the Graces. But Violet is a help. She's getting so good at modelling things in icing that she's practically an employee now.'

'I bet you're paying her way over the odds. They'll be loaded with Acorns.'

I laughed. 'Yes, more than a squirrel in winter!'

'What are you doing with yourself? Have you had even a vestige of a social life since the wedding?'

'No, to be honest, though we didn't have much of a one before, really. We always enjoyed each other's company best . . .' I paused. 'Of course, I've been out to Mark and Stella's to pick up the co-op order and drop off vegetables, and they always give me tea and cake. But even they haven't invited me

241

over for their Thursday evening gathering since Ben left. That's a bit odd, isn't it? It's only just struck me. And we used to go and meet them in the pub, sometimes.'

'Other women don't want you around if you're single. You become a threat,' Libby said. 'Never mind, I'll be back soon and I know you don't have any designs on Tim!'

'He wouldn't look at me if I had. He's too madly in love with you.'

'I know,' she said, and sighed luxuriantly.

'Perhaps you should just enjoy that right now, rather than rush into a pregnancy?' I suggested deviously, because I still needed to phone Gloria and try to get to the bottom of what she'd said at the reception, even though I was sure I'd misunderstood what she was implying.

'Actually, we've come to much the same conclusion,' Libby said, 'though I daren't leave it too long. But anyway, how else are you filling in your time, between gardening and good works?'

'I made fourteen jars of mixed pickles, defrosted some organic lamb and cooked lots of individual Lancashire hotpots with shortcrust pastry lids. Harry is very partial to them and his freezer was looking a bit empty. Then I had a rush wedding cake job—a manga cake with a sort of grown-up cartoon on the top. There are still all the finishing touches to put on the Goth cake too, and now I have a ski cake order, which is quite a challenge.'

'That does sound pretty busy,' she conceded, so presumably she will now stop imagining I am drinking myself to death in her absence. I wouldn't have time even if I had the inclination.

'Yes, so busy I was really late with my last

instalment of "Cakes and Ale". I had to rush something out and I don't think I was at my best. I had to say the Artist had decamped, but kept it light.'

'I hadn't thought about how you would handle that. I suppose you couldn't very well just never mention him again, when he was in all the episodes that had gone before.'

'No, but at least I have you and Gina to write about now, if only in guarded terms!'

'How do you think Gina is settling in?'

'As if she's always lived in Neatslake. She comes to buy eggs and vegetables, though we don't have many eggs just now—the hens aren't laying—and stays for a chat and a cup of coffee. She says you should order a produce box weekly, until Tim and Dorrie can get going with your own hens and kitchen garden.'

'Tim and I think Dorrie should have some kind of allowance for helping with the gardening, so she will be less poverty-stricken from now on.'

'That will be a relief. One less Acorn to worry about so much,' I agreed.

'Meanwhile, Gina will be doing most of the cooking, so it's up to her where she gets things from. I don't suppose you have a lot of stuff to sell at the moment, anyway?'

'No, not really—carrots, winter vegetables, that kind of thing. And she can have any amount of jam, relishes and pickles she wants too.'

After a bit more chat she rang off, but I felt much better for having talked to her, even if I hadn't been entirely truthful about Noah, or informed her that although I'd renounced all interest in men, I went out with a bang.

243

*   *   *

I was starting half to expect Russell's late night calls. That night he told me that the mysterious smell from Ben's studio was permeating the whole building and they think that whatever died did it deep inside one of Ben's three-dimensional works, though they can't pinpoint which one . . .

'Maybe there was a mass mouse suicide pact?' I suggested, feeling rather guilty. But I supposed the stink wouldn't last for ever. Surely eventually it would wear off.

I couldn't believe I'd done something so vindictive! Perhaps I should have confessed, so he could remove the offending bits of prawn head and help get rid of the smell sooner.

But no, on second thoughts, I couldn't possibly . . .

When Russell had been wittering on for a bit, I asked him directly if Mary knew he was calling me so often.

'Of course she does!' he said, going all hurt. 'She would phone you herself, except that she's still feeling guilty about not telling you about Ben and Olivia—and she's easily upset now she's expecting. But I'm sure she'll get over it once the baby arrives.'

I thought I must have been mistaken about Russell and he was just being kind and keeping in touch.

Chapter Nineteen

Driven

*I can't believe it's suddenly December! I have
barely started preparing for Christmas and, since
almost all of my presents are edible, I usually
have things well in hand by the end of November.*

*Still, at least there is not a lot to do in the
garden, this month . . .*

'Cakes and Ale'

I was glad when Libby and Tim returned, because
keeping a brave face on everything was a bit
wearing and at least with Libby I didn't have to
pretend . . . though admittedly there *were* one or
two things I'd been holding back on.

I also hoped to astonish her with my svelte new
figure, which was entirely due to having lost my
appetite, but still filling my days with even more
hard work. Now each night I instantly fell asleep
with the unconsciousness of exhaustion once my
head hit the pillow.

Libby invited me over to see the wedding
pictures, which had been awaiting their return, and
when I'd admired them she said, 'I've got a couple
of Noah's too—and this came with them for you.'

She handed me a stiff brown envelope with my
name on, and inside were two pictures of me, not
at the wedding but the first time we had met, on
the Green. In one I was barefoot and windblown,
clutching Aggie the hen under one arm and doing
that angry pointy finger thing at Noah, like a

fishwife. The other must have been taken at the moment when I caught sight of Ben in the doorway behind him, for I looked entirely different, my face lit up with love . . .

'Noah says I have to wait until Christmas for prints of the rest of his photos,' Libby said, leaning across to have a look at mine. 'I might get a second album for them. Those are very good of you, aren't they? What are you going to do with them?'

'I thought Aggie might like them pinned up in the henhouse.'

'You are joking, aren't you? You can't possibly do that to photographs by Noah Sephton! They're worth good money, you know. He's quite famous.'

'Money doesn't mean that much to me, Libs— but relax, I was joking. Actually, I like this one of me with Aggie, even if I do look furious.'

'It says something on the back,' she pointed out, and I turned it over. In pencil was written 'Militant angel!' It didn't say anything at all on the back of the other one.

'You look prettier in the other. Glowing. What are you looking at? It's not Noah, is it?' she asked suspiciously.

'No, it was Ben,' I said shortly, and turned it face down. 'I got a job lot of frames from the charity shop the other day and I'm sure there's one about the right size—so you see, I really wasn't serious about the henhouse.'

'I didn't think you were. In fact, I thought you might treasure it, because I have a strong suspicion that you and Noah got much friendlier than you're telling me about, Josie Gray!'

'Well . . . a bit,' I admitted. 'Nothing serious. We'd both had a bit too much to drink and had a cuddle, that's all.' I felt myself blushing hotly.

'Ah-ha! Just wait till I see Noah Sephton!' she exclaimed. 'I told him to keep an eye on you, not seduce you!'

'It's not his fault. Because I looked OK, he didn't think I was seriously upset about breaking up with Ben. And what's more, I *told* him I wasn't, so you can't really blame him. No, if anyone was doing the seducing, it was me,' I confessed, 'though if he hadn't tried the peapod wine, he'd probably have managed to resist.'

'Josie, that's so unlike you!' Her blue eyes were round with surprise. 'But I suppose it was just the rebound and the booze—and thank God it wasn't Rob Rafferty, because that would have been much worse.'

'Oh, Libby, I'm still amazed he asked Pia for my phone number!' I said, diverted. 'I mean, I don't at all want to see him again, but the fact that he fancied me was so good for my morale!'

'Don't get carried away, because apparently nothing even vaguely female is safe from him,' she said dampeningly. 'But *Noah*—I mean, you're not his usual tall, leggy young blonde. Maybe he really likes you?'

'No, I told you, it was the peapod. He did phone me to see if I was OK later, though, after he ran into Pia in London, which I suppose was kind of him,' I added grudgingly.

'I'm still cross with him,' Libby said. 'You were vulnerable and a one-night stand was the last thing you needed.'

'Actually, you're quite wrong, Libs. I felt a bit horrified when I woke up next morning, it's true, but after that, I felt *much* better about everything and more able to cope. It was like a catharsis.'

'I hope you didn't tell him so?'

'I may well have done . . . I certainly remember saying making love with him had proved to be a sort of emotional enema,' I admitted. 'He sounded a bit peeved.'

She giggled. 'I wish I could have seen his face! But if you're sure you're all right, I suppose I'll have to forgive him, though won't it be a bit awkward if I invite him to stay now?'

'Not really. I probably won't need to see him, will I? And I'm sure he'll be as happy to forget about it as I will, because Pia thinks he's still going out with that model, Anji. I feel a bit guilty about her.'

'Don't be. You didn't know. Pia's probably got it wrong anyway, because I had the distinct impression he'd gone off her.' She was still looking a bit worried.

'Really, it wasn't important, Libs,' I assured her.

'Except as a catharsis?' She grinned suddenly. 'Oh, Josie!'

*   *   *

When I got back home I did find a frame to fit the fishwife photo, but I slid the other one in behind it—the old, glowing version of myself, hidden for ever. Then Libby rang my mobile, in a panic because it had occurred to her that my having slept with Noah might have had unforeseen results.

'It didn't,' I assured her. 'I thought of that; I'm not totally stupid.' Then I confessed that I'd destroyed the Chinese herbal medicine she'd gone to so much trouble to obtain for me, on the night I found out about Ben's affair.

'I don't think it would have had any effect anyway, really, since clearly I'm barren. I was clutching at straws. But I could have given it to *you*,' I said, before remembering that I really didn't want her to even think of getting pregnant until I'd spoken to her mother!

*   *   *

If I thought I'd been whizzing around keeping myself busy, it was as nothing to the way Libby threw herself into organising Old Barn Receptions: she was like a human whirlwind.

She applied for planning permission and the usual licences, investigated the possibility of having civil marriages performed in the house by a registrar, and negotiated with a catering firm in Ormskirk I'd discovered. Movable Feasts offered organic wholefood event catering, which she was a bit dubious about at first, because she seemed to think that it meant vegetarian. I pointed out that I'm not vegetarian, let alone vegan, just because I try to eat a healthy, wholefood organic diet.

Anyway, they had a business meeting, hit it off and have struck a deal. Now Libby was compiling a glossy brochure, with very clever artist's impressions of what the interior of the Old Barn would look like when it was finished. I chose which of my cake photographs to include in the back section, where she recommends me among other suppliers, including Hebe Winter for rose petal confetti, the couple who make handmade paper invitations and Dorrie's floral arrangements. The Graces also feature as the purveyors of heirloom embroidered wedding tablecloths for under the cake.

'Such a good idea, if you think people will be prepared to pay so much for a tablecloth, dear,' Lily said doubtfully, when I suggested it.

'People are prepared to pay for lovely, handmade things, and the price takes into account all the time you will spend embroidering and Pansy crocheting the edging.'

'Well, if you really think so, perhaps we will start to make a stock of them now, ready, so that we will just have to personalise them with the happy couple's names as the finishing touch.'

I wished that I could lay in a stock of cakes ready too, but I never knew what shape or size I would need next. But then, that is why I enjoy making weird and wonderful cakes and I would hate the monotony of turning out three-tiered white confections.

Lily is also going to provide A Stitch in Time, a sort of have-needle-will-travel emergency service, for any last-minute crises to the bride or bridesmaids' dresses.

* * *

By the start of December the brochure proofs had arrived—Libby certainly doesn't let the grass grow beneath her feet—and I went over to Blessings to help her go through them. Very grand it all sounded too.

'For weddings at St Cuthbert's church in Neatslake, the services of a vintage Bentley and chauffeur are available for a small extra charge, to drive the happy couple back to the reception at Blessings,' I read.

'That's me,' said Tim, beaming. He'd arrived home a little while earlier and immediately changed into jeans, trainers and a fleece gilet. His white-blond hair seemed to be going in six directions at once, due to his habit of running his hands through it when excited or worried about something.

'We've had to organise special insurance for that,' Libby said, 'and bought yards of silk ribbon to decorate the car, because chances are that Tim will only be driving the happy couple the few yards back from church when it rains, so they'll get soggy each time.'

'Do you know, darling,' Tim said, turning to Libby, 'I think there might still be a chauffeur's uniform or two in the attic!'

'I think that would be going a bit too far, Tim. A smart dark suit will do and, goodness knows, you've got enough of those for work.'

'I expect the uniforms are made of that stiff sort of wool that itches anyway,' he agreed, though with a shade of regret. I suspected he liked the idea of dressing up.

'My job will be to organise everything on the day and make sure it runs smoothly,' Libby said. 'And Josie is my second in command.'

'So what am *I* doing, apart from driving the car if requested?' asked Tim.

'Ensuring Dorrie has enough flowers and foliage for her table decorations beforehand, either from the garden or the florist in Sticklepond. Then you will be doing the meeting and greeting at the receptions,' Libby told him, 'which you couldn't really do dressed as a chauffeur. That's really your forte and you will be brilliant at it—making sure

251

everyone has a drink, showing them where in the gardens they can take the best photographs, that kind of thing. Just like a host at a party, really.'

'Oh, right!' Tim said, looking relieved. I'm not sure quite what he thought Libby would have had him doing.

'Before the wedding season, the most important thing you can do is help Dorrie get the grounds picture-perfect again, especially the lawns and rose garden nearest the barn. We've had to take soft-focus pictures for the brochure, but by next spring I hope it will all look much better. When I contacted *Glorious Weddings* magazine they were very interested in doing an article about the business, maybe in the June issue, so I'm sending them a brochure as soon as it's printed. It will be great publicity.'

'And you get a mention in the article they did about my cakes,' I reminded her. 'That one's supposed to be out in March.'

'Yes, that's true. Perhaps we should advertise Old Barn Receptions in the same one? It all means lots of lovely coverage—and if advance bookings are good, which I'm sure they will be, then you can give up the soliciting and garden full time, Tim.'

'That would be wonderful,' he said wistfully, but not unhopefully. 'Do you really think it will work?'

'Absolutely! Remember all the trouble I had finding anywhere for our reception, though admittedly it was short notice and late in the year. But there's clearly a dearth of places in the area, and Blessings will be terribly classy too: *the* place for receptions. "Reception to be held at Blessings, Neatslake",' she added grandly. 'I mean, how good does that sound?'

'And all the receptions will be as ecologically low impact as possible,' I said happily, because I'd insisted on it. 'That will probably be popular. Everyone's interested in doing their bit these days.'

Gina came in and removed the tea things and Tim went off to have a word with Dorrie. 'I'd better get back too,' I said. 'I need to do a bit more to the Goth cake tonight, though it's nearly finished. I think it's quite a success, in a weird sort of way. Once I start helping you with the receptions, what with all the cake-making, baking, preserving, writing my articles, the gardening *and* delivering the veggie boxes and eggs, there won't be a second left in the day!'

'Just as well,' Libby said. 'Less time to brood over things. And you'll be better off, financially.'

'I'm already rich in all the important things—especially good friends. I don't need more money; I've got enough of that.'

'Maybe, but like I said, you could go out and buy yourself some decent clothes. You can't be my second in command looking like an escapee from *The Good Life*.'

'When I'm not doing anything messy, I'm actually terribly stylish these days, I'll have you know!' I said indignantly. 'Or I am if the boho look is still in. Stella gave me some lovely hippie clothes and one or two of the dresses would probably do for the receptions, once Lily Grace has taken them in a bit.'

'There's nothing smart and fashionable about the old hippie look,' Libby said firmly. 'No, we'll go and buy you something new.'

'But I think I'd be happier, and feel much more like me, in one of Stella's long Indian paisley

253

cotton dresses and a big frilly pinny,' I insisted mutinously.

'I could do you out like a Victorian parlour maid in a long striped dress, if you really want to look retro,' Libby suggested. 'Or maybe you could go Elizabethan to match the house, like the re-enactment society in Sticklepond.'

'I'm definitely not wearing a farthingale, but if you want me to look sort of medieval, I could wear my bridesmaid's dress?'

'Yes, and your hair loose, with a circlet . . . that would look interesting. But then, I would probably have to dress up too. It would look odd if only one of us was, wouldn't it? So maybe not. We would both be better neatly dressed and blending into the background.'

'OK,' I agreed, thinking that actually it was probably just as well, because after being tossed aside on the night of the wedding, my bridesmaid's dress had been very creased, though I was working on that. Lily Grace had told me an old trick: you hung the garment in a steamy room to sort of relax the crumples away. It had been in the bathroom ever since, and it did look better every time I had a shower or bath. I just hoped it didn't get mildew before it was crease free.

I went out by way of the French doors and found Tim and Dorrie standing under a carriage lamp, impervious to the cold and the dusk, discussing the garden.

'That Rambling Rector has rambled quite out of order,' said Dorrie. 'It needs a firm pruning back, and then it should make a glorious backdrop by next year. Now, in front of it, there used to be a magnificent herbaceous border, if you recall, but

254

it's well and truly overgrown. Disgraceful! I just couldn't keep it under control at all, and Moorcroft was worse than useless.'

'Could we salvage the perennials?' asked Tim.

'I should think so. Between us we could go right through it and save what we can, then plant it up again next spring.'

The moonlight showed the path through the rose garden to the distant gazebo, which I had noticed on the day of the wedding was sadly shabby and in need of a good coat of paint.

Tim must have been thinking the same thing, because he said, 'The gazebo would be a perfect spot for photographs of the happy couples. If we get some dry days, I could start repairing and painting that myself.'

'Harry would give you a hand, with advice, if not anything terribly physical,' I offered, then, finding it a bit chilly for standing around, went home.

Behind me their voices started up again, debating the merits of whether to try to recut the croquet lawn out of the rough grass.

* * *

'Our Sadie's sent more photos of what she calls the granddad flat,' Harry said. 'It's come on a treat— nearly finished.'

'You can't say she isn't doing her best to entice you over there, Harry,' I said. 'I'm sure you'd be very comfortable. Maybe you should think seriously about it. I mean, I know it would be sad to leave your friends, but think of the fun you would have with all your family, especially the grandchildren.'

'Nay, I couldn't leave you on your own, lass!' he said, though his gaze lingered on the photos spread out on the kitchen table.

'I . . . well, I would hate to see you go, Harry, but I'd be fine, absolutely fine!' I said encouragingly. 'If you change your mind about going, you mustn't worry about me. After all, I've got Libby here now, ordering me about, and once the wedding season at Blessings starts, my time's going to be fully taken up. I'll probably be making lots of extra cakes too, as well as doing my usual work in the kitchen and garden.'

'It's getting too much for you. I'm that worried about you, you're looking so peaky.'

'But I love being busy, you know I do.' I paused. 'Harry . . . you *wouldn't* stay here just because of me, if you really wanted to go to New Zealand, would you?'

'No, but I don't want to leave my friends either— or what's left of them. And this is the place I've lived in all my life, man and boy, except for the war. And what about poor old Mac here?' He reached down and gave the dog a pat and Mac licked his hand.

'Oh, that's OK then,' I said, relieved and feeling happier. It suddenly occurred to me that it was ages since I'd emailed the MOD and there was still no reply, but if they thought I would quietly go away if they ignored my letters, then they were wrong! But I supposed it *might* have gone astray?

Anyway, when Harry had gone off into the garden again, I emailed them another:

2 December

Dear Clive Wapshott,

On 8 November I sent you an email. We're now into December and so far you have not had the courtesy to acknowledge that you have received it, let alone replied. In case it did not reach you, you will find it below. If you did receive it, but it has been filed in the box marked 'ignore her and she will go away' then I suggest you retrieve it and pass it on to someone who attained their present position through the exercise of their intellect, rather than by any other means and/or has the good manners to reply to their correspondence.

If you would like to telephone me instead, you can reach me on the above number. I am not feeling terribly happy about the efficiency of your department, but of course if the first email didn't reach you, then I may be maligning it . . . slightly.

Yours sincerely,

Josie Gray

The lack of response hadn't improved my temper, but I thought perhaps they would deign to reply to this one. I can't really believe my first email went astray and their lack of response made me even more furious than I was before. How dare they treat Harry, who had served his country so bravely and deserved his medal, in such a shabby way? If they didn't deign to answer this email, then I would phone them up and tell them so!

257

Chapter Twenty

Faithful Friends

At this time of year, having lots of leeks and potatoes, I make batches of vichyssoise and freeze it. You can eat it hot or cold; it just needs a generous swirl of cream in it before serving. French onion soup is another good one for winter, especially after a year like this, when I have strings of onions hanging everywhere. A good soup is economical, filling and, above all, comforting.

'Cakes and Ale'

Although I would have liked to forget Christmas altogether that year, unfortunately that was not really an option. Usually I love it, from carol singing to the last dark, rich cake crumb, and for several years it had followed the same pattern.

Harry and Mac would come round at about two for a Christmas dinner of free-range chicken (not ours) and flaming pudding with brandy butter and white sauce. Then Harry went back to his cottage to fall asleep in front of the TV, until I took him some sandwiches and mince pies later. Ben and I walked off our dinner with Mac, then played Scrabble and Monopoly in front of the roaring woodstove.

This year it would be just the two of us—three if you counted Mac.

I discovered I was dripping tears into the old sweet tin full of Christmas cake decorations, which

258

I was rummaging about in, trying to find some extra fir trees for the Skiing wedding cake. 'You daft bat,' I admonished myself aloud, mopping my eyes. 'Just get on with it.'

So I put the finishing touches to the Skiing cake, which I thought was quite impressive, even if the pair of figures did look as if they were going to launch themselves into space once they reached the bottom of the very steep, tree-edged run.

But then, I suppose that's symbolic of marriage really, so quite appropriate—*and* relationships, since Ben certainly went well and truly off-piste, so it was his own fault if an avalanche of all the things he didn't want, like marriage and fatherhood, crashed down on his head.

Having got the decorations out I thought I might as well carry on and ice all my Christmas cakes. There were several, in different sizes, from tiny to large, since I give them as gifts. Ours was usually huge, since Ben loved Christmas cake, especially accompanied by a good chunk of Lancashire Crumbly cheese, but what would have been ours was now destined as a present for Libby and Tim. I'd told her not to buy one. Harry wouldn't miss out because he always had a small one to himself, decorated with the same little igloo, white-clad Eskimos and slightly out-of-scale polar bear every year.

My four Acorns had fallen into the habit of passing Christmas Day together and pooling their resources, and it was easier for Dorrie to go to the Graces than the other way round. Now that they were spending so much less on food, drink and other necessities, they could afford to turn the heating on and light a roaring wood fire in the

259

sitting room if they felt like it, though I expected Dorrie thriftily turned her heating off whenever she went out. I ordered their large, free-range chicken at the same time as mine—they paid me in Acorns, and I paid the people who supplied them—and I always gave them a Christmas cake and a large plum pudding.

Dorrie took soup as a starter, and brandy and brandy butter for the flaming pudding, plus an old video of Charles Dickens's *A Christmas Carol*, which they watched right after the Queen's speech. Then, after a cold collation of chicken and stuffing sandwiches and sherry trifle, Dorrie went home.

They know how to live it up in Neatslake.

Chopping wood for our stoves and Harry and the Graces' open fires had been one of Ben's chores, and it occurred to me to check how much firewood there was left. This turned out to be very little, though there was a dauntingly enormous supply of large logs in the lean-to store, a whole winter's worth.

If I didn't want everyone (including myself) to freeze, I'd have to do it myself, and sooner rather than later. Resignedly, I fetched the axe and set to. By spring, I would have muscles like Mr Universe.

*   *   *

After a while Harry came through the fence with a big tin mug of hot tea for me.

'I heard you chopping. But you shouldn't be doing that, our Josie—it's too hard for you,' he said, looking worried.

'I really need the exercise, Harry,' I lied, wiping my brow with the edge of my fleece jacket. 'But the tea is wonderful—just what I need.'

I drank it down, then scooped up Aggie, who had followed him through the gate, and handed her to him, together with the empty mug.

'Dratted hen,' he said, and trudged off to see where she had got out this time.

Reluctantly picking up the axe, I was just about to set to again when I heard my mobile, though it took me a couple of minutes to find it, fallen among the logs. Lucky I hadn't chopped it in two, really.

'Hello?' I said, snatching it up. 'Josie Gray, Weird and Wonderful Cakes.'

'*Hello*, Josie Gray, Weird and Wonderful Cakes,' enunciated a voice like Golden Syrup. 'I've run you to earth at last! This is Rob—Rob Rafferty.'

'I—yes, I recognised your voice,' I said faintly, sitting down on a large, upended log, since my knees had gone a bit funny. 'How did you find my number?'

'Remembered that someone told me you made cakes, so I put "Josie Gray cakes" into an internet search engine, and there you were.'

'That's very clever of you. And . . . *do* you want a cake?'

'No, I want *you*,' he said, in that smooth, warm, hard-to-resist voice.

'M-me?' I said nervously.

'Yes, the *Cotton Common* cast are having a Christmas bash in the wine bar in the old Butterflake Biscuit factory over at Middlemoss— do you know it? I thought you might like to come with me.'

I stopped silently opening and shutting my mouth like a landed fish and said, as firmly as I

261

could, 'That's very kind of you, but really I can't. I—'

'You're doing something else tonight?'

Flustered, I blurted, 'Well, no, but—'

'Then you could spare an hour or two, so we can get to know each other better, couldn't you? I've been thinking about you ever since Libby's wedding, Josie,' he added, his voice going a little throaty.

Flattering though his invitation was, my heart was racing with panic as I frantically tried to think of a way out.

'How nice,' I managed, primly. 'But actually, I am terribly busy with cake orders and then later Libby's coming round to discuss business. You know she and Tim are starting up a wedding reception venue at Blessings?'

'No, but you can tell me about it later. After all, it's just for a couple of hours, Josie. The cakes and Libby can wait, can't they? So I'll pick you up about eight?'

He didn't wait for an answer, but rang off. I'm sure the thought that I might really not want to go out with him never even entered his handsome, golden head, because he probably has a mirrorball for a brain, endlessly reflecting his own ultramasculine beauty back at himself.

Quickly I called Libby and told her what had happened.

'Rob Rafferty did *what*? But, Josie, are you mad? He's the playboy of the west Lancashire world. Why on earth did you agree to go?'

'I didn't, I was just too stunned to get out of it before he put the phone down. And there's just something terribly attractive and compelling about his voice. In fact,' I confessed, 'there's something very attractive and compelling about him, so I'm really afraid he might mesmerise me into doing something silly and then I would regret it.'

'I'm sure he would love to show you a good time, if you let him,' she agreed, 'but is that what you want?'

'No, of course not! The Noah thing was a one-off and I certainly am not about to have casual sex with every man who comes my way, however gorgeous they are. I just never had the opportunity to learn how to say no, that's all.'

'Then you'd better learn fast because I don't think you can get out of going to the wine bar with him now,' Libby said thoughtfully.

'I did tell him I had a business meeting with you tonight, Libs, but he said you could wait.'

'Oh, *did* he? Then I'll phone you about nine thirty and say some crisis has blown up and you have to come home. You'll need to be terribly firm and tell him you have to put the business and your friendship with me first, and then jump into a taxi. But I'll be waiting for you here, in case he drives you back himself.'

'Thanks, Libs,' I said gratefully.

'And if he asks you out again, you'll just have to say that you've put your social life on hold, because of your own cake business and helping me to get Old Barn Receptions off the ground,' she suggested. 'He'll get bored with you eventually and go and find someone else to play with.'

'Yes, and if he hadn't caught me on the hop and steamrolled me into going, I'd probably have managed to put him off in the first place.' I sighed. 'I could do without this complication.'

263

'Lots of women wouldn't think being invited out by Rob Rafferty a complication,' she pointed out.

I grinned. 'I suppose not. I mean me, Josie Gray, and Rob Rafferty!' Then I had a thought. 'What on earth shall I wear tonight?'

'A chastity belt?' she suggested.

* * *

My new jeans, being quite tight, were as close to that as I could get, and I teamed them with a burgundy and gold Indian cotton top Stella had given me.

Rob picked me up in something long, low and red—don't ask me what, I'm not good at recognising sports cars—and although I felt really shy and nervous he talked enough on the way for both of us. Just as well, since I was silently recovering from his greeting kiss, which had involved an alarming amount of body contact. 'Thorough' was the word that sprang to mind; I felt as if I'd been rotovated.

The bar was very full and rather dark and I was pleased to see that most other people there were fairly casually dressed too. I've never watched *Cotton Common*, but I still managed to recognise several of the actors from it and, even if I hadn't, Rob introduced me around and told them all I made wonderful wedding cakes.

There were some TV production people there too, and a young, attractive, dark-haired woman called Claire Flowers immediately said, '*Josie Gray?* What, the Josie Gray who writes for *Skint Old Northern Woman* magazine as Country Mouse?'

I nearly dropped my glass. 'Yes, but . . . how do you know?'

'I saw that article in *Country at Heart* magazine.'

'Oh . . . yes, that did blow my cover once people had twigged.'

'That's the internet for you. A couple of people make the connection, and it spreads like wildfire.'

Rob, who had been standing looking puzzled, said, '*Skint Old Northern Woman*?'

'It's a cult women's magazine. It went online at the start of the year and the circulation's gone massive. Just everyone gets it. Josie writes this brilliant column called "Cakes and Ale", all about her struggles to be self-sufficient. Urbanites love it because it makes them think of a lifestyle they would love to be living.' She looked me up and down. 'But I really didn't expect you to be tall and . . . well, *pretty*, if you don't mind my saying so. I really thought you'd be a quiet, plain little country mouse, like your pseudonym.'

'Well, I'm tall, but apart from that I *am* the complete country mouse bit,' I said, embarrassed.

She started to ask me about my lifestyle and I found myself telling her all about how we'd tried to be self-sufficient for years, but the twenty-first century kept intruding, and the cake-making business and all the rest of it. I even mentioned Uncle Harry next door and how the Artist had gone off to live in London.

'That's a pity,' she said thoughtfully. 'I liked the bits about him. It sounded so idyllic, the two of you, a bit like *The Good Life*.'

'My best friend has moved back to the village, though, which is good,' I said. 'Did you read about that in "Cakes and Ale"?'

'Yes, and that would make an interesting angle . . .' she mused, seemingly deep in thought.

'For the articles, do you mean?' I asked, puzzled. Rob, bored, had gone off to get another drink and not come back, and the noise level in the bar was rising, though most of the voices were enunciating with right-to-the-back-of-the-hall clarity. It made it a bit deafening.

Claire looked at me with bright-eyed enthusiasm. 'No, what I'm actually thinking is that you and your life in Sticklepond would make a really great TV series. Sort of self-sufficiency with a twist!'

'I live in Neatslake actually. It's a couple of miles from Sticklepond and it's very quiet, so I don't think it would make terribly exciting viewing.'

'*Seasons in Sticklepond*, starting with *Sticklepond Spring*,' she said dreamily. 'That could be the first series of, say, six episodes of half an hour each. And if that takes off—which I'm sure it would—*Sticklepond Summer, Autumn, Sticklepond Christmas* . . .' Her cheeks had gone quite rosy with excitement. 'You know, it's just what the current market needs! Everyone wants to know about growing vegetables and fruit, and making things and saving money, but without giving up *all* the comforts of the twenty-first century.'

'Do you think so?' I said doubtfully. 'Wouldn't it be terribly intrusive, though, and people would come and descend on me? I've already tried to keep the more personal angle out of my columns since the *Country at Heart* article.'

'I don't think Hugh Fearnley-Whittingstall has much problem with visitors,' she said. 'And, of course, they'll think you live right in Sticklepond, won't they? So they'll go there, if anywhere.'

'Yes, I suppose there is that,' I agreed. 'And now they've found that Shakespeare document at Winter's End, they must be used to masses of visitors to the village, so a few more wouldn't make much difference. There's already a new teashop and craft gallery.'

'I really think this could work, Josie,' Claire assured me earnestly. 'It will have everything— gardening, cooking and preserving, wedding cakes, a cute hen . . .'

'You mean Aggie?'

'Yes, she's obvious star material. And then your friend's wedding reception business—showing you involved in that would add an interesting twist.'

'I'm sure Libby would like the publicity,' I agreed.

'It's just a pity about the love interest.' Then a thought struck her. 'Unless you and Rob . . . ?'

'Gosh, no!' I said hastily. 'This is just a quick drink. I'm right off men, really.'

'Yes, I suppose you would be, with your childhood sweetheart leaving you like that.'

'I really don't want to talk about that angle on the TV.'

'OK . . . I suppose we can manage without. *You* will be the star—your life and struggles to balance economical green living against surviving in the twenty-first century.'

'And Aggie in a supporting role. My uncle Harry's dog is very photogenic too,' I offered.

'So are you,' she said, looking at me again and smiling, so I thought it was probably too dark in there for her to see that I wasn't really.

We must have been discussing it for ages because Rob was both narked and a bit drunk when he

267

came back. And by the time he managed to get a word in, Libby called me as prearranged and I had to tell him I needed to go. 'But you don't have to bother driving me back. I'll ring for a taxi.'

'No, if you must go, I'll take you,' he insisted, to my alarm.

'You've had a couple of drinks, Rob,' Claire said forthrightly, 'and you don't want to lose your licence again, do you? I'll run Josie home so we can talk some more. I'm thinking of featuring her in a TV series.'

Rob looked even more miffed, so I suspected he had been planning a detour, maybe to his home. But he did suggest we have a night out together soon, and when I told him that I couldn't because I needed to concentrate on mine and Libby's businesses, I could see my goose was cooked.

Claire came in to meet Libby when we got back, and loved the interior of the cottage, though of course it was too dark for her to see the garden. I was still a bit doubtful about the idea, not to mention the invasion of what privacy I had left, but Libby was all for it, especially if Old Barn Receptions was going to get the occasional mention.

'I'll pitch it now and then we could start shooting in the early spring,' Claire said. 'I think this could be *massive*, with book deals and all kinds of spin-offs . . .'

'Don't you think it would be more like that *Island Parish* series, on the Scilly Isles, where nothing much happens but it's all very slow-paced and addictive,' Libby suggested.

'Well, that has a cult following too,' Claire said. 'This could be very lucrative for you, Josie, so you will do it, won't you?'

'I suppose so—but I don't know what I would do with more money.'

'Invest it for security,' suggested Libby. 'Employ someone to come in and do heavy jobs for you from time to time? Trips to London because you are a media star? You'll find a use for it. Anyway, you haven't got it yet. Don't count your chickens before they're hatched.'

We worked out some kind of story line and then Claire said she would go straight home now and do a treatment . . . or maybe she said she would *give* it the treatment—I don't know. But she was still bubbling with enthusiasm. I felt quite exhausted.

When she'd gone Libby and I opened a bottle of elderflower champagne and toasted *Sticklepond Seasons* and all who sailed in her. I was sort of excited but very apprehensive. I think total anonymity suited me better, really.

But then Libby pointed out that I really enjoyed sharing all my knowledge about living well on very little, and this way I would be reaching audiences, and helping people way beyond the readership of *Skint Old Northern Woman* and *Country at Heart*, which made me feel a lot better.

But on reflection, maybe that was the elderflower champagne?

*   *   *

By next day I had convinced myself that Claire wouldn't sell the idea of the TV series, so I needn't worry about it. I mean, my life isn't that exciting, is it?

'No, but a series like that is just what the current

269

economic climate needs,' Libby said when I shared this hope with her. 'The way you live on very little is quite aspirational, and they will think if you can do it, anyone can.'

'Well, they're right, they can do it if they put their minds to it.'

'I don't suppose most of them will, they'll just enjoy the idea of it. Now,' she added, 'can we get back to the matter in hand?'

We were standing by the loose boxes next to the Old Barn, an area destined to become rather swish loos. Libby was holding various sanitaryware brochures having, with typical thoroughness, immediately become an expert on the matter.

I was finding it hard to whip up much enthusiasm for Victoriana versus ultramodern, but I nodded at appropriate moments—or even inappropriate ones, like when she mentioned black granite basins. And then, when I could get a word in edgeways, I said, 'I really don't think the toilets are that important, Libs. You don't need to spend huge amounts of money on them, and if you go for classic, durable white porcelain then you can tart the cloakrooms up in any style you like.'

'I suppose you're right,' she conceded. 'I was getting a bit carried away and it's already all costing a lot more than I thought it would. And there are so many rules and regulations to comply with that you would think the government didn't want people to start up new businesses at all! Still, Tim thinks we'll get permission for it, so long as none of the neighbours objects. I don't see why they should, do you? We aren't going to hold evening receptions. I want everything over and cleared away by late afternoon!'

'I'm your nearest neighbour and I won't be objecting. But some people do like to have an evening party too, or their wedding might be quite late in the day.'

'Then they can have it somewhere else,' she said firmly. 'We're going to be terribly exclusive and expensive and do things on our terms. They can take it or leave it—but I'm sure they'll queue up to take it.'

'I expect you're right. It's astounding how much money people are willing to shell out for a wedding, especially these days, when half of them don't last much longer than it takes for the confetti to hit the ground,' I said cynically.

But neither that, nor Ben's defection, had prevented me from carrying on with my habit of hanging out near the church with the Grace sisters, whenever the bride and groom were about to emerge: we're still suckers for sentiment.

'Come on,' Libby said, 'I'm freezing. Let's go in and have some coffee to warm up.'

On the way to the house we came across Dorrie, heeling in new rose bushes, her faded blue beret over one eye.

'They look like a bundle of dead twigs right now, don't they?' I said, as we paused.

'Yes, but come spring they'll be fine. It's late in the year to put them in, but it's mild enough at the moment.'

'It doesn't feel mild to me! We're going to go and warm up with a cup of coffee, Dorrie, are you coming in?' invited Libby, but Dorrie said no, she'd rather carry on.

'You never know what the weather will do next at this time of year. Better to get them all in now.'

'I'll get Gina to put some in a flask, then, and bring it down,' Libby promised.

Gina brought us a plate of those crunchy Italian amaretti biscuits with ours—she spoils Libby—and then said to me, 'Your uncle Harry, he says he loves the minestrone and I say he never taste the real thing so I make it now, and take him some later.'

'Gina seems to be settling in,' Libby said when she'd gone back to the kitchen. 'Pansy Grace has invited her to join the Neatslake WI and the Folk Society, though I'm not sure she's quite grasped what either of them is about. Her niece is coming over for Christmas with her husband and baby, so she's looking forward to that and showing her flat off. What are you doing for Christmas this year, Josie? I mean, it's going to be a bit . . . different, isn't it? Do you want to come to us for dinner?'

'That's really kind, Libby, but I think I'll just keep it low-key and have Harry over as usual—chill out.'

'Well, come here for tea in the afternoon then, at least?' she suggested. 'Or on Boxing Day. I must pop down to London and do some present shopping soon. Time is rushing by.'

'Tell me about it! At least I seem to have run out of wedding cake orders for the moment but I usually make most of my presents, so I'd better get on with it.'

'Is Russell still phoning you up late at night?'

'Yes, though I don't always answer the phone now. I *think* he's just being kind, but I really don't feel I want to know how tired and grumpy Mary is getting, or that Olivia's still looking slim and

272

elegant, apart from the bump, which he let slip the other night. Tact is not his middle name.'

'No, too much information—and presumably she was with Ben when he saw her.'

'Yes, I assume he's still living with her but, knowing Ben, that's probably from sheer inertia because he couldn't be bothered trying to find somewhere else.'

'When's Mary's baby due?'

'About the end of April, I think—and Olivia's a couple of weeks after.'

'I hope she has twins and her stomach has more folds than a concertina afterwards,' Libby said vindictively. 'Can't you tell Russell to stop calling you?'

'Not really, and I hope Mary will start talking to me again once the baby's here, instead. We'll never be on the same terms ever again, but our friendship does go way back.'

'I think she's already chosen sides, Josie. Olivia putting her on to that herbalist was probably the clincher.'

'Yes, perhaps you're right. That's the point when she should have come clean to me about what was going on, if she was ever going to. I still feel guilty about destroying my pills and potion. They probably cost you a lot.'

'Well, don't feel guilty, it doesn't matter. And if you find someone else and want to try again, I'll buy you some more!'

'That's not going to happen, Libs—and since it's obviously me that's barren, it probably wouldn't work anyway.'

'Oh, I know lots of women who didn't conceive with one partner, but did almost instantly with

273

another,' she assured me, though she had forgotten that it certainly hadn't happened after my one illicit night of peapod-induced sin with Noah. It made me remember something I wanted to ask her, though.

'Libby,' I said casually, 'could you give me Daisy's number? It was nice seeing her again and I said I'd give her a ring.'

'OK,' she said, looking slightly surprised, because Daisy is quite a bit older than we are and I hadn't really ever had much to do with her.

But she jotted it down on a bit of paper and I said, more to distract her than anything, 'Ben still phones me too, without the least encouragement. He seems to feel the need to talk through ideas for his work and tell me about his successes.'

It was just as though Nemesis, in the form of an increasingly expanding forty-two-year-old blonde, had never come between us.

'He wants me to tell him everything going on in Neatslake too, as though he's missing instalments of a soap.'

She eyed me narrowly. 'You're not thinking of taking him back, are you?'

'No, of course not. I'm managing perfectly well on my own, though he seems to think he'll persuade me to eventually, no matter what I say. I get quite snappy with him and then he goes all hurt and puts the phone down, though a few hours later, there he is again, as if nothing had happened.'

'That's men for you,' she said largely, though all hers had turned out to be peaches, while mine was like a stored apple that looked fine on top, but was sweetly rotted underneath.

The Ski cake was duly delivered in Harry's old car, which is not quite as convenient as the van, but does well enough if I wedge tall wedding cakes in the front passenger footwell with giant bubble wrap. But I spoke too soon about not having any more wedding cake orders.

Frederica Willis, whom I knew slightly, came to see me. She was a fifty-year-old spinster who kept the Ponderosa Dog-breeding Kennels just outside Sticklepond, and she was going to celebrate her nuptials with a retired, widowed colonel just before Christmas, in a small church ceremony.

She was in a rosy glow of love, and I suddenly thought what a perfect subject she would make for Noah's photographs—especially when she said she bred cavalier King Charles spaniels and her kennel maids, holding her brood bitches on ribbon leashes, would form a guard of honour outside the church.

In fact, she had brought a lovely ruby bitch called Dodo with her, a colour I hadn't seen before. They are the sweetest little dogs and, except that Mac would probably eat it, I would love to have one myself!

The colonel, who sounds besotted, had told her she could arrange things entirely the way she wanted them, and had apparently taken the news of the nuptial reception committee with equanimity. I only wished he worked in the medals department of the MOD; he sounded terribly sensible and nice.

The cake was to be a simple, stacked two-tier

one—that is, the smaller one placed directly onto the lower, without columns. The edges of both the top and bottom tiers were to be decorated with a line of outwards-facing seated cavalier spaniels, like canine caryatids, plus the words, 'FAITHFUL COMPANIONSHIP AND LOVING HEARTS'; and on top, instead of the bride and groom, would be a larger pair of spaniels.

I liked Frederica very much—or Freddie, as she asked me to call her—so I said I would do the cake despite the rush, and for a fraction of my usual price, though she wasn't aware of that. Actually, I'd taken some icing sugar paste round to Violet straight away, together with some pictures of cavaliers that I got off the internet, and she was going to make all the little caryatid ones.

The happy but dogged couple I would do myself. A hint of veiling on one, and a military cap on the other, perhaps.

* * *

In the few days since I'd met Claire Flowers she had been bombarding me with excited and enthusiastic emails, most of which didn't seem to require an answer, luckily.

There was also finally a reply from the MOD! Not that it did anything more than patronise and annoy me, which is pretty much what I expected. It went as follows:

14 December
Dear Ms Gray,
    Your email to Clive Wapshott has been passed to me. I am the person in charge of the

276

MOD Medal Office. I note all that you have said and in particular that you are not satisfied with the assessment of medal entitlement carried out on behalf of your uncle. However, your first email was not a question, and so consequently was not acted upon.

My job is to uphold the integrity of the United Kingdom medal system, and I am sorry to say it, but there are those who do not qualify for a medal for the want of a single day, let alone seven days. The rules governing the awarding of WW2 medals were written by those who had first-hand knowledge at the time. They were then approved by HM the King in 1948. It is against these rules that medal entitlement is assessed. There is no doubting your uncle played his part in the war effort.

Please be assured that each application for a medal is treated with due diligence. May I suggest that if you would like to appeal against the assessment provided by Clive Wapshott, you write to me at the address below.

Yours sincerely,
Ronald Horeshay
Lt.-Col. (Retd)

Patronising git! I thought, on first reading this pompous little missive, though when I showed it to Harry he seemed unsurprised—even amused.

'Typical of the Forces top brass, that is! You'll not get anywhere with them, but I'm going to see if I can get the medal second-hand. Then I'll weigh it, and file off the bit of it I'm not entitled to—seven days' worth!'

'No, don't do that, Harry. Let me get you one for Christmas instead,' I suggested. 'I bet I can find one on the internet.'

'Well, all right, so long as it's not too dear.'

'Oh, I'm rolling in filthy lucre these days—all these cake orders. And I'll probably have so much money I won't know what to do with it, if that TV series comes off,' I reminded him, having told him all about it earlier, and he chuckled. He doesn't think anyone would be interested in watching film of me digging the garden and making parsnip wine either!

I gave him a printout of the latest letter to show his cronies, together with a copy of my reply to the MOD, which I had dashed off immediately, in a froth of rage.

14 December

Dear Ronald Horeshay,

Having been brought up with a modicum of good manners, I tend to reply to all my correspondence whether I have been asked a question or not. This was obviously an important issue on which I felt—and still feel—strongly, and which clearly merited an answer.

However, your reply is just the sort of idiotically jobsworthy one I was expecting. If the rules are so set in stone that someone who lacks even one single day's service does not qualify, then clearly there is something wrong with the rules. 1948 is rather a long time ago and I don't particularly care whether the then king approved them or not. The rules have become a moronic, moribund dinosaur and the sooner they are extinct the better. Where does common sense, compassion and intelligence impinge upon the 'diligent' scrutiny of medal applications?

What really upsets me is that clearly you have been sending out this sort of slap-in-the-face letter to many war veterans who, elderly and perhaps in poor health, have found their thoughts increasingly turning to the war years, to friends lost and all the old horrors. They will be wondering whether sacrificing so much was worth it, and there you are, telling them clearly it was not: they were weighed and found wanting. I expect many just turned their face to the wall at this point. Did you ever think of this as you sent out your brusque little dismissals?

And, as a taxpayer, I am colluding in this betrayal by helping to pay your wages. I don't like that one bit.

My uncle, having a sense of humour, has framed your first letter of rejection in a nice gilt frame and given it pride of place on the wall. He is considering buying a second-hand medal and, having worked out exactly how much of it he is not entitled to, snipping the requisite bit of metal off and hanging that on the wall too. If that is a treasonable act and you want to shoot him, you had better move fast—he is 82 and has severe health problems. In fact, since I will probably give him the medal for Christmas, you might have to shoot us both.

Your department has the facts already, but clearly your answer is already set in mud the consistency of concrete. To what would I appeal? Compassion? Justice? Good sense? Do they exist anywhere in the MOD? It

279

certainly does not sound like it. The exercise would be pointless.

Never mind, I expect you were afraid that if you had quietly slipped my uncle his so obviously undeserved medal, you would have been crushed in a stampede of Ancient Mariners . . . if there are many left who would qualify. Not to mention all the other elderly ex-servicemen.

At least you had the grace to reply, even if you only trotted out a few lame phrases. You will observe that there are several questions in the above letter but I absolve you from any need to engage your brain further on the matter: let us draw a line for the moment underneath your whole sorry excuse for a department.

Yours sincerely,
Josie Gray

Even if I hadn't actually expected to get Harry's medal out of them, it was still a free country and I was entitled to express my opinion, and I had, forcefully. I hoped my emails at least rattled their cage a bit, though I doubted they would puncture their complacency.

The whole correspondence had at least amused Harry, his friends and most of the village, though, so that was a positive outcome.

Chapter Twenty-one

Visiting Rights

Most of the Christmas presents I give are edible, from cakes to sweets and biscuits. Home-made petits fours, *fudge and peppermint creams are always popular, though if you are going to post them, the weight can be an issue!*

I always ask the recipients of the Christmas cakes to keep the decorations, so they can be reused the following year. Some that belonged to my grandmother are practically antiques . . .

'Cakes and Ale'

I misjudged Rob Rafferty's sticking power, because he turned up on my doorstep just as I was taking some cheese scones out of the oven and I was too flustered not to let him in.

But anyway, after he had eaten three scones liberally coated with melting butter, licking his fingers afterwards like a schoolboy, and got round to asking me to go out with him again, I'd made up my mind to be frank with him.

'To be honest, Rob, apart from being really busy with my wedding cake business and helping Libby to set up Old Barn Receptions, I've only just broken up with my long-term partner and I'm not ready for any kind of relationship yet.'

'I'm sorry, I didn't know that,' he said with easy sympathy. 'But still, there's no reason why we shouldn't be friends, is there?'

'*Just* friends?' I asked cautiously, opening the

nearest cake tin and offering him a slice of Battenburg cake, since he was still hungrily eyeing the remaining scones and I didn't want to have to make a whole new batch.

'If that's what you want,' he agreed through a mouthful of cake. 'Or what you want right now, anyway. Who knows, maybe you'll change your mind later. But meanwhile, there's nothing to stop us going out for the occasional meal or drink, when you have time, is there? And now I know you can bake like this, you'll probably find me on your doorstep more often than you want!'

I was so relieved I told him he could drop in whenever he felt like it, and actually I did enjoy his company once I'd relaxed my guard.

Libby said I was mad and it was like thinking I could be friends with a lion, but I'm positive she's wrong—it's my baking he's now lusting after.

*   *   *

My phone line has suddenly gone all crackly, despite BT saying there is nothing wrong with it.

Could the MOD now be tapping my calls, because they have me down as some kind of subversive?

But if Big Brother is watching me, he isn't going to find me terribly exciting, unless you count surfing the internet, looking for a minesweeping medal. And luckily, I found one, though it cost me a lot more than I would tell Harry it did!

*   *   *

Libby went to London to do her present shopping
282

the week before Christmas and came back with Pia, which I knew because I happened to be outside when they were arriving, and Pia waved.

I'd been chasing Aggie round the Green again, with Violet on her trike trying to head her off on the other side. It was amazing how fast a hen could run when she put her mind to it, even a fat one. One minute she was ambling along aimlessly, and the next she was haring off like an Olympic sprinter.

But she was too plump to keep that pace up for long, so with a bit of help from Violet I finally caught her and went to try to find how she'd got out of the run this time. I was starting to think she could materialise on the wrong side of the netting any time she liked, which is a trick I hope the local fox doesn't learn.

A bit later Pia popped over to see me and said she thought she might stay at Blessings for all of Christmas and New Year.

This would be providing she didn't fall out with Libby, of course—and they did seem to have been getting along together much better lately. Also, it sounded as though Pia intended spending all of her time over at Middlemoss with Jasper Pharamond. They'd been engaged in a long-distance courtship of texts and emails since they met, so she must have made quite an impression on him at the reception once she'd grasped that the way to get his attention was through our ancestors' stomach contents.

I carried on working while she told me all about it with all the self-absorption of a teenager in love, and it was some time before she showed any interest in what I was making.

'What are those?' she asked finally.

'Marzipan fruit and nut *petits fours*,' I said, stuffing a pecan into an oval of natural marzipan and then placing it in a recycled paper case (I mean that the cases are made of recycled paper, not that they have been used before. I draw the line there!). 'I give them as Christmas gifts every year and sometimes I do fudge, rum truffles, or coconut ice too—all kinds of goodies. But because this year I've had a couple of rush wedding cake orders, I'm making only these.'

Pia ate a bit of marzipan. 'I don't think you've ever given me any, though there's usually a sugar mouse and a chocolate watch in my parcel.'

'You can have some this year if you like, and I suspect Father Christmas will still give you the mouse and chocolate watch, even if you'll be nineteen by then,' I assured her, and in fact, I'd already made the mouse and several watches, using my brown Bakelite mould.

'I've always loved getting your presents, God-ma. I never know quite what to expect!'

'I just collect bits and pieces I think you might like all through the year, so there's usually a box full that I can divide up for your birthday and Christmas, in the hope there'll be at least one or two things that you'll really like.'

'Oh, I've loved everything you've sent me, however weird,' she assured me. I racked my brains, trying to think of anything particularly odd I'd sent her . . . Maybe it had been that dried scorpion trick, when she was eight?

'This year it's a bit different. You've got just one main birthday present,' I said. Pia had so admired my rainbow knitted hoodie last time she was here that I'd got Pansy Grace to knit her one too. And she was getting the matching mittens, long scarf and Peruvian-style hat with earflaps for Christmas.

The kind of present *I* prefer is one that's been made just for me, lovingly, even if it's a peg bag or one of Pansy's stranger knitted toilet roll cosies, so I hoped Pia would feel the same way.

'Mum told me there might be a TV series about you doing gardening and stuff,' she said. 'Cool!'

'Oh, I don't think it will actually come to anything. I'm not that exciting.'

'*And* she said Rob Rafferty tracked you down and you went to a party with him!'

'Just drinks in a wine bar. I didn't want to, really, but he wouldn't take no for an answer. Anyway, Claire Flowers, the woman who's keen on doing the TV series, monopolised me and then drove me home after an hour or so. But Rob's dropped in to see me since then, and after I told him about breaking up with Ben, he suggested we became just friends.'

She stared at me. 'Well, be careful, God-ma!'

'It's all right, he's only after my pastries.'

'A likely story,' she said, as disbelievingly as Libby, while making inroads on the pistachio nuts. 'Did Mum tell you Noah's coming to Blessings for Christmas?'

'Noah? Noah *Sephton*?' My hands stilled, I stared blankly at her.

'Of course—how many other Noahs have you ever met? She saw him in London and invited him. I don't think he usually does much at Christmas. I don't mind, to be honest, because I'll feel a bit of a gooseberry up at Blessings with the two lovebirds.'

'You don't sound as if you intend to actually be

there very much,' I pointed out.

'No, well,' she blushed. 'I hope not, if things go OK with me and Jasper. I think he's pretty convinced now that I'm not the empty-headed party girl he first thought me. He didn't know I could cook, for a start, even if it's only Italian cooking that Gina taught me.'

'There's more to you than meets the eye,' I agreed solemnly, but inwardly I was digesting the news about Noah. I found I really, really didn't want to see him ever again . . . Why on earth had Libby invited him?

'When is Noah turning up?' I asked casually, stuffing an almond into a date, and then encasing the date in marzipan. I'd have done more pistachio ones, but Pia had now finished them off. I pushed the hazelnuts nearer to her—at least they were cheaper, if she wanted to binge on something. 'And, I mean, is he coming alone? Didn't you tell me he was going out with someone?'

'Oh, Uncle Noah's always going out with somebody, but they never last long. Though, actually, come to think of it, I did see a magazine picture recently of him with that Anji, so she's still around. But he's definitely coming on his own and arriving on Saturday, my birthday—though I'll probably be out, because I'm hoping Jasper will take me somewhere. He's coming here tonight too, and then we're going to the Griffin,' she added dreamily.

I gave her the parcel containing her rainbow cardigan before she left, telling her not to open it before her birthday, but it wouldn't have surprised me in the least to hear she'd been seen wearing it ten minutes after she got back to Blessings.

* * *

Next morning I phoned Libby up to ask her why she had invited Noah.

'He usually just goes to stay with a cousin and his family in Cornwall, but they couldn't have him for some reason this year, so he was at a loose end,' she said. 'I couldn't let him spend Christmas on his own, could I?'

'He doesn't seem the sort of man who'd have to spend *any* time alone, unless he wanted to,' I pointed out. 'Pia said she thought he was still going out with that model, the blonde one who was with him the first time he turned up here.'

'I don't know, but he certainly wasn't expecting to spend Christmas with her.'

'Just as well,' I said, relieved. 'I would feel terribly guilty if I met her. It's going to be awkward enough if I run into Noah. I'll have to try and stay out of his way.'

'I think it would be better to do the opposite—get the meeting over with and carry on as though nothing had happened.'

'Libs, it will be hideously embarrassing! Especially since *I* know that *you* know.' A thought struck me. 'But does *he* know that you know?'

'I think I'm losing the plot,' Libby said. 'I was going to tear him off a strip, but since you seemed perked up by the experience, I decided not to. So no, he doesn't know that I know—I don't think.'

I sighed. 'Perhaps you're right. He's a friend of yours, so I'm bound to see him occasionally and I'll just get it over and show him that I've forgotten all about getting peapodded with him. He'll probably be relieved I don't want to hang around his neck or make trouble with this Anji.'

'His girlfriends are never serious; that's why I warned you about him,' Libby said. 'You were honoured if Pia came to visit you. I've hardly seen her since I brought her back. Jasper came and picked her up yesterday and she didn't come home until late—though I suppose I should feel grateful that she came home at all. And this morning, when she finally showed up for breakfast, she said she was going to apply to study at Liverpool University, where Jasper is.'

'Study what?'

'She didn't say. Art history, perhaps?' she suggested doubtfully. 'Don't they all study something like that, if they don't really know what to do? In our day, it was teaching or librarianship. But whatever it is, I suspect it's only a ruse to stay near Jasper.'

'But he must be more than halfway through his degree and she will just be starting, so isn't it a doomed manoeuvre?'

'No, he plans to do his masters there afterwards. She's borrowed my car now and gone over to Middlemoss. Goodness knows when I'll get it back.'

But she didn't sound quite as frazzled as usual when Pia is about, so mother/daughter relations did seem to be improving. Maybe love had mellowed Libs a bit.

'Did you ever phone Daisy?' she asked casually now.

'*Daisy?*'

'My sister—remember, you asked me for her number?'

'Oh, yes, but then I forgot! I'll do it after Christmas. I expect she's busy.'

'Yes, there's always so much booze around at Christmas that she has her hands full with Mum,' Libby agreed.

*   *   *

Ben's poisonous mother rang and accused me of trying to 'entice Ben back again'. She said if I hadn't been pathetic and needy, so that he felt guilty about me, he would have fixed a date for the wedding with Olivia by now.

The only time I was ever pathetic and needy was just after Granny died, so it seems that he has been telling the same lies about me to his mother that he told to Olivia.

You know, I think jealousy of my mother, combined with acute ingrowing snobbery and bile, has completely unhinged Nell Richards over the years, and she's entirely lost her grip on reality.

'Just leave him alone,' she finished, after a stream of invective. 'You were never good enough for him!'

'I'm not trying to entice him back, and I don't think it's particularly me he's missing, Mrs Richards,' I said patiently. 'He seems to find it difficult to create new work away from Neatslake. And *he* has been phoning *me*. I haven't called him once.'

'That isn't what he told me,' she snapped, and put down the phone.

Perhaps Ben was trying to use me to get out of having to marry Olivia, which he clearly didn't want to do. Who knew? And did I care?

The conversation left such a nasty taste in my mouth that I had to resort to damson wine to dispel it.

* * *

Violet had performed miracles by producing what seemed like hundreds of little icing cavalier spaniels within a few days, and I painted them in the various cavvy colours with natural food dye and stuck them all around Freddie's cake.

The bridal pair for the top had come out magnificently, I thought. I'd given the groom spaniel a top hat, which sat jauntily over his long ears, and the bride a little tiara with a touch of net veiling (which I hoped no one would attempt to eat) and a bouquet of tiny flowers.

Well, I delivered that on the Friday before Christmas and Freddie loved it so much that she invited me to the wedding on Christmas Eve and the reception party at the Ponderosa Kennels afterwards (in the living room, not the actual dog runs).

After that I loaded up and delivered the Christmas cakes to the Graces, Dorrie and Libby (I had already given Harry his little one), and then drove out to give Mark and Stella theirs, as usual. They'd been a bit strange since Ben moved out, considering we'd been friends for such a long time, but perhaps they didn't know quite how to talk to me any more. Or perhaps, like Mary, they'd decided they could give allegiance only to one side, and it wasn't mine.

* * *

I was spot-on with that suspicion, because when I walked into their kitchen, it was to find Ben sitting there with Stella, which stunned me practically witless. My very own Spirit of Christmas Past, come to rattle his chains.

'What on earth are *you* doing here?' I gasped, clutching the cake to my bosom.

He got up, looking pale and strangely unfamiliar, like someone you knew very well a long, long time ago. 'Just visiting. Actually, I stayed here once before on my way to Liverpool, but this time I came hoping to see you—and here you are!' He took a long stride towards me. 'God, I've missed you, darling!'

Seeing he was about to take me in his arms I backed away, holding the cake between us. 'Don't!' I said sharply, and he stopped dead. My hands were shaking and the cakeboard must have tilted, because a snowman dropped off onto the quarry-tiled floor, and Stella stepped in and removed it from my grasp, before anything else did.

'Oh, a cake—how wonderful! But you shouldn't have!' she exclaimed, as if I hadn't been bringing one every year for at least the last ten years.

'Yes, happy Christmas in advance,' I said automatically, while Ben—the big, tousled, amiable, trustworthy-looking Ben that I used to adore—was standing off with an expression like a puppy who knew he had done wrong, but was sure he would be forgiven if he looked winsome enough. And he did look very, very appealing . . .

'I thought you might be pleased to see me by now, Josie!' His hazel eyes, soft and pleading, held mine and I felt my resistance weakening a bit—

291

and my knees. Part of me wanted to put back the clock and be enclosed in those warm, loving arms again . . .

He must have seen my face soften, for he came closer and tenderly embraced me, pulling me close. 'We belong together, Josie! I've been such a fool, but I'll make it all up to you, I promise. You need me. Just let me come home with you and life will be just the same as it always was—'

The spell was suddenly shattered and I pulled away, furious with him—and with myself for weakening even for a moment. 'I don't need you. I've been managing perfectly well on my own,' I snapped. 'And what do you mean, life can be the same as it was? How can it ever possibly be the same as it was? You can't just slot back into my life like a missing bit of jigsaw, you know. And, anyway, you belong in another one now. You don't fit here.'

Mark, who had come into the kitchen in time to hear this, looked reproachful. 'Ben just really, really wanted to say he was sorry face to face, Josie. He feels so terrible about betraying your trust, especially now he realises it was you he loved all along.'

'Yes, he really *needs* you, Josie!' urged Stella. 'And he does fit here. It's where he *has* to be.'

Ben ran his fingers through his hair in a gesture that used to make me go weak at the knees. It didn't have quite the same effect now that it was cut into a shorter, spikier, fashionable style.

'Without you, Neatslake and my studio, all the things here that I love, I just can't seem to work any more. I was OK when I could recharge my batteries at home and then go back to London, but

292

now I feel—trapped. Dead. Like a fly in amber,' he added, with surprising imagination for him.

'I can see Olivia in the sticky amber role, so I know where you're coming from there,' I said drily, 'but you flew into it with your eyes open.'

'Look, Josie, I've talked it all through with Stella and Mark—they've been great! I can see I was stupid to give in to an infatuation and not realise I risked losing everything I most valued. But I've come to my senses now and I understand how much I've hurt you. So I want you to know that if you take me back, I'll never give you a moment's worry ever again. I'll make it all up to you, darling!'

All three of them looked expectantly at me, but I didn't seem to know my lines. Had I inadvertently stepped into an insane episode of *The Archers*, a story of seriously deluded countryfolk?

I heard myself say, not without regret and sadness, 'It's too late, Ben. Way, way too late.'

'No, don't say that. Of course it isn't too late,' he said. 'I can tell you've been missing me—you look thin and pale. You need me just as much as I need you.'

'And you have to think what this means to Ben's *work* too,' put in Mark.

Now that did make me feel a bit guilty, but that was mainly over the ongoing rotting crustacean thing.

'Perhaps we should go and leave you alone for a bit,' suggested Stella with a meaningful look at Mark, 'to *discuss* things.'

'There's nothing to discuss, because Ben's living with another woman and she's pregnant with his child. That's where his responsibilities lie now and he can't just throw up his hands and walk away. In fact, his mother just rang me and said he would have married Olivia if he hadn't felt so sorry for me. She wanted me to leave you alone, Ben—though actually I haven't contacted you at all since you left, have I? It's all been the other way round.'

'If I married anyone, it would be you! We still *could* marry. What do you think? Shall we tie the knot and to hell with everyone else?' he demanded. 'My parents can stick their allowance and their approval where the sun doesn't shine. Being here in Neatslake with you is all that matters to me now.'

I had so longed for Ben to ask me to marry him, especially when Granny was alive, but this hardly ranked as the proposal of my dreams . . . And then the meaning of what he had said percolated through and I said slowly, 'You mean . . . can you *possibly* mean that you never married me simply because your parents would have cut off your allowance, Ben Richards? That it wasn't because you didn't believe in marriage, or all the other things you used to say about not needing to prove our love by signing up to an outdated institution?' Tears came to my eyes. 'I respected your principles, however much it hurt me—and upset Granny—and yet all the time it was to do with money!'

'No, of course it wasn't!' he blustered shiftily. 'That's not what I meant at all! I *didn't* believe in marriage, but now I can see how selfish I was and what it would mean to you. Please, please marry me now, Josie, and let's settle back down as we were.'

'No, I don't think so, thanks. Try Olivia.'

'Look, my mother and Olivia have got together and think they can force me into something I don't want, but they can't,' he said, starting to look impatient and harassed. Just how much of an easy pushover had he expected me to be?

'I've been looking for somewhere else to live, but it's not easy in London and I really, really just want to come back home,' he pleaded.

'I'm sorry, Ben. I do forgive you for what you did, but I don't want you back. I've written you out of "Cakes and Ale" and out of my life. I've moved on. You need to do the same now,' I said sadly, but with finality.

'I didn't think you could be so hard, Josie!' Stella exclaimed, sounding shocked. 'You'll drive him away and into marrying Olivia, and *then* you'll be sorry.'

'No, I don't think I will be sorry,' I said, and turning, walked out.

I'm not sure quite how I drove home. I've no recollection of it at all, but I think between them, Ben and his mother are about to turn me into a lush.

Chapter Twenty-two
Unwanted Presence

Some people put sugar in their shortcrust pastry when they are making mince pies, but I don't. Granny always made them in thin pastry shells with a generous filling of home-made mincemeat —sweet, but still slightly tart—and now that's the way I do it. The cult of sweetness seems to have gone too far. When I am given bought bread at friends' houses I am amazed at how sickly sweet that is too. But why would people want sweet bread? Or do they have such a sweet tooth that they don't notice?

'Cakes and Ale'

When I got home I just carried on with what I had to do, but on automatic pilot because my mind was replaying the scene in Mark and Stella's kitchen over and over again, on an endless loop. I could see Ben's face—puzzled, hurt, and hopeful; hear his once-beloved voice, cajoling, explaining, and trying to smooth away what had come between us—this troublesome wrinkle of infidelity in the fabric of our lives.

Maybe he should try hanging it in a steamy bathroom, like my bridesmaid's dress?

But was I being unreasonable, as Mark and Stella seemed to think? *Was* it possible to forgive him and start over again? It wasn't that I didn't long for the clock to be put back, for everything to be as it was, but how could that happen? I'd

296

thought I'd known him through and through, but not only had he betrayed me with Olivia but also, it seems, lied about why he didn't want to get married.

Olivia wasn't the type to butt out gracefully, either, even without the small but insuperable matter of the baby. We couldn't pretend that had never happened, or that Ben's child wasn't out there, growing up without a father.

No, despite that momentary weakness when I had yearned to be safe in his arms again for ever, I was sure I'd made the right decision in tearing him up by the roots and leaving the place where he once was in my heart to lie fallow.

And one thing was for sure: I would never completely trust a man again.

Libby thought I'd made the right decision about Ben too—the only possible one—when I rang up and told her all about it, which was comforting. But then she said she had to go because Noah had just arrived—the man, after Ben, I least wanted to see ever again.

'Libby, if he mentions me, tell him I've gone away for Christmas!' I said urgently before she rang off, but she just laughed.

*   *   *

Later, while I was making more mince pies with a large glass of last year's parsnip wine at my elbow, there was a knock at the door. Subconsciously, I'd been half expecting Ben to turn up, but really, really hoping he wouldn't. He couldn't see me, because the curtains were shut, so I wondered if perhaps I could ignore him and hope he would go away . . .

But no, there was a thunderous repeat of the knocking and anyway, he still had a key and could get in if I didn't answer. Wiping my hands on my apron I opened the door, resolutely prepared to send him away again, only to have the wind taken right out of my sails when it wasn't him.

'*Russell?* Well, this *is* a surprise!' I exclaimed, peering past him to look for the car. 'Where's Mary? Are you on your way somewhere for Christmas?'

'No, I thought I'd just pop up for a night, to see how you were coping,' he said, with his familiar, toothy smile. 'Can I come in? It's freezing out here.'

'I—well, I suppose so,' I said, because I couldn't very well leave one of our oldest friends standing on the doorstep in the biting wind, could I? Anyway, I needed to check the first batch of mince pies and put the next lot in, so I did that while Russell dumped the holdall he was carrying on the floor and divested himself of his outer layers.

'Those smell good!' he said, as I manoeuvred steaming mince pies out of the tray and onto a wire rack.

I smacked his hand away before he burned it. 'Russell, did you say you'd come all the way up here just for one night?'

'That's right.'

'Well, that's very kind of you, but really, you didn't need to. I feel quite guilty now! Where are you staying?'

'Here, of course,' he said, looking surprised. This time he managed to snatch a mince pie before I could stop him, then shifted it from hand to hand

298

like a hot chestnut.

'*Here?* Oh, no!' I exclaimed in dismay. 'I mean— it's lovely to see you, but I wish you'd told me first, because you can't stay here tonight, not without Mary. It wouldn't look right.'

Russell stared at me from his muddy-brown eyes with some astonishment. Frost was melting into drops of moisture on his moustache and beard, and the Arctic explorer look didn't really suit him. 'I didn't expect you to go all Victorian and prudish about putting me up, Josie! And Mary won't worry because I told her I was visiting an old friend, one she doesn't like.'

'That just shows you know she wouldn't like it, Russell. I mean, if you'd come all this way just to visit me for a few hours, and she knew about it, that would be *one* thing, but to sneak off for the night with a lie is quite another.'

'I thought you'd be pleased to see me,' he said sullenly. 'I don't see why we can't be cosy together tonight, if Mary knows nothing about it.' He tried a smile that he obviously thought alluring. 'Come on, Josie, you know you've always fancied me! I thought you'd give me a warmer welcome than this.'

If I'd known he was after something that hot I would have let him burn his mouth on the mince pies.

'No, I haven't always fancied you, Russell—I can't believe you could even think that! We've known each other a long time and I'm quite fond of you,' I said, though I was a lot less sure about it at that moment, 'but I've never fancied you in the least!'

'You just don't want to admit that there's always

been a spark between us.'

'Only in your drunken imaginings! You always did tend to get a bit overfamiliar when you'd had too much to drink, but I didn't think anything of it, except that it irritated Mary.'

'You're protesting too much,' he said, coming round the table with obvious intentions. 'Let's kiss and be friends.'

'Let's *not*,' I replied, edging away. 'If you don't leave right now, I'm going to scream!'

'What, and give old Harry a heart attack?' He grinned confidently.

'OK, then I'll phone Mary and tell her what you're up to.'

'I'll deny everything,' he said, though to my relief he stopped moving towards me.

Then he made a sudden lunge and grabbed my wrist. Startled, I did let out a yell, though by then I'd remembered that Harry would be at the Neatslake Seniors' Club in the parish hall, playing in a dominoes tournament.

More to the point, I snatched up an empty metal mince pie tray with my other hand and crashed it over his stupid head with as much force as I could, considering it was my left hand and an awkward angle. He yelped and the tin hit the flagged floor with a noise like nearby thunder.

In the resulting silence a smooth, deep, familiar voice enquired from behind me, 'Am I interrupting something, or in the nick of time? Only the front door was on the latch and I wasn't sure which would be more tactful—to come in, or go away.'

'*Noah!*' I gasped gratefully. Russell released his grip and I shot across the room like a homing pigeon and grabbed his arm, before realising quite what I was doing.

He looked mildly surprised at my enthusiastic welcome, but said, 'Hi, Josie,' and kissed me on both cheeks, smelling of that delicious aftershave.

'Who the hell are you?' demanded Russell belligerently.

'This is—' I began to say, but Russell answered his own question.

'*I* know who you are—that photographer, Noah Sephton!' Then he looked suspiciously from one to the other of us. 'But I don't see what you're doing here? How do you come to know each other?'

'Noah is an old friend of Libby's. He was the usher at her wedding and I was the bridesmaid.' I tried to sound casual, but since this was the first time I'd come face to face with Noah since then, I felt myself go a little pink.

'And you got *friendly*, perhaps?' Russell suggested. 'So friendly, he just turns up and walks straight in, sure of a warm welcome? No wonder you wanted to get rid of me quickly!'

'You have a nasty mind, Russell Brown!' I said with dignity. 'And I really think you've outstayed your welcome.'

'All in good time. Have you told Ben you've replaced him so quickly? Only he seems to think you've been going to pieces without him and you're dying for him to move back in.'

'I haven't replaced Ben and nor am I about to go to pieces,' I said, loosening my grip on Noah, but staying nearby. 'I've got a lovely home, a successful business and good friends—that's all I need. Now, if you'd like to clear off back to London, we'll pretend this sorry interlude never happened. Or alternatively, you could give Ben a ring and go and explain what you're doing up here. He's staying nearby.'

'Ben's here too? Does he know about . . . ?' He jerked his head at Noah.

'There's nothing to know—and none of his business, or yours, if there were. Goodbye, Russell.'

Russell gave me a dirty look but picked up his bag and left, slamming the door after him, leaving me and Noah alone together in the sudden silence.

What do you say to a man you don't really know, apart from one night of wild, drunken, marvellous sex? One, moreover, who's just rescued you from an attempt on what's left of your virtue?

'Do you want a cup of tea and a hot mince pie?' I offered tentatively, and his thin, dark face split into that attractively lop-sided grin.

'Anything except peapod wine.'

I blushed again, more hotly. 'I went off alcohol for a bit, though as you can see that's wearing off again.' I gestured at my half-full glass on the table. 'But that's only parsnip. What brought you to my door so opportunely?'

'I thought you might be in need of another emotional enema,' he said, a glint in his light grey eyes.

I couldn't get any redder. 'No, seriously?'

'I'm just being friendly. Since Pia told me all about you and this Ben, your teenage sweetheart and the love of your life, I've felt guilty about what we did. I just wanted to apologise and make sure you're really OK.'

'I'm absolutely fine and I knew what I was doing: Libby'd warned me about you.'

'Warned you about *what*, exactly?'

302

'Only that you have lots of casual affairs, you don't get involved—and you admitted as much to me yourself. Which was fine,' I assured him hastily. 'In fact, it was just what I needed to shock me out of wallowing in my misery and set me on the road to getting on with my life. So you needn't feel guilty, because I felt quite grateful afterwards, if it makes you feel better. Now, let's just forget all about it, OK?'

He looked a bit stunned, to be honest. 'So, I'm just a casual philanderer who moves on from woman to woman, without a backward glance? Some kind of Casanova?'

'Well, no, actually I think you seem quite kind. You did leave me your phone number and then contacted me to see if I was all right. And then here you are again, still concerned. But you needn't be, because as I said, sleeping with you helped me come to terms with everything.'

'Gee, thanks,' he said drily. 'I can see my concern was misplaced.'

'Actually, Pia said you're still going out with that model you turned up here with the first time we met, so I'm the one who should feel guilty.'

His face looked inscrutable. 'Did she? Well, you needn't feel guilty on Anji's account. She shares her favours with all her friends.'

I couldn't tell from his voice if he minded about that or not—but maybe that sort of thing is the norm in the circles he moves in. If so, there is not so much a cultural chasm as an abyss between the social mores of Neatslake and those of London.

'So, what's happening with the Ben situation now?' he asked me. 'Presumably he's staying locally in the hope of seeing you? I hope I haven't messed that up?'

I looked down at the steam rising from my mug. 'He already has seen me. He was in a friend's house when I went round earlier. He asked me to take him back again, but I told him it was over. He was having an affair for months, you know, and now this other woman is pregnant.'

'Yes, Libby told me.'

'Ben says he misses being able to come back here to recharge his artistic batteries and it's affecting his work, as if it is my fault. And he can't seem to get it through his thick head that I'm not part of his life any more. How stupid can he be, to think that everything could ever be the same again?'

'*Very* stupid. In fact, I can't imagine why he ever looked at another woman when he had you,' Noah said gravely.

I looked at him doubtfully, pretty sure he was paying me back for what I'd said about enemas.

'Olivia—that's the other woman's name—is trying to pressurise him into marrying her, and his parents are all for it too, especially his mother. He offered to marry me instead, though he's always said marriage was an outdated ritual that he wasn't going to pander to—and then he let slip that he'd only been against the idea before because his parents would have cut off his allowance, not because it was against his principles! One word and he'd have come straight home with me.'

'But you didn't give that word?'

'No,' I sighed. 'It was all a bit surreal. He looked like Ben, but inside he was a stranger, someone I didn't know at all. I don't believe in love any more,' I added gloomily. 'Or not romantic love. I'm like you, I suppose.'

'Oh, no, I'm a real romantic at heart,' he said, to my surprise *and* disbelief. 'I know it's possible to fall in love—truly, head-whirlingly, dazzlingly in love.'

'You *do*?'

'Yes, didn't Libby tell you I was once married?'

'That's right—she did! And she said it was all tragic, like *Love Story*. I'm so sorry I forgot! How selfish of me to be so bound up in my own troubles when something so very sad has happened to you.'

My newly acquired cynicism obviously didn't run terribly deeply yet, because I had to dab a sentimental tear or two from my eyes. When I looked up his face was unreadable but he said, lightly enough, 'So you see, I know what it is to love and be loved. I don't expect I will strike that lucky again, but it doesn't stop me hoping.'

He sounded insouciant enough about it, but I did wonder if he was more involved with the beautiful, if seriously unfaithful Anji than he was making out.

I sighed. 'Libby says I never fell in love with Ben properly: we were too young. I was only just thirteen when we met and he was a year older and—well, it was like meeting the other half of myself, somehow. I knew—we both knew—it would be for ever. Or I thought it would be for ever.'

'If you'd been together ever since and he never had a chance to sow his wild oats, I suppose it does partly explain why he went off the rails when another woman showed an interest in him,' Noah suggested.

'Libby said that too, and that if I played my cards right I could get him back. Which I could, except that I don't want him any more. I've done with love, and anyway, he wouldn't be the Ben I thought he was, would he? He's changed. And I *haven't* changed, which might have been the problem. He seems to have told everyone I was emotionally needy, so that I've started to wonder if it is true!'

'I don't think you're emotionally needy,' Noah commented. 'In fact, I thought at the wedding you were the most serene woman I'd ever met. Which is why, I suppose, I believed you weren't motivated by being on the rebound when you lured me into your bed, you little siren.'

'I did *not* lure you!' I exclaimed indignantly.

'OK, dragged me, not unwillingly, into bed. I was by no means as drunk as you were, even if the peapod stuff had gone to my brain a little. I just couldn't resist you. You're very beautiful, even if you don't seem to know it.'

'Me?' I went red. 'Rubbish! Libby's the beautiful one.'

'Libby's pretty—but you, in your own, unusual way, are quite lovely. But then you go and hide it most of the time with ghastly clothes like the ones you're wearing now,' he added.

'Pansy Grace knitted this jumper for me specially, and I love it!' I said indignantly.

'Did she *have* to put pom-poms on the hood and ties? You look like a mad elf.'

'It doesn't matter what *you* think. I'm not dressing to please you—'

'Or anyone else,' he interrupted.

'There you are, then. It's because I don't want to attract any more men . . . though actually it doesn't seem to have put Rob Rafferty off because—' I stopped dead and blushed furiously again.

306

'You've been out with Rob Rafferty since I saw you last?' Noah asked incredulously.

'Only *once.*'

'Oh?' He eyed me thoughtfully. 'Maybe I got you wrong. I hope *he* was a cathartic experience too?'

'It was nothing like that at all,' I snapped. 'Just a drink in a wine bar with the cast of *Cotton Common*. I told you, I've given up on men—and I never thought I'd ever end up discussing aspects of love with you, Noah Sephton!'

'Why not? It's what all my exhibitions are about, love in its various forms. My next one will be about weddings—the triumph of optimism over intelligence.'

'But you said you still believe in true love, even if you don't really expect to be struck by the same bolt of lightning twice yourself—while *I'm* not convinced it really exists at all any more.'

'It's true I don't expect something that good to come round twice. So,' he shrugged, 'I take what I can get.'

'I'm not going to be anyone's second best—not Ben's, or yours, or anyone else's. I'll just quietly live my life alone from now on.'

'And lonely?'

'Not at all. I have my uncle Harry, Libby and all my friends. And I might get a cavalier King Charles spaniel puppy one of these days, for company.' Then somehow I found myself telling him about Freddie of the Ponderosa Kennels, and her doggy wedding arrangements. I knew he would appreciate it.

'I don't think a puppy is quite the same as a lover,' Noah said finally, unconvinced by my arguments, 'but since we both know where we

307

stand now, could we be friends, do you think?'

'Maybe,' I agreed cautiously.

'With the proviso that if you ever feel the need of another cathartic moment, I'm your man for the job?' That teasing glint was back in his grey eyes.

He stood up, his dark head not quite brushing the wooden rack overhead. Ben was forever knocking into it . . . *had been* forever knocking into it.

'Take some of those mince pies back for Libby. If she intends getting pregnant one day, she'll find it easier if she isn't practically anorexic,' I said absently, thinking that Noah's handsomeness lay not so much in any one individual feature, but deep in the fine bones of his beautifully shaped head . . .

'*Is* Libby trying to get pregnant?'

'What?' Then, guiltily, I realised what I'd just said. 'Forget that. It just popped out,' I urged him. 'I hope she doesn't try for ages yet. She and Tim should have a bit of time together first.'

And I should really do something about contacting Gloria and putting my mind at rest before it got that far, stupid though I knew my suspicions were. In fact, I wouldn't put it off till after Christmas; I'd do it tomorrow, if I could catch Gloria instead of Daisy.

'I'd love her to have children eventually, of course, so I can be a pretend auntie again. I'm Pia's godmother, you know. I can't have children myself, you see. It's another thing that really hurt about Ben—that Olivia should be the one to get pregnant.'

'I'm sorry. I regret not having them too,' Noah said sympathetically, and I smiled at him.

308

'You know, you're the strangest man! Not a bit the way I imagined you were. Well, actually I suppose you are, really, only your motivation is different.'

'So is yours, and I warn you that I'm still no angel—but then, even angels want to singe their wings occasionally, don't they, Josie?'

I turned away, on the pretext of finding a tin for the mince pies. 'I thought we weren't going to mention that night again?'

'Yes, but it's a bit irresistible teasing you sometimes, darling. But if you like, I promise I'll only do it when we're alone.'

'After Christmas, that will probably be never.'

'Never say never again,' he replied. 'Look, I'd better go. Gina's whipping up some special pasta dish for dinner that she's convinced is my favourite, though anything she cooks is fine by me.'

I handed him the mince pies and saw him out, and if his parting kiss landed right on my lips in a more than friendly way, I didn't fend him off. I didn't encourage him either.

'*Ciao!*' he said, and sauntered off, the big, battered red cake tin rather spoiling the soigné effect.

I stared absently after his elegant back as he passed beyond the streetlights and vanished up the lane towards the gatehouse, then was just about to go in again when a familiar figure the approximate size of a grizzly bear moved from the darkness at the side of the house.

'Ben?' I called. 'Is that you?'

'Yes.' He walked slowly into the circle of light cast by the lamp over the door, and I could see he was in one of his rare fits of rage by the way he was clenching and unclenching his hands.

'Russell rang me up to say he'd called in to see you on the way somewhere or other, and caught you with another man, and I didn't believe him. But it's true, Josie, isn't it?' He laughed shortly. 'All that about how betrayed and hurt you were, when in reality I was hardly gone five minutes before someone else had taken my place.'

I opened my mouth to rebut the allegation, then realised that actually that was *exactly* what I had done!

'You're not denying it, I notice,' he said, moving meancingly closer, and I edged back, ready to whisk inside and slam the door.

I found my voice. 'Is there any point in my telling you that Russell is the one who thought I would welcome him into my bed if he turned up here?'

'No,' he said uncompromisingly. 'Russell said it was Noah Sephton he caught you with, of all people—and I saw him kiss you myself, so I know he was telling the truth.'

'It was just a friendly kiss. He's a friend of Libby's and I like him.'

'Yes, bloody friendly!'

'Look, he only dropped in for a chat and a cup of tea, not anything else—and it was lucky he did, because he was just in time to rescue me from Russell.'

'Don't lie to me!' he bellowed, grabbing my shoulders and giving me a shake, his fingers digging in, painfully.

'Why not? Isn't that what you've been doing to me for months!' I yelled back. 'And whatever I choose to do now is none of your business, so let me go!'

He opened his hands and I fell back against the doorframe. 'I loved you,' he said flatly. 'You were always my girl. You never even *looked* at anyone else.'

'I looked at Rufus Sewell quite a bit on the TV,' I said, with a mistimed attempt to lighten things, but it didn't seem to register.

'Tell me truthfully, Josie, *did* you sleep with him?'

I've never been great at lying. My throat closed up and I froze to the spot, just looking at him. After a moment he pushed his fists down into his jacket pockets, as though afraid he might hit me, and strode off.

* * *

To add that final wonderful touch to the day, Mary called me, quite hysterical, and demanded to know if Russell was there with me. I was happy to assure her he wasn't, but I'm not sure she believed me.

She hadn't known about all the late night phone calls until she saw the phone bill and put two and two together and now accused me of encouraging him to call me and trying to entice her husband away. There was no reasoning with her and I thought Russell deserved everything he would get when he finally arrived home.

I was totally drained after this, absolutely reeling. I certainly didn't need alcohol or anything else to send me to sleep.

Chapter Twenty-three

Family Way

My friend has decked her new home with swags and swathes of greenery from the grounds and installed a huge, colour co-ordinated tree, like something out of Ideal Home *magazine.*

Decorating the tree is another thing I have left to the last minute this year, and in any case, my approach is slightly different. I have inherited an ancient artificial tree, made of twisted wire and shiny, thin green paper that has gold cord from long-eaten chocolates still tangled among the fronds. The decorations are equally old and several have been carefully repaired, while some of the tinsel strands are bald in places—but no matter, once the tree is finished it always looks beautiful.

'Cakes and Ale'

The days when I opened my eyes on a new dawn with the optimistic expectation of a busy and happy day before me seemed long gone, but next morning was worse than usual.

I suppose that was hardly surprising, given the events of the previous evening. And perhaps some part of me had secretly been nurturing a tiny flame of hope that I would one day awake to find everything suddenly switched back to how it used to be, with Ben shaking me and saying, 'Wake up, darling—you're having a nightmare!'

He certainly shook me the previous night, just

not in a good way. And now he knew that I'd been unfaithful too . . . though can you be unfaithful if you're not any longer with your partner? I mean, there was a slight difference between what *he* did and my actions, wasn't there?

Things didn't get any better when Harry came in with Mac, and confessed that *he'd* had an argument with Ben the previous night too! Ben had gone to the Griffin, got drunk and then started calling me a tart (a case of the pot calling the kettle black) until Harry offered to fight him. When you consider that he's half Ben's size and in his eighties, that was brave but a little rash, though of course I knew that however drunk he was, Ben would never hurt Harry.

Mind you, I never thought he'd hurt *me* either, but he'd come perilously close to it the previous night.

Harry had sprung to my defence, though I was, if not a tart, then certainly guilty of a bit of drunken wantonness, and the ready tears sprang to my eyes. 'Thanks, Harry—but I'm really not worth fighting over.'

'Nay, lass, don't cry—of course you are. I can't think what got into him.'

So then I had to explain about Russell turning up on the doorstep with a lot of misguided assumptions, and Noah calling in, perfectly innocently, in the nick of time to save me from a serious affront to my dignity, if nothing worse.

'I was trying to bang some sense into Russell's head with a baking tray at the time, so I was pleased to see him. But then Russell leaped to some ridiculous idea that Noah and I were having an affair, and he rang Ben's mobile and told him.'

'Russell mustn't have known he was up here staying with your friends, Josie. He wouldn't have tried it on, otherwise.'

'No, but he managed to make *his* visit sound innocent and Noah's not, which was the opposite to how it really was, and so Ben rushed down just in time to see Noah kiss me goodbye on the doorstep—you know what Londoners are, forever kissing each other.'

Harry nodded. 'They're getting worse than the French for that. A lot of sloppy ducks, they are.'

'So when Ben saw that, he thought Russell was right and got mad.'

'He should have known you better than to think that of you—and there was no call to go badmouthing you in the Griffin either.'

'No,' I said a bit guiltily. 'I expect it will be all over the village now.'

'No one will believe it,' Harry assured me. 'They'll see it was all jealousy and he was roaring drunk. The landlord threw him out and I saw that Mark and Stella come in a Land Rover and drive him away.'

I hoped he was right about no one believing it, but that didn't stop me feeling I had a big H for Harlot written across my forehead when I took Mac out for a walk later, especially when I bumped into Mrs Talkalot from the post office, and she asked me some probing questions about an intriguing rumour that had reached her ears of Rob Rafferty being seen on my doorstep . . .

*   *   *

I'd put it off until the last moment, but I was just

314

climbing down from the loft with the box containing the Christmas tree and decorations, when the phone rang, so I was a bit breathless by the time I'd galloped downstairs.

'Josie?' Olivia's brittle voice held an ominous note of triumph. 'I just wanted to thank you for turning out to be such a slut that Ben came straight back here and proposed! Now we're getting married in early January and his parents are delighted! And aren't you the dark horse—Noah Sephton, of all people! Of course, it won't last, I can't imagine what—'

I slammed down the phone before she could add anything else. I thought they deserved each other! I didn't suppose Olivia had quite grasped yet what it was like to live full time with an artist like Ben, who always thought of his work and himself in relation to it, before anything or anyone else. Far from sustaining an ideal environment for him to create in, like I had done, she probably expected him to fit in with her London life.

But somehow this wasn't much consolation and I felt so full of furious energy that I decided I might as well burn it off in a useful manner by chopping more logs, though I put my gloves on this time. I still had blisters from the last session.

It was very therapeutic, though I was tiring by the time Noah suddenly leaned over the gate behind me and volunteered to carry on.

'Are you sure?' I asked doubtfully, because I didn't think he would make much of a go of it. 'It's pretty hard on the hands if you're not used to it.'

Actually, it's pretty hard on *everything* if you're not used to it!

'I've got gloves in my pocket,' he said, giving me

my empty red cake tin, which I supposed was the reason why he'd come. He hung his padded down jacket on the corner of the wood shed and at least he was wearing jeans and sweatshirt this time, even if he did still manage to look elegant in them.

I watched him critically and discovered to my surprise that while he might be a slightly built townie, he did seem to know what to do with a wood axe. It's all in the rhythm . . . and he has *lots* of that. I sat on a big log and watched, and so did Aggie, who had escaped yet again and was peeping round the corner.

I'd obviously got him on his mettle, because it was ages before he stopped for a breather and to drink the mug of tea I'd made him.

While I was crumbling bits of ginger biscuit for Aggie, he said he'd remembered my description of Freddie's wedding tomorrow and wangled an invitation, and he offered to drive me there.

'How did you manage that?' I demanded, amazed.

'Dorrie knows her, so I rang up and told her I was a photographer and offered to take some pictures for free, if she agreed to let me use some for my next exhibition. You said it was a low-key wedding, so I thought she might not have a professional wedding photographer booked.'

'No, I'm sure she said one of the kennel maids was going to take pictures. I don't think either she or the bridegroom has a lot of spare cash.'

'So, since we're both going, I might as well pick you up about ten,' he suggested, and I agreed. You mightn't think I'd be in the mood for a wedding after Olivia's little bombshell, but I did want to see the spaniel guard of honour and what everyone

316

thought of my cake. And the idea of a wedding still, somehow, cheered me up, and probably always would, however illogical that was. I hoped Freddie and her colonel hadn't economised on bells . . .

Harry came out after a while and, after peering short-sightedly at Aggie, scooped her up under his arm.

Noah paused again, to mop his face and be introduced.

'How do?' Harry said, favouring him with a rheumy, thoughtful gaze from under his hat brim, so I expect he remembered that Noah was the subject of Ben's jealous rage. 'Saw you at Libby's wedding, didn't I?'

He seemed to like the look of him, though—and so did I. I liked my men hot, ruffled and pared down to a close-fitting T-shirt . . .

'Josie's doing too much,' Harry said, watching the way Noah swung the axe with approval. 'She shouldn't have to chop all this wood and she takes barrowloads of it across for the Grace sisters. It's not right. *I* can't do it any more, nor the heavy digging.'

'I'm no frail flower,' I protested. 'I like digging, and I expect chopping wood is doing me good.'

Noah looked up. 'I think Harry's right, you are doing too much. I noticed you were getting thin and you know what they say.'

He paused and, despite myself, I asked, 'No, what?'

'Never trust a thin cook.'

Harry chortled. 'He's got you there, lass.'

'Libby told me about the projected TV series too, and you don't want to look like a rack of ribs

317

for that, or it will put the viewers right off the good life.'

'Oh, I don't think the TV series will come to anything. It was just a young TV producer—or whatever she was—getting carried away with an idea.'

'You never know,' Noah said. 'But this is one chore I can take off your hands while I'm staying here. I'll come round and chop firewood for you every day.'

'No, really, you don't need to,' I protested. 'Anyway, you can't chop wood on Christmas Day, and didn't Libby say you were going back after Boxing Day?'

'Yes, but I can at least leave you with a good pile to keep you going.'

'Never look a gift horse in the mouth,' Harry told me, and went off to shut Aggie back into the run.

*   *   *

When Noah finally went back to Blessings for lunch I dug out the slip of paper that Libby had written her sister's phone number on and rang it, hoping I'd get her mother instead. I wasn't quite sure what I would do if Daisy answered . . . engage in inane chat, probably.

But my luck was in, if you can call it that, because Gloria picked up after a long wait, just as I was about to replace the receiver. She didn't sound entirely sober, but seemed pleased to hear from me.

'Daisy's had to go to the dentist and I didn't feel like going with her,' she said. 'I said I'd stay at home and rest.'

'That's all right. I wanted a little chat with you anyway. It was lovely to see you at the wedding. You looked terribly smart!'

'Daisy got our outfits off that eBay. They were a snip.'

'Yes, it's amazing what you can find on there,' I agreed, thinking of Harry's medal. 'Libby's was a lovely wedding and reception, wasn't it?'

'Yes, our Libby looked like an angel, but Daisy would insist on dragging me off to that place we were staying at hours before I was ready to leave!'

'She'd driven a long way to get there, so I expect she was tired,' I said tactfully, wondering how to lead in to what I wanted to ask.

'We were having such an interesting chat just before you had to go too,' I lied inventively. 'I'd just said that opposites usually attract, yet there were Libby and Tim, both fair and blue-eyed. And you said yes, they had more in common than they knew . . . ?' I prompted. 'You used to know Tim's father quite well, I think.'

Gloria giggled. '*Very* well! Robert—Tim's father—put some money in the bank for me when I told him, provided I didn't make a fuss, which I wouldn't have anyway,' she said good-naturedly. 'And afterwards, he was always generous if there was a gas bill to pay or something like that.'

'Told him *what*? That you . . .' I gulped hard, 'that you were having his baby?'

'Yes, but I never asked him for maintenance, because that would have made trouble, and I knew he'd see me right, like a proper gentleman. Then he married that harpy and when she found out about our bit of fun, the money dried up.'

Oh God, this was worse and worse!

'But, Mrs Martin, shouldn't you have told Libby before she married Tim?' I gasped, appalled.

'No—why spoil a happy marriage for a little slip in the past?' she said, and giggled again. There was a glassy clinking noise and the sound of pouring. 'Must go, our Daisy'll be back soon. Cheery-bye!'

She left me so stunned I was shaking. I knew Gloria's moral standards to be a little different from mine, but still . . . this was going *too* far! What on earth was I going to do? How could I possibly tell all this to Tim and Libby, and tear them apart? But then, how could I not? What if I didn't say anything and they had children and they—

Oh, it didn't bear *thinking* of !

But of course, I did keep thinking about it, until it occurred to me that maybe it was all a figment of Gloria's permanently sozzled imagination. Then I felt slightly—but not much—better.

I should have waited to speak to Daisy instead. Gloria was bound to have said much the same to her when she was well and truly plastered and had no control over what came out of her lips. Not that she seemed to have a lot of control when she was sober, either.

So I waited until I thought she would be safely home, and then rang the number again. My fingers were trembling slightly: this had to be the most difficult call I'd ever made.

'Daisy Martin,' she said, in the sort of voice you get when your lip is still numb from the dentist's anaesthetic.

'This is Josie.'

'What, Libby's friend, Josie?' She sounded slightly surprised.

'Yes,' I said, and managed a few disjointed enquiries about the dentist and how she was before plunging into the subject most on my mind.

'Daisy, your mother said something at Libby's reception that made me think . . . well, that she and Tim's father had been having an affair at one time.'

'Yes, I know all about that, of course,' she said. 'I'm not sure you could call it an affair. You know Mum—she got about a bit—but he was always generous and gave us a lot of financial support when I was growing up. He played hard, did Robert Rowland-Knowles, but he was prepared to pay for his fun.'

'But what about *Libby*?' I exclaimed.

'Oh, Libby doesn't know anything about it, and Tim doesn't seem to either. I told Mum not to mention it, but she got tanked up at the reception and blabbed.'

'Only to me, and I haven't told anyone, of course. But, Daisy, shouldn't you have—I mean, don't you think you should have told Libby and Tim *before* they married?'

'No, that sort of thing doesn't really matter in this day and age, does it? But I thought it was better to leave it a secret. No harm done.'

No *harm*?

'But . . . what if they have children, Daisy?'

'I think that's unlikely, don't you? Pia was an accident and Libby's getting a bit long in the tooth. But if so, we'll all be related, won't we—one big happy family!'

Clearly Daisy's moral code was as weirdly offbeat as her mother's was, or she couldn't possibly think any of this was OK!

321

But now she seemed to feel that we had exhausted the subject, for she started to tell me about the holiday she was going to take in the new year to Morocco with some girlfriends, when Libby had promised that Gloria would be stowed safely away to dry out yet again.

I presume I made all the right noises, because she said it had been nice having a little chat.

*   *   *

I desperately wanted to talk all this over with someone, but the only person I could do that with was the person most involved!

And unfortunately, when Libby came round later with a lot of very chic little Christmas parcels to put under my tree, her mind seemed to be running on the idea of babies, though luckily not in the very near future.

'Tim and I are really enjoying being just the two of us at the moment,' she said.

'If you can call it being alone, when Gina's around all the time, Pia is to and fro, and Dorrie pops up at the most unexpected moments,' I pointed out, getting a grip on myself and trying to sound normal. 'But no, I really think you should give yourselves a couple of years first.'

That should safely take her into the realms of diminishing fertility!

'A year, perhaps,' she agreed. 'I ought to get Old Barn Receptions off the ground first. But I can't afford to wait too long, because your chances lessen with every year past thirty.'

'Well, just give it a *bit* longer,' I suggested, and I suppose my manner must have been jumpy and odd, because she gave me a very suspicious look, as if she knew I was hiding something, and asked me if I was feeling OK.

'Fine—just a bit tired. Have you heard about my love triangle? Ben, Russell and Noah, with me as piggy-in-the-middle?'

*　　　*　　　*

Mary phoned me again, but this time to shame-facedly apologise for her earlier accusations, now that Russell had arrived home and explained everything.

He was obviously sharper-witted than I'd ever given him credit for!

'He called me from his friend's house in Liverpool, right after I'd spoken to you, so he *was* where he said he would be! And before I could ask him, he told me that he'd called in to see you on his way up, but only stopped briefly because it was getting so late.'

'*That's* true,' I agreed.

'Then I asked him about all those late night phone calls to you and of course they were just because he was feeling sorry for you.'

'Of course,' I echoed.

'He wanted to be sure you were all right, but he thought I would be upset if I knew he was calling you.'

'Yes, I expect he *did* think that.'

'And then,' she added, her voice seeming to wobble suddenly on the verge of hysteria, 'he said when he called in he found *Noah Sephton* with you, being *very* friendly and—you won't believe this bit, Josie—'

323

'Try me,' I said morosely.

'Well, it's just that he seems to have the insane idea you two are having an affair!' She giggled. 'I mean—*you* and Noah Sephton!'

'Yes, it's unbelievable, isn't it? I barely even know him. He's just a friend of Libby's, that's all.' I summoned up a hollow laugh. 'Unfortunately, Russell seems to have shared this mad idea with Ben.'

'Oh, I'll put him straight, next time I see him, don't worry. They're both as daft as each other, if they believe something that stupid. Anyway, according to the current copy of *Simply Secrets* magazine, he's been having a sizzling affair with this absolutely gorgeous model for ages and—'

'Anji. Yes, I know about her,' I broke in.

'– and it quoted some of her friends as saying a wedding was on the cards.'

'Oh? But that might have been a bit of wishful thinking,' I said doubtfully. 'He's a widower, but I don't think he's ever found anyone to measure up to his late wife and he didn't sound serious about this Anji.'

'Maybe not, but he's hardly likely to look at *you* when his taste runs to the blonde, leggy and beautiful, is he?'

'You never know. I had a date with a soap star the other day—Rob Rafferty.'

She giggled again. 'In your dreams!'

After she'd gone, I went and looked in the mirror: no makeup, sulky mouth, tangled hair, sallow skin, blue-grey eyes. Yes, same old Josie, the one a man like Noah Sephton couldn't possibly fancy. It must have been entirely the power of the peapod. Though that doesn't account for Rob, of course . . . But come to think of it, Libby did say he wasn't at all discriminating, so being female and youngish is probably all the criteria he looks for.

The conversation with Mary hadn't done a lot for my self-confidence, but the good thing was that Mary and I were now tenuously on speaking terms again and it had provided a distraction, however temporary, from my other worries.

Chapter Twenty-four

Handsome Cavaliers

It always amazes me the things people buy at Christmas that they could easily make themselves. Take bread sauce, for instance. This takes a matter of minutes to prepare, about the same time as opening a packet and mixing it with water, but it will taste a hundred times nicer. And good, thick Lancashire-style gravy, easily made with the juices from the roasting tin and a little cornflour, is ambrosia compared to the granulated abomination sold in supermarkets.

'Cakes and Ale'

Now that I had Libby's ghastly secret to worry about as well as my own problems, even exhaustion couldn't make me fall asleep that night. I spent most of it making and icing about a million gingerbread biscuits in the shape of stars and threading them on very thin green string.

My tree and Harry's were now groaning under the weight of them and I gave what was left as festive gifts to the Graces and Dorrie, and to Gina for her very own little tree in the flat. I didn't think Libby would want me ruining the colour scheme on *her* tree, which was a silver one with purple-shaded baubles.

I'd taken Mac with me while I was out delivering the biscuits, but he wasn't terribly impressed by the notion of this as a walk, so then I had to go right up the lane and back by the footpath, which made it a scramble getting ready in time for Noah to pick me up for Freddie and her colonel's wedding.

Luckily I'd already decided what to wear— another of Stella's almost circular, velvet, wraparound skirts, this time in a plum colour, with my favourite burgundy and gold patterned Indian cotton top. I haven't got a smart winter coat, so borrowed Libby's velvet jacket again.

Harry, who saw us off, said approvingly, 'You look pretty as a picture, our Josie!'

'Yes she does,' Noah agreed, 'in her own unique way!'

I gave him a look and he returned it with a bland smile, having got out to open the passenger door of his old Jaguar for me. Inside, the scent of old leather mingled with that subtle aftershave of Noah's into an almost aphrodisiac blend. I tried to pin it down, but again, limes and a hot summer's day by the cricket pitch on the village green, was as close as I could get. Don't ask me where the cricket comes in.

'I think I owe you an apology,' Noah said, as he drove me with exaggerated slowness out of the village towards Sticklepond. 'Libby told me about the scene with Ben. She said the whole village knew, because he got drunk and badmouthed you in the pub, so *I* might as well know too.'

'I don't see why you should apologise. It wasn't your fault that Ben got the wrong end of the stick.'

'Maybe if I hadn't kissed you good night . . .'

'That was nothing. Anyway, by then, Russell had already half-convinced Ben I'd plunged straight into an affair with you after he left. He was quite unreasonable.' I shivered. 'A bit nasty too, though he's not really like that usually . . .' I trailed off.

'Jealousy does strange things to a man,' he commented. 'But he couldn't know for certain about—well, about the night we had together, could he?'

I might have remarked tartly that it had only been half a night, if that. But we *had* packed rather a lot into it . . .

When I remained silent he said, 'Well, could he? You didn't tell him?'

'No, but he asked me point-blank and I just couldn't say anything at all—I froze. So then he decided he was right and that's when he really flew off the handle.'

'That doesn't make me feel any less guilty, Josie, because if he had come to Neatslake in the first place to make it up with you, and you wanted him back, then I've spoiled it all. If I'd kept clear of you last night, this would never have happened.'

'But I don't want him back! And what I did or didn't do, with you or anyone else, is no longer his concern.'

He turned and glanced at me. '*Was* there anyone else? I wondered, when you said you'd been out with Rob Rafferty too.'

'No, of course not,' I said shortly. 'It was always only Ben, until you came along. And afterwards.'

'That's what I thought.'

'After Ben stormed off, he went straight back to London and proposed to Olivia and they're marrying in early January.'

'How do you know?'

'She phoned me up and told me, highly pleased with herself. She knows about you and me too and I expect she's spreading the news around. Consider your reputation shattered.'

'I didn't know I had one, though it *may*, of course, mean demotion from the Fifty Most Eligible Bachelors list next year,' he said lightly.

He glanced at me in time to catch my Gorgon glare. 'I meant your reputation for only being seen with beautiful young models!' I said. 'And speaking of which, what about your girlfriend, Anji? The one you've been pictured with in London recently? There are lots of rumours that it's serious.'

He shrugged. 'Not put about by me! But I don't cut my old girlfriends dead in the street, you know. Most of them stay good friends.'

Or maybe more than friends?

I looked at him doubtfully, feeling suddenly sorry for poor Anji if she'd fallen hard for Noah and was trying desperately to hang on to him. I expect he'd been entirely open with her about just looking for no-strings-attached fun, as he had been with me, but perhaps she had assumed she could change his mind? Reforming a rake has always been an attractive proposition.

Noah gave me a sideways smile. 'You realise if we keep being seen together like this, it will give the gossips lots more ammunition?'

'Well, since my life was so boringly blameless up until now, it's probably time I gave them something to talk about, isn't it?'

'You won't have to when you're a TV personality; they'll make things up about you, instead.'

'I don't *really* think that's going to happen,' I said doubtfully. 'Though Claire Flowers is still bombarding me with emails and she seems pretty convinced. She's talking about starting filming in March.'

'That sounds very positive to me. She must have someone seriously interested in the idea,' he said. 'Here's the village—where do I park?'

'Anywhere along the lane here.'

The church in Sticklepond, while not quite as large or as old as St Cuthbert's in Neatslake, is very pretty, and we arrived just as the kennel maids were lining up outside with the spaniel guard of honour, all wearing large satin ribbon bows.

Of course I lost Noah instantly, because he was off taking photographs, but I joined forces with Hebe Winter and Dorrie, who were also guests, having got to know Freddie through the Women's Institute meetings. They said they'd come straight on from the annual Christmas Eve morning bash at Winter's End, which is apparently quite an event. Hebe was her usual tall, hawk-nosed, dignified self, but Dorrie's best beret was tipped over one eye and her cheeks were flushed, so I suspected she'd been at the festive punch.

However cynical about love I might have become, I have to admit that Freddie, her healthy outdoors complexion innocent of any makeup apart from a dusting of powder and a dab of soft pink lipstick, looked absolutely glowing in a cream

329

silk shantung suit. Her colonel, silver-haired, handsome and upright in neat tailoring and a regimental tie, beamed on her with fond and proud eyes.

Afterwards we all repaired back to the Ponderosa Kennels, where there was much sherry and a buffet of tiny pork pies, triangular sandwiches and vol-au-vents filled either with scrambled egg or what looked suspiciously like undiluted condensed mushroom soup.

The Cavalier cake stood on a table of its own and Noah photographed the happy couple cutting it. It was much admired and all the kennel maids wanted a slice with a spaniel sitting on it, which I noticed they wrapped up in paper napkins to keep, before eating the rest of the cake.

You never knew where Noah and his Leica would turn up next—or from what angle you would suddenly find yourself being snapped, a sagging vol-au-vent halfway to your mouth—but his antics seemed to amuse the guests rather than annoy them. In fact, I barely spoke to him until late in the proceedings, by which time I had managed, without any effort at all, to click with a good-looking young farmer. It's amazing what a few new clothes and a bit of slap can do . . . and maybe just a smidgen of confidence in your powers of attraction.

Maybe Libby was right about using some of the money I was making on augmenting my wardrobe and updating my makeup.

Anyway, I was just getting the hang of flirting when Noah broke abruptly into the conversation and dragged me off to Neatslake, saying we would be late for dinner! He meant *he* would be late for

330

dinner, for despite Libby showering me with invitations over the Christmas period, I'd accepted only the one to go to tea on Boxing Day. Dorrie accepted a lift back with us, since it would save Hebe driving her home, and sat in the back, flushed with sherry and goodwill, quietly singing something jolly and repetitive in French.

'It's still quite early; I don't know what the rush is,' I complained to Noah.

'Sorry if I dragged you away from your latest conquest,' he said shortly, 'but if you didn't manage to exchange phone numbers, I expect Freddie can help put you in touch.'

I turned my head and looked at him in astonishment. 'Don't be silly. He must be at least ten years younger than me, even if I was seriously interested—which I'm not. And neither was he. It was just a bit of a flirt!'

'Like Rob Rafferty?'

'Well . . . yes, I suppose so, though since I explained to Rob about having just broken up with Ben, he said he's happy just to be friends.'

'I bet he is,' Noah said darkly. 'Good tactics.'

I laughed. 'After he dropped into the cottage and tasted my scones and cakes, he's now much more interested in my baking skills than me personally! And that's fine by me, because I don't want any more than that. I keep telling you—I'm done with love. Love *sucks*.'

That last bit came out very forcefully—I must have drunk more dry sherry than I'd realised.

Noah's face, which had been fixed into a frown as he stared ahead over the steering wheel, relaxed into a grin. 'Down with love?'

'Long live love!' suddenly chimed in Dorrie from

331

the back seat, stopping singing for a moment. *'Vive l'amour!'*

'Quite right,' Noah said, pulling up outside my cottage. 'I'm all for it.' He told me to wait while he got something out of the boot, then handed me a large, flat, gift-wrapped parcel, kissed me chastely on the cheek and departed. It was just as well I'd left a last-minute present for him at Blessings, when I dropped off Libby's gifts!

In my absence Harry had been in the cottage and left a large gift under the tree too, so what with Libby's presents and those from the Graces, Dorrie, Pia and even Gina, there was quite an exciting-looking array of them. There must be still a lot of the child in me because I adore getting presents and, despite Ben's absence, could hardly wait for morning!

After all that rather odd party food I wasn't terribly hungry, but I prepared the sprouts ready for next day and put the whipped cream on the sherry trifle, which Harry is very partial to, and decorated it with little edible silver balls and hundreds and thousands.

Then I watched some mindless telly before going to bed on a great, comforting wave of elderberry 2005. On top of all that sherry, it certainly did the trick, and even if Santa had got stuck in the chimney, I would have slept right through it.

*   *   *

I was up early on Christmas morning, but not as early as Harry, who I could hear outside whistling 'I Saw Three Ships' as he fed the hens.

I made porridge with nutmeg and honey, the way

332

I like it, then put on my Christmas music CD before allowing myself to open my presents, sitting on the floor by the stove in the living room, a cup of coffee on top to keep hot. Thanks to Noah there was a whole basket of firewood ready nearby; I didn't have to stint.

With a feeling of gratitude I opened his gift first. As I'd guessed it might be from the shape, it was a nicely framed photograph of me at Libby's wedding. I remembered him taking it, on the steps when I had just come out into the sunshine. Unlike the ones of me with Aggie, this was in colour. My eyes were wide open and startled and the wintry sun had made my dark auburn hair glow like a dark flame. I looked startled and half poised for flight, the heavy dress swirling out at the hem.

I hadn't realised I could look like that. It was odd, like seeing a stranger.

Setting it down carefully on top of the sideboard, I started opening the rest. I loved everything: Pansy's crocheted shrug with the bobbly buttons, Violet's jam jar string container, Lily's patchwork holdall and the tiny hanging cupboard with a fretwork top and little drawer underneath that Harry had made.

Dorrie had given me a bar of rose soap with petals pressed into it, which I think she got from Hebe—she makes a lot of that kind of thing to sell in the Winter's End gift shop when the house is open to the public. Libby and Tim's gift (though I would be surprised if Tim had any idea what he had given me) was a gardener's radio shaped like a watering can, and Gina's a big box of those crunchy amaretti biscuits, which might be a bit like coals to Newcastle when I bake so much myself,

333

but I expect she noticed how many of them I ate when I was at Blessings!

Harry and I had a very cheerful chicken dinner with all the trimmings, neither of us mentioning Ben's empty chair at the end of the table, or past Christmases. One of his jobs had always been to carve the chicken, but this year I did it myself, not trusting Harry's eyesight with a sharp carving knife.

Under the table, Mac noisily chewed on the rawhide bone that had been in his doggy stocking. Harry was wearing his minesweeping medal pinned onto the warm jumper I'd got Pansy to knit for him, and she'd made him matching socks from an excess of the same wool.

After we'd eaten ourselves practically into a stupor, he went off back home for a snooze and to follow his usual Christmas afternoon habit of telly and snacking before the fire, while Mac and I set out for a walk.

It was a grey, cold day, with the lights already on in several of the houses and not many people about. I walked quite a long way with Mac, feeling solitary but not lonely, as if I'd suddenly reached a poignant but tranquil place.

Noah had been around in my absence and pushed a sprig of mistletoe through the door with a note saying, 'Consider yourself virtually kissed!' And when I went round to take Mac home and lock the hens up, so Harry didn't have to go out into the cold again, there was another big basket of chopped firewood by the back door and a new heap in the woodshed.

When I phoned Libs up to wish her happy Christmas, I asked her to thank him.

Boxing Day was pretty much a repeat of the day before, in that Harry and I ate a huge lunch and then he retired to his house, while Mac and I tried to walk off the excess calories.

But in the afternoon I went up to Blessings for tea. Harry was invited too, but instead went to see the widow of his friend Bob, and said he would have his dinner at the Griffin later—they do a good meat and potato pie there, with mushy peas and gravy—then have an early night in with the telly.

At Blessings everyone was gathered in the Great Chamber, including Dorrie and Noah. Pia had just been dropped off by Jasper and was actually wearing her rainbow jumper, hat, scarf and mittens so that it seemed my birthday and Christmas presents had been a resounding success.

I'd given Libby a knitted French poodle toilet roll cover in Lurex-spangled white yarn, so she could start her own collection (whether she liked it or not), and all the menfolk rum and raisin fudge I'd made at the last minute, plus a long narrow striped scarf apiece—a muted, manly version of Pia's. Luckily Pansy knits them one after the other on automatic pilot when she's watching telly, so always has a good stock to hand.

When Gina came in, she said my wine and *petits fours* were just what she needed, now her family were here and eating her out of house and home, and I thanked her for the amaretti biscuits (most of which I had already eaten; I was sure I would have regained all my lost weight by New Year!).

335

We all ended up playing board games, because there's something about Christmas that seems to make you want to, though perhaps it's just having the leisure to do that kind of thing. I'm not bad at Scrabble and Cluedo, but with Monopoly I always buy the colours I like best, so that I'm either a resounding winner or, more often, lose my shirt. It was all fun, anyway, right up to the moment, over the Earl Grey and Christmas cake, when Libby dropped a bombshell.

'Noah's going to rent the gatehouse for a few months,' she said, pouring tea from a large, flowery pot. 'His next exhibition will be photographs of wedding receptions, so he's going to be taking pictures at most of the Blessings ones—and he's going to include one or two he took at ours as well.'

'And Freddie's,' he put in. 'I think I got some good ones there.'

I turned and stared at him. 'You're going to live in *Neatslake*?'

'Well, I'll be going up and down a bit to my studio in London during the week,' he said. 'I'll divide my time.'

He sounded just like Ben, with one foot in the country, and one in the metropolis. I think I was probably scowling, because he added, 'But I won't if you *hate* the idea, Josie!'

'You've no objection, really, have you, Josie?' Tim looked surprised, as well he might.

'Me? Not at all—why should I? The people in your photographs might, though, Noah. Some of your angles are not exactly flattering.'

'Oh, no, they'll be so made up that the great Noah Sephton is going to photograph them that

336

they'll sign a disclaimer,' Libby said. 'Or most of them will, anyway.'

Noah smiled modestly at me, which for some reason made me feel like hitting him over the head with the Monopoly board . . .

'What's more, he's going to update the gatehouse a bit at his own expense,' Tim put in, 'have a shower put in, and so on. It's a bit basic right now, to say the least.'

Noah shrugged. 'I like to be comfortable and, who knows, if I like living here enough I might take out a long lease on it, if you'll let me. I intend moving in sometime in March, just before Old Barn Receptions is launched. I want to be here from the first!'

He sounded terribly enthusiastic now, but I expected that once he'd got enough pictures, he would be hightailing it off back to the bright lights again.

'How *is* the barn coming along?' I asked Libby. 'I've been too busy the last few days to go and see.'

'There's still lots to sort out. A permanent stage and sound system are going in next, but the workmen aren't here over Christmas, of course. I'll be lucky if they're back after the New Year!'

'What about that advert you were going to put in *Glorious Weddings*?'

'It'll be in the February issue, which is out in mid-January, so we should start getting some early bookings,' she said hopefully. 'And I'll be starting local advertising in the New Year too, when the brochures have arrived from the printers.'

It did sound as if it was all pretty well on track and she didn't really need my help that much, except as a sounding board, prop and stay, which had always been my main function as Libby's friend! However, she did tend to get carried away with the finer detail instead of sorting out the basics first, so once the New Year was over I would have to make sure she hadn't missed out anything vital.

After tea, Pia and Noah both said they would like some fresh air and elected to walk me home, then came in for a glass of wine. Pia ate a gingerbread star and two chocolate watches from the tree, while telling Noah about some of the zanier presents I'd given her for Christmas and birthdays over the years.

'One year, when I was about eight, she sent me a little Paddington Bear fibreboard suitcase for Christmas, and she'd filled it with lots of tiny wrapped presents.'

'How sweet,' Noah said. He looked quite at home on the sofa, lying back with his long legs stretched before him, ankles crossed, a glass in one hand and a half-eaten gingerbread star in the other.

'Well, the suitcase was, but I was into practical jokes about then—a horrible childhood stage— and so there were things like severed fingers and plastic doggy-do. I'm not sure Mum has quite forgiven either of us for the fake ink blot, because I put it right in the middle of a brand-new huge cream leather sofa and she nearly had a seizure. Then there were the realistic plastic bluebottles ...' Pia, who had been a little imp, smiled reminiscently.

'Not so sweet, then,' he said, amused.

'Ah, but it was the very last little parcel in the suitcase that was the best thing—the dried

338

scorpion.'

'Josie sent you a *dried scorpion* for Christmas?'

'That's what it said on the brown paper packet. Only when I started to undo it, it made a horrible scrabbling and rattling noise as if it was alive in there and trying to get out, so I screamed at the top of my lungs! I was petrified.'

'I didn't mean to frighten you,' I apologised.

'Oh, I loved it! And of course when it stopped making a noise and I found out it was just a wound-up piece of elastic and card, I tried the trick on everyone and it got them all going every time. I'm surprised I didn't scare you with it too, Noah. I mustn't have seen you until the novelty wore off and I'd moved on to something else.'

'I'm glad I missed that one! But I do seem to remember you playing tricks on me at one time, and now I know who to blame.' He raised a quizzical eyebrow at me.

'I think I must be the world's worst godmother,' I said guiltily.

'No, the very best,' Pia said warmly.

When they left, Noah lingered slightly and said, 'I'll say goodbye for the moment, Josie, because I'm off early in the morning. I did chop you extra wood today, to keep you going.'

'Yes, I noticed, thank you for that. I'm going to miss you,' I added.

'I'd be flattered if I thought that was for myself, rather than my wood-chopping abilities,' he said ruefully.

'No you wouldn't, you'd run a mile. It's much better just to be friends, you said so yourself.'

'Did I? Well, I'll be up occasionally to see how the gatehouse renovations are coming along, then

339

I'll be settling in by March, so you won't have to do without my log-splitting skills for long.'

He bent his dark head and kissed me goodbye and, perhaps because of Pia's interested gaze, it was *almost* brotherly.

Then he wound the striped scarf I had given him around his neck and sauntered off, looking as if he'd sprung out of an Armani advert.

Chapter Twenty-five

Chicken

Sprouts are best picked and eaten fresh the same day—or at least they are when they are not frozen hard to the stem! However, when I have a glut of them I do freeze a lot, especially the small ones.

I know the New Year has really begun when there are Seville oranges in the shops (not something you can grow in our climate!) and I have jars of jewel-coloured marmalade lined up in the larder once again.

'Cakes and Ale'

Harry and I spent a quiet New Year together, after which he retired to his shed and filed seven days' worth of metal off his minesweeping medal before displaying it, framed, on his living-room wall, together with the entire MOD correspondence. So many people had been to see the collection that he was thinking of charging an admittance fee.

My days were fully occupied with the usual busy round, including making lots of jars of lovely, deep-orange marmalade—plus keeping Libby grounded over the Old Barn conversion.

Then there were lots of enquiries about wedding cakes, most of them generated by that article in *Country at Heart* magazine. But I took Libby's advice and put my prices up, turned down any boring commissions or troublesome-sounding customers, and stuck to my guns about only delivering locally. Having to collect the cake put a lot of people off.

I still get internet fan mail too, though I thought it would have tapered off by now. It still seems odd to me that I should have a cult readership interested in the way I live *my* life, just as Ben and I once pored avidly over John Seymour's self-sufficiency books and Lizzie Pharamond's *Perseverance Cottage Chronicles*. We were too late for the first great wave of self-sufficiency, but now I'm a kind of guru to the next generation!

I suppose my lifestyle seems more accessible than that of the earlier self-sufficiency experts, since I live a truly green life only about eighty per cent of the time, if I'm lucky, so even city dwellers can follow some of my ideas.

After all, when Ben, Mary and Russell were doing their MA courses at the Royal College of Art in London and we all lived together in a basement flat, I still managed to grow loads of fruit, herbs and vegetables in containers liberated from skips. I sprouted mung beans, made jam, and baked bread, pies and cakes with wholemeal flour too.

And whatever Ben says, I never *hated* London. I may not have been much of a party animal, like him, but I used to love meeting Libby for lunch in

341

the Museum of Garden History, or going out to Kew Gardens for the day, plus there were all those lovely parks. There are worse jobs than selling bunches of flowers all day in a florist's too.

* * *

Rob Rafferty called in today for a chat and Noah was quite wrong about him, because he made no attempt to pounce on anything except my cakes, though I am sure the whole village is now talking about all the men visiting my cottage. Still, at least it will distract them from raking up old stories about Libby's mum's colourful past, which they have had a tendency to do since the wedding . . . Thinking about that reminded me of my horrible little secret, though I hastily pushed it out of sight.

* * *

Noah was still in London, but a few days into January I started to get all sorts of little hen-related gifts in the post, like a plastic wind-up chicken that laid eggs—and they just *had* to be from him, because I didn't know anyone else who would do something so daft. Then one day I got home from walking Mac to find a fresh stack of firewood and a cockerel weathervane on the woodshed roof, which was a bit of a giveaway, coupled as it was with a note from Noah saying he'd found Aggie halfway to Blessings and returned her to her run, though he couldn't guarantee she would still be there on my return. (Though by some miracle she was.)

I phoned him up to thank him and then I asked,

'Noah, have you been sending me lots of hen stuff in the post?'

'Hens? Who, *me*?' he said innocently. Then he asked me if I'd like to go with him to see the Antony Gormley sculptures of a hundred iron men, facing out to sea along the beach at Crosby, near Southport.

I'd wanted to see them for ages, but not got around to it, so I agreed and, despite the icy breeze blowing along the sands, I was glad I had, because they were very impressive. They had all the dignified presence of the Easter Island statues and, like them, looked as if they'd been there since the dawn of time.

They were also stark naked and Noah said they made him feel shy and distinctly lacking in the undercarriage department—as well they might—but I wasn't about to bolster up his ego on that point so I just nodded agreement. I expect this was why he chased me round and round one of them with a smelly dead crab, though he didn't catch me, thank goodness.

Gina had sent a packed lunch of sandwiches and Thermoses of hot coffee and soup, which we had in the car to thaw us out before the drive back. All in all, it was the best day I'd had for a long, long time, right up to the moment when Noah dropped me off at home, windblown, tired and relaxed from the warmth of the car.

I opened the front door and scooped up the post waiting for me on the mat as Noah tooted his horn and drove off, dumping three circulars and a letter from *Reader's Digest* (telling me I had won a huge amount of money—*perhaps*) straight into the recycled paper bin.

343

That left one handwritten envelope, which contained only a newspaper cutting from *The Times*, announcing that Ben and Olivia's nuptials had taken place at a register office. The envelope was postmarked Wilmslow, so I knew Ben's mother had sent it.

The sun seemed to go out of the day with Ben's mother's act of spitefulness. I never did anything to deserve all the enmity Nell Richards has directed at me over the years, but I hoped this would now be an end to it, for Ben and I were irrevocably parted. What more could she want?

To round the day off, Ben himself phoned me up in the evening, drunk as a skunk, to tell me his marriage was all my fault and he hoped I was satisfied.

'I don't see why I should have to take the blame for any of your actions, Ben Richards,' I told him coldly. 'As far as I know, you're an adult, even if you don't behave like one.'

But then his voice went all choked as he said he hadn't done any new work of any significance since we had parted and he didn't feel as if he ever would. 'I never really appreciated that our life together in Neatslake was the wellspring of my inspiration until it was too late, Josie. My creativity is shrivelling, here in London!'

'Well, presumably it shrivelled a bit whenever you were down there, Ben—and you've spent a lot of time in London in the last year, though admittedly *not* painting.'

'I thought you'd understand,' he said reproachfully. 'You always believed in my art!'

'I still do,' I replied, with a guilty thought for the rotting prawns, though I hoped by now they were

344

little more than a faint, unpleasant tang on the air. 'But now I come to think of it, you never did any really brilliant work while you were at the Royal College of Art, did you? It wasn't until you moved back to Neatslake that you were truly inspired again. I hope you get your mojo back, though, Ben, I really do—only it will have to be without any help from me.'

'My work can't have been that bad, because I got my MA!' he said indignantly, but then, with an effort, he added that he understood my bitterness (he has *no* idea!), and if he'd driven me into the arms of another man he forgave me (which was very big of him), and so surely *I* could forgive *him* for his little slip too?

He seemed to have entirely forgotten that he'd married his little slip. And if he still thinks I had a fling with Noah, then either he hasn't seen Mary since I spoke to her, or if he has, she didn't manage to convince him his suspicions were as unbelievable as *she* found them!

Unless, of course, village gossip has reached his ears via Stella and Mark, and he has drawn the wrong conclusion? And according to Libby, the village now seems to suspect I've got a thing going with Rob as well, but Ben mustn't have heard that fresh titbit . . .

I couldn't think of a thing to say, but luckily I didn't have to, because at that point there was the sound of a sharp-edged, by-now-familiar female voice saying, 'Ben? Who are you talking to?' and the phone went dead.

*   *   *

345

Noah came over to chop more wood next morning, before going back to London, arriving just in time to catch me about to trundle a heavy load of it over to the Graces in the wheelbarrow.

'Why don't you fill your car boot with it?' he asked curiously.

'Because the car was Harry's pride and joy, and I'm trying not to make too much of a mess of it.'

'Well, luckily I'm not so precious about my Jag—I'll take it across,' he offered, and he did too, though I insisted on lining his boot with henfood sacks first.

When he came back we had a cup of tea and a slice of treacle tart and I found myself telling him about Ben marrying Olivia and then phoning me to tell me it was *my* fault—that everything, including his losing his inspiration, was my fault—only suddenly, through Noah's eyes, I could see the funny side of it for the first time.

Before he left, I showed him the rush WAG wedding cake order I'd just finished making—a football topped with a pair of icing sugar Manolo Blahniks and a handbag. It was pretty straightforward, except that I had to buy a special cake tin for the football, though I expect it will come in handy for all kinds of designs now.

Because of the firewood the Graces now think Noah is wonderful and a 'dear boy', and Pansy asked me if I thought he would like one of her handknitted sweaters as a thank you. I said I was positive he would love one, especially if it had big, cheerful stripes, because he was very into that sort of thing.

*　　　*　　　*

346

Since Ben's call I knew he'd come up and stayed with Mark and Stella, because he'd been seen in the village. And once I thought I saw him in the distance myself when I was out walking Mac, so I turned and made off in the other direction, just in case.

It made it a little awkward about the co-op order too. Stella was very cool when she next rang to ask what I wanted. Then she called again when it arrived to tell me how much I owed her and where she would leave the order for me to pick up, so I haven't actually seen her since the day I ran into Ben in their kitchen. And that's OK by me. My true friends are the ones who have stuck by me, like Libby and Harry.

* * *

I was wrong about the TV series, because it looks as though at least the first six episodes will be shot. I had to drive over to the wine bar in Middlemoss to meet Claire Flowers for a big discussion over lunch—not that I actually *discussed* anything much, since she did most of the talking.

By the time we'd eaten a plate of seafood linguini (one little plateful cost as much as I could have fed twelve people with!), she'd thrashed everything out to her satisfaction and I was committed to the project and, if truth be told, starting to get a little excited about it too.

'So we'll start shooting in early March then, and hope for a good dry bright spell. The budget will be tight,' she began, then broke off and waved at someone behind me.

347

'It's Rob,' she said. 'I wonder if he would like to make a brief appearance in an episode—free.'

'He might, but he'd serve no useful purpose, except decoration,' I said, twisting round to see him. 'He—'

'Josie!' Rob swooped down on me like a golden eagle, scooped me up and kissed me with his usual enthusiasm. Then he did much the same to Claire, only by then I'd noticed the tall, slim, blonde girl standing behind him.

'This is Anji,' Rob said, coming up for air. 'She's got a cameo role in an episode of *Cotton Common* and when Claire said you'd be here for lunch today, we thought we'd come over because Anji really wanted to meet you.'

'*Me?*' I said, baffled and a bit embarrassed. Close to, Anji looked even more beautiful than she had the first time I'd seen her but, although there was a social smile on her lovely lips, her eyes were icy and my heart sank into my boots.

'Yes, you—my friends have told me *all* about you,' she said pointedly, 'and I'd *love* to have a little chat!'

* * *

'And then Claire had to leave and Rob went to buy drinks and Anji more or less told me to leave her boyfriend alone!' I told Libby, who'd come over with some curtain material samples she couldn't make her mind up about, just after I got home, limp as a rag.

'What, Noah?' Libby exclaimed. 'Good heavens, rumours *do* get around!'

'It must be Olivia spreading them, because Mary

348

certainly doesn't move in the same circles,' I said. 'Anyway, Anji said they'd been seeing each other for months and everything had been fine until he came to Neatslake for your wedding, and now he was blowing hot and cold and talking about spending half his time down here, so she wanted to know what the big attraction was.'

'What on earth did you say?'

'That the attraction certainly wasn't me—and by then, I think she was having trouble believing it herself. I mean—she is *stunning*, Libs, and even though I'd dressed up a bit for the wine bar I still couldn't hold a candle to her. In fact, I expect she just frightened Noah off a bit by getting too serious too soon, but I expect she'll get him back if she settles for what he's prepared to offer.'

After all, I certainly did, and you couldn't say he wasn't upfront about the lack of seriousness of his intentions!

'So what did she say next?' Libby enquired, fascinated.

'That now she'd seen me again, she couldn't really square the rumours with the reality, but if I *did* have any designs on Noah, to lay off! And I said I didn't, and anyway had only just broken up with my long-term partner and so wasn't interested in men, except as friends. Then Rob came back and I said I had to go, and escaped.'

'What an exciting life you're leading!' Libby said. 'I do think Noah dumped Anji before he had his little moment with you after my reception, though, so you needn't feel guilty about that on *her* account.'

'Maybe not . . . but then, he was with her in London when you ran into him before Christmas, wasn't he? And Pia saw in a magazine that he'd been to a charity event with her, so they must still be pretty friendly. Really, I don't know what to think. But it's his problem, it doesn't matter to me.'

'Oh, no?' she said, looking at me thoughtfully.

'No!' I said, and then after a pause added, 'I got another hen thing in the post today. Chicken and rooster oven mitts.'

'I've never known Noah to be like this. He must really like you!'

'I think it's more of a long-running joke, because of the way we met, when I was trying to catch Aggie. But we get on fine now we know where we are. Like Rob, too—he's happy just to be friends.'

She looked as unconvinced as Noah had about that.

'And the TV series is all signed, sealed and ready to start shooting?'

'March, early on, and I'm hoping they include a bit about the reception business, even though it won't have opened by then, because it would be good publicity, wouldn't it?'

'Yes, brilliant.' She fingered the swatches of material that had been her reason for visiting and said, 'Could you possibly come back with me now and help me make my mind up about these? Or did you say you had to wait in for someone to collect the WAG wedding cake?'

'No, that's all right. The bride's mother came all the way from Knutsford in a taxi for it this morning. She couldn't see it, because it was encased in giant bubble wrap by then, but she handed me an enormous cheque without a blink— if she'd been *able* to blink; her false eyelashes must have weighed a pound each. I hope the cake got there in one piece.'

'Must have done,' Libby said, 'or they would have rung you up by now.'

'I've got another one to make. I couldn't resist it.' I got out my design book and showed her a rough sketch. 'He's a marine biologist and she's a Butlins redcoat—isn't that a lovely mix? There's going to be a seaside rockpool scene on the top tier, with below it a sort of candy-striped, scalloped tented effect, folded back to reveal the happy couple sitting in deck chairs on the bottom tier.'

The rockpool would have a shiny, crackle-glazed surface, starfish, seaweed, a seagull, spade and bucket—the works. Even a dead crab, which suddenly reminded me of my day out at Crosby beach with Noah . . .

'Come on,' I said, getting up. 'Let's go to the Old Barn and compare fabric samples *in situ* while there's still daylight.'

* * *

There were no workmen around when we got there. The main bulk of the alterations were now done and the Old Barn was acquiring its finishing touches, with the permanent stage and the sound system going in, plus a large screen where any civil ceremonies in the Great Chamber could be relayed to the rest of the guests. I'd thought this was rather an extravagance, but Libby had insisted.

The barn now had lots of subtle, rather medieval-looking lighting, a dark oak floor and a couple of large reproduction tapestries, which all gave it a sort of indeterminate historical feel that

351

should be a good backdrop to any kind of wedding.

The former tackroom next to it was now a food preparation room, with huge fridges, worktops, sinks and a dishwasher, while the very swish new cloakrooms were done up like the Savoy, with expensive liquid soaps, a full-length mirror and piles of fluffy white towels. There were even changing cubicles (my idea!), in case the bride and groom wanted to put on their going-away clothes and leave for their honeymoon straight from the venue. This was where the fabric samples came in, though actually there was no reason why they shouldn't be the same fabric as the cloakroom curtains, and he had lots of that left over because he'd bought a whole bolt of it off the internet.

After Libby had come round to my way of thinking we went outside so I could tell her about a brainwave I'd had.

'When it was pouring with rain the other day, I suddenly thought how difficult it was going to be for the bride and groom to get from the car into the barn without getting soaked. There would have to be lots of dodging about with big umbrellas, and you can't get out of a car fast if you're wearing a meringue dress and yards of net.'

'That hadn't occurred to me,' she admitted.

'But if you had little metal rings sunk into the cobbles in front of the doorway, which would be quite unobtrusive, you could put up an awning-covered walkway whenever necessary.'

'Now, that *does* sound like a good idea, Josie, and it could be stowed in one of the stables when we don't need it.'

'It would be better in some kind of synthetic material, so the mice don't eat it.'

352

'*Would* they do that?'

'They'd probably chew holes in it. Come on, let's have a walk around the garden while the sun is shining. I think I need some cold, fresh air to blow away the cobwebs.'

The grounds were by now emerging from their years of neglect too, and Tim was devoting as much time as he could to helping Dorrie transform them back to their former glory. Seth Greenwood, Sophy Winter's husband, had resurrected the small knot garden near the house as a wedding present (that's what he does for a living). Although he'd had to put in a lot of new box planting, which would take time to grow together, it was defined with coloured gravel, so it already looked charming.

But the greatest bonus, I thought to myself as we walked around in the wintry sunshine, was that Libby had been so involved in the mad scramble of getting the business ready for opening at the end of March, that I was quite sure any idea she'd had about starting a family was pushed right to the bottom of her to-do list. Perhaps in the end she'd even decide she couldn't do both—and she might even go off the idea. I mean, it wasn't like Libby in the least!

I'd relaxed about my guilty secret a bit by now, since I'd come to the conclusion that there was no way I could ever *tell* her, so there was really nothing I could do about it. It might be an ostrich-with-its-head-in-the-sand approach, but it worked for me.

Chapter Twenty-six

Subtleties

It seems somehow immoral to me that people are prepared to spend thousands of pounds on lavish weddings. I often hear them referred to as 'fairytale', but they seem more the stuff of nightmares. The most romantic wedding I ever went to was a very small affair in a nearby village church, with only close family, friends and pets in attendance. The bride's silk suit had been run up by a local dressmaker, she carried a small posy of winter roses from her garden tied with ribbon, and came out of the church to a peal of bells and a shower of dried petal confetti. The reception was held in the bride's home, where friends and family had provided the buffet.

But then, of course, who am I to talk, when the newest dichotomy in lifestyle is that I'm assisting my friend to set up her new and terribly upmarket wedding reception business.

'Cakes and Ale'

Noah hadn't been down to Neatslake since I had the unfortunate encounter with Anji—and there had been no more fowl presents. Was this cause and effect—they were back together again and so he was too preoccupied to play chicken any more?

The Old Barn Receptions advert appeared in *Glorious Weddings* in the middle of January and soon Libby and I were stuffing brochures into envelopes and mailing them off. I suppose there will be even more publicity when that article about my cake business comes out, complete with pictures of the Pisa wedding cake. The *Sticklepond and District Gazette* did an article about the new venture too, so there were lots of local enquiries and it was all looking very promising for the launch in late March.

*   *   *

The first firm booking came towards the end of January, and Libby thought it should be a fairly easy reception to cut our teeth on, since the bride's mother was firmly in charge and not interested in any of the extras in the brochure, including my cake. Apart from the venue and the catering, she was organising everything herself. In fact, it all seemed to have been organised for months, except that the hotel where they had planned to hold the reception had just gone into receivership. Finding Libby's advert in *Glorious Weddings* had been the answer to a prayer when they were at their wits' end.

That booking was followed by a steadily increasing number of others, and then one day Libby phoned me in a panic to say she'd been asked if she could do a themed reception.

'Themed? What kind of theme?' I asked.

'Elizabethan.'

'Well, that shouldn't be too difficult, should it? The inside of the barn does look vaguely Elizabethan already. It just needs a few extra touches.'

'That's what I thought, but I'd still like you to be at the discussion tomorrow. They said they wanted

355

you to make the cake anyway. You *will* come, won't you?'

'Yes, of course. I can't wait to see what they think the Elizabethans had as a wedding cake!'

*   *   *

Already we had discovered that the reception was usually organised by the bride and her mother, but sometimes the happy couple would make the arrangements instead. That day, the would-be Elizabethans had come alone, though it was clear from the start that, behind the scenes, Daddy and his expanding wallet would be bankrolling anything his little princess set her heart on, however absurd.

'Did you have any particular reason for wanting an Elizabethan-style wedding?' I asked as Libby unlocked the door to the Old Barn and led the way in. I thought they might belong to a re-enactment society, or be historians or something similar.

'No, we just thought it would be different and fun, didn't we, Kevin?' said the prospective bride, who was a small, skeletal creature, mounted on the highest stilettos I'd ever seen. I hoped she didn't fall off, because there wasn't an ounce of fat on her anywhere to cushion the blow. 'All my friends seem to be having themed weddings, but no one's thought of anything quite like this!'

Her fiancé, who had the sort of head that would have looked better with hair on it, nodded obediently. 'When Laura said that's what she wanted, I Googled "Elizabethan wedding" on the internet and they're big in the USA, so we got lots of ideas.'

356

'And I looked up Elizabethan banquets,' I put in, 'so we should have some interesting ideas between us.'

'We're having invitations that look like parchment, with big wax seals,' Laura said, 'and telling everyone that they can come in costume if they want to.'

'What date is the wedding, did you say?' asked Libby, switching on all the lights and ushering them in.

'The first Monday in April. It's the only day the church at Middlemoss could fit us in at short notice,' the bride said, 'but once Kevin proposed I wanted to get married right away. I can never bear waiting for anything, can I, Kev? I'm just *too* impatient!'

'No,' he agreed, looking long-suffering.

'Then we couldn't find the right place for the reception until Fee—my best friend—spotted your advert in a wedding magazine.' She stood in the middle of the room and slowly spun around on her heels.

Libby winced a bit—probably thinking about her new wooden flooring.

'And it's just how I imagined it! It only needs a few details to be really Elizabethan, doesn't it? Maybe straw on the floor? Candlesticks? Lutes playing, that sort of thing?'

'I think oak floorboards are fine for the upper classes of the period, who would be the only ones able to afford a lavish wedding feast, anyway,' I said quickly. 'Straw would look a bit downmarket and the long skirts would drag in it.'

'Perhaps you're right,' she conceded. 'Candlesticks?'

357

'I'll look into it,' said Libby. 'And actually, if your budget will run to it, there is an Elizabethan re-enactment society in Sticklepond who could be hired to add a bit of extra authenticity. They could serve the food, move among the guests and even do an exhibition dance from the period. They've got a collection of music from the time that you could play in the background, and might even know some suitable musicians.'

'Great!' Laura said.

'But I think we ought to have a DJ,' Kevin objected. 'You can take things too far.'

'No, that's at the evening party, when we've all changed back into ordinary clothes again, dumbo,' she said. 'Don't you ever listen? I've already booked that. They have function rooms at the old Butterflake Biscuit factory at Middlemoss. Do you know it?' she asked us.

'I do,' I said. 'It's very nice and only a few miles away.'

'Of course, it would be easier to have both events in the same place, but you said you didn't do evening events?'

'No, I'm afraid not,' Libby said firmly. 'We need the time to get ready for the next day's wedding.'

Laura flicked open a tiny mobile and relayed everything we had discussed without letting the person at the other end get a word in until right at the end. Then she snapped it shut. 'Daddy says I can have whatever will make me happy,' she said with a satisfied smile.

Libby had been making copious notes and now she got out the brochure and turned to the back. 'There are a few more extras you might like to consider, like floral decorations for the tables.'

'Bunches of herbs were popular,' I said, suddenly remembering my research. 'Rosemary featured a lot too, especially gilded.'

'Did it?' Laura said doubtfully.

'We have an expert flower arranger—you can safely leave it to her to produce something pretty,' Libby assured her.

They also ordered one of the Graces' tablecloths, to be embroidered, at my suggestion, with love knots and other Elizabethan symbols of love and fidelity.

Then the bride-to-be said to me, 'And of course we want *you* to make the wedding cake!'

'Actually, at that time they didn't have a wedding cake as we know it. In fact, I think it was around then they broke a thin loaf over the bride's head instead. But they did have what they called "subtleties", which were three-dimensional constructions in sugar, often with biblical meaning. What about something like that?'

'No,' said Laura decidedly, 'I want one shaped like a giant pomander studded with roses, just like my bouquet.'

'But, darling, don't you think that would look a bit odd?' began Kevin.

Laura's small foot began to tap on the floor and there was a glint in her eye and a rising note to her voice as she snapped: 'I *want* it. I can *see* it. It will look *beautiful*!'

Kevin hastily agreed.

'Mostly *white* rosebuds,' she added.

'I can make you exactly what you want,' I said, and what was more, I would be able to utilise the football cake mould again. How convenient!

Libby promised to have the plans and menus

with them soon, for approval, and they went away happy. Or the bride was happy, anyway. The groom looked as if he had suddenly been seized by the love knots, so I expected the reality of spending a lifetime with Laura had begun to sink in.

But then, how many marriages lasted a lifetime these days? The more I saw, the more cynical I felt about it all!

*   *   *

Libby got Jasper Pharamond on board as Historical Food Consultant for a small fee, to see which banqueting foods of the time could be updated for modern tastes. Then he got together with the proprietors of Movable Feasts, and they devised a menu consisting of a crab and salmon ring with pomegranate seeds, glazed roasted chickens and rastons, which were a sort of stuffed bread-wrapped morsel. There would be platters of salads too, and the desserts would be rose petal ice cream and open apple tart with cream.

Well, it was a nod in the direction of the right century.

I suggested they cook one of the peacocks, which would be traditional, especially if they dressed it up again in its feathers before serving, but Libby told me not to be silly.

Jasper also suggested some drinks of the time, but, anachronism or not, by the bride's decree it was to be pink champagne in the loving cup.

*   *   *

By now, Libby was quite blasé about showing prospective customers around the Old Barn and only called me in if they were thinking of ordering one of my cakes, or if she needed some kind of backup.

It still amazed me how much people were prepared to spend on a wedding, especially on a dress they would wear only once, but it seemed to me that it was the ones prepared to lavish the most money who had the least chance of their marriage lasting past the first anniversary.

Libby also thought I'd turned into an old cynic. Well actually, she said I was an embittered old cow, but she was joking . . . I think. Anyway, *she* was almost as bad, because we'd started taking bets on which couples would make it past their first anniversaries—or even if their marriages would last longer than the last bite of wedding cake—though how we'd ever find out which of us had won, I wasn't sure.

*   *   *

Libby said Noah rang last night to see how his gatehouse renovations were going, and she told him about the Elizabethan wedding, which she thought would make for interesting pictures, especially the bald-headed groom with the eagle tattoo on the back of his neck and a large tongue stud, dressed up in doublet and hose.

'He said he'd been too busy to come down, but he looked forward to moving in soon.' She paused. 'So I told him your pile of firewood was dwindling by the day and he said he'd heard that you were seeing a lot of Rob Rafferty, so maybe *he* could take over the wood-chopping duties.'

'What! Who told him that?' I demanded.

'That's what I asked, and he said Anji'd told him she saw you and Rob in a wine bar together when she was down here recently, and you were obviously more than friends—and then Claire Flowers told her you had been seeing a lot of each other.'

'But that is twisting the whole thing right round,' I exclaimed. '*She* arrived with Rob, not me. I was already there with Claire. And Claire knows Rob is only a friend, nothing more. How devious!'

'All's fair in love and war, Josie, but don't worry, I put him straight.'

'I'm not worried. I don't care what he thinks!' I declared, but wondered if perhaps this was why the hen gifts seemed to have dried up.

'*And* I told him that although you were friendly with Rob, you were certainly not on wood-chopping terms.'

'Thanks—I think. You know, it never even occurred to me to ask Rob to chop wood.' I giggled suddenly. 'I expect he'd have to study for the part, first!'

*   *   *

I baked the round Pomander cake (the mould was in two halves so it was quite easy to make, really). There was a flat bit on the bottom, of course, so that it wouldn't roll away.

Violet had already started to make icing rosebuds and foliage, because it would take quite a lot to cover the surface entirely. I was quite looking forward to putting it all together! I

362

emailed Claire Flowers about it, and she said she hoped to film me putting the finishing touches to it in the programme, so I suppose I had better try to time the icing for when the film unit descends on me. That, or make another, just for the cameras.

* * *

It had been cold and damp lately and Harry had had a tendency to pore over the pictures of New Zealand that his daughter kept sending him, while crankily telling me what the temperature was over there. I think it was just because his rheumatism was playing him up, though, not because he was seriously thinking of uprooting himself and emigrating!

I had had to start chopping wood again too, because we'd almost run out. It was a task I could do without when I was so busy, but I expect the exercise was good for me, and anyway, Harry found a fire comforting when he felt all achy, and my stoves ran on the stuff, so it had to be done.

* * *

I had a phone enquiry about a cake from friends of the Goth couple I made one for last year. They were Goths too, and were trying to find a venue where they could have a themed civil wedding ceremony and reception, so I suggested Blessings and gave them Libby's number. 'She's registered for civil ceremonies and the house is Elizabethan, it's lovely.'

Libby phoned me later and said, 'I never thought our first civil wedding ceremony would be a Goth one! They're coming round to discuss what they want at ten tomorrow morning—and *you* have to be here. I don't know a thing about Goths.'

'Neither do I, really, but they sounded nice so it will probably be fun, Libby. And Pia will think it's wonderful; she's half-Goth herself.'

'Now *that's* a worrying thought,' Libby said.

*   *   *

The couple arrived early, because I saw them drive slowly past in an old black hearse with running boards while I was still washing up cake tins, and by the time I'd whipped my pinny off and run round to Blessings, they were already in the Great Chamber with Libby.

They made a striking couple: the man, who introduced himself as Marty, was tall and thin, wearing black trousers and waistcoat, and with a top hat over his long, blue-black hair; while Lola, his fiancée, had on a long dress of dark red velvet, the same colour as the lipstick that stood out like a gash against her white face.

Gina, fingering her crucifix, hovered protectively until firmly sent away by Libby to make coffee, and we got down to business.

Libby needn't have worried, because they already knew exactly what they wanted, from the parchment invitations to the going-away vehicle (their own hearse). They'd brought a ring-binder full of notes and photographs, which they proposed leaving with us for reference.

'It'll be perfect in here, if the curtains are drawn and perhaps the room is just lit by candelabra?' suggested Lola happily.

364

'Funnily enough, we've just bought a pair of electric candelabra for an Elizabethan-themed wedding. They look just like candles, but are much safer. We could use those,' Libby suggested.

'Great,' said Marty.

The floral decorations for both the Great Chamber and the Old Barn were to be dark flowers and ivy—basically, anything in black, blood red or deep purple would go down a treat—which I expect Dorrie would find an interesting challenge. The soundtrack music to *Edward Scissorhands* would play during the ceremony and the buffet meal.

'Then we've got a DJ who'll play a mixture of Goth and eighties pop, later,' Marty said. 'Another friend will be doing the photographs in black and white, like a diary of the day.'

When we told them that they would probably have a second photographer taking pictures, in the form of Noah Sephton, they seemed highly delighted.

'And did you say the wedding ceremony could be relayed live to the guests in the barn, the ones who won't fit in the Great Chamber?' asked Lola, and seemed pleased when Libby said that was no problem, so maybe she was right about installing that screen in the barn after all! And when we showed them the barn they loved it.

'We'll need only the wall lights on to give the right ambience,' Marty said, taking in the cavernous interior.

'Yes, and we can cover the tables with crimson cloths without the usual white ones on top,' suggested Libby, who was getting into the swing of things. 'What about the buffet? Will you need anything different there?'

'No, I don't think so,' said Lola. 'Food is food. And we will have a choice of red wine or dark grape juice in red goblets. We've already bought enough of those. They're plastic picnic ones actually, but they look good.'

'Fine,' said Libby, scribbling that down.

They also ordered dark red rose petal confetti and they loved the idea of the heirloom tablecloths—if the Graces would embroider one with cats, bats, dragons and fairies and give it a nice, black edging. I assured them that the sisters liked a challenge.

So that just left the cake design to be decided. They wanted a stacked, two-tier hexagonal black and white one, decorated with a Celtic knot design around the sides and embellished with suitable motifs like bats and a dragon.

'And we'd like Gothed-up bride and groom figures on top,' said Marty.

'With wings,' added the bride.

'The dragon?' I questioned.

'No, me,' she said. 'I'll be wearing black feathery wings on the day.'

*　　　*　　　*

On Valentine's Day hen mania (and perhaps Noah's sanity) resumed, because I got a big, chicken-shaped card that opened out to reveal the message 'Clucky in Love'.

In fact I got two cards, because Ben also sent me one. Like the other, it was unsigned, but I knew who'd sent it. For a start, it said inside 'Forgive me?' And then, it was handmade, like all the

Valentines Ben had ever given me, with various kinds of seeds stuck onto card in the shape of a heart. It must have taken ages, but unfortunately he hadn't dried out the melon seeds properly and they had gone mouldy, so I put it straight onto the compost heap.

I kept Noah's out on the dresser, though, despite feeling angry with him for so easily believing Anji's lies about me. But unfortunately, when Libby saw the card she became convinced that he was romantically interested in me.

'No, he's just being silly again,' I told her. 'I think he was a bit piqued when I didn't instantly fall head over heels for him after our night of passion, like all his other conquests, but we get on well enough together when he isn't trying to flirt with me. He can obviously get anything else he needs elsewhere.'

She looked unconvinced, especially after a tiny but very ancient-looking oil painting of a chicken arrived—but so far as I know, even the Victorians didn't ascribe any romantic meaning to poultry other than turtledoves.

Libby and Tim—and even Noah, in his way—had enriched my Neatslake life, and although I was resigned by now to always living alone, it didn't mean that life couldn't be fun. After Ben left, it seemed impossible that I would ever feel happy again, but after Valentine's Day, I found my spirits rising with every day that took me closer to spring.

Chapter Twenty-seven

Spring Fever

March came in like a lamb, so I hope it isn't going to roar out like a lion, since I've planted my early potatoes, sown my leeks and summer spinach and put in strawberries and some new raspberry canes. I adore raspberries! According to an elderly friend, during the war strawberry and raspberry jam was really nothing of the kind, but gooey mixed fruit, with tiny wooden pips put in, to take the place of real ones. Can that be true? Fake pips?!

'Cakes and Ale'

As a wet and dismal February turned to a brightly optimistic March, things started to blossom with the promise of fruition.

I supposed Mary and Olivia were doing much the same in London, for they were due to give birth some time in late April and early May . . .

Mary rang occasionally now, but I hadn't asked her specifically when.

As usual, I had lots of other things to think of. There was the garden, for a start. By March I was really starting to gear up for a whole new cycle of planting and harvesting, and there was loads to do getting new beds ready and that kind of thing. Cleaning out the henhouse had also now fallen to my lot, but at least the hens were repaying me by laying again.

And then Claire Flowers and a film unit

descended on me, for the first of the six episodes of *Sticklepond Spring*. It was very odd: at first it seemed so intrusive, all these people shoving muffs on sticks at me and pointing cameras and trailing wires, not to mention drinking my tea and eating all the cakes and biscuits. But after a while, I got sort of used to it and most of the time I just carried on as I normally would, except for falling over people's feet. Claire didn't even want me to put on smart clothes. She was perfectly happy with my rainbow hoodie and jeans or patchwork dungarees and spotty wellies.

The filming seemed pretty chaotic, like my days, but Claire said that didn't matter, it would all be chopped up and rearranged later, into several programmes. They must still throw away a lot of film . . . or maybe it was all digital? I didn't notice.

Anyway, they filmed me collecting eggs in the henhouse and, later, chasing Aggie across the Green. (This was not set up for the cameras—she just sneaked out and legged it again.) Violet Grace came over for eggs and was roped in too, with a glowing explanation of our barter scheme. By mid-morning, half the village was loitering outside the cottage, wondering what was going on, but must have been frustrated not to see anything, since by then all the action was going on in the garden—me digging a bed and looking over the last of the winter's stored apples, sweet and wrinkly. The crew ate them all.

Then they did some shots where I was holding up glowing jams and marmalade against the larder window, before finally allowing me to finish icing the Pomander cake. I entirely forgot they were there while I was doing that.

I'd already covered the whole sphere in a layer of white icing and tied a wide white velvet ribbon round it, with a loop at the top, just like a real pomander. Now I began to fill in each quarter with icing rosebuds and leaves, which took rather a long time, but the end result was lovely.

Next day they filmed Harry letting out the hens, me out walking with Mac, and then with Libby at Blessings, slightly self-consciously discussing preparations for the first wedding at Old Barn Receptions. I also had to run up to Blessings to show Libby the copy of *Glorious Weddings* featuring my weird and wonderful cakes, even though she'd already seen it when it first arrived.

In the afternoon I delicately tinted the Pomander cake roses with pale pink and green natural food colouring, and then baked the two hexagonal cakes ready to start the Goth one.

I'd bought bride and groom figurines for the top, which I intended painting in Goth colours when the cameras had long gone, because I needed a steady hand.

All in all, it was an exhausting couple of days, especially since they asked me to do some things over and over until they were quite happy with them. And they got through a lot of cake.

They intended descending on me in April and May too, to add more material, but I thought I'd get used to it.

Libby was terribly excited about it all, much more than I was, but mainly because she thought it would give the reception business lots more publicity. She also said I'd be famous, but I still didn't think my life was terribly exciting, and the six programmes would probably be all there ever

370

were.

I was quite glad to settle down in relative peace and was getting quite hardened about turning down commissions for cakes if I hadn't got the time or didn't like the idea. It wasn't that I didn't like making cakes, it was just that I enjoyed doing other things too, and I never intended to do it full time!

Lola had emailed me a picture of the wedding dress a friend had made for her, so I could paint the models in black and white to match, and then stick on little wings. The groom just needed his suit and top hat painting black, and then once I'd given them pale faces and dark hair, they should look quite strikingly like the happy couple.

* * *

The gatehouse renovations were now finished and Libby let me in to have a look, before Noah finally moved in. I still felt unreasonably miffed with him, probably because he had been prepared to believe Anji's lies about me, but I took him a house-warming gift of a tin filled with home-made biscuits and a bottle of elderberry wine. The tin was actually a catering-sized instant coffee tin that I'd begged from the Griffin, hand-painted by Violet with big colourful spots on a cream ground.

Since Noah hadn't been down since January, he had missed all the excitement of the filming, but as I said to Libby as she let us into the gatehouse, I expect he's quite blasé about all that kind of thing in the arty circles he moves in.

Libby said, 'But you're moving in them too, now!'

'No, I'm just temporarily in the outer orbit,' I said, but she was convinced the TV series would be a huge success and not only would I become a TV star, but Old Barn Receptions would be booked up for the next ten years. I couldn't shake her on it.

The gatehouse had changed out of all recognition. A tiny bathroom with shower and loo had been created out of a corner of the one bedroom, and the lean-to room downstairs off the living room was now a minute galley kitchen. It must have cost Noah a fortune, but according to Libby he was rolling in money and could ask what he liked for his portraits, with people queuing up for them, not to mention his annual sell-out exhibitions of black-and-white photographs.

Libby was delighted with the work that had been done, because she'd be able to rent the gatehouse out as a tiny but intimate holiday let, once Noah didn't need it any more.

* * *

Noah arrived next morning and came round later to thank me for the biscuits and wine. I invited him in, but it was a bit strained at first—none of the easy friendship we had shared previously. I suppose it was because at the back of his mind there was a lingering suspicion that Anji had been right, and I *was* having a mad, passionate fling with Rob Rafferty; and at the back of mine I suspected he was still indulging his no-strings-attached philosophy with Anji.

But then, since I'd just taken a batch of Cornish pasties out of the oven, and it was nearly lunch time, I invited him to stay. I'd already taken one round to Harry, as a quick snack before he went to his dominoes club.

'That's a lot of Cornish pasties,' Noah commented, sitting at the table. 'Two different kinds?'

'Actually, some of them are Chingree Puffs, like a sort of curried pasty. Lily Grace gave me the recipe. And I batch-bake because I freeze a lot of them. Some go into Harry's freezer too. He likes to be independent and gets most of his own meals. Any excess I give to the Graces and Dorrie. All three of them are terribly proud, but I just say I can't fit any more into my freezer because I've got carried away and made too many. Of course, they give me Acorns in exchange.'

'Acorns?'

'Yes, the imaginary currency we use to trade things.'

'Of course, I'd forgotten—Libby told me all about it. You look after your friends well,' he commented, with that attractive, slightly lopsided smile.

'They look after me too, and anyway, I love to cook. I don't have to worry about Dorrie so much now, though, because Libby's always inviting her over for meals, or Gina's popping in with containers of pasta and sauce,' I said. 'Plus Libby and Tim are insisting on paying her for gardening too. But I'm going to miss the Blessings grapes.'

I told him about how the last Mrs Rowland-Knowles never got to see her grapes, since Dorrie whipped them away and bartered them with me for large amounts of Acorns. Dorrie didn't like grapes, but I loved them.

I gave Noah a Chingree Puff to try, and had just bitten into one myself when he said, 'According to Libby, your ex's studio has got electricity and running water, so I wondered if you'd consider renting it to me while I'm in Neatslake?'

'Renting it to you? What on earth for?' I choked, having swallowed my mouthful too hastily.

'I like to develop some of my own black-and-white pictures, and there isn't room in the gatehouse.'

'I—well, yes, I suppose you *could*. Ben used part of it as a darkroom himself sometimes, but it's all a bit ramshackle.'

'Ramshackle is fine. I just want somewhere I can work and spread my stuff out, and the gatehouse is bijou, to say the least.'

'Yes, I see what you mean.'

'I can come and go by the side gate and not disturb you. And I'll pay you rent, of course.'

'I don't need rent! The studio isn't doing anything useful at the moment, though I thought I might use it for extra storage next winter.'

'I'll be using your electricity and water,' he pointed out.

'All right then, we'll call all that wood chopping you did for me the rent.'

'I did that for love,' he said. 'It doesn't look like anyone else has.'

'No, I've chopped my own as I've needed it,' I said, meeting his eyes fair and square.

His light grey ones searched mine for a moment and then he smiled again, but more warmly. 'You won't need that much wood once it gets warmer, will you? I'll have to pay you back some other way . . .'

'Well, there's always a lot of heavy digging at this time of year,' I suggested, though not seriously. Some of the tension between us seemed to have evaporated at last and we were falling back into our previous casual friendship.

*   *   *

The reception bookings had gone from a trickle to a steady stream and, even before the official opening day at the end of March, there were clear signs that the venture would be a huge success.

That didn't stop Libby worrying about it, though. 'This simply *has* to work,' she said, as I helped her to manoeuvre the trestle tables into a horseshoe arrangement for our very first reception the following day. 'It's cost us a fortune.'

I straightened my aching back and looked around the barn. 'Everything looks wonderful. I don't see how it can fail, do you?'

'It had better not, because Tim's just told his partners he's had enough and is leaving at the end of the month!'

'Well, that might have been a bit rash, but it shows how much faith he has in you. Did you say the bride's mother was making the wedding cake for this first reception, Libs?'

'Yes, that's what she said. It's supposed to be arriving in the morning. She's bringing it before she goes to the hairdressers. And they've hired a string quartet to play during the meal, so they will arrive early too, to set up.'

'I think I'd rather have the Mummers, even if you do have to unplug their electric violins and drag them off the stage eventually. You certainly get your money's worth.'

Libby turned to me, looking suddenly anxious. 'Oh, Josie, we've put so much into this! You do think it will take off, don't you? You're not just saying that?'

'Yes, of course I do, you idiot! It will be a huge, *mega*-success,' I reassured her, because Libby was normally such a tough cookie, on the surface at least, that I knew she must *really* be worried to ask me that. 'Everything looks lovely, and you've organised it to perfection. In fact, I don't think you really need me at all tomorrow,' I joked. 'Even Pia is going to be here, helping!'

'Yes, it's lovely how she's taken an interest in the business,' Libby agreed, brightening, 'and she says she'll work for me all over the summer holidays too, peak wedding time—though I suppose that's with the proviso that Jasper is at home, and not off digging somewhere, or she'll simply up sticks and shamelessly follow him.'

'I'd like to see her getting her manicured nails full of earth in an archaeological trench,' I said. 'The things we do for love!'

'You *will* be here nice and early tomorrow, won't you?'

'As soon as I've made sure Harry is OK and walked Mac,' I promised. 'Is Noah going to be around, taking pictures?'

'Yes. He happened to be here when the mother was fussing about last-minute arrangements and asked her, and she was terribly flattered. They will all be putty in his hands, just you wait and see. In fact, practically every woman seems to be putty in his hands when he's exerting his charm, except you, though it doesn't seem to stop him flirting with you, I've noticed.'

'I think that's just a reflex action—I am *so* not his type,' I said. 'Rob Rafferty's much the same. They agree to be just friends, but can't resist trying it on sometimes to see if they get a reaction. But since I know they're only looking for casual, uninvolved sex, that's hardly a flattering or enticing prospect, is it?'

'Oooh, Little Miss Blasé, with her two celebrity menfriends,' Libby said, and I grinned.

'I suppose it does seem a bit strange,' I admitted, then cast a last glance around the Old Barn. 'It all looks perfect—the stage is set, we're just awaiting the actors! I've got that feeling in the pit of my stomach that I always get in a theatre, before the curtain goes up.'

'Yes, that's it exactly! There's an air of hushed expectancy and I feel sort of hollow as well, though I think that's nerves.'

'It will be fine, you'll see,' I assured her again, though truth to tell her last-minute jitters were infectious and now I was feeling nervous too. 'At least I talked you out of making me wear some kind of smart dress and tights, because a plain black T-shirt and trousers, covered by a big white pinafore, is much more my cup of tea.'

'You're still a bit too thin,' Libby commented. 'And you know what they say about thin cooks.'

'I didn't until Noah told me. And can you be too rich or too thin? There isn't any meat on *your* bones either.' But it was true that my clothes were still a bit loose despite my getting back my appetite. I suppose I was physically working much harder.

'Nature made me small and thin, but she made

you taller and bigger-boned. I don't think you ought to lose any more weight.'

'I can't help it. I must be burning off more calories than I eat. All that digging and planting and hoeing . . .'

'Do you *need* to grow so much now?'

'Probably not, but old habits die hard. Dorrie says she and Tim will soon have Blessings fairly self-sufficient with the new fruit and vegetable garden, and what you don't grow you can barter apples and pears with me for, like Dorrie has been doing. But maybe not the grapes.'

'*What* grapes?'

'The ones off the vine in the old greenhouse,' I said guiltily. 'Dorrie doesn't like them, so she used to barter them with me. Tim's stepmother never got to see any at all.'

'Well, hands off my grapes from now on,' Libby said severely.

'OK,' I agreed. 'Didn't Tim say he'd ordered a henhouse for spring?'

'Yes, so maybe the peacocks will chase the chickens instead of me,' she said optimistically, because one of the two lonely males had recently taken a fancy to her—Claudius, I think.

'Really, I only need to grow enough to feed the Graces, Harry and myself. I don't barter stuff with Mark and Stella any more. The only contact we have is by phone when I give them our co-op order, and I expect they would have dropped that, except it's cheaper the more people come in with them to bulk buy.'

'There's nowt so queer as folk,' Libby said absently, and I could see her mind had wandered away and she was picturing the scene tomorrow,

378

with the guests milling about, the food set out on the buffet tables and champagne cooling in the ice buckets . . .

'It'll be fine, don't worry, Libby—absolutely fine!'

*   *   *

That afternoon I started on a Bed of Roses wedding cake commission, which was going to be the happy couple depicted in a four-poster bed, with a coverlet of roses. Violet, who had come to collect more sugar paste, because she was making lots of the flowers and foliage, was chatting to me as I beat the mixture.

'Isn't that that nice Noah Sephton in your garden?' she said, peering through the living room to where she could see the path beyond the French doors.

'Yes, he asked me if he could use the studio as a darkroom.'

'Oh? I thought everyone used those digital cameras now, though come to think of it, I noticed his looked like an old one at Libby and Tim's wedding.'

'He says he likes the quality and controllability of his old Leica with black-and-white film, especially for portraits, and he also prefers to develop and print them himself. He does use digital too, though, for the colour ones.'

'Well, I expect it will be very nice for you having someone around, for company,' she said kindly, and I only hoped her romantic little heart wasn't cherishing the same mistaken hopes as Libby's did when Noah was inundating me with chicken gifts and chopping my firewood.

We watched as some deliverymen carried boxes of stuff into the studio—chemicals and things, I suppose—and then a table and chairs and a few other bits and pieces. He certainly seemed to be making himself at home.

'He's already paid me rent in advance, as far as I'm concerned, by chopping firewood, but he says he'll do some heavy digging too.'

'He's very kind, but he mustn't spoil his beautiful hands,' she said, to my surprise.

'He *has* got rather nice hands, but they're already a bit callused from chopping wood,' I said guiltily. 'He even manages to look elegant with an axe; it must be in the bones.'

When the deliverymen had gone, Harry came through the wicket gate, followed by Mac, and stood talking to Noah. Then they both went into the studio, so I supposed Noah was showing him what he was doing to it.

'It will be nice for Harry to have another man to chat to occasionally,' I said to Violet. 'I'm sure I've left him alone an awful lot lately, since I've been helping Libby with the barn as well as being snowed under with cake orders.'

'You can't be everywhere at once, dear,' she remarked. 'Now, how many roses would you like me to make?'

*   *   *

Mary phoned later in the afternoon, mostly to tell me that the last stages of pregnancy are hideously uncomfortable, which was hardly tactful of her since this was clearly something I was never going to experience.

And call me a nasty person, but when she said Olivia had suddenly loosened her rigid grip on her diet and ballooned to the size of a walrus seal, I rejoiced.

That seemed to be the budget of her news, except that she said *Simply Secrets* recently reported that Anji was the latest in a long line of broken-hearted ex-girlfriends of the fickle Noah Sephton. 'So watch your step!' she giggled, as a parting shot.

But you can't believe everything you read in magazines, so who knew what the real status quo was? I suspected she had settled for what she could get.

Chapter Twenty-eight

Three Tiers for the Bride

Now that my cakes have featured both in a wedding magazine and in the glossy brochure of my friend's wedding reception business, I am getting even more enquiries. But making weird and wonderful cakes was never something that I intended to do full time and so I only accept commissions I really want to make.

And something I quickly learned is that when delivering a cake myself, it always pays to keep a little repair kit, including icing sugar and ready-made fondant icing, with you, for any little accidents en route!

'Cakes and Ale'

It was about ten next morning when I went over to Blessings, already dressed in my black trousers and top, with my snowy apron folded in my bag, and by that time I'd already had three frantic phonecalls from Libby. Much ado about nothing: she'd organised the whole thing to such a degree that there simply wasn't room for error—or not on her part, anyway. She had no control over what the bridal party would do.

I arrived at a crucial moment: a large lady with a scarlet mouth and a face like a doughy, flour-dusted bap, was just placing the third and final tier of an elaborate wedding cake into place.

'This is Mrs Fosdyke,' Libby introduced her. 'She's the bride's mother and she's made the cake herself. Isn't it lovely?'

'It's certainly very impressive,' I agreed tactfully. It was the traditional white job, all icing swags and flourishes. On top, a pair of bride and groom figures seemed to be cowering in the shade of an over-large vase of silk flowers. The tiers were supported by slender silver columns . . . *very* slender.

'Is that straight?' asked Mrs Fosdyke, still clasping the top tier between bejewelled hands.

Libby, standing nervously in front, said, 'Yes, it looks fine.'

The woman cautiously let go and then came round to view her handiwork. 'There, isn't that just as good, if not better, than any bought one? I told my daughter we needn't go to the extra expense of ordering a cake when I have been to all the icing classes and knew I could make one myself. Of course, she wanted a bought one, but I told her that your charges had been so extremely high that some economies simply had to be made, after losing our deposit on the first venue.'

'There *are* cheaper places,' Libby said mildly.

Mrs Fosdyke clearly hadn't economised on herself, for she was dripping with jewellery and the car parked outside probably cost about what my tiny cottage was worth.

The cake, though, was indeed perfectly adequate, if uninspired—and it isn't easy making a traditional wedding cake, even if you *have* been to icing classes. I hoped there was enough support under those slender columns, for that part could be tricky for a novice to get right . . .

But even as the thought crossed my mind, the pristine white tower seemed to shift slightly to one side and tremble . . . And then suddenly the top two tiers tilted and started sliding downwards in slow motion, like a glacier calving. They hit the floor with a soggy series of thumps, and rolled.

Only the base layer stayed put, with a row of partly sunken silvery columns sticking up like a ruin. It *was* a ruin.

There was a horrible silence. Mrs Fosdyke had gone as white as the cake and her eyes had glazed over. I bent down and picked up the two tiers, which had luckily come to rest with the tops uppermost, and quietly laid them on the table.

Libby cleared her throat. 'Oh dear!' she said inadequately.

Mrs Fosdyke, getting her voice back, came out with an unexpectedly obscene expletive—presumably the 'something blue' needed at every wedding—then turned on Libby, saying, 'This is all your fault!'

'*Mine?*' Libby gasped, taking a step backwards.

'Yes, of course. The table legs must be uneven, or the floor, and—'

'No,' I interrupted, 'it was none of those things. It fell simply because the columns were unsupported and the weight of the upper tiers made them sink into the cake. You should have inserted dowelling in the layers underneath, where the columns were to rest.'

'*Dowelling?*' she exclaimed, in very Lady Bracknell tones. 'I never heard of such a thing! You are making excuses.'

'I'm afraid you'll find I'm correct. I make wedding cakes for a living,' I explained, though I didn't tell her mine were weird and wonderful. I might not enjoy making the traditional kind, but I did know how to do it, and sometimes I used the technique for fairytale castles. In fact, the upper thin cake layer of my four-poster Bed of Roses cake would have to be supported in the very same manner, disguised as bedposts.

Mrs Fosdyke seemed, reluctantly, to accept the truth. She stopped blustering and started wringing her hands over the sorry remains, instead. 'But it's ruined! The icing swags are all knocked off and the sides are battered and—' She stopped, and her eyes widened. 'Oh my God—Penelope! What is she going to say? And it's not even as if you can pop down to the nearest bakery and buy one off the shelf, is it?'

'You don't need to,' I said with more assurance than I felt, spurred by the entreating looks Libby was shooting at me—miracles, my speciality. 'Luckily, the tiers came to rest on their bases and the bride and groom figures are OK, though the

384

vase and flowers are past mending. If you leave it with me, I'm sure I can do something with it, so it'll pass muster at the reception. I haven't time to re-ice it, but I *can* hide the damage.'

She looked at me uncertainly, but with dawning hope. 'Are you sure?'

'Yes, perfectly.'

Then she glanced at her watch and yelped, 'Look at the time! I'll simply *have* to trust you; I can't do anything else!' And off she shot.

When she'd gone, Libby looked at the ruins of the cake and said, 'How on earth are you going to do something with this? It's a ruin.'

'At least the floor is so clean you could eat off it, so it isn't dirty,' I said. 'Come on, help me put the layers back in the boxes, with what's left of the decorations, and I'll take them home and see what I can do. Here's Pia—she can come back with me and help. You don't really need me for a bit, do you?'

'I suppose not. The buffet food has arrived and the girls are having coffee in the tackroom before they set it all out,' she agreed. The three enterprising young women who run Movable Feasts not only help make the buffet food, they also serve it and clear up afterwards.

We explained to Pia what had happened, and she helped me carry the boxes of ruined cake back to my cottage.

There, she watched me while I laid the three tiers out on the work surface, carefully removing the last broken fragments of icing decorations. Underneath, the base layer of icing was quite soft, which wouldn't have helped support the columns. Amateurs either get it so hard it won't cut without

385

a hacksaw, or so soft it practically runs off the cake.

After dusting them down with a clean pastry brush, I filled in a couple of gaps with ready-made fondant icing, polished the joins with icing sugar, and then rebuilt the tiers by placing them directly one on top of the other.

'It's not so tall and impressive like this, but I haven't time to put dowelling supports in for the columns—it's tricky to do,' I explained. 'This is how wedding cakes used to be made; it's much simpler.'

I tied a wide, stiff, silver organza ribbon around each tier, finishing with big, neat bows at the front. It was starting to look austere but impressive.

The bride and groom figures were fixed firmly back into place on top; I was so glad that hideous vase of flowers had got broken! Then, after a glance at the chicken-shaped clock on the wall (another anonymous gift) to see how time was going, I got out a box of little icing roses and fixed them round the edge of the top tier with more sugar paste.

'I got Violet to make me lots of these, for a cake someone has ordered. I'll have to make some more, now.'

'It looks lovely,' Pia said admiringly. 'You are clever!'

'Not really,' I said modestly, though actually it had come out much better than I had expected. 'Come on, I'll get the car out and then we'll drive back with you holding it—and I'll take my icing repair kit, just in case anything else drops off!'

*   *   *

But nothing did drop off. In fact, the bride thanked her mother for the beautiful cake with tears in her eyes.

'Yes, so clever of you to do a Victorian-style stacked cake. I've hardly seen one, except at the smartest London weddings,' Libby said innocently.

Later Mrs Fosdyke did take me aside and thank me for saving her bacon for her, though not with any great graciousness. She didn't offer to pay me for my efforts, either, though actually I had done it more for Libby's sake—and the bride's.

There wasn't really much for me to do at the reception, except mop up guests who had liberally thrown their food or drink over themselves, or needed a sobering cup of coffee—that kind of minor emergency. Anyway, Pia was proving surprisingly good at helping out too. I think she's likely to become just as decided and assertive as her mother, given time.

Noah, in one of his lovely suits, took a couple of posed shots of the simpering (and distinctly pregnant) bride with her groom, but after that unobtrusively circulated, photographing the guests as the fancy took him. It seemed to take him a lot.

I remembered that Libby had once said to me that he was handsome, but you didn't always notice that at first, and she was right, because he seemed able to blend into the background when he wanted to, even when in reality he was the handsomest and best-dressed man in the room.

* * *

387

When the last, lingering guest had gone away and Movable Feasts had quickly and efficiently packed the remains of the day in plastic hampers and departed, Tim opened a bottle of bubbly just for us and we all sat among the wreckage, exhausted.

Noah must have gone back to the gatehouse to change out of his suit, for he now reappeared in jeans and the brightly striped sweater that Pansy had knitted him as a thank you for all the firewood he'd delivered. On him, it looked like a fashion statement, so clearly my little joke had backfired.

We all agreed that the reception had gone very well, for a first performance. 'And you do realise we have to do it all over again tomorrow?' Libby said.

'So do Movable Feasts. I don't know how they keep it up!'

'They have other people doing most of the baking,' Pia said. 'I asked. Isn't it surprising how many guests took doggy bags away with them? Usually the richest-looking ones!'

'Yes, that surprised me too,' Tim said. 'Movable Feasts seemed prepared; they had all those little containers ready.'

'I know,' I said guiltily. 'I've got one with some smoked salmon in it. It's a treat I don't often get a chance to eat.'

Mind you, I don't often get a chance to eat seafood either, but since the Prawn Incident I seem to have lost my appetite for them.

We couldn't sit there for long, because we had to clean up the debris, strip the tables, put the linen in hampers for the laundry, and clean the preparation room and the toilets. Gina came in to see how things had gone on and wanted to help,

388

but Libby wouldn't let her.

'No, you have plenty to do already with the house and the cooking, Gina. In fact, I can see we need to factor a cleaner into the business; we can't do *everything* ourselves. I'll go and give Dolly Mops a ring and see if they can send someone tomorrow after the next one!'

'At least the cake will be all right. It's sitting in my larder now,' I said. Tomorrow's reception was for two dog-breeding friends of Freddie's, who had met at Crufts. 'Apart from having to model a Boxer and a Dachshund bride and groom in icing, and edge the tiers with daisies, it was a doddle.'

'Why daisies?' Noah said.

'The bride's name is Marguerite. They're all over the tablecloth they ordered from the Graces, too.'

'Has that got dogs on?' asked Tim with interest.

'One or two, among the daisies and the more traditional wedding symbols. That's nothing, Tim. They have had to embroider bats and spiders on the Goth one, and Pansy's crocheting a special black border in a cobweb pattern.'

'Well, let's not worry about the Goth wedding yet,' Libby said wearily. 'We've still got another four receptions to go before we have to get ready for the Elizabethan one next Monday.'

'Yes, let's take them one at a time,' I agreed. 'Have you got the rose petal confetti from Hebe Winter for tomorrow, Libby?'

'Yes, that's here already, and Dorrie's got the flowers for the table decorations in her outhouse. In fact, tomorrow's reception might prove to be easier than today's—I suppose because we're more in control.'

'And much nicer people,' I agreed. 'But by this

time next week we will be old hands and take even the oddest reception parties in our stride!'

Chapter Twenty-nine

Good Reception

The best thing about April is early asparagus. Oh, the joy of eating fresh, tender little green spears dipped in melted butter! Uncle and I usually pig out on the first bunch and this year the Photographer, who has rented the Artist's empty studio, joined us.

Aggie, my favourite hen, seemed to be under the impression I had invited her to the asparagus feast too, because she followed him in through the garden door and was very reluctant to leave.

'Cakes and Ale'

By the end of the first week we were getting the hang of things a bit, and there had been no major incidents since the bouncing cake, other than Lily having to be called in urgently, in her Stitch in Time sewing repairs persona, to hastily reattach the ripped bodice of a wedding dress when the groom had clumsily stood on the hem while dancing.

Harry and I celebrated my first day off by having our annual asparagus feast, when we greedily devoured the first tiny, tenderly nurtured shoots with melted butter, and since Noah had again, entirely unasked, resumed his wood-chopping duties, I invited him too, as a thank you.

I don't know why Harry liked Noah so much, yet was always warning me against Rob Rafferty! It seemed to me they were much the same . . . but anyway, it was unfortunate that Rob turned up just as we were finishing off our lunch with plum ice cream and coffee.

He swept me off my feet and planted one of his smacking kisses full on my lips before he actually noticed Harry and Noah sitting at the table in the kitchen.

'Oh, sorry, didn't know you had company,' he said easily, putting me back down again, slightly rumpled.

Harry grabbed his stick and levered himself to his feet, jamming his hat back over his eyes. 'If you mean me, I'm off,' he said tersely. Mac uncurled himself from under the table and followed him out, but Noah didn't look like he was about to move any time soon. 'Hi, Rob,' he said. 'If you came for the asparagus, you're too late.'

'Asparagus?' Rob echoed. 'No, actually, I came to see if Josie wanted to come to a birthday party tonight for one of the *Cotton Common* cast: Viola Stewart—you met her when I took you to the wine bar. It'll be fun.'

'That's very kind of you,' I said, acutely aware of Noah's sharpened gaze on me, 'only I'm really tired! Libby's wedding receptions began this week and this is the first day off we've had. I've loads to catch up on.'

'All the more reason for an evening off, then?'

'No, really, like I said, I'm way too tired—sorry!'

Rob gave me his full-wattage smile. 'Oh, I'm *sure* I could persuade you!' he drawled throatily.

Noah drained his coffee cup and got up, his chair

scraping back along the quarry tiles. 'Thanks for lunch, Josie, but I'd better get back to work again. See you later—unless you've gone out, of course,' he added. 'See you, Rob.'

Rob watched him leave by the French doors into the garden and walk off down the path towards the studio with a puzzled expression. Then he turned to me, one eyebrow raised, for an explanation.

'Noah's using the studio at the moment. There wasn't enough room at the gatehouse to spread his pictures out or do any developing.'

'Wasn't there? Well, I'm sure he's doing a lot of developing now,' Rob said, slowly and thoughtfully.

Then he said he couldn't stay, he'd only popped in with the invitation, but he could see I was too tired. Even the offer of a slice of rich fruitcake wouldn't tempt him.

*   *   *

We spent all of the following Sunday afternoon transforming the barn for the Elizabethan-themed reception. Libby, of course, had it all planned out in her notebook, like a military campaign.

First we arranged the tables into one big 'T' shape—and everyone not on the top bit of the 'T' was going to be *literally* below the salt, because Dorrie fetched a pair of shell-shaped silver and deep blue glass salt bowls from her cottage. 'And make sure you don't let anybody make off with them,' she instructed. 'They're an heirloom.'

Since the use of herbs had been widespread for decoration as well as flavour at that time, she made up simple bunches for the tables of

392

rosemary, thyme, lavender and parsley, together with a few flowers, which she called tussie-mussies. They looked very pleasing in simple (if totally anachronistic) glass vases—but then, the bride seemed to be happier with an updated version of the Elizabethan theme, an adult excuse to revisit the dressing-up box.

'Rosemary for remembrance and fidelity,' Dorrie said, watching Tim up on the stepladder attaching a kissing knot of gilded rosemary, ribbon and leaves so that it was suspended above where the bride and groom would sit at the wedding feast. More bunches of the gilded rosemary twigs, tied with ribbons and called Bride's Laces, would be offered to guests as they arrived, and also surrounded the elegant glass cake stand that stood on a cloth embroidered with love knots, awaiting the arrival of my Pomander cake.

A pair of large brass candelabra with twisty electric candle bulbs were placed one on either side of the stage. Then, when we had finished setting out large platters that looked like wood, but were not, archaic-looking cutlery and goblets, all on loan from the re-enactment society, our job was done. As we switched off the lights and left the barn in darkness, it smelled, not unpleasantly, of herbs.

*　　　*　　　*

Next day, when the bridal car (a bizarre choice of a white stretch limo) drew up outside the Old Barn and the bride and groom emerged, a very regal Hebe Winter, dressed up convincingly as Queen Elizabeth I, offered them the loving cup as they

393

crossed the threshold.

Gentle lute music was playing as the rest of the guests filed into the dimly lit interior, where Shakespeare shyly proffered a quill pen with a gel nib and invited them to sign a large, parchment book.

The groom looked morose in a fur-trimmed robe over doublet and hose, but his bride was radiant in a jewelled and billowing gown, decorated with love knots of ribbon. I suppose half the guests were dressed in variations of the same style, the women in heavily brocaded and ornamented overgowns closed at the top, corset-fashion, while the skirts were left open to reveal the underskirts below. Few of the men had followed the groom's example, but a doublet and hose, it has to be said, did not suit everyone.

The Pomander cake was admired and cut, and several buxom wenches from the Sticklepond re-enactment society carried round the platters of food and filled the goblets. Then, once the speeches were done and the noise level was rising as the champagne sank, the Virgin Queen led a few of her courtiers in a stately dance to the music of lutes, a viola and fiddles.

It was, in a strange way, quite magical, and Noah and his Leica were *everywhere*.

* * *

The last week of March had merged seamlessly into the beginning of April in a blur of wedding receptions, gardening and cake-making, but when I did have time to think, I felt a growing sense of unease. I saw a film once where the main character

394

kept catching glimpses of someone out of the corner of his eye, and you were never quite sure if what he was seeing was real or if he was being haunted. It was terribly atmospheric and eerie and . . . well, that seemed to be happening to me with Ben, because unless I was imagining it, he was almost *stalking* me. He must have come to stay with Mark and Stella from time to time, because he wasn't always around, thank goodness.

But maybe I was imagining things, because Harry hadn't mentioned seeing him in the Griffin, and I was sure he would have, if he had. Unless, of course, my very own Spirit of Relationships Past was avoiding all his old haunts?

*　　*　　*

We had hardly had a chance to recover from the Elizabethan reception when it was time to get ready for the Goth extravaganza, which was, of course, to be the first wedding ceremony in Blessings.

Still, at least that meant the Great Chamber could be prepared for the ceremony a day in advance, with a suitable table for the registrar covered with a dark velvet throw and set with the brass candelabra. Tim had cut lots of dark ivy for Dorrie to arrange, together with dozens of darkest red roses from the Sticklepond florist. Once the crewel-work curtains were closed and the central light switched off, the effect should be just what a Goth couple dreamed of—dark, velvety and lush.

Unfortunately, there was a reception in the Old Barn the day before the Goth reception that wasn't cleared away until after five in the afternoon, so that we were only just starting to transform it when a by-now-familiar hearse pulled up in the courtyard and out poured several pallid and raven-haired young men, who had brought the red wine goblets and a large, vellum-style book with a quill pen, both remarkably like the ones Shakespeare had been offering to guests only a few days before.

They stayed to help move the tables, and then at Dorrie's bidding, carry the table decorations of more dark ivy and roses in black glass vases, before finally flitting silently off into the night.

*   *   *

I took the cake over first thing and set it on the Graces' tablecloth, embroidered with bats, cats, dragons and fairies as well as a smattering of dark roses and Celtic knots. The black crochet cobweb edging was amazingly fine. Pansy had surpassed herself.

Come to that, my cake wasn't half bad either. I considered the dragon a masterpiece.

The room was dark, lit only by the wall sconces plus a small light where the hook-nosed DJ was setting himself up on the stage in a nest of ivy, like a strange bird.

Movable Feasts, as a concession to the event, had removed the white pinafores over their black tops and trousers and blended into the darkness behind the buffet table, where they had started filling dark red goblets and putting them on trays as the guests arrived.

The groom came first in his hearse, with the best man, and they went straight to the Great

Chamber, both wearing dark suits, black top hats and gloves.

But there was a small crisis as the bride arrived in her white, black-embroidered dress and cute wings—one of which had been caught in the car door and was drooping. I had to phone for Lily to come over urgently, but it was soon fixed in the cloakroom; there was just a ripped stitch or two where the wings attached to a stiffened part of the dress.

I watched the actual ceremony on the screen in the Old Barn, though since the chamber was so dimly lit, it made for mysteriously shadowed viewing. Only a few brightly clad people stood out, like the bride's mother in pastel floral and big hat, and of course all those very white faces—plus the regular flicker of camera flashes, as Noah and the bridegroom's friend recorded the moment.

After that, the reception was pretty much like a darker version of the Elizabethan affair, and although I didn't expect there to be a lot of hopeful joy about a Goth wedding party, it was a surprisingly cheery and happy occasion.

It was hard to keep track of where Noah and his camera were among the shadows, though, what with his dark hair and suit, and at one point I'm sure I heard him whisper: 'Wings would suit you too, angel!' though when I turned around, there was no sign of him.

Afterwards, the happy couple changed into something even more outlandish and drove away in the hearse, a collection of rubber bats, black shoes and cans trailing in their wake.

Libby and I both agreed that the couple were so well-matched that the chances of this marriage lasting the course were a lot higher than most of the previous ones, and there was no point in taking a bet on the outcome.

Chapter Thirty

Tried and Tested

I've ordered my tomato plants. I adore seed and plant catalogues and always want to order the unusual new varieties of everything, even though I know the reliable, tried-and-tested old ones are the best!

'Cakes and Ale'

Easter week was slightly easier from the reception point of view. I suppose the churches have so many special events and services that they simply can't fit in lots of weddings too.

But we did have one reception the day before Good Friday, and in a mad moment I had rashly accepted a commission to make the happy couple an Easter Bunny wedding cake.

The bride was one of those soppy, Madeline Bassett types, who should have stayed safely incarcerated in a P. G. Wodehouse novel telling people that the stars were God's daisy chain. She showed a distressing tendency to refer to her husband-to-be as Peter Rabbit and in return, he called her Bunnykins. Urgh!

I did manage *not* to throw up while discussing the design, but it was a near-run thing. Still, the cake was easy, since I'd done rabbits before (appearing out of a magician's hat, that time), so creating a vegetable garden with a picket fence around it and Peter and Bunnykins in the carrot patch together, sugar sweet, was not a problem. Violet moulded lots of tiny carrot tops that I planted in neat rows to look as if they were sticking up out of the ground, and I made a wheelbarrow full of bunches of them with green leafy tops. Around the sides I lettered 'Peter and Bunnykins lived happily ever after'. It was a huge success—most of their family and friends appeared to be as wet as they were.

On Easter Sunday Noah presented me with a huge, organic milk chocolate egg tied up in Cellophane. Inside, when I'd nibbled my way in, there was a fluffy, speckled hen that clucked when pressed. I had come to the conclusion that he was quietly, handsomely and elegantly stark, staring bonkers.

I'd half expected *something*, though, so in return handed him a large, marzipan rabbit—here's one I prepared earlier.

As usual, Pansy and I made lots of little chocolate eggs and chicks, using my set of Easter moulds, then concealed them all over the parish hall for her Brownie troop to discover.

*   *   *

Mary rang for another pregnancy bulletin that I didn't want to hear, and then she said, 'I did *tell* Ben the very idea that you were having a thing going with Noah Sephton, of all people, was insane, you know. I mean, it would be like suddenly discovering you were shacked up with

David Bailey, practically. And Noah Sephton's gorgeous!' She cackled like a hyena.

'Yes, you're right. What on earth would he see in *me*? I have got to know him a bit, because he's Libby's friend, but he's just kind, that's all.'

I wasn't going to say *how* kind he'd been after Libby's wedding . . .

'When Ben said he *knew* it was true, because you didn't deny it when he accused you of it, I told him, "You're mad! Josie must have been so gobsmacked by your insane suggestion that she was speechless!" '

Mary laughed again and I joined in, rather hollowly.

'His latest idea is that you're having a passionate affair with Rob Rafferty too! He's mad, quite mad.'

*   *   *

Claire and the film unit descended on me again for two hellish days, when they were underfoot at every turn. I take back what I said about getting used to this, though Aggie seemed to bask in the limelight, and even Harry was turning into a bit of an old ham . . .

*   *   *

Even though Old Barn Receptions became hugely popular almost instantly, we did have some time free. Never having given much thought to the matter before, I hadn't realised that some days are more popular for weddings than others.

Saturday was *the* day. Every single one of them

was now booked until the end of the season (and some of next season). I expected Sunday would be too, except that a lot of churches hadn't got time to fit weddings in on that day. The next most favourite were Friday afternoons and Mondays, but on other days there were only occasional weddings, which was just as well, because it meant we could catch up a bit. This suited Noah, too, because he was often in London in midweek, coming back for long weekends.

Libby now kept a good supply of Hebe Winter's natural petal confetti and Dorrie was able to create table decorations and fill vases at the drop of a beret. Even the Graces were trying to lay in a stock of tablecloths, ready to personalise to taste, but unfortunately this wasn't something I could do with my cakes, since I rarely knew what was next.

Pia was spending part of her time in Liverpool, where she'd enrolled on an NVQ in catering! She was living there with Jasper, but she came back most weekends to help out, unless they were off somewhere. When she was here, Jasper often was too, helping Dorrie in the garden. Dorrie said if any of the guests spoke to him (which they did, because he was such a good-looking young man) he told them he was the under-gardener. But he didn't ever get tipped, unlike Tim, who seemed to be raking in the money whenever he got the Bentley out.

With Pia there and Tim to boss about, Libby didn't *really* need me, except at the start of the receptions until the cake had been officially cut, because it's amazing what little accidents—and big accidents—can happen to a fragile, icing sugar confection, especially when it's sitting on a table in a room containing several drunken and not altogether steady guests.

There was the occasion, for instance, when mischievous twin pageboys ate all the icing off the back of the lower tier of a cake (luckily not one of mine), and then sicked it up on the groom's shoes while he was telling them off . . .

But it was not always the guests that caused the accidents. At one reception Caesar, the stupider and more amorous of the two peacocks, took such a fancy to the bride as she got out of the car that he ran after her into the barn and chased her round the tables, rattling his tail feathers impressively. Of course the bride managed to bash into the table holding the cake during the pursuit, but by the time she had been coaxed out of her fit of hysteria (she had a bird phobia) and Tim had put out the peacock, I had it looking fairly respectable again.

And, despite my disenchantment with the whole idea of love, if it was a local wedding I couldn't resist running over with the Graces to stand outside St Cuthbert's as the happy couple emerged. The pealing of the bells drew me across the Green like invisible wires.

*　　　*　　　*

I was still sometimes getting the feeling of being watched, and one morning (a non-wedding reception day) when I came home from taking Mac for an extra-long walk, I just *knew* someone had been in the cottage. Someone other than Harry, that is. He had a key, of course, and could come and go if he pleased, though he seldom did if

I was not there.

It was hard to put my finger on what first alerted me, it was just that some things didn't seem to be exactly where I'd left them, and there was a lingering scent on the air that reminded me of the aftershave Ben had suddenly taken to wearing while he was having the affair . . . Was I imagining this too? Or *had* Ben been in the house—and if so, what was he looking for?

The idea that he could come and go as he pleased was very unsettling, so next day I decided to have all the locks changed, including the one on the studio door. I really should have done it before.

Noah was in London and it's amazing how quickly I'd got used to him being in the studio, so that it felt odd when he wasn't there. I think Harry missed having him around to talk to, as well.

When he did come back, and I heard the squeak of the side gate, I went out to give him the new studio key.

'I've had all my locks changed. I just thought I'd like better security now I'm living alone,' I said, following him into the studio.

'Oh?' He cast a swift look around the room and then said, acutely, 'Or maybe you thought Ben might let himself in?'

'How did you guess that?' I demanded.

'Because I'm pretty sure he—or someone—has been in here while I've been away, and I don't suppose it was you?'

I shook my head. 'I wouldn't come in when you weren't here. You're right, only I thought I might have been imagining it. I do think he's been in the cottage.'

'I knew I hadn't left that pile of photographs out of the folder, and I did close the door to the darkroom. But I don't think anything's been damaged.'

'Oh, no, he would respect your work too much to do that!' I said, shocked. 'He must just have been curious.'

'And maybe jealous?' Noah suggested.

'No, I don't think so. My friend Mary thinks she's now convinced him that the very idea you and I were having an affair was totally ludicrous—and he'd heard the even sillier rumour that I was having a fling with Rob Rafferty too, so she put him straight about that, as well. Of course, she thinks the whole idea is so ridiculous that she can hardly help laughing when talking about it.'

'And *is* it so ridiculous?' Noah asked gravely. 'Rob seemed very sure of his welcome that time he called by when I was there.'

'Don't be daft,' I said shortly.

'That's what Harry said too. He said you had more sense than to take up with a rascal like that.'

'I don't know why he hasn't seen that you are just as much of a rascal, leaving broken-hearted girls behind you in swathes.'

'Not intentionally,' he said mildly, 'and that's a slight exaggeration.'

'Anji?'

'You'll have to believe me when I say that that affair was on its last legs by the first time I met you, I was just trying to let her down lightly. Then she told all those lies about you and Rob, and had me convinced for a while that you weren't the girl I took you for—especially when I could see you were on such friendly terms with him.'

404

'They're *just* friendly terms,' I said coldly, though now I came to think about it, I hadn't seen him for ages and ages. 'And strange as this may seem to you, I don't care what you believe, Noah Sephton!'

'Don't you? But to get back to Ben, don't you think, if he now knows I'm using the studio and around the place a lot, he might be wondering if he was right first time? Perhaps he was looking in the cottage for signs I was living with you?'

'That's ridiculous! And anyway, even if he still had a right to be jealous, which he doesn't, there wasn't any evidence for him to find,' I said.

He seemed to be back to his usual self, because he gave a wicked grin and said obligingly, 'I don't mind providing some!'

Being used to his teasing by now, which probably came automatically, I ignored that one. Instead, since I hadn't been in there for a while, I wandered about looking at the prints that were hanging up, or laid on every surface.

There seemed to be an awful lot of me, not only in the background at the receptions, but caught at various unguarded moments, in that annoying way he had of practically shooting from the hip when I least expected it. There were some of me working in the garden that I had no idea he had taken at all . . .

'You seem to have become my muse,' he said casually, watching me.

'But I look so serious in all the pictures!'

'Yes, that's why you make such a perfect foil for all that hopeful joy,' he agreed blandly.

* * *

Despite my little ups and downs with him, it was lovely that Noah and Harry got on so well. Once Noah showed that he could chop wood and dig a trench with the best of them, Harry thawed rapidly. But I kept warning Harry that Noah was only here temporarily, and not to get too used to having him around, though he didn't seem quite to have grasped that fact yet.

But I hadn't realised just how matey they had become until one morning in late April when I'd been out to collect the latest co-op order, keeping a sharp eye out at Mark and Stella's for the van, in case Ben was there. When I got home I could see the studio door was open, so I knew Noah was about, and I could hear Harry's voice talking to someone on the other side of the fence.

I was just about to call out when his next words stopped me in my tracks.

'That first summer she lived here with her granny, after her parents were killed in the car crash, she followed us around the garden like a little dog. She was angry—at fate, with her granny, with me—but she came to like helping out and baking and that. And then, on her first day at the local school she met Libby, who might come from the wrong side of the track, as they say, though no one takes much notice of that these days, but was like a breath of fresh air and full of ideas!'

'She's that, all right,' Noah's voice agreed, but slightly muffled. I thought he might be in the henhouse.

'She had Josie doing all kinds of things. She'd decide she needed to learn to ride a horse, say, and persuade Josie to go and help out at the stables on Saturdays in exchange for lessons. And then

406

tennis—she got them invited to the vicarage tennis parties . . . Yes, it was always something new with Libby.'

'And when did Josie meet Ben?'

'Oh, same day as Libby, at school. He's a year older, but he was a tall lad even then. They were nigh on inseparable after that, until this last year or two, despite his mother and father trying to put a spoke in the wheel.'

'Did they? What on earth for?'

'They thought their son was too good for her, what with her granny being a cleaner and all. But Nell Richards trained as a nurse with Josie's mum, and they were friends before Nell married this doctor and got all these uppity ideas. But that was after he'd made a play for Josie's mum and been turned down. Nell got him on the rebound, and it filled her full of spite.'

'But she could hardly blame Josie for that!'

'You'd think not, but there was no logic to the woman. And if the Richardses thought Josie was beneath them, you can imagine what they thought of her best friend, Libby . . . and Ben never seemed too keen on Libby either, that I could see, though she's a grand lass and it's not her fault what sort of upbringing she's had.'

'No, it certainly isn't,' Noah agreed. 'You know, I still can't imagine why Ben's parents wouldn't have welcomed Josie as a daughter-in-law with open arms.'

'Nor me, but they never managed to part Ben and Josie.'

'But you said they weren't quite so inseparable the last year or two?'

'No . . . it was after Ben won that big art prize—

Turner, was it?—the rot started to set in, I reckon. He suddenly got to like the bright lights and the things money can buy. But then, he'd always been a bit like that.'

'It's strange they never married. Josie seems, from what Libby keeps telling me, to be a very marrying kind of girl.'

What the hell was a 'marrying kind of girl'? And was it good or bad, I wondered.

'They were as good as married,' Harry continued, generously spilling my store of secrets, 'but "as good as" wasn't really enough for Josie's granny, though she came to accept it in the end. Josie would have had him like a shot, I reckon, if he'd asked her, but it was him who seemed to be against the very idea and if she questioned that, she was questioning how much he loved her.'

'Hmm . . .' Noah said thoughtfully.

'Then it turned out he'd been stringing her along all this time. His parents had threatened to cut his allowance off if he married her. That was the only reason for his stubbornness.'

I heard Harry heave a deep, heart-felt sigh. 'She loved and trusted him all these years and look where it got her. She's that soft-hearted too, for all she tries to pretend she isn't—and I won't stand by and see her hurt again,' he said, a note of warning in his voice.

Oh God! I hoped Harry, too, wasn't starting to think Noah had any serious intentions towards me . . . or even any intentions at all!

'Rob Rafferty—' began Noah.

'Forget him, lad! She told me herself that though she likes him, he'd never be more than a friend, and she's nothing if not truthful.'

'Blunt, even,' Noah agreed. 'Yes, that's what I thought, really.' The henhouse door slammed. 'That's that done, anyway.'

'Thanks, Noah. It'll save Josie a job and she hates cleaning out the hens. She'll be back soon, I shouldn't wonder.'

I dodged back indoors quickly and a couple of minutes later made a noisier exit, calling: 'Harry? Kettle's on!' and then acting all surprised when Noah appeared too.

What I'd overheard had given me a lot to think about, though. I'd no idea that Harry knew so much about me! But then, Granny had probably discussed me with him, and he could see for himself how things were.

At least he'd put Noah well and truly straight about Rob, though I knew that shouldn't really matter to me. It was just a pity he didn't think to grill him about his love life, that was all!

*   *   *

In late April Mary called to tell me that Olivia had been rushed into hospital and had her baby, though I don't know why she thought I would want to know.

'It was due two weeks after mine, but it arrived before she could have the elective Caesarean she'd booked,' she said, almost indignant that Olivia had pipped her to the post. 'She rang me from the hospital—some swish private one. No National Health for her!'

'I would have thought Ben would be in charge of telling everyone about the baby.'

'Yes, but that's just the thing—Ben's been

409

spending more and more time away from her. Once they were married she got so possessive, it was as if she'd bought him. She wanted him to stay around all the time, to know what he was doing and where he was. He couldn't take it. He said some very cruel things to her as well, about looking ugly and unattractive when she was hugely pregnant.'

'That was pretty blunt,' I agreed. 'But he's very self-centred and goes his own way. So he wasn't there when she suddenly went into labour?'

'No, so she thought he might be with us, only he wasn't. He's renting a room—or I suppose that should be a cabin—on a houseboat, and Russell went and checked that out first. He told us not to tell Olivia about it, so we haven't, because he's one of our oldest friends. But then, so are you. I think our loyalties have been a bit muddled . . .'

'Never mind,' I said. 'So was he there?'

'No, but then Russell thought he might be with those friends of yours up in Neatslake—what are they called? Old hippie couple?'

'Stella and Mark. I know he does stay with them sometimes.'

'Yes, and that's where he was. He's renting a room and studio space in one of the outbuildings from them, so he can divide his time between Neatslake and London, like he used to.'

'I was sure I'd seen him about more lately, but I thought I was imagining it. And there was that day when I thought someone . . . But never mind that,' I added.

'Olivia keeps asking me if he's seeing you. Things seem to have turned on their head, don't they?'

'Yes, I suppose they have. It's a sort of role reversal that his wife is now worrying about me. But she needn't; I wouldn't take him back now if he came gift-wrapped in five-pound notes. *Especially* if he came gift-wrapped in five-pound notes. So he does know about the baby now?' I added, 'And you didn't say whether it's a boy or a girl—or whether it's all right.'

It wasn't the poor little infant's fault that it had been born, after all, and it had been two or three weeks early.

'It's a boy and it was quite big. Olivia really let herself go and ate for quads. She's going to regret it when she tries to get her figure back. Ben's parents rushed to the hospital and they're hopping mad with Ben, though I don't suppose that's much consolation to Olivia.'

'I expect he's in the middle of painting something,' I suggested. 'He'll *intend* to go down, but just won't get round to it until he's good and ready.'

'He might be, but he's not painting much lately and it's not very good when he does—his last exhibition sold hardly any—so I shouldn't think it's that. I don't know how you ever put up with him!'

'Neither do I, looking back, but when you love someone and you've been together for years, you don't really think about it, do you? You've just sort of grown used to each other's little ways. His work might have gone off latterly, but he's a genius artist really, so I didn't mind looking after him— and we did share a love of good, home-grown food and a simple lifestyle, until he started to veer off the rails.'

'You looked after *all* of us when we were

411

students at the RCA,' Mary said. 'I don't think I appreciated that enough at the time.' She sighed. 'If I don't start contractions naturally by Monday I've got to go in and be induced. I'm the one who should have given birth by now!'

'Can't you jump up and down, or eat curry or something?'

'That kind of thing doesn't really work,' she said gloomily. 'It has been nice talking to you again, Josie. You are very forgiving, considering I was such a disloyal cow—and then I even accused you of having something going with Russell!'

'Don't worry, at least you know the truth now and we can be friends again. I only have time for my mad, passionate affairs with Noah Sephton and Rob Rafferty. I simply can't fit in any more celebrity lovers, even though they are lining up at the door.'

'Oh, don't!' Mary begged me with a hysterical giggle—and then suddenly yelped. 'Oh!'

'What?' I asked anxiously.

'My back's been aching all day and . . . Josie, I think my waters have broken! Oh, thank you, *thank you*!' she exclaimed and rang off, though not before I heard her yell, 'Russell! Get your ass down here!' at the top of her lungs.

I put the phone down gently. I'd been all right while I was talking to Mary, but now the reality of Olivia having Ben's baby really hit me—the unfairness of it all—and I suddenly sank down onto the sofa and sobbed my heart out.

I didn't know that Noah had come in through the French doors until he sat down next to me and put a comforting arm around my shoulders.

I turned to him and had my cry-out in his arms,

412

then eventually sat up and gave him a watery smile. 'Sorry. It's just that Olivia has had her baby and . . . I don't know why I'm so upset, because I'm over it all, really. It's just—feeling the baby should have been mine and knowing I'll never have that experience.'

'That's perfectly understandable, Josie,' he said gravely, handing me a large, soft white handkerchief.

'Thanks for being so kind, Noah. I know,' I added brightly, mopping my damp face. 'Let's have a glass of something!'

'As long as it isn't peapod,' he agreed cautiously, but accepted a glass of Violet's special rhubarb, before settling back onto the sofa next to me, with his long legs elegantly crossed.

I found he had turned his head and was surveying me in a puzzled sort of way.

'You know, what baffles me is why you're so devastated at not being able to have children yourself, yet I've several times heard you trying to persuade Libby not to rush into pregnancy, as though you're trying to put her off. It seems so unlike you to be selfish about it, so it's not that . . . so why?'

'I don't know what you mean,' I protested. 'Of course I would *love* Libby to have a baby—it's just that she's so busy right now that it doesn't seem sensible until the business takes off.'

'Perhaps that's so,' he agreed, 'but I still think you're evading the issue. What is it really, Josie?' he asked softly, and I found the tears rushing to my eyes again. I longed to tell him the truth, but how could I? Sharing the secret would only burden him with the knowledge too.

413

'Don't start crying again,' he said, putting his arms around me.

'I'm not!' I said, trying to blink back the tears.

'Then it's raining in here,' he said, and kissed me lightly on the lips—and I kissed him right back, though far from lightly. The feel of his warm mouth on mine and his strong arms tightening around me was terribly familiar and comforting, somehow . . .

It was just starting to look as though our friendship might be about to suffer a sea change, when he pushed me away and sprang to his feet.

'This is *so* not a good idea, is it?' he said, looking a bit pale. 'I must remember to refuse your wine in future, or I'll be taking advantage of you again—and Libby told me you weren't that sort of girl.'

Everyone seems to have been telling him what kind of girl I was! But I wasn't a girl—I was a woman—one who just wanted to lose herself in his kiss again for another dose of that magic medicine . . .

Yes, it was Return of the Slut.

Shoving her firmly back into her Pandora's box, I said lightly, 'Oh, I know you were just being nice to me because I was upset, Noah, nothing more. And Violet's rhubarb wine is pretty innocuous!'

He looked relieved, but it wasn't flattering that he'd backed off at the first sign that I felt more for him than friendship, even if it was just temporary lust. It's just like I told Libby—he's not interested in me that way, despite the flirting, and he'd run a mile if he thought I was *really* falling for him.

414

Chapter Thirty-one

May Day

I am so enjoying fresh salads again, but I will know May is really here when I can find enough pignuts to make them really tasty. They aren't really nuts, but a small root tuber that grows wild. They taste a bit like pine kernels and are a little-known seasonal delicacy.

There has been lots of digging to be done, though the Photographer has been a great help. The hens are let out occasionally to feast on any exposed insects and, as always, Aggie stands affectionately close to whoever is wielding the spade, making me fear she will get just that bit too close one day!

'Cakes and Ale'

Russell called me early next morning, the first time I had spoken to him since he turned up, unannounced and unwanted, at my cottage before Christmas.

He sounded embarrassed, as well he might, but also angry—though if anyone should be bearing a grudge about the actions of that night, it was me. And I wasn't; I just wanted to forget about it, especially now Mary and I were speaking to each other again.

'Mary insisted I rang you, to say she's had a little boy. Nine pounds, and they're both doing well,' he said stiffly.

'That's wonderful! Give her my congratulations,

won't you? What are you going to call him?'

'Pablo.'

'Ah, yes, I'd forgotten you were such a huge Picasso fan.' Pablo isn't a name that goes particularly well with Brown . . . but still, there are lots of odd name combinations about these days, so that probably won't matter.

'They're going to let her bring the baby home tomorrow, so you might be able to speak to her yourself then. Her mother's coming to stay,' he added. He sounded profoundly gloomy, considering he'd just become a father.

'I'll let her settle in with the baby first,' I said. 'Tell her I'll ring in a couple of days.'

'I'll *have* to go,' he said, as if I was physically hanging on to him with both hands. 'I've got a whole list of people to ring.'

'Thanks for letting me know, Russell,' I said, but I was talking to empty air.

Little Mr Huffy.

*   *   *

'I can't believe it's the first of May tomorrow and already we've been in business for over a month,' Libby said, as we cleared up the debris after yet another reception, ready for the Dolly Mops team to come in and clean the place. 'Why does so much food end up on the floor? Are people so drunk they miss their mouths entirely? But then, it happens at even quite sober weddings too.'

'So far it's been a big success and it's going to be even busier from now on, isn't it?' I agreed, picking up a half-eaten bread roll, which fortunately had landed butter side up. And butter

416

side up was the story of Libby's life, once she'd got herself past the dodgy start, so I hadn't really expected Old Barn Receptions to be anything but a blazing triumph.

'Yes . . . and here comes high wedding season, with blossom and church bells and romance in the air,' she said dreamily. 'Maybe I should have a second, summery wedding?'

'You haven't got time, and you'd have to squeeze your reception in on an unpopular day of the week, like Wednesday, because those are the only ones we've got free,' I pointed out.

'It's all right, I wasn't really serious! Anyway, we need our occasional rest days to catch up with everything else, like having a life. It's a pity there's only one Saturday a week, because we could book those ten times over.'

'Thank God there aren't! I don't really think you could cope with more receptions than you are doing now,' I said, and she had to agree.

'It's the May Day celebrations on the Green tomorrow morning, Libby. Do you remember what fun they were?'

She regarded me with astonishment. 'Of course not, because I was never mad enough to leave my warm bed at that hour of day to watch some ditzy folk dancing round a painted stick! But feel free to catch a chill in the wet grass, provided you're here later. Tomorrow's reception is the biggest we've catered for yet.'

'Yes, of course I'll be here, though not terribly early. I'll have to be up before dawn for the dancing round the maypole and I usually sell hot toddy to the people watching to make money for the donkey rescue centre. You should really come, you know. It's great fun.'

She shuddered. 'Maybe not.'

'You don't know what you're missing!'

'I think I have a good idea. I don't expect Pia will fall out of bed in time for it either—assuming she *is* actually in her own bed and not over in Middlemoss tonight. Or maybe Jasper's coming here and I'll fall over him at breakfast instead. He's always underfoot in the kitchen, talking recipes with Gina. She thinks he's wonderful.'

'You don't mind about him and Pia, do you?'

'Not really, he seems to be a nice boy, and the relationship's making her change rapidly in a good, if slightly odd, way. Now she seems as fascinated by the history of food and cooking as he is, and reading all kinds of stuff about it. You know, I used to consider her a complete featherhead, but what with this research and her being so useful in the business, I'm starting to think I never knew her at all!'

'Oh, Pia's very like you in some ways. I mean, once she knew what it was she wanted, she went all out to get it—or maybe that should be *who* she wanted!'

'You married young, Libs,' I reminded her.

'I'd like nothing better than to see her walk down the aisle with Jasper at some point, but she's too young. They're both too young, and Jasper hasn't even finished his degree yet.'

'You'll just have to wait and see, and not jump your guns, Libs.'

Her face lit up. 'Here's Tim. He must have finished washing down the Bentley. The peacocks had left footprints all over it and they must have been jumping in muddy puddles first.'

418

'At least the new ducks on the lily pond won't do that, but they *will* give you eggs,' I said.

The only point of the peacocks seemed to be that the guests often liked them to be in the photographs. Well, apart from the bride that one of them chased, that is, and I had a horrid feeling that Noah took a picture of that.

There'd been a return of that tension between us since he'd kissed me, not all due to the brisk way he distanced himself, because it was partly me doing it too. My Inner Slut was a very slippery customer.

Anyway, he'd been in London for a few days and he wasn't due back until tomorrow, so he would miss the May Day celebrations.

*　　*　　*

Next morning I was out on the Green waiting for dawn to break with all the other mad maypolers, including the Graces and the members of the Neatslake Folk Society.

I'd set up the usual little table on the edge of the Green in front of the house, where I sold my cups of hot toddy from a sort of insulated bucket that I use every year. Harry, well wrapped up, was sitting on a folding chair next to it, taking the money. Mac was curled up underneath, twitching his eyebrows from time to time in an amused kind of way at the humans' mad antics.

'There's Noah,' Harry said, pointing across the Green.

'So it is. But he wasn't due to get back from London until tomorrow and I wouldn't have thought this would be his kind of thing anyway.

419

But I see he's got his camera, so maybe that's the explanation.'

Indeed, he now appeared to be taking pictures of the Graces, especially Pansy, who was dressed in a dirndl skirt and wool shawl, with a red and white spotted handkerchief over her head. She looked a bit like one of those Russian wooden matryoshka nesting dolls.

I spotted another unlikely figure too. 'Good heavens! There's Pia with Jasper! He must have insisted they come.'

I was right, for on spotting me they came straight over for a cup of hot toddy and Pia said, 'What a god-forsaken hour of the morning, God-ma! But Jasper wanted to see the maypole dancing.'

'Yes, they don't do it in Sticklepond,' Jasper agreed.

'I didn't realise it would be so cold.' Pia shivered and he put his arm around her.

'It'll warm up soon, when the sun's on the Green. It looks as if it will be a lovely day,' I assured her.

'A nice day for a white wedding, perhaps—and right on cue, there's Rob Rafferty,' she exclaimed. 'But who is that girl he's with? He's all over her like a rash!'

I followed the direction of her gaze, my own eyes widening. 'She's called Anji and she's a model.'

Pia turned and stared at me. 'What, *Noah's* girlfriend?'

'Well, she was, but he says she isn't now, and it looks like he was right.'

'But I thought Rob was after you!'

'Not really, not when I made it plain I only wanted to be friends.'

'He had a pash on my mum too, at one time,'

420

said Jasper unexpectedly.

'What, Rob Rafferty?'

'Yes, but she didn't take him seriously, thank goodness. I much prefer Nick as a stepfather!'

'Yes, he's much nicer,' Pia agreed. 'Oh, look, they seem to be leaving already. It hardly seems worth getting up if they are only staying for five minutes.'

'From the look of them, I'd say they hadn't been to bed yet,' I said tartly. 'They must have just stumbled across the May Day celebrations by accident on their way home from somewhere.'

And they were indeed on their way for, even over the music, the noisy roar of the sports car could be heard before it vanished into the distance.

'There's Noah too, near that oak tree,' Pia said, waving, and he flapped a languid hand back, but didn't move from where he was. I expect it was a good vantage point for taking snaps of the unwary, like a lion at a watering hole waiting to pounce. I wondered if he'd seen Rob and Anji, and if he had, whether he had cared . . .

As dawn began to warm the edges of the sky over the tall chimneys of Blessings, the dancers took their place around the pole and, as always, I felt terribly envious. I did attempt to learn how to do it once, but had to give up due to a tendency to go right instead of left, and in instead of out, tangling the whole thing irretrievably up into one huge knot.

The morris dancers shook out their handkerchiefs and formed a set nearby. Then the fiddler and an accordionist struck up—and they were off.

I *love* this bit; there's something archaic and exciting about the music and the dawn, the intricate patterns of the dancers and the merry jingling of the morris men's bells . . . My feet were tapping along to the rhythm of the music.

When the maypolers had finished and the morris men had performed a couple more dances, everyone formed into a big ring round the pole to dance, including all the onlookers.

'Come on,' said Jasper, dragging a reluctant Pia off.

I took off my apron and folded it as Noah wandered across and came to a stop in front of the table, looking at me quizzically. Then he held out his hand: 'Come on—you *know* you want to!'

I laughed, because he's a constant surprise to me, so that, as Elizabeth Bennet once said of Mr Darcy, I could never quite make his character out. I think the feeling was mutual. 'Yes, of course, I was about to join in. I always do; it's the high spot of my day.'

'I'm staying here with Mac to look after the toddy,' Harry said. 'You can leave your camera with me, if you like. It'll only get in your way.'

Noah, the elegant, urbane and sophisticated, threw himself into the proceedings with abandon, whirling me wildly round until I was dizzy. He had to hold me upright at the end of the dance and I'm sure I was pink in the face and hot, though he looked cool as a cucumber and his short dark hair was no more ruffled than it usually was. He might have been a little distant since we shared a kiss the other day, but now he was smiling down at me with that old, teasing expression in his light grey eyes and I was smiling right back . . . until out of the

422

corner of my eye I glimpsed a tall, thickset and familiar figure skulking on the edge of the onlookers.

Noah followed the direction of my gaze. 'What is it?'

'Ben,' I said.

'Ah, yes. He does a good line in glowering, doesn't he? Very Heathcliff. It seems to be directed at me.'

'At *both* of us. Perhaps I'm not supposed to have fun, any more? But even though he can't possibly still think we're having any kind of affair, after Mary put him straight, perhaps he still blames you for everything, in a perverse sort of way? I suppose that's easier than blaming his own actions.'

'Very profound, Dr Gray!' he said.

'I wish he would just stay away from Neatslake altogether. He should be with Olivia and the baby, not stalking me like this.' Some of the joy seemed to have gone out of the morning and I turned and set off briskly back towards Harry.

'Josie, wait!' Noah said.

'I can't. I've got to pack the toddy things up,' I tossed back over my shoulder.

'Well, you don't have to do a hundred-yard sprint first, do you?' he said, following in my wake. 'I don't remember that being the finishing touch to any May celebrations I've ever been to before.'

'That was Ben, that was,' Harry said as we got back, 'but Pia just went and spoke to him, and he's gone now. I don't know what he thinks he's playing at, hanging around glaring at you like that. In fact, what's he doing here at all, if he's just become a dad, that's what I'd like to know?'

'I don't think he's taking well to marriage and

fatherhood, Harry. He's done a runner, according to Mary, and is staying up here a lot with Mark and Stella.'

I gave Mac the last biscuit from the plate and put the lid on the toddy container, which was empty apart from a few dregs and a half-drowned sprig of borage in the bottom.

'I just told Ben he should be in London with his wife and baby,' Pia said, arriving with Jasper in tow. The Three Graces, I noticed, were also heading in my direction, all wearing strange little rubber boots with low heels against the dampness of the grass.

'You really shouldn't have done,' I told Pia.

'Yes, but Mum said you thought he'd been hanging around watching you lately, which is creepy.'

'He could have turned nasty, Pia,' I said, because the old, easy-going and laid-back Ben seemed to have vanished inside this angry stranger. 'What did he say?'

'Mind your own business!' she said indignantly, turning pink.

'I told you not to,' Jasper pointed out. 'He's right.'

'Yes, it is my business. Josie's my god-ma, and I love her!'

'Here are the Graces—let's not worry them with it,' I suggested.

'We're stretching our legs,' Lily cried gaily, though I would have thought they'd already stretched them, since I'd noticed all three were dancing earlier.

'Yes, and we thought we'd help you carry everything back into the house,' said Pansy, 'only you seem to have lots of helpers already.'

'But the more the merrier,' I said.

Mac uncurled himself from under the table and I stooped and got Noah's camera and handed it to him. 'There you are. I suppose you'll be taking pictures later, at the reception?'

'I'll look in, but they sound, from what Libby says, to be a very stuffy and uninteresting lot. I wish they could all be like Freddie's wedding!'

'Well, the one on Monday might be more fun,' I said, picking up the big bin of used brightly coloured plastic tumblers, which would be washed and put away, ready for next year. 'They're marrying in St Cuthbert's and there will be one of my cakes—a bed of roses. They've chosen a rose theme for the whole day, from rose petal confetti, like Libby had, to roses on the table and cupcakes with crystallised rose petals on them. Roses, roses, all the way.'

'I think that is *so* romantic!' Lily said.

'Did you see your girlfriend with Rob Rafferty, Uncle Noah?' asked Pia cheekily, and Jasper nudged her in the ribs.

'*Ex*-girlfriend,' Noah said, 'and he is welcome to her. In fact, I'm delighted.'

Seeing Harry struggling to rise from the folding chair, he unobtrusively took his elbow and helped him to his feet, before picking up the insulated toddy container and following me into the cottage. In fact, Harry, Pia, Jasper and the Graces *all* trooped after me, carrying the folding chair and table and all the other bits and pieces, which made quite a crowd in the warm kitchen. Mac got under the table, out of the way.

'I've told Jasper you make the best cakes in

Neatslake,' Pia said hopefully, so it was just as well there was a whole fresh fruitcake in the tin, which I have discovered is Noah's favourite, and a malt loaf that just needed buttering.

'What about a bacon sandwich first, lass?' suggested Harry, putting the kettle on. It looked like becoming quite a party.

Chapter Thirty-two

Raspberries

I had the first duck eggs from my friends' new flock—if you can call several ducks together a flock? A gaggle, or maybe that should be a waddle, of ducks?

But anyway, they made a nice change and in return, I gave them some raspberries, since they don't expect to be picking their own before next year.

'Cakes and Ale'

The Bed of Roses cake was a big hit and the reception was perhaps the prettiest yet, though with an excess of pink for my personal taste. But since I'd just put pink icing on a couple of hundred cupcakes, that might have jaundiced my views slightly.

I did pop across to join the Graces outside the church before the reception, to see the bride emerge, and lovely she looked too, in a dress trimmed with palest pink silk roses and Swarovski crystals. She carried a bouquet of yet more pink

426

roses and even the table decorations at the reception continued the theme.

Perhaps you *can* have too much of a good thing?

When the official photographer had gone, Noah insisted on taking some pictures of the bride in among the rose beds in the garden and, such is his charm—or maybe his fame—she did it without a second thought about the dangers of getting the hem of her dress or her white satin shoes grubby.

When I saw the photographs later, she looked as if she were trying to fight her way out of a thorny bower, but I think that's the effect he was after.

*   *   *

After May Day Ben must have gone back to London, because that feeling of being watched vanished, which was quite a relief . . .

It's a pity I don't feel the same when Noah isn't here. Despite my best intentions, I've so got used to him being around, working in his studio, popping in for a chat, or doing the hard chores around the garden without being asked . . . *especially* cleaning out the henhouse, my least favourite job of all!

He says he doesn't mind that chore in the least, because he is in love with Aggie, and wants her home to be beautiful. And actually, they do seem to have a bit of a thing going. He talks to her, and she answers, in hen language. I feel quite jealous; it used to be me she followed around all the time!

I tend to forget Noah is this smart, rich London photographer, until some sudden languidly elegant movement of his hands, or passing mention of some famous person who is going to sit for his

427

portrait, jolts me back into remembering.

I keep telling myself that I mustn't get too used to him being around, because once the wedding season is over at Blessings, I don't suppose I will see much of him at all.

Harry will miss him too, but when I said as much to him he gave me a strange look and said, 'No, I won't, then, you daft lass,' so either he is in denial about how much he has enjoyed Noah's company, or he's starting to lose his marbles.

I told Libby and she said it was me who was losing my marbles, and then asked me, if I had to design my own wedding cake, what I would choose?

That was changing the subject with a vengeance.

'I have no idea,' I said, staring at her in some surprise. 'I've never thought about it . . . but it's never likely to be a problem I have to face anyway, is it?'

*   *   *

Funnily enough, though, once she'd started me thinking about the subject, I kept pondering what sort of wedding cake I would like. A garden trug with trowel and secateurs? Jam jars and wine bottles supporting a tabletop covered in cakes?

Anyway, I was standing dreamily pondering this among the raspberry canes later that day, while absently stuffing my face with the fruit rather than filling the basket by my side, when Noah came through from Harry's garden. He made me jump, because I hadn't known he was around.

He laughed. 'You needn't look guilty—why shouldn't you eat your own fruit?'

428

'No reason, I suppose. It's just that I came out to pick them for the Graces and Dorrie, as a little treat. They haven't got any at Blessings yet and the only edible thing the Graces have in their garden is rhubarb.'

'There looks to be plenty for everyone. I'll help you pick them,' he offered, though I noticed he put more in his own mouth than in the basket, so he obviously loves them as much as I do.

When we'd finished I thought he would go back in the studio, but instead he said, 'Any chance of a cup of coffee?'

'Yes, of course.'

I washed the raspberry juice off my hands and put the kettle on, then got out the cake tin as well as the biscuits. For a slender man, Noah can certainly put away a bit of food. So can I, come to that, now my appetite is back to being as hearty as it used to be. Just as well I am so busy that I must burn thousands of calories off every day!

'I've got something I wanted to discuss with you,' Noah said, sounding quite serious, and my first thought was that perhaps he'd decided he had enough wedding pictures and was leaving Neatslake or . . . well, I didn't know, but he'd got me worried.

'That sounds ominous!' I said, sitting down opposite him.

'Not really, it's just that Harry's been showing me the latest photos of the annexe his daughter's had built onto her house, in the hope of persuading him to go and live with them in New Zealand.' He paused. 'He talks about it a lot.'

'Does he?' I said, surprised. 'He's hardly mentioned it to me for ages.'

'He showed me some photographs he took when he went out there for three months too. He seemed to really like it.'

'Yes, he did, but he said he was glad to come back and that he doesn't want to leave his friends or his home, and spend his last years so far away.'

'Doesn't he?' Noah looked steadily at me, one dark eyebrow raised.

'What?' I demanded. 'He *doesn't*! He told me so!'

'But perhaps he was just saying that because he was worried about leaving you alone.'

'No, because I asked him that myself, and I said that if he changed his mind, he mustn't think about how I would manage without him, because I would be fine.'

'You may have told him that, but I don't really think he believed you. And although at first he resisted the idea of making such an enormous change to his life, he's been slowly coming round to the idea. But once Ben deserted you, he didn't feel that he could too.'

'But it wouldn't be deserting me—and I don't see why he told you and not me,' I said indignantly. 'Admittedly, I might have been a bit clingy after throwing Ben out, because it felt like Harry was the only person I had left who really loved me—but not now.'

'Well, that's OK then, because I've told him I'll keep an eye on you if he goes, so he needn't worry.'

'*You!*' I stared at him, and he looked very seriously back at me.

'Yes, me! I've fallen in love with Neatslake and I'm going to buy a cottage here—*Harry's* cottage,

430

in fact.'

I think my mouth was hanging open with surprise, and I was feeling a bit cross too! How dare Harry arrange all this behind my back?

'You mean, *you* will be my next-door neighbour?'

'Lock, stock and hen coop,' he agreed.

'Neatslake isn't really holiday cottage territory,' I pointed out.

'That's all right, I'm not looking for one of those. Perhaps you haven't noticed, but lately I've been packing all my London commissions into segments of a few days every couple of weeks, so I can spend more time here. But I won't buy Harry's cottage if you actually *hate* the idea of me living next door, Josie.'

I looked away. 'I—well, no, I don't suppose I will *hate* it . . .' I conceded.

'Good. And you know, once I've moved in, Libby and Tim could let Pia have the gatehouse for a bit of independence. She and Libby are getting on much better now Pia's helping out with the receptions, but there's still a bit of friction. I suppose it's inevitable, really.'

'I can see you've got everything all worked out,' I said slightly sourly, feeling outmanoeuvred and ruffled, but then I had a thought. 'What about Mac?'

'Harry's daughter's even offered to pay for him to go out there too, which helped Harry make his mind up.'

'They are very attached, though I would have had Mac with me, if Harry had wanted to leave him.' I sat back and looked at Noah, who was unconcernedly eating cake as if he hadn't just reorganised my life into a whole new pattern: out

431

with the last of the old, and in with the disturbingly new.

But I think I must be finally growing out of my fear of change, because I didn't feel half as upset about it as I thought I would. There was none of that feeling that I was standing on quicksand at all. OK, so the grass under my feet was a different kind from the usual Neatslake turf, but at least it wasn't quivering.

* * *

As soon as Noah had left, I went next door to talk it over with Harry.

'You should have told me when you changed your mind, Harry,' I said. 'I really don't mind—though of course I'll miss you dreadfully.'

'I wouldn't have gone and left you alone, lass. But now Noah's going to take care of you, you'll be fine.'

'He is not going to take care of me. I can take care of myself,' I protested, and he grinned.

He has old-fashioned ideas sometimes and obviously felt I needed a man to keep an eye on me.

And come to think of it, Noah tended to butt in and take over when he found me doing anything strenuous in the garden, as if I were some fragile little flower, so perhaps he did too.

It was the exact opposite of how Ben treated me. He liked to be warm, comfortable and well fed, but he was so wrapped up in his painting that he didn't seem to notice what hard work it was for me to keep things the way he liked them.

Noah was different. He was serious about his

photography, goodness knows, but not to the extent where people come second.

'What really made you change your mind about going to New Zealand, Harry?' I asked.

He looked guilelessly at me, from under his hat brim. 'One day I thought: I wouldn't want to get to ninety and find myself wishing I'd gone out to New Zealand when I was only eighty-two, and young enough to make a new life for myself.'

Chapter Thirty-three

Family Matters

Forrest Gump might have thought life was like a box of chocolates, but mine is more like a compost heap, with ever newer and stranger layers being added . . .

'Cakes and Ale'

Luckily there was no wedding reception at Blessings that day, because I was dying to discuss Noah's bombshell with Libby. But as it happened, I met her halfway down the drive heading towards my house on the same mission . . . Well, same *mission*, but different news.

'Josie—thank goodness! I've got something I want to tell you,' she exclaimed, grabbing my arm. 'Let's go to the gazebo—Dorrie's in the rose garden.'

'I've got something to tell you too,' I said, then with foreboding noticed the strangest of expressions on her face. 'You first,' I added hollowly when we got there.

'Oh, Josie, I'm pregnant!' she said, her face glowing. 'I've only told Tim so far—and he's delighted, of course, even if we didn't intend it to happen so soon.'

I stared at her aghast, which was not quite the reaction she was expecting.

'What's the matter, aren't you pleased for me?' she demanded.

I recovered and gave her a hug. 'Of course, I was just stunned, that's all! It's—great, absolutely great.'

She hugged me back. 'I know how you're feeling: pleased for me, but wishing you could have a baby too. But you can share mine! In fact, I intend unloading my offspring on you at every possible opportunity once the novelty has worn off.'

'If I can get it away from Gina. She's going to be ecstatic,' I said, summoning up a suitable smile— or I hoped it was suitable. 'Of course I'm pleased about it, if you are—but right in the middle of your first wedding season, Libby! How are you going to manage?'

'I don't suppose it will make any difference,' she said optimistically. 'I'm only *just* pregnant and even by the end of the season it will probably barely show. I don't see why it should slow me down, either. You know, I probably couldn't have timed it better if I'd tried, because I'll have had it well before the start of the next wedding season, especially since we're opening in May next year.'

'I hadn't thought of that. You're right,' I agreed, only half-aware of what I was saying.

'And if I do get morning sickness, or something—

which heaven forbid!—then I have you to help me and Pia . . .' She paused, looking worried. 'I'll have to tell her about the baby soon, though I don't know how she's going to take the news.'

'I should think she'll be fine about it,' I said, getting a grip on my wandering (and slightly appalled) thoughts. 'She's so madly in love with Jasper, she'll probably barely notice! But I do think you ought to try to take life a bit easier now, for the first three months at least.'

'That's what Tim said, but I'm fit and healthy and I don't see why I shouldn't stay that way, so I'm not about to wrap myself up in cotton wool for the duration. And I'm not going to have any tests done either, other than the usual scans, because I want this baby, no matter what.'

'It'll be fine, you'll see,' I reassured her—or maybe that should be myself—and when she asked me for my news, I managed to chat away about Harry, New Zealand, and Noah moving in next door, as if it was the only thing on my mind.

'I feel the pair of them have been conspiring together behind my back!' I said indignantly. 'You'd think Harry would have told me, rather than a comparative stranger, that he'd changed his mind.'

'He probably didn't know how you would take it, Josie,' she said, then added enthusiastically, 'and that's a great idea of Noah's about letting Pia have the gatehouse.'

'Yes, he's full of brilliant ideas.'

'Cheer up, Josie. It'll turn out fine, you'll see. Neatslake may not be the most obvious place for a second home, but Noah's been mentally moving in for months, and he's certainly got his feet under *your* table. No wonder Ben started getting second thoughts about whether you two had a thing going.'

'I don't think he did get second thoughts, really—and even if he did, he wouldn't find any evidence of it when he snooped around the cottage because we *haven't* got a thing going,' I said. 'Noah only fancies me when he's had a couple of drinks too many, and that's only because I'm the nearest female, or he's feeling sorry for me.'

'I think you must be suffering from low self-esteem,' she said, looking at me critically.

*　　　*　　　*

Libby went off to spread the glad tidings of great joy, and I went straight home and phoned Libby's sister, Daisy, though since her line was engaged I had to drum my fingers for ten minutes before I could speak to her.

'Daisy, Libby's pregnant!' I blurted out without any preamble.

'Yes, I know. She just phoned me,' she replied, sounding slightly surprised.

'I don't know how you can sound so calm, then. I really think we'll *have* to tell her about Gloria and Tim's father now. We can't keep it secret any longer.'

There was a pause. 'Well, I don't really see *why*, but you obviously feel strongly about it, Josie, and you're her oldest friend . . . So OK, I'll call Libby and say I'm coming up for a couple of days and then we'll tell her together. I'll book Mum into the Pines for a little drying-out session. I'm not trusting her here on her own.'

'Perhaps you should tell Libby by yourself?' I suggested. 'It is a family thing, after all.'

'Oh, no, if you're not there, I don't think I can do it,' she insisted. 'I mean, I don't really know Tim at all yet and I don't know how he'll take it, so I need backup. Anyway, it's *your* idea!'

So in the end I had to agree, however reluctantly.

After the call I stood gazing into space for a few minutes, wishing this was all some nightmare, but then a slight movement drew my attention and I saw that Noah was standing in the doorway, his blue and white striped mug in one hand.

'I've run out of milk,' he said mildly. 'I thought I could cadge some. And no good fairy tripped down to the studio with something good to eat today, either.'

'Sorry,' I said, 'I—I forgot.'

'Yes, well, obviously you've got something else on your mind,' he agreed. 'I couldn't help overhearing some of what you were saying. I take it Libby's expecting?'

'Yes. I'm sure she would have told you herself later.'

'And that was her sister, Daisy, you were talking to?'

I nodded.

'And far from being delighted about Libby's news, you're so worried about it that Daisy has to drive all the way up here tomorrow in order to tell her sister—*what*, exactly? Is there some big secret you're going to hit Libby with?'

All at once I felt my defences crumbling. It would be such a huge relief to share my worries with someone else—someone other than the horribly sanguine Daisy!

437

'Oh, Noah, when Gloria got drunk at Libby's reception, something she said made me think she'd had an affair with Tim's father! He was a bit of a womaniser, according to local gossip.'

He knitted his dark brows. 'Well, that's not a crime, is it? Unless . . . Oh, do *please* tell me I'm wrong, and you aren't harbouring the mad idea that Tim and Libby share the same father?' he demanded, staring at me incredulously.

'*I* thought it was a mad idea at first too,' I said defensively, 'but then I rang Gloria and asked her, and although she didn't come right out and say so, she inferred it. And even then I couldn't bring myself to believe it, so I asked Daisy too, and she said she knew all about it, but didn't think Libby needed to know! She just doesn't seem to feel the way she should about it—but then, neither does Gloria.'

He frowned. 'I don't think anyone could think a thing like that wasn't important. There's something wrong here, Josie.'

'You don't really know Gloria—and Daisy is obviously more of a chip off the old block than I realised! I wonder if there's insanity in the family?'

'The only insanity seems to be yours,' he said, though I couldn't blame him for not believing me, because I'd been in denial myself for months.

'I still think you've got it wrong, Josie.'

'No, unfortunately I haven't. Daisy's driving up in the morning—there's no reception tomorrow, thank goodness—so we can tell Libby and Tim then, together. Weren't you going back to London tonight, for—'

'I'm not going anywhere,' he stated. 'Not until this has been cleared up!'

438

I didn't see how it could be—it wasn't something you could simply sweep under the carpet—but there was nothing else to do until Daisy arrived the following day, and summoned me to Blessings.

* * *

I hardly slept all night and was on tenterhooks until she called.

'Can you come up now, Josie?' she said, sounding strained, which was not surprising given what she was about to do. 'I've told Tim and Libby there's something we need to tell them, so we're just waiting for you. We're in the Great Chamber. Libby says to come straight round.'

When I got there, Libby and Tim were looking slightly puzzled, and Noah, sardonic.

'I don't know what you're doing here,' I said to him, but he just smiled sardonically and didn't show any sign of taking the hint and going away.

'Have a ringside seat,' Libby said gaily, not looking a bit concerned. 'Daisy's about to reveal some serious news, but she didn't want to do it without my oldest friend present—probably because she's going to announce she's about to get married again and foist Mum back onto me, and knows I'll kill her if she does.'

'Actually, it's nothing like that, Libby. This is something really serious,' I told her, and she looked enquiringly from me to Daisy.

'I can't imagine what's the matter with you two. You look like a pair of conspirators! So come on, out with it!'

'This is all Josie's idea. I'd have carried on keeping it a secret otherwise,' Daisy said, giving

439

me an unloving glance and shifting uncomfortably.

'But you can't keep it secret any more, you must see that? They need to know,' I said. 'In fact, they should have known before the wedding.'

Daisy sighed. 'Oh, well, here goes: Libby, Mum had an affair with Tim's father years ago—well, more a bit of a fling really, you know what she was like. Tim, *your* father put it about a bit too.'

Tim nodded. 'I'm afraid so.'

'Well, thanks for sharing that unsavoury little family link, Daisy,' Libby said drily, 'but I think I could have lived without the knowledge.'

'There's more,' Daisy confessed. 'Mum got pregnant by him—and *I'm* the result.'

'Oh my God!' gasped Libby.

Tim wrinkled his forehead. 'You mean, you're my *sister*?'

'Half-sister.'

I gulped, hard, then said incredulously, 'But you told me he was *Libby's* father!'

Daisy stared at me as if I'd run mad. 'I never did. Her dad was a commercial traveller Mum met down at the Griffin. She told me so—and she hadn't been seeing anyone else at the time. After she fell pregnant with me, Tim's dad did help support her financially, but they didn't . . . you know . . . carry on any more.'

'Told you so,' Noah said to me smugly. 'I knew there must be a rational explanation.'

Libby looked quite gobsmacked. 'Why didn't you tell me?' she said to Daisy, and then she turned on me. 'And why didn't *you* tell me what you suspected? I could have sorted it out months ago.'

'But it was only something your mum said at the

440

reception that made me suspect it, and I tried to convince myself it wasn't true for ages. And then when I finally asked her, she must have thought I'd somehow found out about Daisy. I can see now I must have been mad to think what I did—but how could I tell you that the love of your life might be your half-brother?'

'So that's why you kept discouraging me from getting pregnant?' To my relief she had started to see the funny side, and laughed. 'But, Tim, how do you feel about all this, darling?'

He was starting to look pleased, in a baffled sort of way. 'Fine. I've got a half-sister I never knew about, but *you* aren't related to me at all, which is the main thing.'

'It certainly is,' I agreed, and then a thought struck me. 'Will Daisy be the baby's aunt on both sides?'

'Well, yes, but we don't need to tell anyone else that, do we?' Daisy suggested, relieved that the ordeal was all over.

'No,' Libby said. 'Let's keep all this in the family.'

Chapter Thirty-four

Gestures

It's amazing how much wine I have got through this year, considering I have drunk most of it on my own! I suppose that is a pitfall of producing your own drink, in that it is always to hand, but I have resolved to cut down a bit. Anyway, it is so hot at the moment that home-made lemonade is much more refreshing . . .

'Cakes and Ale'

I stayed at Blessings for a celebratory drink and I certainly needed it, because I felt like a wrung-out dishcloth after all that emotion.

Then I made an excuse and went home and Noah, uninvited, came with me, though he didn't say anything until we got back to the cottage. I kicked off my sandals and sank onto the sofa with a long sigh. 'I think I need another drink!'

'For once, I think you're probably right. And *I* need one too. I feel as if I've been taking part in a badly written soap episode. Melodrama wasn't in it.'

He fetched a bottle of wine from under the stairs and, sitting down next to me, poured us each a good slug. This was getting to be a habit. I sank mine in one—apple wine, the good year—and refilled my glass.

'Tell me, would you ever have told them if Libby hadn't got pregnant?' he asked, leaning back and turning his dark head to regard me curiously.

442

'I—well, I don't know. Probably not,' I confessed. 'They love each other. What would *you* have done if it had been true, and you'd known about it?'

'I expect I'd have taken the coward's way out too, and hoped they didn't procreate!' he said frankly.

'I'm not a coward! I just wouldn't want to hurt my best friend, that's all.'

'You're such a sentimental idiot underneath that cool, calm exterior,' he said meditatively. 'I think perhaps that's why I've grown to love you so much!'

I stopped with the glass suspended halfway to my lips. 'Don't be silly!'

'Oh, I'm not silly,' he said quite calmly. 'I *do* love you.'

'As a friend, perhaps?'

'A bit more than that . . . a *lot* more than that. And I'm hoping that you've got over Ben now, and are used to having me around, instead?'

'Well yes, but—' I stammered uncertainly. 'I mean, how can I believe you when I know you've still been seeing Anji until recently and—'

His grey eyes flashed. 'I have not! God, you're so cynical!'

'And you're not? You told me yourself you only went in for casual affairs, so how am I supposed to believe you now?'

'I went in for casual affairs simply *because* I'm a romantic. I knew true love existed, I just didn't expect to feel that way ever again. Then I fell for a disillusioned, dippy, embittered wedding cake maker, of all people!' he added bitterly.

Removing the glass from my hand he pulled me into his arms. 'So, little Miss Cynic, how do you

443

feel when I do this?' he demanded, kissing me, and of course my Inner Slut made a mighty bound for freedom at the touch of his lips.

'Dizzy,' I said truthfully at last, when I could speak, looking up into his darkly handsome face and intent grey eyes. 'I'm dizzy. And confused, because you know you aren't in love with me really. You can't be, because you kept backing off every time I showed any interest! And anyway, you told me that your wife was the love of your life and you never expected to feel that way again!'

'Yes, but I was wrong,' he admitted. 'I just said so. I did love her, and I'll never forget her, but that doesn't mean I can never fall in love again—and I have, with you. After all, you loved Ben for years and you've got over him. Now I'm hoping you're feeling a different kind of love for me.'

'You're certainly *different* all right, Noah,' I said, because he was quite right: my feelings *had* slowly changed, I just hadn't wanted to admit it to myself. 'And that's why it wouldn't work—really it wouldn't!'

'So am I flattering myself by thinking you might have fallen for me just a little bit? Do you think I could become more to you than just some kind of cathartic agent or a dose of emotional medicine?'

'Perhaps that wasn't the most tactful thing I could have said to you at the time,' I admitted. 'In fact, I suspected later that you were only flirting with me to try and get me to fall for you because you felt piqued!'

'It certainly got my attention. And perhaps I did think I'd see if I could get you to fall in love with me at first, but that all changed as soon as I started getting to know you. In fact, to know you is to love you.'

'That's the most romantic thing anyone has ever said to me,' I sighed, and he kissed me again. It seemed to be becoming a habit—the sort I could live with. The sort I might not be able to live without . . .

'Well, maybe now you'll believe me when I tell you I'm a romantic,' he said then, releasing me, got down on one knee. While I stared at him in wide-eyed astonishment, he took a ring from his pocket and pushed it onto my unresisting finger, while asking, very seriously, 'Will you marry me, Josie?'

I was too stunned to do anything except nod dumbly, with a diamond as big as the Ritz casting rainbows on my hand and tears glittering in my eyes.

Then I threw my arms around his neck and gasped, 'Oh, it's beautiful!' It was a moment I had often secretly dreamed of, but never expected to experience.

'Well, don't cry about it!' he said, then got up and refilled our glasses for a toast. 'Here's to us— unless you're going to refuse me, of course? You haven't actually *said* yes.'

When he looked at me like that, I found it hard to refuse him anything . . . though I soon discovered that he seemed to have the oddest idea that we should postpone any bedroom activity until after the wedding . . .

But as I pointed out a little later, if the horse had already bolted, it was too late to close the stable door.

'I knew I shouldn't have let you open that peapod wine,' he said, propping himself up in bed and smiling ruefully at me.

445

'It wasn't, only apple. You can't blame it on the peapod this time, Noah Sephton!'

'Maybe not . . . So,' he added suavely, 'how was that for you? An emotional enema? Bit of a catharsis?'

I blushed. 'You're never going to let me forget that, are you? Oh, this is all so mad, I can't believe it's happening!'

'Believe it!' he said, looking down at me very seriously. 'Just remember, Josie, that I'm not Ben, and when I commit, I commit totally. I'll never leave you for anyone else . . . and in any case, I think you can safely say I've already sown *my* wild oats!'

'So have I, now—with you! But I still don't know how this will work out, Noah, because you'll still be spending a lot of time in London and I'll be up here . . .'

'But you'll love my house in Chelsea! It belonged to a Victorian artist, so it's got a long garden at the back, a bit like yours, with a studio at the end of it. I'll want you there with me sometimes, Josie, so I think you may have to cut back on the cake orders a bit.'

'I don't mind that, but what about my garden and the hens?'

'I'm sure Tim and Dorrie could look after things for a couple of days whenever we're away, and you can catch up with it all when you're at home. It will keep you occupied when you *can't* come with me, and I have to leave you alone. And meanwhile, I'll be cramming all my appointments into as short a time as possible, so I can rush back to you. It'll work, you'll see.'

'Yes—we'll *make* it work,' I agreed, and then a

446

sudden thought struck me. 'What's Ben going to do when he finds out? Not that I've noticed him lurking about for ages, and he hasn't rung me up, but I keep expecting him to reappear . . . unless he's finally given up on me?' I added hopefully.

'Don't worry about that. You can leave it all to me, now,' Noah assured me. 'And I'm going to put a notice of our engagement in *The Times* so everyone will soon know about it. In fact, let's go and see the vicar tomorrow about having the banns read.'

I sighed happily: 'The Graces are going to *love* this!'

Chapter Thirty-five

Wedding Belles

The Photographer and I have put our relationship under the zoom lens and decided to press the shutter. This doesn't mean that I will be abandoning my garden and my principles—on the contrary. Uncle has decided to live with his family in New Zealand, and the Photographer is moving into his cottage, though eventually we hope to combine the two into one. I also have designs on the garden of his London house . . .

'Cakes and Ale'

Noah and I saw the vicar first thing next morning, before Noah set out for London.

Oddly enough, I'd missed a call from Ben while Noah was with me, which was hardly surprising

447

because I never even checked until he'd left for London and even then I hardly wondered what he wanted. My mind was taken up with other, happier, things.

* * *

Telling Harry the good news was a bit of a damp squib. I said carefully, 'This might be a bit of a shock, Harry, but I'm engaged to Noah.'

'I know,' he said. 'Congratulations!'

'You *know*? How can you know? I only just know myself!'

He twinkled at me. 'He asked my permission to marry you weeks ago! He said I was as close to a father as you'd got, and he wanted to do everything by the book. That Rob had him worried for a bit, though, until I put him right.'

I'm not sure which book Noah was going by, but it seemed to be of Victorian vintage.

'Your granny would be that proud of you!' he added, making me go a bit tearful. 'And she'd like Noah, I'm sure she would.'

'Yes, I think so too. We've already been to see the vicar about putting up the banns, because we want to get married as soon as we can.'

He ran his fingers around the inner band of his hat, obviously troubled by something. 'The only thing is, Josie, once I told our Sadie I'd made up my mind to move over there, and how easy it would be to sell up now Noah's taking over the cottage, she went and booked my ticket—and Mac's. So I might not be here for your wedding.'

'Well, I'd have liked you to be there, Harry, but it doesn't matter. I know you'll be thinking about us

448

on the day. And if you're not here to give me away, I'll take a leaf out of Libby's book and do it myself!'

* * *

In fact, the news of my engagement didn't seem to come as a surprise to any of my Neatslake friends, though Libby nobly refrained from saying, 'I told you so' when I told her, which I did right after telling Harry. She also offered me a free reception at the Old Barn and the use of her apartment in Pisa as a honeymoon venue.

'But you'll have to have the reception on a midweek day, if it's August,' she said, 'otherwise we can't fit it in.'

'I'd already thought of that and it's a Wednesday—just a small wedding, with only our local friends. I want to walk across to the church with Noah, so I hope it doesn't rain on the day!'

'What about a wedding dress?'

'I'm going to look in the attic this afternoon to see if I can find the trunk with Granny's in. I think it should fit me—we were about the same height—and I remember it was a lovely, heavy embossed satin. And would you like to be my bridesmaid—with Pia too, if she will?'

'I'll be matron of honour,' Libby agreed. 'You'll have to ask Pia yourself, but I'm sure she will, because she won't be sulking about your wedding.'

'I think Pia would fit into my bridesmaid's dress and then we would only have to get you something in pink, but I don't think it matters if they match or not.'

'You'd better leave that to me,' she said. Then

449

she grinned. 'Oh, Josie, who would have thought this time last year that you would be about to marry Noah Sephton and I would be expecting a little Rowland-Knowles!'

*   *   *

I intended to drop in at Poona Place and tell the Graces next, but I ran into Violet as I came out of the lane—or rather, she almost ran into me. She said Tinkerbell's brakes needed adjusting.

'I was never a bridesmaid,' she said wistfully, once all the exclamations and congratulations were over. 'Of course, had dear Lily's fiancé not have been killed, both Pansy and I would have been. He was a naval officer, you know, on the Russian convoys—went down with his ship.'

'No, I didn't even know Lily had been engaged,' I said, surprised and touched. 'She's never mentioned it.'

'She doesn't very often, though she still has his picture on her bedside table. It does make a bond between her and Dorrie though, both having loved and lost their young men in the war.'

'Yes, I should think it does.' Then on impulse I asked, 'Would *you* like to be one of my bridesmaids, Violet? Only I'd like my dearest friends to support me on the day and I've got Libby and possibly Pia, so it would be lovely to have you as well.'

Her small face lit up. 'How wonderful! And how much I would like that!'

'Do you think your sisters would also . . .?' I let the question hang in the air, thinking that at this rate, there would be more bridesmaids than guests.

450

'No, I don't think they have ever felt the longing to do so that I have, and I am sure they would be happy that I should represent them—if you really mean it?'

'Yes, of course I do! Now, you'll need a dress. I thought Pia would fit the pink one I wore at Libby's wedding, and Libby's going to look for a dress that will tone in with that colour, even if it isn't exactly the same shade.'

'There is no need,' Violet said. 'If she can find a suitable pattern and some material, Lily will make up both our dresses.'

So now my three bridesmaids will be pretty in pink, and neatly represent the Three Ages of Woman.

Noah, when he rang me from London—not for any particular purpose, just to say he loved me—laughed and approved the arrangements. He will ask Tim to be best man and perhaps Jasper will do the usher's role again, though there are not going to be many guests to organise.

'I'll be back tomorrow, but it sounds like you've been too busy to miss me,' he commented.

'I have been busy and I'm about to start making the base for our wedding cake, but I've still missed you.'

'What kind of cake?'

'Wait and see. Claire and the film crew will be able to take some pictures of it when they come next week for a last day's *Sticklepond Spring* filming. It starts to run on the TV soon, which will be very odd.'

'I think it'll be a cult success, like your magazine column,' he said. 'Is Claire still trying to get me to agree to feature in the next *Sticklepond* series?'

'Yes, I'm afraid I told her we were getting married, and she said she'd like to include a bit of filming on the day for the next one, *Sticklepond Summer*!'

* * *

Ben called again and, in a voice like someone who had just discovered that the Mafia had put a horse's head into his bed, announced tersely: '*I know about the prawns.*'

Then he put the phone down.

I'm only surprised it took him so long to suss out, really.

* * *

When Noah got back, he confessed that he'd tracked Ben down to his studio in Camden.

'Really, Noah, there was no need to do that,' I said. 'In fact, he rang me after you'd left and I got the feeling he'd . . . got over me. Completely,' I added with finality.

Noah grinned. 'Yes, when I told him we were getting married, he said his eyes had been opened to your true nature and I was welcome to you, which wasn't quite the reaction I'd expected, to be honest.'

'Did he tell you why?'

'Yes. He'd just discovered that you'd spiked all the artworks you'd sent down from Neatslake with prawn heads, which had stunk the place out for weeks. Very inventive revenge, Josie! I'll have to take care not to annoy you.'

'I can't think what got into me!' I said guiltily. 'I

know I did a bad thing, but I hoped the stink would have vanished by now.'

'That sort of smell does linger, but now he's removed the offending items and sprayed fabric freshener about inside, he's hoping that will clear the last lingering redolence, so he can finally sell them.'

'I *love* the way you say "redolence",' I sighed dreamily. 'Say it again!'

He looked at me severely. 'I'll have you know that Ben said he'd never thought you'd touch his precious artworks and I should watch my back. He also said what you'd done had killed any vestige of love he had for you and he's moved on.'

'Well, about time too! Even Anji's managed to get over you and shack up with Rob Rafferty.'

'That was the good news. The bad is that Ben's moving back to live at Mark and Stella's permanently and they're setting up some kind of residential painting holiday centre.'

'That doesn't sound like Ben at all,' I said, astonished. 'He's always hated the idea of teaching!'

'I don't think he's got much choice. His work isn't selling terribly well at the moment. But he hopes, once he's back near Sticklepond, that he'll find a new direction. And I must say, having seen his creations, that I hope he's right! Nasty, aren't they?'

I agreed. 'But what about Olivia and the baby?'

'I didn't ask him about them, but I didn't have to. He said marriage might be all right for me, but his had been a serious error of judgement and Olivia and London between them were stunting his artistic soul.'

'Oh?' I said, then lost interest in Ben—or indeed, in anything else—for quite a long time . . .

Later, when I told Noah what arrangements I'd made for the wedding and asked him if he wanted to honeymoon in Pisa, he said yes, but we could also have a second honeymoon next year, in New Zealand, to see how Harry was getting on!

*   *   *

It seemed impossible, but life got even busier after that. Between arranging for our wedding, bouts of cake-making, gardening and helping Libby, I was also assisting Harry to pack up his belongings, including his filed-down medal and the MOD correspondence, and dispatch the things he would want in New Zealand.

He was leaving a lot of the heavier furnishings in the house as a wedding present, and Noah was paying him the full market price for the cottage and has already had an architect look at ways of turning the two properties into one.

Then the sad day came when we went to the airport to see Harry and Mac off. As the poor dog vanished to be swallowed up in the bowels of the aircraft in his special travelling crate, I wished I could have explained to him what was happening, and what a lovely time he would have when he arrived in New Zealand.

Harry looked small and sprightly as he set out on his last adventure, his hat brim at a jaunty angle and his hand luggage full of Yorkshire Tea, in case you couldn't get it out there.

'You daft lump!' he said fondly, as I wept over him.

454

'You will ring me as soon as you get there, won't you?' I begged. 'Just quickly, to let me know you're all right?'

'Yes, or I'll get Sadie to do it if I'm tired,' he said. And then he hugged me, shook Noah's hand and went resolutely off through the barrier, only turning for one last wave.

'Cheer up,' Noah said, putting a consoling arm around me. 'I think he's made the right decision and you'll be able to see for yourself next year.'

*   *   *

Ben moved into Ranter's End with Mark and Stella, and I saw his tall, sad, surprisingly run-to-seed figure shambling about in the distance sometimes, but he didn't come anywhere near me.

I expect he was out searching for his mojo.

By then, I'd found another co-op group to join, in Sticklepond.

*   *   *

I'd put the finishing touches to our own wedding cake while Claire and the film crew were here, but now I led Noah into the kitchen for his first sight of it.

'Ta-dah!' I said, taking my hands from over his eyes.

'Good grief!'

He took in the two-tier vegetable garden, with ivy growing up the sturdy, twisted columns, the henhouse on top, decked with a fat and happy Aggie, and the lettering right around the sides . . .

'"Clucky in Love"?' he queried mildly. 'And "I

455

Should Be so Clucky"?'

'It's what it said in the Valentine's Day card you sent me,' I explained.

Noah whipped me down to London in the Jaguar, to see his house in Chelsea. After the noisy bustle outside, it surprised me by being a haven of quiet calm—and also by being a taller, more elegant version of mine, right down to the studio at the end of the garden, though his is brick-built and sturdy. I had great plans for that garden and I was sure it would spark off lots of ideas about green and economical living in cities, that I could pass on through my 'Cakes and Ale' column. Claire Flowers, of course, was desperate to persuade us to let her film us doing it, but we will see . . .

Maybe we should just keep the Chelsea house as our own private escape . . .

Pia had also escaped. She'd taken over the gatehouse as her own domain, since Noah was now living in Harry's cottage—or nominally living there. When the two became one, I would have to get used to my living space doubling in size . . .

Lily was making good progress with the two bridesmaids' dresses and she'd also altered Granny's lovely wedding dress to fit me, so I felt that in a way Granny would be with me on my big day.

And our wedding presents had started to arrive, including the promise of a ruby cavalier King Charles puppy from Freddie! We were to receive it when we got back from honeymoon, but I'd already seen it and it was the sweetest little thing.

And we'd got a rooster so now Aggie was nurturing a brood of little speckled chicks, which temporarily curtailed her escapology.

Everything seemed to fall so beautifully into place, it was as if the pattern was preordained.

Perhaps it was.

Chapter Thirty-six

Fruits and Leaves

I had the most ecologically friendly wedding possible—apart from flying to Pisa for our honeymoon, of course. However, the Photographer promised that on our return we would donate a sturdy oak sapling to the village green, to replace the tree that blew down in the winter's gales, so I hope that goes some way to making up for it!

'Cakes and Ale'

Noah and I spent the night before our wedding separately in our adjoining cottages, as a nod to superstition.

I had a hen party at home, with the Graces, Libby, Gina, Pia and Dorrie, but Noah went to the Griffin with Tim and Jasper.

And I was very glad I was alone first thing next morning, because there was something I *urgently* needed to do, before Libby and Pia arrived to help make me look lovely for my big day . . .

*　　　*　　　*

Hand in hand, Noah and I walked across the sunny Green to the old church, where my trio of

457

bridesmaids, pretty in pink, awaited us. They all looked lovely in their way. Violet's small face was suffused with such joy, she looked almost luminous.

But then, my thin shell of cynicism had been entirely blown away by Noah's love.

Pansy had lined up her Brownies on the path in front of the steps, so that we passed under a bridal arch of paper flowers. As we walked down the aisle, I could hear them rustling behind me and lots of giggling, as they all crammed into the back pews.

When I turned to face my handsome bridegroom at the altar, I felt as if this was all a dream and I might wake up at any minute—and I didn't want to. But then he smiled at me, that now familiar, slightly twisted smile—and I knew I wasn't dreaming after all, and that this would be for ever.

*   *   *

Since I'd pointed out the difficulties of photographing his own wedding, Noah had drafted in a young and nervous assistant instead, who was now trying to marshal us into a group on the church steps.

'You look extra ravishing,' Noah said, his arm around my waist, 'as though you'd been lit from within.'

'Do I?' I said, trying to keep the big smile off my face and feeling just like the cat who'd got all the cream.

'Yes. In fact, you're also now wearing a guilty expression that I'm starting to become familiar with,' he added suspiciously.

458

I looked up at him. 'Actually, I *do* have something to confess, Noah, and I'm not quite sure how to tell you this . . . but I'm afraid there are going to be three of us in this marriage. I'm having a baby.'

He stared at me for a moment, his light grey eyes widening, then his face broke into an expression of pure delight and he snatched me right off the ground, swinging me round and round.

'Oh, Josie—and you kept that to yourself!' Libby exclaimed, when he put me down, and gave me a big hug.

'I only did the test first thing this morning.'

'And you managed to get pregnant without taking the Chinese herbal medicine, or anything?'

'Oh, I found a better medicine than that!'

'Or do you mean an enema?' Noah asked wickedly.

'I take back what I said about you being romantic, Noah Sephton!' I said.

If you've enjoyed reading about Josie's cooking in *Wedding Tiers*, why not try out some of her recipes for yourself?

Wedding Cake

Because the fruit is left to soak in the alcohol before the cake is cooked, this is a quick cake to make at short notice, though of course it tastes even better if made well in advance. This makes one eight inch round, rich, dark, fruit cake that can also be used for Christmas cake.

Ingredients:
Naturally dried fruits are preferable. The dried fruit plus glacé cherry element of this recipe should total two pounds in weight, though you can safely vary the different quantities of the ingredients within that to include, say, more mixed peel and less cherries, or more sultanas and less currants. The following is one combination.

1lb mixed dried fruit including peel
4oz sultanas
4oz currants
4oz raisins
4oz glacé cherries, halved
Quarter of a pint of medium sherry

6oz unsalted butter
6oz soft brown sugar
Grated rind of one lemon and one orange
(unwaxed)

460

3 eggs
1 tablespoon of treacle
2oz chopped almonds
4oz plain flour
2oz self-raising flour
1 level teaspoon mixed spice
Quarter teaspoon ground nutmeg

Method:
Put the fruit and cherries into a bowl and pour in the sherry. Cover the bowl and leave for at least twelve hours, but preferably three or four days.

To make, preheat the oven to 300F/150C/gas mark 2. Grease, and then line with greaseproof paper, an eight inch round cake tin.

Cream the butter and sugar in a bowl together, and then stir in the lemon and orange rind, beaten eggs, treacle and almonds. Sieve in the flour and spices and mix everything together until blended. Finally, stir in the soaked fruit and sherry.

Spoon the mixture into the cake tin and smooth the top.

Bake for two hours and then reduce the heat to 275F/140C/gas mark 1 for a further one and quarter hours, or until a warm skewer pushed into the middle comes out clean. If at any point the cake seems to be getting too brown on top, cover tin loosely with foil.

When the cake is cold, wrap it well in greaseproof paper and store in an airtight tin or box.

Turn over when icing it, if you want a really flat surface.

Peapod Wine

Use young, fresh, empty pods. If you haven't got enough at one time, freeze them, but make sure they are dry before using. You need about four pounds of peapods to make one gallon of pale green wine.

Ingredients:
    4lb of green peapods
    2lb of granulated sugar
    7 pints water
    2 unwaxed lemons
    2 unwaxed oranges
    Quarter teaspoon of tannin
    1 teaspoon of yeast nutrient
    Wine yeast

Method:
Cut up the peapods and thinly peel the oranges and lemons while bringing the water to the boil. Add the peelings and peapods to the water and boil gently for half an hour. Remove from heat and allow to cool.

Put the tannin, yeast nutrient and sugar in a large bowl and then strain the liquid from the peapods over it. Stir until all is dissolved. (Discard the pods and peelings onto the compost heap.) Add the juice from the oranges and lemons, stir and then add the yeast.

Pour into a fermenting jar, topping up with cool water if necessary, and fit an airlock. Leave in a cool place until fermentation is complete, then rack into bottles and age for at least six months before tasting . . . Goes well with fish, cold meats and salads.

Quince Jelly

Quinces can be grown as a bush or trained along walls and fences. The fruits are high in pectin and very tart, and the jelly goes well with cold meats, especially duck, goose and roast pork. Quince wine is also very good.

Ingredients:
  4lb ripe quinces, roughly sliced
  1 pint water
  Lemon juice
  Granulated sugar

Method:
Put the water and quinces into a preserving pan and bring to the boil, then simmer for forty to fifty minutes, until the fruit is tender.

Pour the quince pulp into a jelly bag suspended over a bowl. Allow the juice to drain through overnight and then discard the pulp.

Measure how much juice you've got and then put it back in the preserving pan. For every pint of liquid, add 1 tablespoon of lemon juice and 14oz sugar. Stir over a low heat until sugar is dissolved.

Bring to the boil and keep it boiling briskly, without stirring, for ten minutes, or until the mixture reaches setting point. (To find setting point, drop a teaspoon of liquid onto a cold plate and then push with your finger—if it wrinkles, it's right.)

Skim any foam off the top with a slotted spoon. Ladle the jelly into hot, sterilised jars, leaving

1 inch space at the top. Cover, label with date and store in a cool place.

This makes about two and a half pounds.

Tipsy Truffles

Ingredients:
4oz dark cooking chocolate, broken into pieces
3 tablespoons dark rum/whisky/alcohol of your
    choice
2oz butter
3oz icing sugar
3oz ground almonds
Chocolate vermicelli/cocoa powder

Method:
Melt chocolate in the top of a double pan, or in a bowl over simmering water. (Do not get water in the chocolate!) You can also use the microwave on a very low setting.

When melted, remove from the heat and stir in the butter, sugar, alcohol and almonds. Keep stirring until the mixture is blended smooth.

Allow to cool a bit and then form into balls about three-quarters of an inch in diameter. Gently roll them in the vermicelli or cocoa powder (don't use drinking chocolate!), then put them in paper or foil sweet cases.

Chill. When packed in a container between layers of waxed or greaseproof paper, they can be stored in a cool, dark place for up to two months.

Nut Constellations

This is a quick and easy treat—unless you shell your own peanuts, which takes time!

Ingredients:
  4oz chocolate, dark or milk as preferred
  2oz shelled peanuts
  Paper or foil sweet or *petits fours* cases

Method:
Melt the chocolate in a bowl over simmering water, a double pan or in the microwave on a low setting, as before.
  Stir in the shelled peanuts.
  Drop spoonfuls into the sweet cases and put somewhere cool to set. Store as the truffles.

Battenburg Cake

This is fiddly, but the end result is pretty. You will need a seven inch square cake tin and greaseproof paper.

Cake ingredients:
  6oz butter
  6oz caster sugar
  3 medium eggs, lightly beaten
  4oz self-raising flour
  Natural red food colouring
  Natural vanilla essence (optional)

For the covering:
  Apricot jam
  8oz natural almond paste

Heat the oven to 325F/160C/gas 3. Grease the cake tin and then line with greaseproof paper. When lining the base, cut the paper about four inches wider than the tin, then pull the excess up into a fold in the middle of the cake tin, to divide it into two.

In a large bowl cream the butter and sugar together until fluffy and then beat in the eggs, one at a time. Gently fold in the flour with a wooden spoon.

Divide mixture into two bowls. Add a few drops of natural vanilla essence to one bowl, and a drop or two of natural red food colouring to the second bowl, to turn it pink.

Put pink cake mixture in one half of the cake tin

and plain in the other. Smooth the surfaces.

Bake in the oven for 35–40 minutes, or until it has shrunk slightly from the sides of the tin and feels firm when pressed with the fingertips.

Turn out the cake onto a wire rack, removing the paper, and leave to cool.

Trim the edges of each half and cut into two long strips each. Warm the apricot jam and use to stick the cake strips together, alternating the colour.

Roll out the almond paste into an oblong large enough to wrap right around the cake and then brush one long side with apricot jam. Press it down onto the almond paste. Brush the other three sides with jam and press the almond paste over it, to cover, finishing neatly up one edge. Leave the ends uncovered to show the chequered cake.

Slice into little squares to serve.